Puppets On A Stage

Ψ

A Pandora Belfry Adventure
(Book Four)

Kristina Schram Ph.D.

Mischief*Maker*Media

Published by Mischief Maker Media (USA)

First printing: November, 2018

Cover Design, Interior, and Technical Expertise: GorKee

Cover Photos from iStockPhoto

Play excerpts from: Shelley, Mary. *Frankenstein - Original 1818 Uncensored Version (Includes illustrations + audio links)*. Enhanced Classics. Kindle Edition.

ISBN: 978-1-939397-31-7

Visit Kristina Schram on the World Wide Web at:
www.KristinaSchram.com

Acknowledgements

A big thank you to my generous and helpful beta readers: Elizabeth Schram, Ian More, Heather Duane, and Dan Unzen! I'm quite aware I can be a bit like Pandora myself, always trying to go it alone. But you don't let me, and for that, I am more than grateful.

You complete me...

~~~~~~~~~~

To those poor souls who suffer beyond what
any being should have to...

~~~~~~~~~~

Sometimes the job of a writer is to reveal the truth, and sometimes it's to create a more palatable truth. In writing about the residents of Nepenthe Manor, I have attempted to do both. While I hope to turn a light on the very real issues with which the mentally ill struggle every day, I also want to give these unique individuals a chance at a life I imagine few get to experience in the real world—one full of adventure, mystery, healing, and plain old fun.

1

Head Popped Off

PANDORA AWOKE TO a throbbing head and the sound of some-one singing in a soft, lisping voice. Well, the singing started out soft, but grew louder and more animated with each word. "Mama had a baby and its head popped off!" A wicked chuckle filled the air, fol-lowed by another recitation, and a deeper, even more wicked, chuckle. The singing seemed overly loud, as though echoing inside Pandora's head, and she hoped that her own head would pop off, if only to end the torment.

She cracked one eye open and saw through the blurred slit a bright room, and nearby, little Lucy sitting in a chair, her short legs swing-ing back and forth. In one pudgy hand she held a bunch of wilted stems, only one of which was still attached to a flower. A bright yel-low dandelion.

Groggy and out of sorts, Pandora watched as Lucy chanted at the re-maining flower, then her stubby thumb popped its 'head' off. More delighted laughter followed.

"Please stop," Pandora managed to push out, though even this mini-mal effort was an irritant to her aching head.

Lucy's head swung up. "It's about time you woke up, Panda Bear! It's been years and years. So whose head is actually popping off?" She held up the denuded stems. "Mama's? The baby's? Whose?"

"Whoever you want," Pandora muttered irritably. "You can even sing, 'Miss Polly had a dolly and its head popped off.' Definitely the doll's head popping off on that one." She wanted to add that maybe Lucy could go pop off herself, but decided the effort, which would be ignored, required more energy than she was up to producing.

Lucy snorted derisively. "That's boring. It has to be a real person or it's no fun."

Pandora rolled her head on a stiff neck and looked around. Realizing where she was she swallowed hard. She was in a hospital. What had happened to her? Why was she here?

Lucy slid off her chair and shoved the flower stems into Pandora's face. "Dr. Steele begged me to come with him to see you, so I brought these flowers for you." She threw the stems onto the bed. "Now get up! It's time to come home. Birdy's dying from internal pains she says are from missing Skippy so bad. Charles is having spasms in his chests from his anger zieties, and Sinclair's gone back to his stupid counting crap." She pulled at Pandora's shoulder, displaying a surprising amount of strength for such a little body. "Now come on!" Pandora started to sit up, but then her head did a loop-de-loop, blackness filled her mind, and she fell backward. Lucy's insistent voice, thank all that is good in this world, faded away, as did the pain.

The next time Pandora awoke, it was to murmuring voices. Neither of them was Lucy's. Maybe there was a God. "She definitely had a concussion, and is still suffering from the effects of it," a masculine voice stated with confidence. "I've learned through my work with brain-traumatized patients that concussions can influence a person to do things they wouldn't normally do. Head trauma can cause excessive moodiness, anxiety, depression, and changes in personality. It could very well be that having a concussion is what made her do what she did."

Pandora knew that voice. It came from the intriguing, though some-what troublesome Dr. Steele, the new therapist at Nepenthe Manor, and the sadist who had brought Lucy to see her. She had a feeling he was currently on her shit list, but she wasn't sure why. Her brain didn't feel right, like it was filled with wet cement and spider webs. Was this what it was like to be on drugs? To be crazy? She didn't know. All she knew was that she felt like kicking someone, and would have done so if her head didn't ache so badly.

"Are you sure?" a feminine voice interrupted Pandora's wandering thoughts. For once in her life Vicki actually sounded like a worried mom. This wasn't her typical demeanor. She was more likely to let Pandora fend for herself, consequences be damned. "According to my mother, Pandy yelled, 'It's the only way!' then jumped off the bridge. I know my daughter's dramatic, and prone to doing impulsive acts, but that seems a bit extreme, even for her."

"As only your mother, you, and myself know what Pandora shouted, I say for the moment we keep that information to ourselves. I want to assess your daughter and see what comes up, but for now we'll treat her behavior as a result of her concussion. I told Dr. Gara what hap-pened during the basketball game—that Pandora hit her head really hard, then vomited—and she agrees with my conclusion. That's what she'll be writing in her report, anyway, with the implication that Pan-dora fell off the bridge, not that she jumped. However, between you and me, I want to be sure about that."

"So you're saying we keep this off the record?" Vicki sounded relieved. She never did hold much with the idea of mental illness, ironic, being that she was the *Director* of the Nepenthe Manor Funny Farm, aka Insane Asylum. She and her mother shared the same opinion, though Vicki's main prejudice centered on her belief that with enough hard work and rational encouragement people will get better. According to her great wisdom, talk therapy is a waste of time.

And yet her husband, Professor Robertson, had been mentally ill. He'd gotten brain damage from crashing his motorcycle on the way to Pandora's birth, and that had turned him into a nutter. He'd survived the crash and lived another fourteen years, only to die from pneumonia a day or two ago. Poor Professor Robertson. Pandora felt a sudden urge to start bawling and promptly bit down on her tongue, which made her gurgle in pain.

"Pandora?" Dr. Steele leaned down to peer into her face. Her eyes were closed, but she knew exactly what he was doing. She could feel him. His proximity made her skin go all itchy, and while normally she found him physically compelling, right now she just wanted him to go away. "Are you awake?"

"Do I look awake?" she grumbled.

"What the hell were you thinking?" Vicki demanded, joining Dr. Steele, who was hovering over Pandora's bed like the Grim Reaper.

Like she was going to answer that loaded question. Pandora reluctantly opened her eyes, then promptly squeezed them shut again. "Can you turn off the lights, please? And move back? I can see your nose hairs."

"It's just the light from the sunset coming in through the window," Vicki explained, using her patronizing voice, which sounded quite similar to the one she used with the inmates.

"Then please shut the curtains!" Pandora practically shouted, anger welling up inside her like a blocked toilet about to overflow. It was weird to get so mad about something so trivial, but she couldn't seem to help herself.

"No need to yell!" Vicki responded with her usual sensitivity, then went to close the curtains, metal scraping against metal as darkness descended. Pandora knew it was her mother who'd done the closing because her weird flowery perfume—a new addition since Dr. Steele had arrived—dissipated. When the light had dimmed to a more bearable glare, Pandora opened her eyes just a bit and let them flit around the sterile looking room. Except for the empty bed next to hers, it looked exactly like the room where her dad had died. Not a good sign.

"Irrational anger," Dr. Steele noted, his unwavering, intensely blue eyes assessing her like a specimen in one of his studies. As interesting as playing the role of specimen sounded, she wasn't up for it. "One of the side effects of a concussion. Dr. Gara thought she might have suffered a second one when she hit the water. New research is showing that concussions can be more dangerous than we thought. That's why we'll have to keep a very close eye on your daughter for the next few days."

Based on what she'd heard so far, Pandora now knew why she was in the hospital and why her head hurt so badly. Though she recalled very little of what had happened to get her here. The basketball game she remembered, probably because they'd won a decided and delicious victory over the town kids and Jimbo, her nemesis. She wished she could forget Vicki telling her right afterward that the professor had died. Skippy's father had come for him, too; she'd been there for that and would never forget the ugly scene. Then she was almost kidnapped by a guy named Baker, followed by Grandmother Belfry taking her away in her white Cadillac. After that, Pandora's mind went fuzzy.

So she'd jumped off the Pine River Bridge, had she? Sounded like a brilliant plan to avoid having to stay with her grandmother.

It had been a plan, though, hadn't it? She couldn't remember exactly, or at all, actually, and that didn't sit quite right with her. She hadn't really tried to kill herself, had she? She didn't believe in offing herself. Not even during this last week, with the ghost stirring things up and getting stalked by her grandmother and her goons, not even when she'd felt like she'd been losing her tenuous grasp on the world she lived in. She wanted to live. Didn't she?

"I'm right here," Pandora growled, not wanting to face that particular question right now. "So stop talking about me like I'm not."

Dr. Steele straightened up, a spark in his eyes. "Ah, there she is. The Pandora we know and love, thank goodness."

Pandora swallowed. *Know and love?* Was he just throwing crap at her to distract her from his real intentions, or did he really mean all that? It was doubtful he meant it. The world was very good at throwing crap at her.

"What exactly do you mean about keeping an eye on her?" Vicki asked worriedly. "Dr. Gara said she's going to be all right, and I've got to get back to the manor. I missed so many days with Professor Robertson's illness, and then there's the funeral to plan, and Mayor Daft and Hank Jackson are using Pandora's little *stunt* to bolster their argument that we need to be shut down, and I have to figure out what I'm going to do next. With all that, *with my life...*" The last three words were spoken in a whisper, as though Vicki both wanted to say them out loud and did not. But as everything came through so loudly and clearly for Pandora right now, she easily heard what her mother had said. She wasn't sure, however, that she wanted to know what Vicki meant by it…

"The hospital has staff for that sort of thing," Dr. Steele pointed out, unnecessarily. Of course they had staff for that sort of thing. It's what people do in a hospital. This conversation was getting really irritating. "And I'll check in on her whenever I can."

Oh, goody, thought Pandora sarcastically, and then, less sarcastically, *oh goody*.

"Go do your thing, Vicki," Pandora spoke up, her tone as martyr-like as she could make it. "It's what you've always done. Why change now?" She said this while watching Vicki's face closely. Her mother's curly hair was a mess, all oily and wild, and dark circles under her green-brown eyes made her look ten years older.

"I didn't mean I wouldn't come visit, Pandy. Of course I will. It's just that I can't stay here all day. You know I have people counting on me."

"Like your daughter."

Vicki pulled back her shoulders, opened her mouth to say something undoubtedly reproving, then clamped it shut. After taking a deep breath, she gave Pandora a tight smile. "I'll be back later. Want me to pack a bag for you?"

"No!" Pandora shouted, then regretted doing so. Loud noises were her head's current enemy. "I mean, I'll be all right." No way was she letting her mother go through her stuff. Though she'd probably do it anyway. Then again, maybe not. She was a busy lady, after all. She'd most likely forget.

"Well, you won't be needing a brush for a while," Vicki remarked, one corner of her mouth quirking up.

Pandora looked back and forth between them. "I don't get it."

"Oh." Vicki actually looked chagrined, as though she'd been caught making fun of a cancer patient. "You don't remember."

Pandora glanced at Dr. Steele. "Remember what?"

He gestured toward her head. "You cut your hair. Really short."

"I did?" She reached up, slowly, as any sudden movement set off stars in her head, and patted her skull. It felt all bristly, as though someone had taken a weed whacker and gone at her. For some reason the fact that she'd cut her hair made her more nervous than the jumping. "Why did I do that?"

"I believe you were protesting something I did," Vicki answered dryly, her arms crossed tightly across her chest.

"Oh, yes. I remember now, and you're wrong, Vicki. It had nothing to do with you. I was protesting my father's death." Was that right? Because it sounded good.

Vicki looked down at her feet, paused, then looked back up, her eyes blazing. "Don't you dare make this about him." Her arms dropped to her sides and her posture straightened, as though her body was filling with resolve. "Now, I'm going back to the manor to take care of things. The funeral will likely be in a few days. Make sure you're ready for it. Afterward, you'll be going to my mother's house until I decide what to do with you."

Instead of answering back, as she normally would, Pandora turned her head away.

"Did you hear me, Pandy?"

Pandora remained silent.

"Well, I know you heard me. I'm standing five feet away. I won't be changing my mind, you know. A lot of things have gone wrong lately. I won't let you be one of them."

"Too late," Pandora whispered when the silence was too loud to bear, but Vicki was already gone.

Dismembered Body Parts

2

DR. STEELE PATTED her arm, but she wouldn't look at him. She remembered now why he was on her shit list. He hadn't stopped her grandmother from taking her away from Nepenthe Manor, hadn't stopped Skippy's dad from kidnapping his son, either. He had simply stood there and allowed these travesties to happen, all because he believed the inmates, and herself, should leave Nepenthe Manor and go out into the real world, *for their own good*. What a load of crap.

"I think now would be a good time to start my assessment," he said in a soft, calm voice, but even so it sounded like a warning.

Pandora made her eyelids flutter dramatically, rolled her eyes back, then closed them with a deep, shuddering breath.

"Nice try, Pandora. But I know you didn't just pass out."

She didn't move.

"We can do this now, and speed up your discharge, or later, when I have some time. That could be awhile."

It was not an effective threat, being that the alternative was going to her grandmother's. The hospital was safe, and besides, she really didn't feel like herself, or even that well, for that matter. She ached all over and her head wouldn't stop hurting and she felt on the edge of losing her temper every passing moment. Wouldn't it be nice to have people looking after her for once? To not care about anybody but herself? To not feel the weight of responsibility, which she felt like she'd been carrying around like a sack of dismembered body parts for as long as she could remember?

Yes, it most definitely would.

Two more minutes passed in silence, then Dr. Steele sighed. She had to hand it to him. He had lasted longer than most people did. People don't like silence, and when appropriate, she wielded it like a weapon.

"All right. I'll try again tomorrow, but if I don't catch you awake, I'll have to do the assessment Monday evening. It's the best I can do since I have meetings and patients the whole day. When I took over as director while your father was in the hospital I got behind in my paperwork." He paused. "You're sure you don't want to try now? I thought you'd want to get back to your friends." He paused again. "Yes, I know what your mother said about making you stay with your grandmother when you got out, but I'm sure she won't really send you off now, not after all this."

He obviously didn't know Vicki, but then he hadn't been at Nepenthe Manor all that long, and was stunningly naïve about things. At best the man struck Pandora as a foolish optimist. She'd done her damndest to cure him of his positive attitude, to no avail. He just didn't get it, not often enough anyway, and someone like that was not to be trusted or relied on.

However, while that all sounded well and good, it was a dictate she struggled to hold herself to when it came to the good doctor. Like the wily wolf, he had a way of sneaking past her defenses, which was why she definitely didn't want him doing an assessment on her. Who knew what he might find?

She felt his hand lift from her arm, sensed him moving away from her. She didn't need her eyes to know when he paused in the doorway and looked back at her. She could practically hear him breathing. She wanted him gone, and yet, she hoped he'd stay. He might be an optimistic fool, but he kept the ghosts at bay.

There were footsteps out in the hall, brisk, healthy thuds, and Dr. Steele cleared his throat. "I was just getting out of your way, Nurse Abrams."

"Oh, Dr. Steele, you know you're welcome to stay as long as you want. Regular hours don't apply to you." The nurse gave a little giggle that grated on Pandora's nerves, like claws down a chalkboard. "And if you have any questions, just ask. I'm here for you."

Good Lord, woman, Pandora scoffed. *Hold on to some of your dignity!* Yes, Dr. Steele was gorgeous with his dark hair and piercing blue eyes, and his wee bit of an Irish accent was the absolute cream on top. *But this is a hospital! For the sick and dying! Not a bar, you floozy.*

"Well, yes, thank you." Dr. Steele, Pandora was pleased to note, sounded slightly wary. "I'll be sure to ask."

"You do that. Now go get yourself some shut-eye. You look all worn out!"

"Sleep sounds pretty good right now. It's been a long day."

She tutted sympathetically, and Pandora could see through slitted eyes the nurse patting Dr. Steele on the arm. "I heard one of the manor's inmates passed away on Friday. One of your patients?"

"No. But he was a long-time resident and will be missed."

"Of course he will." There was a brief moment of silence, as though in tribute. "And they don't like change, do they, that lot at the asylum? Brings out the worst in them, in my experience. We get them here sometimes. You'd think it was the end of the world when all that happened was someone doing something a little bit different. We once had a patient who flipped out when his mother changed the color of his toothbrush. They'd run out of his favorite at the store, you see, so he bashed his head against the mirror. Twenty stitches, it took, to fix him up."

"Yes, well, change can be hard, but it can also be good, once you adjust." He yawned. "Sorry, I really am bushed."

"I can see that." Arm squeeze. "You can have your wife or girlfriend fix you up a nice cup of hot chocolate or warm milk to help you sleep."

Pandora had to refrain from retching. So much for the woman hanging on to her dignity.

"I'm afraid I'll have to make that hot chocolate myself. Good night, Nurse Abrams."

"Good night, Dr. Steele." Nurse Abrams' voice held a satisfied, almost seductive burr. Damnit. Despite his initial wariness, the man couldn't resist setting the nurse straight on his relationship status, could he? Or was his fatigue clouding his ability to deflect unwanted attention? And it had *better* be unwanted attention. The woman was an idiot.

Pandora opened her eyes as the nurse approached. "Subtle, Nurse Abrams."

"You're awake." She took Pandora's wrist in her cool, soft as marshmallows, fingers, her eyes focused on her watch. "And what's that about?"

"Your approach to Dr. Steele."

"Oh, that." She grinned, showing a gleaming row of rather lengthy teeth. "I've learned from far too many years of experience that subtlety is overrated."

"Not with a guy like that."

Nurse Abrams smirked at Pandora, dropping her wrist as she did the mental calculations to figure Pandora's pulse rate. Judging by her furrowed brow, she was struggling with the math. "We'll see about that." *Not if I can help it.* "Ninety-six." She finally got it.

"Say, can you up my dose?" Pandora nodded at the IV bag hanging on the pole by her bed. "My head is killing me."

"Not a chance. Any more on top of what's already in you, and you'll go to sleep and won't wake up." She assessed Pandora with suspicious brown eyes. "Unless that's what you were aiming for?"

How much did she know? Pandora wondered, feeling a little breathless. *What was the official story?* "I just want this headache to go away."

The suspicion melted away. "It will, with time. Best thing to do right now is to eat something solid. Think you can do that?"

The thought of food made Pandora's stomach curdle, and she shook her head. The simple movement was enough to set off the pounding again, and she wanted nothing more than to shut it off. "Not yet."

"Shame," the nurse tutted. She stuck a glass thermometer under Pandora's tongue, then busied herself straightening up the bedding, checking the IV, and writing down important updates on Pandora's chart until a minute had passed. At last she plucked the glass tube from Pandora's mouth just when Pandora thought she was going to pass out from lack of oxygen. Nose breathing had never been one of her strengths. "Got a fever, I see. 101. Not bad, not great." She shook out the thermometer, then pocketed it. "I'll check on you later, but I'm hoping you'll be asleep by then." She wrote down the number on the chart.

"Me, too," Pandora muttered as the nurse strutted out the door.

But now that she was awake, she couldn't get back to sleep. Her head ached, her stomach gurgled, and her pulse had escalated to the speed of a revving engine. Her whole world was falling apart and she was stuck here, waiting for Dr. Steele to return to assess whether or not she'd tried to kill herself. Problem was, she wasn't sure she knew herself. Nothing seemed sure.

And just like that it no longer felt safe to stay in the hospital, where questions could be asked, and hopefully evaded, but maybe not successfully enough given her current buggered up state of mind. People might start to think she had a serious problem, and that would put a major damper on her freedom at Nepenthe Manor. Besides, what if that Baker guy came for her here, where there was no security and nowhere to hide? Grandmother had hired him, after all, to forcibly remove Pandora from her home. She might try using him again, even though she had seemed surprised to hear that Baker had used the threat of a stun gun to subdue Pandora. Plus, Vicki knew Pandora wouldn't go to her grandmother's without a fight, so she wouldn't care if Baker came back and finished the job. It seemed Pandora's only recourse was to run away and hide out at the manor.

A shadow darkened the doorway. "You're still awake."

Pandora, deep into her inner musings, jumped. Her mother had returned. Styrofoam cup of coffee in hand, she stepped into the room, bringing the smell of the potent brew in with her. "I can't sleep, my head hurts," she replied, and Vicki looked relieved. It was a weird thing to be relieved about, but sadly believable.

"I decided I needed to sort things out with you before I return to the manor." Ah, she was relieved Pandora was still awake so they could have their little talk. That was a little less insulting, but not exactly heartwarming, either.

"Like what?"

"Like what the official story is."

"Official story?" Pandora echoed, pretending ignorance.

Vicki's mouth tightened. "Let's cut the crap, Pandy. You and I both know why you jumped. So you wouldn't have to stay with Mother."

Pandora summoned up her 'hurt' expression, though a part of her wondered if it was completely put on. She kind of did feel hurt that her mother would assume something like that, even if it was plausible. She made what Pandora had done sound so tawdry.

"That's not why I jumped," she responded in a soft voice. "I jumped because I wanted to die." She mentally assessed the statement. Did it feel true? She wasn't sure, and that scared her.

Hearing her words, Vicki reared back, startled. "Shush! You did not!" She looked over her shoulder, checking to see if anyone had overheard, then shut the door.

"But I did want to die," Pandora persisted. "It was all my fault, and my head got messed up at the basketball game, and I just couldn't see any other way out."

"What was all your fault?" Vicki asked warily.

"Professor Robertson's death. What else?"

"How could you possibly think that, Pandy? Who would make you feel that way?"

"Um, *you*, Vicki? You implied that I was the one who killed him. I suppose it was because we got into an argument in his hospital room, about me going to stay with Grandmother Belfry when I didn't want to, and he heard us, and it sent him over the edge. How can I live with that on my conscience? Knowing I'd killed an innocent man. How?"

Pandora assessed this statement, too. Sometimes she couldn't distinguish between when she was telling the truth or making stuff up for effect. But if she truly did believe she was guilty, it lent credence to the idea that she'd tried to kill herself.

Vicki rubbed her forehead. "It wasn't your fault, Pandy. I overreacted, all right?"

Pandora shrugged, feeling cold despite her fever. "I guess."

Vicki came close to the bed and leaned forward, her voice low. Her breath smelled heavily of stale, bitter coffee. "So you can tell Dr. Gara and Dr. Steele that you didn't jump. Tell them you fell."

"But maybe that's not what happened."

Vicki's eyes remained steady. "I'm sure it is. You had a concussion, remember? Just tell them you fell, and I won't send you to Mother's."

Pandora's interest was caught. "I don't have to leave Nepenthe Manor?" Was she actually happy about that? Only minutes ago she'd welcomed the chance to hide out in the hospital and escape her life for a while. But that was before she'd started seeing the ramifications of staying here, where people might start to think the wrong thing.

Or the right thing.

"I don't know why you wouldn't jump at the chance of getting out of that place." Vicki shook her head. "Sorry, bad choice of words. But anyway, I'd leave tomorrow if I could..." She trailed off, her eyes staring blankly at the wall over Pandora's head.

Pandora didn't like the sound of that, especially considering the earlier statement Vicki had made, about needing to figure out what to do with her life now. "Well, it is my home, and staying with Grandmother sounds horrid."

Vicki gave a tight laugh. "Imagine growing up with her." She set down her coffee and took Pandora's hand, something she never did; her slim fingers were cool and dry. "Say it was an accident, don't do it again, and you get to come back to Nepenthe Manor. All right? Do we have a deal?"

Pandora nodded. She looked down at their hands together, wanting to both pull away and for the contact to never end. "You won't go back on it?"

"As long as you don't give me reason to."

"That's not acceptable."

Vicki sighed. "It's the best I can do, Pandy."

Pandora wondered if she should push her luck, then decided not to. Her mind wasn't as sharp as it could be right now, and she didn't want to mess this up. "All right. I'll take it."

Vicki pulled her hand away, grabbed her coffee, and headed for the door, opening it wide. "Good. I'll send someone to pick you up when you're released. Shouldn't be more than another day or two."

Pandora watched her mother leave, something fishy tugging at her mind, but she couldn't find the source. As the effects of the painkillers caught up to her again, she slipped into the darkness, and the disturbing feeling that she'd just made a bad bargain followed her into her dreams.

3

Great Day for Swears

PANDORA AWOKE TO the irritating sound of voices. *Again*. Why couldn't people just let her sleep? Dreamland was such a nice place to visit, the exception being when she dreamed about Baker popping the heads off babies, using his stun gun as a lever.

Thanks, Lucy.

"I told you her hair looked like a pile of horse doody," the devil herself declared in her deluded idea of a whisper, then added more loudly, "Pandora Poohead already talked to me and said she was coming home just for me. That's how cool I am, you guys."

"Oh, stuff it, you shrimp," Birdy snapped. "We've all heard how you threw a fit so Dr. Steele would take you with him yesterday." Pandora could smell the overwhelming sweetness of Birdy's grape Bubble Yum, along with her perfume, *Love's Baby Soft*, which had to be the stupidest name in the history of names. "Anyway, if I know Pandora—and yes, that butch job makes her look like a concentration camp victim—she's going to stay here as long as she can and milk as much attention as possible out of this whole joke of an accident. She's totally pulling a Bodkin." Mrs. Bodkin was the manor's resident hypochondriac and whenever a person thought someone was faking it, well, they'd use that phrase. "I'm the one who should be in the hospital. I'm suffering horribly. My eyes hurt, my chest hurts, even my feet hurt. I'm in deep mourning, and I don't think staying at Nepenthe Manor is healthy for me right now. I'm having flashbacks." Leave it to Birdy to 'forget' Pandora was actually in *true* mourning.

"But if you leave, Birdy," Charles said in a soft, breathless voice, "there'll only be a few of us left." He started wheezing, his dicky heart unable to handle his growing agitation. "And then what? Maybe Nepenthe Manor will close because nobody will be left but me. Am I going to get sent back home then? To my grandma?"

God forbid. That woman couldn't look after a hamster. Unfortunately, she was all Charles had since his mom and dad were both dead. Poor kid. With all the changes happening lately, it was only natural he was scared of having to live with a woman who wouldn't leave the house because she was afraid of aliens probing her nether regions. It didn't help the poor sap that he had a bad heart, thought he was a superhero, and had the mental toughness of a mushroom.

She was about to open her mouth and rescue him when a completely unexpected voice cut off her attempt. "I can assure you that no one is going to close Nepenthe Manor."

Dougie Daft? What the hell was *he* doing here?

"Shows what you know!" Birdy exclaimed triumphantly. "Word is out that we're going to have to shut down because we've run out of money and your asshole dad wants the property for condos."

Lucy clapped her hands and giggled. "Birdy said asshole!"

"We're not at Nepenthe Manor," Birdy stated matter-of-factly, "so I can say what I want, especially since Mayor Daft truly is an asshole."

"But you're under my authority, Birdy," Dougie corrected her, "and rules are meant to be followed for a reason." Pandora nearly scoffed out loud, giving away her condition. Rules were the last thing Dougie Daft followed, and if he did follow a rule, it was for his benefit, not society's. "Besides," he went on in his soft, yet strangely authoritative voice, "a beautiful *woman* such as yourself doesn't need to use profanities to liven up her speech. Your luscious lips already do that." He paused and Pandora could imagine Birdy pushing out her gloss-covered lips to emphasize his point, then getting all riled up with hormones because a male had said something flattering to her. "It's unfortunate I work at Nepenthe Manor now," he went on, cleverly moving to shut down said riled-up hormones. "Or I'd snap you right up."

Work at Nepenthe Manor now? Had Dougie lost his mind? He must be joking. Of course he was joking.

"But if I weren't a patient we could, you know..." Birdy, little tramp that she was, just had to throw that possibility out there, and extend what had to be a joke.

"Then you would be back under your mother's thumb, wouldn't you, and you don't want that, do you?" No, she didn't. Birdy was in constant competition with her mother, and the latest contest between them involved securing the worst mental health diagnosis possible. Personally Pandora thought they both should win the prize, which would be a one-way ticket to a correctional facility. Crime? Wasting everyone's time.

Birdy sighed despondently. "Well, it wouldn't work out between us anyway. I'm in love with Skippy."

"You are very loyal."

"I am, aren't I?" she replied perkily, easily shrugging off her sorrow. Of course it was easy, since she didn't really feel any sorrow anyway. At least not for anyone but herself. "When you're someone like me you can't just turn something like that off."

Pandora thought that if this conversation went on much longer she was going to scream, but she didn't want them to know she was listening so she bit her tongue. By faking unconsciousness she was learning far more than she would by letting on she was awake. Eventually she might 'wake up,' but not until she learned three things: How they'd all gotten to the hospital, what Dougie was up to now, and how he knew about Birdy's mom. That last one concerned confidential information that he shouldn't have access to. Unless he wasn't joking about working at the manor.

He wouldn't dare...

"Aren't you going to say hello, Pandora?" Dougie whispered, and she realized suddenly that he was very near. She could smell the spicy gel he used to slick back his white-blond hair, and his cologne—which was actually rather appealing, if you went for that sort of thing. Sadly, she kind of did. His breath was cool on her cheek, like he was refrigerated on the inside. But it felt nice. It was hot in here.

She sighed and opened her eyes. "What the hell have you done, Dougie?"

"Panny said hell!" Lucy whooped. "This is a great day for swears!"

"I might ask the same of you," he whispered, his eyes on her hair. When she didn't answer, he straightened up and pulled a black leather wallet out of his back pocket. He took out a couple bills, folded them lengthwise, and held them out. "Birdy, I'm about to give you a big job. I want you to take the others out to the vending machine in the hallway and buy everyone a soda and a candy bar. Do you think you can do that?" She reached for the bills and he pulled them back. "I need ten minutes, and I need you to not let anyone get into trouble during that time. You make that happen and the change is yours."

Birdy licked her lips. She got an allowance from her dad, but she was always running short on cash, which she needed to support her make-up, fashion and gossip magazine, and colored contact lens habit. She paid Beetle Steen to buy the make-up she wanted from the local drugstore, a trip typically requested after she received her fashion magazines in the mail. Beetle was the oily son of Frank Steen, Nepenthe Manor's security guard—no, make that ex-security guard now. Pandora remembered that he'd gotten sick and needed surgery. Her brain struggled to recall something else about his being gone, then she mentally snapped her fingers. Ah, yes. Vlad Volkov, the Russian thug her grandmother had hired to kidnap her, was taking his place. Pandora's head spun at the implications of this. One of her would-be kidnappers was now in charge of security at Nepenthe Manor? The whole world was going mad.

"They'll behave," Birdy retorted, glaring at each of them. "Won't you, you little turds?"

Pandora only now realized that Sinclair was in the room, standing quite close to the door. He was back to wearing his normal summer outfit of a short-sleeved white button-up and argyle sweater vest, his rust-colored hair perfectly coifed. He was staring at her, his lips moving. Gone were the dirty t-shirts he'd been wearing these last couple weeks to clean up the labyrinth. His OCD symptoms had actually been improving during that time, and she recalled that she hadn't liked that, knowing it was going to end badly. But now she realized how stupid she had been to worry. Two crises, and he'd regressed back to his old behavior, just like she'd told Dr. Steele he would. The members of the posse simply weren't up to facing the real world. In fact, Skippy was probably already dead from the shock.

"I'm not a turd!" Lucy spat back at Birdy. "You're a turd. You *eat* turds!"

Dougie gave Birdy a stony look that said *handle this* and surprisingly she did. "Fine, Lucy. You're not a turd. But you could eat something that looks like one. Milk duds, anyone?"

"Oooh!" Lucy clapped her hands, predictably distracted. "Milk turds for me!"

Birdy herded them out the door, taking a moment to shoot Pandora a triumphant look before leaving. Like she'd won some sort of contest. Sweet Mary, that girl was delusional.

A second later, Dougie was back at her side, his milky blue eyes fastened on her face like a leech on a pig's testicle. She frowned. Had she just compared her face to a pig's testicle? She really needed to get off these drugs.

"I have a new job."

"I can see that. What are you, some sort of candy striper for crazy people?"

"I'm a psych assistant."

What? "How'd you manage that? You're only sixteen."

"I'm also the mayor's son, and your mother is both desperate for the help, and determined to do whatever it takes to stick it to my father."

"But you don't have any training, and you definitely have no clue what you're doing."

"But I do have training, Pandora," he oh-so-patiently corrected her. "And I know what I'm doing. I know how to restrain clients, and I can administer medication and watch they don't cheek it. I've learned how to fill in charts"—which would explain how he'd known about Birdy's mother—"and take blood pressure readings. I can also make differential diagnoses. I taught myself this last part, and it's been quite the learning experience. Numerous mental illnesses often overlap, and telling them apart can be a challenge, but a challenge I both like and at which I excel. I can also effectively administer CPR. While practicing on that horrid dummy, Resusci Annie, I survived by imagining that she was you. Did you know her face comes from the death mask of a woman who drowned in the 1880s? She's known as *L'Inconnue de la Seine,* and authorities believe she committed suicide."

"Fascinating," Pandora replied, and actually rather meant it. "But how did you learn all that so quickly?"

"Oh, I started months ago, plus I'm a genius."

Pandora felt her control slipping. *"Months?"*

He gave her a smile full of cunning and guile, and it made her feel weird inside, like worms were wriggling about inside her gut. "I've been preparing for this moment for a long time now, Pandora. But recent events, including finally graduating from high school, have allowed me to put my plans into play. My mother insisted I stay in school two years longer than necessary, hoping to force me to conform to societal standards. But as I warned her, it was a waste of time and money. Socializing with those cretins set me back; it did not improve me."

"This can't be right," Pandora said desperately. "Vicki is crazy if she thinks nobody's going to notice a minor working at an insane asylum."

"I'm not getting paid. Dr. Steele says we can call it an internship. Doing so gets around all sorts of rules, as I explained to your mother."

So this is what Dougie had been talking about when he'd told her a few days ago that he had *something in the works.* He meant infiltration. He had infiltrated her world. And he'd done it by getting Dr. Steele on his side, probably by pretending he wanted to help the inmates leave Nepenthe Manor, as Dr. Steele did. Maybe Dougie did want that. Maybe he thought he and Pandora could live together at the manor, just him and her, all alone. She shuddered.

His overly red, vampiric lips twitched as though in pleasure. "Remember when I told you exceptional people make their own rules?"

"Vaguely." She remembered perfectly well. They'd been in his car, after the basketball game against Jimbo and his gang. And she had agreed with him. Because it was, of course, absolutely true.

"Like you, I make my own rules, Pandora, and then I get other people to follow them."

"You won't get me to follow your rules, you devious twerp."

"Of course not," he soothed.

She rubbed at her forehead. "Don't patronize me."

"Your head is hurting. I can help you with that. I've learned several pain relief techniques that I can apply to any given situation. Obtaining that knowledge was an accident, actually, derived from learning about pressure points for, shall we say, self-defense purposes. Allow me."

Dougie stared at her, hands out, until she nodded. Pain relief sounded really good right now. Given the go-ahead, he placed his cool fingers on her temples and started massaging. Ordinarily she'd be completely grossed out by his serpent-like touch, but he was good, and it felt so relaxing and soothing that she was grateful instead. She'd pay the price for giving in to him later, because of course there'd be a price.

But it will have been worth it, said the soon-to-be addict, after taking her first hit.

A few minutes later, Dougie, his magic fingers still massaging, spoke. "My father is working overtime to close down Nepenthe Manor. He thinks I'm going there as a spy for him, which is how I convinced him I needed to not only work at the manor, but stay there, too. Of course I'm not his spy. I might be Machiavellian, but I do have my principles." She gave a disbelieving snort; he ignored it. "So you and I can work together, Pandora, to find a way to get him to back off. Side by side, arm in arm, hand in hand, hip to hip—"

Crikey. "I think we have a bigger problem than your dad," she interrupted, before he moved on to discussing any more body parts touching each other.

The massaging stopped. "And that would be…?"

"I think Vicki is going to be looking for a new job."

The fingers withdrew and Dougie straightened up, his pale features tight. "What makes you think that?"

She would have felt more triumphant that she'd surprised him if her revelation didn't also mean losing the only home she'd ever known. "I'm pretty sure she took the position as director to watch over Professor Robertson. Now that he's dead, why stay? She doesn't really like it at Nepenthe Manor anyway. She's going to want out."

Ahhh… That's what felt so fishy with Vicki. She was going to allow Pandora to stay, but only until she had a new job. How devious of her.

Dougie's pale blue eyes looked darker than normal, or maybe that was because he'd taken to wearing darker colors lately. Today he was wearing a black sport coat over a gray turtleneck. He looked very professional, and very irate. "I see."

"So that means that all your scheming has been for nothing." She closed her eyes, wishing he'd go back to rubbing her head. It had felt so good, and it made her forget. "Besides, there's that guy, Baker, who tried to kidnap me. Vicki will want to get me away from him."

"I heard about him. I've been trying to track him down, but to no avail. Volkov said he never knew much about him, just thought he wasn't very bright. He doesn't like that he was played a fool, and I don't like knowing that someone means you harm."

She waved this off. Sure the idea of someone out there plotting against her made her a little wary, but this wasn't the first time someone had plotted against her, and it wouldn't be the last. People were always trying to douse shining lights like herself. "I'll be fine."

"You don't seem very concerned about your safety." He sounded almost angry. "It makes me wonder if maybe you really did try to kill yourself."

"You can think what you want," she snapped, skeptical of the strange turn their conversation had taken.

"All right, then I think you meant to end your current life."

Current life? "Well, you're wrong."

He leaned in, so close that she could feel his breath on her eyelashes. "Am I?"

"Of course you are. It was all a ruse, and it worked exactly how I wanted it to. Vicki isn't making me go to my grandmother's house anymore. But as I said, it might not matter if she decides to leave Nepenthe Manor."

Was her jumping a ruse or an accident? She'd better make up her mind quickly.

"I'll stop her."

"What are you going to do, kidnap her?" Silence. She opened her eyes. "*Dougie.*"

His cool eyes met hers. "I've already been here to see you, you know. Late last night when no one knew I was here. You were unconscious, and as I watched you sleeping, I was pondering what I would do if you had died jumping off that bridge."

She was almost afraid to ask, but when he didn't continue, she had to, her voice a whisper, "What would you have done?"

"I would have joined you, of course."

"No, you wouldn't have, you idiot!"

"I am not afraid to die, Pandora."

"Well, I am! I didn't want to die then, and I don't want to die now!

Death is the end, and I'm not ready to be at the end of anything." Was this true? Did she really mean it, or was she simply reacting to Dougie's weird declaration? It was the stupidest thing she'd ever heard, and yet so disgustingly romantic she worried she might have gotten seriously brain damaged *just thinking* it was romantic in any sense of the word.

He reached out and smoothed a spiky patch of her hair. His touch, which had once been so revolting to her, she now welcomed, her temples aching for him to start massaging again.

Lord almighty, she had to get off these meds.

"I am pleased to hear that," he said softly. "Now get some rest. You're going to need your strength." He pulled back and headed to the door. He stood for a moment before pivoting around to face her. "I like that we'll be living together, Pandora. It will be good practice."

What? Oh, wait. "Oh, no, it won't!" she shouted at his retreating back. "This isn't practice for us being together, you stalker!" The door shut tight.

Damn him! He'd gotten her again. But, thank goodness the true Dougie had emerged like an imp from under a rock, just in time to smack her in the face and wake her up to his true nature.

From here on out, she had to be at her best or risk getting sucked into his dark and bizarre little world. It wasn't going to be easy. She liked dark and bizarre little worlds.

A Bit of Tinkle

4

AFTER DOUGIE LEFT, Pandora decided enough was enough. If she was going to get out of here, she needed to eat. Her haven no longer felt like one, and things were happening that she knew she had to stop *right now* or disaster would result. Even though she felt weird and not like herself, and even though she'd be returning to the place where Dougie could now get at her 24/7, she had to go back.

She pressed her nurse call button. Twenty minutes, and a hundred button pushes later, a square-shaped nurse entered the room, moving deliberately slow, as though to prove a point...

You might be able to push a button, she could imagine the nurse challenging her directly, *but you won't be able to push* my *buttons.*

Watch me, sister.

As the nurse approached the bed, her steps as ponderous as a sloth's, Pandora's fingers tapped on the bed railing like a row of ravenous woodpeckers. She felt like if she didn't eat something soon, she was going to break things, starting with her own fingers if she kept up this insane tapping. "Sweet Josephine, you took your time, didn't you?"

"I was busy with *real* emergencies."

Pandora's eyes narrowed. "How'd you know mine wasn't?"

The nurse stared at her in defiance. "I guessed."

Pandora gritted her teeth. "Well, there's about to be an emergency if I don't eat soon. I'm really starving"—which was true, her nausea had disappeared—"and I need to eat something before I start cannibalizing myself."

One of the nurse's heavy dark eyebrows, the size of which an 80-year-old man would envy, lifted to show her skepticism. Pandora was tempted to bite her own arm to prove her point, but it probably wouldn't make a difference. Nursie looked a lot like the Hessian, a nasty, butt kissing psych assistant back at Nepenthe Manor, and living proof that Neanderthals had not died out. With their matching low brows, dull eyes, and boxy shapes, the two had to be related to each other, probably more closely than was legal.

"Is that so?" the nurse finally responded.

"That is absolutely so." Pandora smiled sweetly, though in reality she wanted to bare her teeth in a menacing growl. But she knew her sweet smile was actually more intimidating. "I'm that hungry. Say, do you by any chance have a relative who works at Nepenthe Manor?"

"My sister's girl does."

"That explains so much."

"And having met you, Miss," the nurse replied, her words coming out slow and measured, just like the Hessian's, "I now get why she's always complaining about you."

Not bad, Nurse Neanderthal, Pandora admitted. *You've got a little more sass than your niece, I can see. Though I do recall the Hessian having the balls to rat me out to my grandmother, something I owe her for big-time. Gonna have to add her to my shit list…a growing one, it seems.*

"My reputation precedes me," she said, smiling inwardly. "So now that you know what a pain I can be, if you want me gone from this place, fetch me something to eat as quickly as those little legs of yours can go." Pandora made a swift walking motion with two fingers. When the nurse only stared at her, Pandora's other hand started twisting the top sheet tightly into a ball. "Do I need to say that again?"

The nurse heaved a sigh. "I need to get the doctor to sign off."

"Then off you go, and hurry. I've gotten quite good at button pushing these last twenty minutes. I could probably do about a hundred a minute if I set my mind to it."

"I ain't her boss, you know," the nurse grumbled.

"And she won't be yours much longer if you don't get moving."

"She ain't *my* boss, either."

"Ain't ain't a word," Pandora ground out, then rubbed her temples irritably. Somewhere in the back of her mind she knew she was being a brat (though the nurse had started it), and that she was probably going to end up with crap food that someone had spit on, or worse, sprinkled a bit of tinkle on, but she couldn't stop herself. She'd never felt like this before—so out of control and anxious, like something bad was about to happen, and she didn't know what or when or where it was coming from. It was the sort of fear that you can't define, and she didn't like that. In fact, she kind of felt like…

No. Not possible.

She did *not* feel like she was losing her mind. Perish the thought. She needed to eat and get rid of these damn headaches, and then she'd be fine. She would not end up like her father, sticking bugs to a wall and talking to herself.

Oh, crap. Why'd *he* come to mind?

"Ain't is too a word," the nurse muttered under her breath, then pivoted on her white wedge nurse shoes and left the room.

There was a knock on the door and Pandora started out of a dream. She must have fallen asleep while waiting for Nurse Poky-Butt Neanderthal to return. Well, better sleeping than awake and thinking bad thoughts. But she didn't like how tired she felt all the time, and hoped it came from the meds and lack of food.

"Hello, Pandora," Dr. Gara greeted. She was in her late forties, already mostly gray, and had a worn look about her. But she had warm brown eyes and a sarcastic sense of humor that kept her from total decrepitude. Pandora had had many encounters with Dr. Gara over the years, and one could conclude they knew each other quite well. "I would say it's good to see you again, but that wouldn't be nice under the present circumstances, would it?"

Pandora grimaced. "Yeah, well, I'm not exactly thrilled to be here."

The doctor, dressed in a white lab coat and sensible brown shoes, consulted the papers on her clipboard. "So I heard you hit your head pretty hard, then possibly hit it again when you fell off the Pine River Bridge. It's about fifteen feet high, and the water is low right now. Perhaps on a rock?" Dr. Gara's tone was dry, non-judgmental. "Can you tell me what happened?"

Pandora felt a tiny quiver of fear go through her. This was it. The moment of truth. Or untruth, depending. "Well, I don't remember much of anything after I got in the car to go with my grandmother." That much was true, but she did remember what had happened beforehand. Most of it now, anyway. She just couldn't quite recall what her reasoning had been about the jumping.

She admitted she was a bit of a risk taker, but not that kind of risk taker. She could have ended up paralyzed. Or dead. Sure there'd been times when she'd been down about things, and yes, she had thoughts about dying. Not really how she'd go about making it happen, just that people would mourn her terribly afterward and she'd somehow get to witness it all from her little perch of sanctimonious suffering way up high. But she hadn't really wanted to die.

But all that being said, jumping off a bridge after yelling 'there's no other way' still didn't sit right. The simple truth was, she was a little afraid of getting caught out on this one, that this time she'd get into a kind of trouble that she couldn't argue herself out of, mainly because she couldn't remember what she'd been thinking. Even worse, maybe she had lost control of herself, of her own mind. Maybe she'd meant to jump because she'd truly wanted to die.

The best, and only, thing to do, she promptly decided, was steer clear of the topic. Avoid it. Repress it. Make it not real. Besides, she had struck a deal with Vicki. Call it an accident and she could return to the manor. To home.

"Were you upset about going to live with your grandmother?" Dr. Gara prompted, pen poised.

Pandora gave her a look. "Of course I was upset, though that's an understatement. You've dealt with the woman. Would you want to live with her?"

Dr. Gara absently shook her head, then realized what she was doing and stopped. "Your grandmother is a bit difficult, I admit, but I wouldn't harm myself to get out of going to stay with her."

Oh, crap. She knew something, or sensed it. Otherwise she wouldn't have used the word 'harm.' It was a red-flag word, and Pandora knew she was going to have to be very careful here.

"Dr. Gara, if I was going to kill myself, I'd pick a better way to do it. Not one that could backfire and leave me a vegetable. I think I just fell. I remember I wasn't feeling good before I got in the car, and then feeling like I was going to puke, and my mind was probably thinking—because my grandmother would've killed me for ralphing in her car—*get out, get out, for the love of God, get out!*"

Dr. Gara chuckled. "I can understand that. I feel that way sometimes when my twins start bickering, especially when we're trapped in the car. Thank goodness they're older now."

Pandora wasn't the only one who liked living in the land of denial. When they were younger, Dr. Gara's twins, Gigi and Giselle, had been notorious for their outlandish behavior. They were teens now, and from what Pandora had gleaned from Mrs. Hathaway, proprietor of Pandora's favorite bakery, they were still hell on wheels, only sneakier about it.

"Thank goodness," Pandora echoed with a mental eye roll.

"So your appetite is back?" Pandora nodded, both relieved Dr. Gara had accepted her story about why she'd jumped, and maybe a little annoyed she'd let it go so easily. Attention is such an alluring drug. "No nausea?"

"Nope."

"You had a fever earlier."

"I feel fine now."

"Headaches?"

"Sometimes."

"How severe? On a scale of one to ten, ten being your worst nightmare."

"Oh, about a two," she lied.

"So probably about a six," Dr. Gara noted.

"Hey!" Pandora protested, then clamped her mouth shut when Dr. Gara peered at her over her bifocals. "Oh, all right. Maybe a four."

"Six," Dr. Gara repeated. Damn, the woman knew her too well. "Possibly a seven. Food might help to alleviate the headache, but you're also going to have to take it easy for the next couple weeks. How are your ribs, by the way?"

Pandora had forgotten about bruising them during an argument with her half-brother, Xavier. She prodded at them experimentally. "Still sore," she admitted, but only because she knew they wouldn't keep her here. "But livable."

"I heard you were doing quite a bit of physical labor only a week after getting your injury." Her tone was matter-of-fact, but Pandora heard the warning behind it. Still no judgment, but Dr. Gara was determined to make her point.

"Then you heard about our sinkhole. It was a beauty! I wouldn't have minded keeping it, maybe catch me a rogue mayor in it, but it is a bit of a safety hazard for the patients. So I volunteered"—*ha, ha*—"to help fill it in. That's all."

"Hmmm. That's not what I heard." Dr. Gara looked up from her notes, fixing Pandora with a steadfast gaze. If only she'd taken this approach with her twins, instead of feeling guilty for being a working mom and giving in to their every demand, they might be less trouble. "Listen, Pandora. I'm very sorry about your father. He died too young, but he lived a lot longer than what we all thought; he'd been in the hospital several times over the years for pneumonia." Several times? Wouldn't Pandora have known about that? "Your mother kept it quiet," Dr. Gara said, as if reading her mind. "Probably made it sound like a routine visit. She didn't want anyone to worry. But anyway, this time it got him. It wasn't anything anyone did or didn't do."

Pandora's eyes narrowed. "What's your point, doc?"

"Dr. Steele is under the impression that you somehow feel responsible for your father's death. I'm telling you that there is no way you could be. He was a fragile man. I truly am amazed he lived as long as he did after his accident."

Pandora wanted to say, *I wouldn't feel responsible if my mother hadn't implied that I was.* But she kept her mouth shut. Sometimes the truth complicated things too much and worked against your agenda rather than for it. This was just such a time.

"Well, I don't know where Dr. Steele got that idea. I didn't even know the professor was my dad until recently, since that knowledge was kept from me." There. She'd gotten in her dig at her mother without there being repercussions for it. Dr. Gara knew how Pandora felt about Vicki, so this statement wouldn't come as a shocker.

"Well," Dr. Gara said hesitantly, "I'm sure your mother had a reason for keeping his identity from you."

"Vicki always has her reasons. I'm just not sure they're in my best interests, as she likes to claim."

"Yes, well, being a mom is hard, Pandora, and we don't always make the best decisions. We think they're the right ones at the time, then find out later that we messed up. It's not a nice burden to carry around."

Pandora glanced up at the doctor, surprised. This sounded awfully personal. "Yeah, well, at least you admit it. Vicki won't even admit that she poops."

"Like mother, like daughter," Dr. Gara said dryly.

Pandora drew back, as though slapped. "Low blow, doc!"

Dr. Gara laughed. "I'm just saying, don't judge your mother too harshly about this, all right? She has a lot on her plate."

"And I don't?"

"Most of what you have on your plate, Pandora, are the things you put on it. That's not the case for your mother." She consulted her notes. "Now. I'm going to order your food, and then your release for tomorrow. But only on one condition will I let you go…that you promise to take it easy once you leave."

"Promises are for suckers, doc."

"Yes, so you've said to me many times. But Pandora, you've only got one brain. Use it wisely and treat it kindly. All right?"

Pandora sighed. She knew the doctor was right. Why did she feel the need to argue all the time?

Because you think you're so damn smart, but you're nothing but a bossypants! came Birdy's voice in her mind.

Oh, bugger off, Birdy Peacock.

She was going home.

5

A Drugged Slug

IT WAS FIVE o'clock on Monday, and finally time for Pandora to ditch this joint before Dr. Steele showed up and protested her release. When he'd stopped by one time to check on her, she'd been roaming some distant hallway with the aid of a sadistic nurse—basically to prove she could walk without falling over—so she'd managed to evade him. Vicki had come by earlier, long enough to sign where she needed to sign, then took off again without a word. Pandora ended up having to wear the clothes she'd had on when she jumped into the river, which was rumored to be polluted with everything from paint cleaners to human refuse. Everything had been laundered, but her clothes felt tainted and she longed to tear them off and go naked. She didn't follow her instincts, but mainly because she didn't want to give anyone a reason to keep her here any longer.

Nurse Neanderthal had been charged with pushing Pandora's lumpy, squeaky-wheeled wheelchair, and Pandora had the feeling the nurse would happily propel her down every stairwell they passed. No matter. All the greats of the world had their haters. Plus, she was ready to jump to safety, if need be.

As soon as they were out the main doors, Nurse Neanderthal stopped the wheelchair. Pandora jumped to her feet, giving herself a head rush, then whirled unsteadily about to face her nemesis. "I hope for both our sakes that we never meet again."

"Same here," Nurse Neanderthal heartily agreed.

"But if we do, I sincerely hope next time it will be on *my* territory."

Nurse Neanderthal blanched—maybe the lady was smarter than she looked—then whipped the chair around and scurried away, not even stopping to be sure someone had come to pick Pandora up. She was learning.

Pandora scanned the parking lot for the Madmobile, wondering if maybe she was going to have to walk home, as there was no sign of the manor's patient transportation vehicle, or of Lonny or Ronny, its drivers. The twins, who also served as the asylum's gatekeepers, were rather strange creatures, and might very possibly be direct descendants of Ichabod Crane. They generally kept to themselves and were harmless, but their odd appearance and antisocial behavior often frightened

people. If it were up to unenlightened boneheads like Mayor Daft the
twins could easily be asylum residents themselves. The ignoramus
couldn't stand anyone who looked or acted different than himself and
his group of preppy cronies, and because they were soulless robots it
didn't take much to be different from them. The funny thing about
Mayor Daft is that although he wanted to shut down the only place in
the area willing to take in the mentally ill, he'd be the first to scream
bloody murder if he encountered one in public. Damn hypocrite.

At any rate, the Madmobile was nowhere to be seen and it was a hard
vehicle to miss, being the deviant spawn of a hearse and a black stalker
van. It was beginning to look like Pandora had been forgotten. Or
Vicki hadn't told anyone she was coming home because this was actually a devious trap. Soon, the big bad wolf Baker would arrive and haul
Pandora off, with no one about to come to her rescue. Not that anyone would come to her rescue anyway. She'd discovered that unpalat-
able truth when Vlad, the Russian, aka their new security guard and
traitor to her cause, and Dr. Steele both had left her to her fate, stating
inanely that it was for her protection.

Wussies.

Annoyingly, the moment she realized she might be standing in someone's crosshairs her head started to pound, despite her brave words to
Dougie, and she broke into a sweat. Now who was being a wuss? But
she did have a good excuse. While she felt better than yesterday, her
head still hurt and she was weak from lying in bed. Basically she
wouldn't be able to outrun her pursuer, especially if it were Vlad. She
should be able to outrun the plump Baker, though. He might not be
under her grandmother's pay any longer, but he could still be working
for the mystery man he'd mentioned, the one who appeared to be the
brains behind the kidnapping scheme. She needed to know who this
man was, and what did he want with her? Kidnapping is a pretty serious crime, and he didn't seem to care. Maybe she should buy a gun.
Go into hiding. Change her name and color her hair. Maybe she
should—

The sound of a car's engine interrupted her accelerating thoughts and
she turned to see the Madmobile pulling up to the sidewalk. After
coming to a stop, the driver slid out and came around to open the passenger door for her.

"At last," Dougie breathed when he saw her, his pale eyes avid as he
motioned her to get in.

"Where are Ronny and Lonny?" she demanded, feeling like she'd been
sucker punched. "Did you kill them and hide their bodies, Dougie? Be-

cause that's a line I won't cross. Unless I'm crossed, of course, and they've never crossed me."

"While I admire your thinking, the answer is no. They're alive and well. I bribed them, actually. Wasn't really necessary, since I can drive, and I'm an official staff member now. But I thought, what else do they have to fill their dull little lives but the occasional appointment or pick-up here at the hospital? They have to open and close the gate, of course, but not very often. What a tedious life they lead. So I gave them something they needed, and in return they handed over the keys so I could come get you."

"Do I even want to know what you gave them? Because the Madmobile is kind of their baby."

"Get inside and I'll explain everything you need to know on the way." Without waiting for her response, he took her elbow and guided her toward the open passenger door and up into the seat.

"You'll explain everything," she amended his statement as he buckled her seatbelt before she could even reach for it. "Not just what you think I *need to know*."

His smile was devious as he pulled away from her. She'd been about to shove him away, but he was too fast. Or she was too slow. Her mind, her reflexes, all defiled by this concussion. She was like a drugged slug. "How I've missed our little spats, Pandora."

"This isn't a spat. I'm calling you on a detail, which you threw out there to test my wits." *Which are still functioning*, she was relieved to find. "I might have a concussion, but I'm not completely out of it."

"Your head still hurts, though."

"Is that an observation? Cause it's a dick-headed one. Of course my head still hurts. I told you. I have a concussion."

"You look like you're constantly squinting, that's how I can tell," he went on, unfazed by her rant. "You're different in other ways, too, and I'm currently assessing the extent of those changes and whether, as I'm hoping, they offer me a challenge." He looked thrilled at the prospect of said challenge as he left her to go around to the driver's side.

Once inside the Madmobile, he expertly started up the van and shifted into drive, pulling out in front of a car that had attempted to go around them. The driver honked and gave them the finger, but Dougie ignored the irate man as he maneuvered out of the parking lot.

She studied his unaffected profile. "So the rules of the road don't apply to you, either?"

"Not usually, but especially not today. I need to get you home as soon as possible. You are not well, and I find that unsettling."

"What I find unsettling is the image of us getting creamed by a semi-truck."

"So you *do* want to live."

She sighed and rolled down the window. It was suddenly quite hot in the van, and the air felt so heavy. It also smelled like feet. "Who are you trying to beat to the punch, Dougie?"

"I'm relieved to see your deductive skills haven't been too badly affected by your mishap."

Too badly affected? My deductive skills are just fine, thank you very much. "Who, Dougie?"

"Who do you think?"

"Certainly not my mother."

"She didn't even volunteer."

"Dr. Steele?" She tried to keep the hopeful note out of her traitorous voice, but Dougie heard it anyway.

"He wanted to do a suicide assessment on you on the drive back and was quite upset"—Dougie briefly looked the opposite—"when the Director said that I should be the one to pick you up. I didn't even have to manipulate the situation to stay on both their good sides. Your mother did all the work for me. If Dr. Steele is upset, it's with her. Not me."

"So you have them both on your side now," she concluded, feeling dull inside.

"Mostly," he agreed, heeding her tone. "But remember that whatever I do, even if it doesn't seem like it, I'm doing it for you."

"Don't hand me that load of crap, Dougie. You're doing this for you."

He gave a slow, satisfied blink. "All right, I admit that. My current diverted state relies on your presence. I need to keep you safe, and Dr. Steele was going to ask questions that I'm quite certain would be threatening to you at this stage of your recovery."

Sensing something a little off in Dougie's tone, she peeked at him out of the corner of her eye and took in how tightly his pale hands gripped the steering wheel. It was an action far removed from when he'd driven her around in his Lamborghini, and miles from the smooth, cool persona he typically presented to the world. What was going on in that devious little brain of his? And what did it have to do with her, other than the obvious, the little perv?

Dougie glanced over at her, and she looked away, out the windshield. They were approaching the Pine River Bridge, and seeing it made her feel light-headed, almost nervous. She snorted inwardly. This was not like her at all…this oversensitivity. She felt like a delicate baby chick.

Dougie, of course, noticed.

"I'll drive fast."

"Either way." She was pretending nonchalance, but what she felt was fear. Her. Pandora Belfry. Afraid. If this was what her life was going to be like from here on out, might as well just shoot her now.

Dougie pressed down on the gas and they zoomed over the bridge while she gripped the door handle and tried not to look at the hungry black river down below, at the rusted steel girders passing overhead, at the place where she'd almost ended. Once they were over the bridge, Dougie slowed down and Pandora opened her eyes, a thought suddenly occurring to her.

"Who saved me?"

"Jesus?" Dougie replied blandly.

"Very funny. Who saved me from the river? I know it wasn't Grandmother Belfry. She can't swim, and she wouldn't want to mess up her hair. Jenkins is ancient. He'd sink like a stone."

"I can't say."

She glared at him. "You mean you *won't* say. Was it Vlad?" she pondered aloud. "Or maybe it was Xavier. Speaking of my brother, why hasn't he come to visit me? Or has he, and was creepy like you and came while I slept?" And why hadn't Derek visited her, either? Come to think of it, she hadn't received any cards or flowers during her stay. Nothing. The thought made her feel all prickly inside, and she dug her knuckles into her sore ribs to distract herself.

"Did you know that when you sleep you curl up tight like caterpillars do when a bird's shadow passes over them?"

"Oh shut up."

"Sometimes I imagine myself as the bird. A hawk, maybe, or a falcon."

"I said, shut up, sicko. And you're more like a vulture. Now answer my question."

"As your *half*-brother has neglected to take me into his confidence, I have no idea why he wouldn't visit you in your time of need."

"He was probably busy with work. There's lots to do around here."

"And don't ask me about the giant," Dougie warned.

She hadn't planned to, but was delighted to see how much it would bother Dougie if she had asked. Derek was a weapon she could use on him, though sparingly, like a cattle prod.

"I still want to know who saved me from the river."

"And I would like to know why my father is so incredibly vile. But there are certain mysteries in life, Pandora, that are never meant to be solved."

"That's bullshit, and you know it. Your father's an asshole because he was born with the asshole gene." Elizabeth Nepenthe's diary documenting her poor opinion of the Dafts—from a *century* ago—was proof of that.

"Are you insinuating that I inherited that gene, as well?"

"Insinuating? And here I thought I was being so clear." She closed her eyes and rubbed her temples, implying this conversation was over.

Dougie got the hint. "Rest a bit, Pandora," he intoned, sounding like a doctor from a horror movie. "We'll be home soon."

"Just don't stare at me," she mumbled, allowing herself to sink into a doze. "It gives me the heebie-jeebies."

"Well, you give me the urges."

"Oh, shut *up!*"

6

PANDORA JERKED OUT of her doze to the clanging of the manor's gates closing behind them. Then came the sound of the Madmobile's idling engine mixed with the babble of voices. She cracked an eye to see Lonny and Ronny standing outside the driver's side window, both talking at once. She'd never seen the likes of it. The two hardly spoke ten words between them in a typical conversation, and now they couldn't seem to get the words out fast enough.

"We've assembled our group," said Ronny.

"And our master has been chosen," Lonny added.

"We've picked our PCs!" exclaimed Ronny.

"And determined our skills, weaknesses, and necessary weaponry," Lonny finished.

"Very good, gentlemen," Dougie praised the twins. "Keep me informed of your progress."

"Will do," they chimed in unison.

Dougie gave them a little salute, which they returned, then shifted into drive. Pandora quickly closed her eyes. She had never seen the twins look so happy or alive. What the hell were they planning to do? She didn't want to let on that she'd heard, so she moaned and stirred, lifting her arms into a stretch.

"We're home."

It felt strange hearing Dougie refer to Nepenthe Manor as home. He'd done it twice now, and she didn't like it. This was her home, not his. Her sanctuary. From him.

She didn't respond, simply stared out the window as they passed by the labyrinth. How much work had Sinclair gotten done on it, she wondered, before he reverted back to his old ways? She'd have to check it out when she felt a little better, maybe see if he'd show her what he'd done. She kind of felt bad that he'd regressed, even though it meant she'd been right. She didn't like to admit it, but being right in this case didn't feel very fulfilling.

Dougie sped up a little and the barn and the already sprouting field were soon left behind, and a few moments later they pulled up in front of the manor. Built in the 1880s, it was a massive structure and she was glad to see it looked its usual forbidding self. The griffins flanking the stone staircase still served as guardians, and above them were the windows to her bedroom. The faint sound of the ocean crashing against the shore and a strong scent of brine entered the open car window. She was home.

Dougie shut off the van and slid out. He must have moved quite quickly, because he was at her door before it was open halfway, his hand out to help her. She wanted desperately to turn her nose up at his offer, wanted to do things herself, didn't want to get sucked into his orbit. But she soon realized she couldn't afford her pride. She felt sick, and only wanted to lie down in a dark room and sleep. If she didn't want to end up with yet another concussion, she needed his help to get up those stairs without falling down them like Humpty Dumpty, and everyone knows how that turned out.

His hand when he took her arm was cool, as though he were already half dead. A part of her crawled toward the sensation, like worms to decaying flesh. Another part cringed. Dougie Daft was touching her again, and he seemed to be relishing her ambivalent reaction to him. She smoothed her expression to one of indifference.

"I suppose Vicki wants to see me," she said in a calm voice as they entered the foyer. The lingering scent of burnt material reminded her that not too long ago the curtains had caught on fire and nearly burned down the building. Down one of the halls lay the way to Quack Central, where the therapists had their offices. Off to her right sat Vicki's office. Directly in front of them, a spiral staircase led to the other floors and wings, though it was not the only way to reach the different parts of the building. The manor was its own labyrinth, and it felt good to be back. Comforting.

Pandora would feel almost entirely safe if it weren't for Vicki's ominous words about wanting to leave and Dr. Steele's impending assessment of her mental health and Mayor Daft's threats to shut down the asylum and the mystery man who wanted to kidnap her.

"No, but Dr. Steele does," Dougie answered her.

"Super."

She looked up to see Vlad the Russian running smoothly down the stairs. He wasn't very tall, but he was built like a gymnast, all compact and muscled. Acne scars from his youth dotted his face, but instead of marring him, they only added to his mystique. His blue-gray eyes, always scanning for trouble, had settled, ironically enough, squarely on her face. "So the prodigal has returned."

"I'm not talking to you, you rat."

"I told you I needed to make it up to your grandmother after letting you go that first time, when I'd been hired to do otherwise," he said calmly in his strongly accented voice, "and I did as I said I would. I'm only sorry you were hurt in the process."

"You look about as sorry as the Night Stalker after he was convicted of murdering fourteen people."

"I was killing two birds with one stone. No pun intended. The first, my obligation to your grandmother, the second, to get you somewhere safe, away from Baker and his schemes."

"Well, you almost killed three birds."

"You are still alive, are you not?"

"Barely." She swayed a little, and not entirely for effect.

"Help me get her to her room," Dougie ordered, and Pandora thought Vlad would rebel against such blatant autocracy, but he didn't even bat an eyelash as he strode up to Pandora and lifted her into the air. She smelled stale cigarette smoke and his musky deodorant as her feet left the ground and she settled into his bulging arms. It was not an unpleasant smell.

"Wait just one damn minute!" she hissed. "I'm not a package you need to deliver. I can walk!" Her shouting hurt her own ears, and this pissed her off. What also pissed her off was how much she liked being lifted into the air by strong men. First Dr. Steele, and now Vlad. One would think she had a rescue complex. But she was no gag-inducing Rapunzel. Oh, no. She started to fight, struggling to free herself from her oppressor, but Vlad only stood impassively as she squirmed and twisted.

"It is like wrestling the tiger," he said to Dougie, whose eyes were dark with, was that *jealousy*? Was everyone mad here? "A small one, but ferocious nonetheless."

"What's going on?" Dr. Steele called from the Quack Central hallway. "Vlad? Is everything all right?"

"Does it look all right?" Pandora howled. "Tell him to put me down."

"She gave the appearance of someone about to fall over," Vlad explained. "So I help."

"She doesn't look her best," Dr. Steele admitted, coming closer. His eyes swept over her and Pandora immediately stopped fighting.

"I'm perfectly fine," she said with as much dignity as one could muster while being held like a baby. She was not going to let the good doctor use this against her. "Now if you don't mind, I would like to be set down so that I may go to my room and rest."

She waited to be obeyed. She was not obeyed. "I will take you to your room," Vlad insisted, his voice bland.

"I'm coming with you," Dr. Steele said. "Go on ahead. Just let me grab something from my office."

"No! I'm fine. Just put me down!"

"It will be all right, Pandora," Dougie assured her.

"Traitor!" she hissed at him.

He only stared straight ahead, not acknowledging the inflammatory word with so much as a flicker of his reptilian eyelids.

Vlad wouldn't look so unbearably smug if I threw up on him, Pandora thought as he trudged up the stairs. *Unfortunately it's hard to feel triumphant if you've got puke dribbling down your chin.* Based solely on the image this conjured up, she decided to keep her bland hospital meal of rubbery chicken and lumpy mashed potatoes inside her.

The trip up the stairs felt a bit like walking the plank. She knew what was coming... Dr. Steele's assessment, questions she didn't want to answer, didn't feel ready to answer. All she wanted was to be left alone, but it looked like the truth, whatever it was, was going to come out.

A sob hitched in her throat as they neared the top of the steps. So this was her big welcome home. To get treated like a child. To be interrogated by a far too persistent and perceptive doctor. This whole stupid day bit the big one.

Though, really, she should be used to this sort of thing by now. This was how her life worked, and if she didn't suck it up right this instant she'd end up on the wrong side of the gate, so to speak, on soul-wiping meds and with a black mark on her record that would haunt her for the rest of her life.

But she was so sick of sucking it up. Sick of it all.

I just want to go to sleep and not wake up.

Her heart skipped a beat. Did she mean that?

The door to her apartment loomed up in front of her. They had arrived. Dougie placed his hand on the doorknob, then hesitated. He peered past them, toward the stairs, and Pandora turned to see that Dr. Steele had caught up with them. He held something behind his back, something he didn't want her to see. Probably some torture device to get her to confess. Normally that would intrigue her, but not today.

Dr. Steele nodded at Dougie, and he opened the door. It was dark inside the apartment, and he reached in and turned on the light. It occurred to Pandora that he had to be awfully familiar with their place to know exactly where to reach for the light switch, especially being that it was farther from the doorway than would be found in a typical room.

Suspicious.

"Ready?" he asked her.

"Like I have a choice."

"You always have a choice," he reminded her.

"Yes, but sometimes the choice is between two equally distasteful outcomes. Then what?"

His eyelids slowly dropped, as though he were enjoying her discomfiture, then opened again. "Then what, indeed?"

"In we go," Vlad announced loudly, stepping into the apartment... which looked different. It looked *decorated*, as in, for a party.

"Supwise!" Lucy's voice rang out from behind the couch, followed by Birdy's reprimand, "Not yet, you dodo!"

"Surprise!" a chorus of voices shouted over Lucy's heated protest that she was not a dodo, just faster than everyone else. A bunch of people rose up from behind the couch and a few chairs, and turned out to be Charles and Sinclair, Cracker Jack, Carl, the groundskeeper, and the lovely Nurse Devine, who seemed to be standing awfully close to Carl. The surly groundskeeper and perma-bachelor didn't seem to mind Nurse Devine's proximity, made even more apparent when he slung his tanned arm around her shoulders. Pandora was left feeling a bit gobsmacked. Was this the same Carl who regularly berated her for being too soft? Too weak? Too sentimental? All because she spoiled her horse, Shadow, to avoid getting bitten, trampled, or bucked off? How in the devil was she supposed to process this information?

"What is this?" Pandora said aloud, feeling increasingly anxious. "An intervention?"

"You are more suspicious than the KGB," Vlad informed her as he set her down. "It is a party for your homecoming."

"A party? Oh. Well. Huh." This had to be the weirdest, most surreal moment of her life, and she felt her throat constrict. Nobody had ever thrown her a party, and she always pretended not to care when the manor gave parties for the inmates whose families wouldn't, or couldn't, do it. But she kind of did care. Sometimes, while lying in her bunk bed at night, she'd imagine herself attending a party just for her, princess for a day. An evil princess, of course, and she would be surrounded by people who adored her and fawned over her, and who gave her air hugs and seemed so happy she was here on this earth. Which would pretty much be no one at Nepenthe Manor, with the exception of Dougie maybe, and only if you swap out the air hugs for groping expeditions. But still... Her very own party.

Vlad peered at her closely. "Are you crying?"

She dashed a hand across her face. "No! I just thought the only party I'd ever get was when I moved out of here and all the staff would celebrate by going on a week-long bender. Only after I was gone, of course, but it would be in my honor."

He cuffed her shoulder. "You are too dramatic."

She looked sideways at him. "I concede that. But not about this."

He gave her a strange look. "That is very sad, Pandora Belfry."

"That's my life, Vlad," she sighed, looking around her. The posse had already booked it to the table, which had been decked out with all sorts of treats, including a bucket filled with ice and bottles of Coke. She'd never seen so much good food in her life. Too bad she wasn't very hungry.

"Are you surprised?" Dougie asked, watching her closely as he steered her to a quiet corner. "You don't look surprised."

"I am surprised," she admitted. And still not buying it that this was just for her, without strings attached. "Whose idea was it?"

"You can probably guess that my thought processes do not run to parties as a means of celebration. I have other ways of celebrating," he added cryptically. "No, this was Lucy's idea, and I simply made it happen." It now made sense why he knew his way around the apartment so well. "She said you looked awful and needed cheering on—her words—or you'd try to snuff it again—also her words."

"Lucy thinks I tried to kill myself?"

"They all do."

"Crap."

"Yes, well. That's what happens when a person jumps off a bridge. Now come. I'll feed you."

"Holy hell, Dougie! I'm not a newborn. I can feed myself."

"Then pretend I'm your slave, here to meet your every need."

"How is that any different than before?"

"Amusing. I'm offering myself to you, Pandora." He paused, looked at the floor, then back up at her, his eyes brazen. "My services, that is. Let me do this for you."

"You can watch me eat, Dougie. Will that make you happy?"

"That is a state of being I don't quite understand."

"Of course not." She mimed smacking her forehead. "What was I thinking?"

Their plates heaping with food, the posse made a wobbly beeline for her, though it was weird not to see Skippy's tall frame, topped by some kind of hat, amongst them. "Pan-pan!" Lucy lisped as a roll rolled off her plate. She stopped, looked at it, shrugged, then kicked it under a chair before continuing her forward momentum. "You're still alive!"

"Excellent observation."

Lucy turned around. "You owe me five buckeroos, Birdy."

"You guys bet on me?"

Birdy shrugged as she picked through her pile of food for a green olive. Pandora loved green olives. She liked to imagine they were tiny heads. "I was bored."

"Are you wearing a veil?" Birdy was dressed all in black, and wore a little black hat, which dropped a curtain of lace over half her face.

"I'm in mourning. I told you."

Black was Pandora's color. Everyone knew that. Her fingers curled up. Gone for a few days and this is what happens to a person…they get wiped out, removed, erased. "Black is not exactly your friend, Birdy."

Birdy didn't even look up from her search. "Jealous?"

Pandora laughed like an evil villainess. "Of what? Your pasty complexion?"

"Pasty? Please. You're jealous that I have loved and lost and you've never loved at all." She licked potato salad off a black fingernail, then pointed it at Pandora. "I win."

"So glad to be back amongst my *friends*." It occurred to her at that moment that not all her so-called friends were here. Three people were missing from the party. Derek, who she could somewhat understand not being here, since it was Dougie who'd organized the whole thing. He certainly wouldn't have invited this 'giant' threat—ha, ha—to his relationship with Pandora, not that there was a relationship to threaten. Plus, Derek's mother had just been admitted to the asylum, and he was likely with her. So he had a couple of excuses to fall back on.

Vicki and Xavier, however, did not.

7

Veil of Sorrow

"WE MISSED YOU, Pandora," Charles greeted, in between spooning lime Jell-o into his mouth with surprising speed. Maybe he was a superhero after all, and his super power was Jell-o eating.

"I missed you, too, Charles."

"You missed me the mostest," Lucy declared, then shoved a cracker into her mouth and started to chew, crumbs flying everywhere à la Cookie Monster.

Pandora reached out and squeezed a brown pom-pom of Lucy's delightfully frizzy hair. "Right back at ya."

"I didn't miss you," Birdy declared.

"Right back at ya." Birdy mumbled something undoubtedly unrepeatable in front of Lucy, and Pandora turned to Sinclair. "How's it going, Sinclair?" He was the only one who hadn't filled his plate to heaping. He had three items on it, none of which were touching. He looked neat and clean and miserable. His response was a shrug. "Any new projects?" she ventured. Another shrug, though his eyes brimmed with tears as he looked at her, steadily, almost fiercely. Tears? What was going on with him *now*? He was back to 'normal.' He should be happy.

Crikey. This place was filled with a never-ending stream of sorrow and struggle and turmoil, wasn't it? She rubbed her forehead. Why had she come home? Her own mother and brother couldn't even be bothered to come to her welcome home party. Yes, it was nice that Dougie had put it together, but the posse had shown up for the food, not for her.

"Anyone hear from Skippy?" she asked the others, hoping for some good news.

Charles shook his head mournfully. "Nope. But we do have a few new inmates. There's an old guy, Tobias, that keeps talking to us and he says he's the King of Bedlam, which is a silly thing to say"—ironic judgment from a kid who claims he's a superhero—"and a lady named Gloria who has schizophrenia, and is really nice, and a girl, too. The girl won't talk to us, though. I tried to make friends with her and she told me to go away. But with swears."

"She reminds me of you, Pandora," Birdy gave her unwanted opinion with a smug smile.

"I'm so sorry about the professor, Pandora honey," Nurse Devine said as she approached the group, unwittingly saving Birdy from Pandora's fist. "He was a good man." The nurse's arm was looped through Carl's, and she looked different out of her white uniform. Happier. Lighter. Or maybe that was from being with her new boyfriend. Gag.

Pandora had once had so much respect for Nurse Devine, but to fall for Carl, the sadist? Her standards were apparently much lower than Pandora would have guessed. As the *Queen* song goes, *another one bites the dust*, and the refrain left a bitter taste in Pandora's mouth.

"He was," she mumbled, feeling uncomfortable. She preferred it when people didn't mention the professor dying. It made his death real, and right now real was too much to handle. Luckily the posse was either too self-focused or good at repression to bring it up.

"How are you feeling?" She pointed to her head. "Any better?"

"I'm fine, Nurse Devine. Thank you for asking," she added politely. Silence met her response. They were all staring at her, mouths open in disbelief. "What?"

"I don't think I've ever heard you speak without something sarcastic or bossy coming out," Birdy remarked.

"You have potato salad smearing your veil of sorrow," Pandora snapped. "Is that better?"

"Having headaches?" Nurse Devine persisted, ignoring their spat. It was not the first she'd witnessed.

"Sometimes," Pandora admitted.

"Dr. Gara sent over your records. She wants me to keep an eye on you."

Pandora's gaze moved from Nurse Devine to Carl, then back again. "I'm not sure you'll be able to fit me in. Carl is awfully demanding of a person's time."

"And there it is," Birdy declared triumphantly.

"Was that necessary, missy?" Carl asked, stepping forward.

"Were all the times you got on my back about every little thing I did that you didn't approve of necessary?"

"To keep you from becoming a juvenile delinquent? Hell, yes."

"No wonder I jumped," Pandora muttered under her breath.

"Pandora needs some space," Dougie spoke up. "It's been a long day for her."

A wave of anxiety and the urge to cry coursed through her like an adrenaline rush. Nothing was the same. Everything was all wrong. She spun around. The room looked so different. Too much color, too much noise, the smell of the food too strong. Dougie took her arm and pulled her back from the crowd. He found a chair for her and made her sit down, then left her, saying he needed to go check on something. She crossed her arms and watched the proceedings through blurry eyes. Her first party, and she'd scared everyone off.

Way to go, Pandora, she thought miserably. *No wonder you don't get any parties. And now they're talking about me*, she realized as she glared at the happy revelers, who kept looking her way. *Wondering when I'm going to try and off myself next, I imagine. Maybe I should do it and make them all happy.* She bit her lip and looked away, letting her eyes close and her mind wander from the overwhelming scene.

"Why don't we load up a couple plates each?" she heard Nurse Devine saying, as though from a distance. "All right, kids?"

"What's wrong with Pancussion Head?" Lucy asked, sounding mad. Pandora cracked one eye open. "She should be happy. A party is a place to be happy. If she's happy she won't kill herself and leave us all by ourselves."

"Will you shut up about Pandora, you dwarf?" Birdy growled. "I'm in deep mourning and you don't see me trying to kill myself! I could, you know. I have a plan, I have motive, and I'm suffering deeply. But I must remain strong. It's what Skippy would want. Though I sure could use some extra therapy sessions to get me through this." She glanced slyly at Dr. Steele, who smartly avoided eye contact.

"Nurse Devine is right," he said heartily. "Let's dish up and take our food to the rec room. Can we say thank you to Douglas for putting this together?"

"Thanks, Dougie!" the posse chorused. "You're not nearly as big a douche bag as I thought you were," Lucy added.

"Lucy!" Dr. Steele reprimanded. "That is not a good thing to call anyone."

"Even if it's true?"

"Either way."

"It was my pleasure," Dougie said. "Take extra, Lucy. You earned it."

"I did, didn't I? I didn't say one word about Pandora being a big baby quitter, did I?"

Several groans burst out, and even Birdy sounded mad when she said, "Way to hold back, Lucy."

Lucy beamed. "I did hold back, didn't I? So as a reward, I'm taking five cupcakes. That should do it."

As the posse helped themselves to a plate of desserts, Dougie and Dr. Steele spoke to each other for several moments, occasionally glancing her way. She was ready for each look, meeting it with a scowl.

Once enemies, now they're best buddies? And just look at her own self! Sitting like a naughty child in the corner. How humiliating.

"Welcome home, Pandora," Nurse Devine called from the doorway. "I always have plenty of time for you, hon, even if you just want to talk. Carl, too. Isn't that right, baby?"

He gave a quick downward jerk with his head, which apparently was a yes? "Shadow's been waiting for you to come home. Best get yourself better so you can look after her." He abruptly disappeared out the door, Nurse Devine following after him, a plate in each hand.

Pandora heard a nearby floorboard creak and looked up to see Cracker Jack standing in front of her. "You're gonna make it through this, Pandora Belfry. I know this for sure."

"Thank you, Cracker Jack," she replied in a weary voice. "If anyone knows what it's like to go through hard times, it's you." Cracker Jack had fought in the Vietnam War and suffered from shell shock, which they now call post-traumatic stress disorder because it's so much easier to say. He always looked tired, probably from all the nightmares and flashbacks he still experienced, but he seemed to take some comfort from his gardening, which was one small consolation. Not much of one, though, for someone who'd risked his life, then had to return home to a less than welcoming, very ungrateful country. He couldn't get good help because the government programs were behind the times, or they simply ignored the idea of shell shock cause it cost money to treat something they considered a weakness or just plain faking it. What they didn't realize is that in the long run not treating PTSD was going to end up costing them far more. Cracker Jack was one of the so-called lucky ones. He had a good place here, and work to do, and some friends, too. But what would happen to him if Mayor Daft got his way and closed down the manor? In the past, Vicki would have fought the mayor tooth and nail. But now? Maybe the inmates would be better off if Vicki decided to leave. Pandora wasn't sure her mother would battle for them like she had before, when her husband was a patient and needed a safe place to stay.

"We all go through hard times," he said sadly. "We don't all make it through them, but you will. I can tell." With a little salute, he was gone. Pandora wondered what he saw in her that made him think that, because she wasn't so sure she agreed.

After he left, Dr. Steele began herding the posse out the door. Charles gave her a wistful smile. Lucy awarded her a raspberry. Sinclair offered her a view of his stiff back, and Birdy gifted her with a dirty look, which likely would have been her middle finger if she'd had a free hand. Pandora was glad to see them all go. Especially Dr. Steele. No assessment for her today! And not any other day, if she could help it. She'd already figured out a plan. For the next several days she would hole up in the room hidden inside the walls of the manor and use the secret passages to come and go. Nobody knew about them, but her. Well, Derek's mother did, and now he did, too, but she felt pretty sure he wouldn't say anything.

She frowned. Something was nagging at her, something that had happened from before she jumped off the bridge. Something about the secret room. What was it? But she couldn't put her finger on it, so she gave up trying, letting her eyes close for a few minutes as Dougie cleared up.

"Pandora. It's time." She opened her eyes to see Dougie flourishing a pair of scissors in front of her face, and she jerked back in the seat.

"I knew it! You started out with small animals, then moved up to human beings, didn't you? Am I your first human victim?"

"Yes. I've never cut anyone's hair before, but if I have to keep looking at that butch job of yours, I'm going to stick these in my eyes."

"You sounded almost human there, Dougie."

"Yes, and I don't like it."

She pushed herself to her feet. "Fine. Do what you will. I don't care." She led him to the small bathroom, glad to see it didn't look too awful. Maybe Vicki had cleaned it. Or maybe little elves had come and done it, the second possibility being far more likely.

She stood in front of the mirror and studied her reflection. In the past, she would have reveled in how drawn she looked, but today her haggard appearance did nothing to cheer her. Dougie stood behind her, his white-blond hair contrasting with her dark spikes. His elegant black jacket and gray turtleneck stood in stark contrast to her faded skull and crossbones t-shirt.

"You've gotten taller," she noted. "Using a rack?"

"I wish. Unfortunately, it's too hard to do it on myself. Would you care to do it for me?"

"Just say when."

"When," he whispered, his cool breath pooling in the hollow of her collarbone.

"Just cut my hair, Dougie," she growled, feeling strange. He was so close to her, and she felt his closeness all over her body. The sensation was weird and wondrous, and it freaked her out. And yet, she didn't move, and she wasn't glad when he stepped back.

"I will do my best to subdue this disastrous mistake, but you should consider making an appointment with a hair stylist."

"We don't have the money, and no way am I showing my face in town. Everyone thinks I tried to kill myself."

"Then why did you do it?"

"I didn't! I mean, I don't think I did. I told you I want to live."

"But there are times when you don't."

"Not me," she declared stubbornly. "Never."

"I died once."

"And I can see you never revived."

He ignored her jibe. "It made me curious. I was running some experiments with electricity and miscalculated. I was only seven at the time, so I expect I had been sloppy. Anyway, the jolt stopped my heart. I remember floating above my body, looking down at it without fear, without feeling anything but lightness. I felt rather powerful."

"If you loved being dead so much, why don't you do yourself in?" It wasn't entirely a sarcastic question.

"Because I'm not finished with this life yet. And neither are you." He stared at her in the mirror. "Together you and I are going to accomplish great things. I feel this."

"You sound like you found God."

"I found *a* god."

She sighed. "Yourself?"

"No. Now, no more talking. I need to concentrate."

She wanted to ask more about his near-death experience, about finding a god, but did as he asked. She didn't consider herself a particularly vain person, but seeing herself in the mirror looking like a drugged out bag lady, she decided that maybe a trim would be in order. It was a decision that gave her a bit of hope. People who want to die don't care about their appearances, do they?

Maybe I just want to look good for my funeral, she argued grumpily…with herself.

As Dougie worked, a certainty came into her mind. The boy was very good with his hands. Or maybe she liked physical contact more than she'd ever realized. There was no demand from his touch, no agenda, just business, and when she accepted this, she slowly began to relax. What a glorious thing it was to be pampered, and might she even say, cared for? But she mustn't get used to such nurturing. Pampered people end up as wusses, and those doing the pampering might be doing it for nefarious reasons.

"You can open your eyes now," he whispered in her ear. She did, slowly, and focused on her face. Her hair was a little shorter, definitely less choppy, and actually looked quite good. She kind of resembled an elf...the cool kind, not that Keebler dude. "What do you think?" Dougie, so usually self-assured, sounded as though he cared.

"It's not bad," she admitted, though in reality she liked it. "You could be a hairdresser, Dougie."

"Wouldn't my father die of pride."

She snorted. "That would be funny."

"It would." Her eyes slid over to his, which were focused on her face, hungrily. He was nearly side by side with her, so close he could have rested his chin on her shoulder.

She pulled away. "What do I owe you?"

"I get to tuck you into bed."

"That's not at all creepy."

"Is that a yes?"

"I suppose," she gave in, but only because she had exceeded her limit of sassbacks for the day. "But first I need to shower and change out of these clothes."

He nodded. "I will wait in the living room."

After sweeping up the hair, she ran to her room, grabbed her PJs, and took a good, long shower. When she was done, she dressed and went out to the living room, hoping Dougie had left. He hadn't. She cleared her throat. "I'm ready to be tucked in, weirdo."

He pushed a last chair into place. "Good. But I won't be able to do it yet."

"Why not? I'm really tired right now."

"Because you're going to have a visitor soon."

"A visitor?" Please let it be Derek. At the very least, Xavier. Vicki could go suck it for all she cared. "Who'd want to visit me?"

"Dr. Steele, of course. Who did you think?"

In a Dark Place

8

THAT LITTLE SNEAK! "Damnit, Dougie! I don't want to see Dr. Steele."

"I was a little concerned about his motives earlier, but now I'm not. You know perfectly well how to deal with him, Pandora. Simply tell him what he wants to hear and he'll go away and you can rest a little easier knowing he's no longer hounding you on this subject. You know how these things work, and while I admit that Dr. Steele has a somewhat higher than average intellect, he is not at our level."

"I'm not exactly at the top of my game these days, you know."

"Yes, I've noticed that."

She glared at him. "It's because I've had a double concussion, that's why." She liked the sound of that, or maybe she could call it a concussion squared.

"I've already acknowledged your injury and entered it into my equation for getting us through this next step."

His equation? "Thank you for that, Mr. Roboto," she replied, not bothering to keep the sarcasm out of her voice. "But Dr. Steele won't offer me the same mercy."

"Probably not, but remember that I'll be there all throughout the process."

A chill ran down her spine. At precisely what moment had her enemy become her protector? "I don't want you there."

"You need me there," he said firmly.

"I don't need anybody! Just send him away, and be sure to follow him."

The sound of the door opening and closing echoed down the hall. "Too late," Dougie whispered, leaving her. She didn't like how he was suddenly so eager to have Dr. Steele question her. What did he stand to gain from it? Maybe she should book it to her room and escape through the secret passage in her closet. She mentally shook her head. Bad idea. Doing so would give away the fact that she had a secret passage in her room.

There was no helping it. She might as well face her executioner now and hope for the best, even though things typically never worked out for the best for her.

Not wanting to entirely give up without a fight, she left the bathroom and tiptoed down the hall to her room. Once inside, she scrambled up the ladder to her bunk bed and burrowed under the covers, assuming her favorite sleeping position, flat on her back, because it made her look like a dead body lying in a casket. She would feign sleep, or unconsciousness, which was probably more effective, and maybe they'd go away.

"Pandora's room is down the hall," Dougie, the traitor, directed. "Though she is very tired, gentlemen, and needs her rest." Gentle*men*? Who else had come? "Perhaps keeping it short would be best for our little patient." *Patient? Our* little patient? Just who the hell did he think he was? Her own personal physician? And could he be any more patronizing? *Little* patient, indeed. She could kick his ass with one arm tied behind her back, and blindfolded, to boot.

"Your concern is duly noted, Douglas," Dr. Steele said, his tone dry as an old bone. Dougie might think he had the man in his back pocket, but Pandora knew better, even with a head injury to the second power. The doc was quick, and seemed to know all her tricks. His shrewdness was aggravating, and also what made him so alluring. "I promise I'll be careful."

"In here, Dr. Steele, Mr. Volkov." Vlad the Russian? She had to deal with him, too? Was he here to interrogate her? Use some of his secret KGB methods to get her to talk? She perked up. This might be kind of fun.

"We know you are awake, Pandora," Vlad announced, "so sit up like a good girl and listen to what I have to say."

Silence.

"I will come up there."

More silence. After all her experiences with the posse, Pandora possessed the patience of a saint. She could outwait both God and the Devil, and eternity, too.

She felt the bed begin to shake. Vlad, apparently, did not have the patience of a saint. She sat up, almost beaming her head on the ceiling. "All right, already!" She turned to face the room, not looking him in the eye, and he climbed back down. "Happy that you woke a convalescing patient?"

"We need to talk." Vlad went to stand in the middle of the room, his hands on his trim hips and his changeable eyes taking in the state of her room, which was pristine since she'd cleaned it a few days ago. She wasn't the neatest of freaks, by far, so it was not a normal state for her sleeping quarters to be in. But she couldn't quite recall why she had cleaned it, and so thoroughly, too. To prove some sort of point, no doubt. Which was…? She hated to admit she didn't remember.

She sighed, making sure to sound as weak and pitiful as humanly possible. "About what?"

"The threat we feel this place is to your safety." He indicated Dr. Steele, who was sitting at her desk, facing the bed. The doc's expression was neutral as he looked up at her, neither concerned nor threatening nor much of anything. She found she desperately wanted to know what he was thinking. Dougie, she noticed, remained quietly in the doorway, his dark jacket hard to make out in the dim light of the room.

"Birdy might be a pain in the behind," she joked, "but she's not a threat to my safety. I'm pretty sure I can take her."

"You are being funny, but no. We are speaking of that durak, Baker, and whoever he is working for."

She scowled. "Oh, please. I can handle Baker. He's a brute, but strikes me as a bit sub-par when it comes to the bell curve. That means…he's not…too bright," she explained, speaking slowly.

"I know what a bell curve is, and I understand that you are smarter than your average person, but you are hurt and not at your best, am I right?"

"Smarter than your *average* person?" She snorted. "Please."

"Pandora," Dr. Steele spoke up, ending her curiosity as to when he'd stick his perfectly shaped nose in. "This is a serious matter. What happened with Mr. Baker is disturbing. The police have been informed, and Captain Banty, the chief, has Baker's description."

She propped herself up on her elbow. "The police?" Intriguing. "So who else knows about what happened to me?"

He looked apologetic. "I wager the entire town of Bedlam by now."

So everyone knew someone had attempted to kidnap her. Not only was that awesome, it demonstrated that she was enough of a danger that someone wanted her out of the picture. It might even work as an excuse for why she jumped. "Cool."

"It's not cool," he attempted to correct her. To no avail. She knew what cool was. "We probably won't see Baker back, but someone else might come in his place. Who that someone will be, I don't know. A plumber, a new staff member, even a new patient."

Vlad was a new staff member, one who'd already attempted to snatch her, and according to Charles there were three new inmates.

"I don't know what you're getting at," she answered, pretending ignorance. "I'm not leaving. Besides, Vicki said I didn't have to go."

"I know. She told me. Vlad and I don't agree with the Director on this, but she won't budge. She said you've faced worse." *True.* "And she has more—that is, other things to worry about right now."

"You were going to say more *important* things to worry about. Don't protect her, doc. It only makes you look untrustworthy."

"I wasn't trying to protect your mother, Pandora."

She clapped a hand to her chest. "You were trying to protect little ol' me? Like when you let my grandmother, who is quite possibly the second coming of Hermann Goering, take me away?"

"I admit that was a mistake, and I'm sorry. I thought you would be safer with her. That man had a stun gun pressed into your side!"

Pandora pulled back slightly, startled by his sudden vehemence. "Apology accepted," she said magnanimously, feeling somewhat buoyant, and perhaps a little less angry that he hadn't stopped her grandmother from taking her away. "But the point remains. I'm not going anywhere."

"Then you will do us a favor and remain indoors for a while. It'll be good for your recovery, and it will make it easier for us to protect you."

"Sounds a bit like being in prison."

"You do not know prison," Vlad said roughly, and she clamped her mouth shut. Now here was something interesting. She would have to ask him what *he* knew about prison, but another day, when she was up to sparring with a wily Russian. "You will stay indoors unless someone is with you."

"Fine. But only because I don't feel up to going outside right now." She knew she was being childish; she could hear it in her voice, in the stubborn words she spoke, but sometimes a person has to revert to childish defenses because they're all you've got in a world full of adults who have all the power. "I...just don't," she finished lamely.

"Then we are agreed." Vlad turned about and marched to the door, his powerful compact figure a marked contrast to Dougie's slightness. "Come, Daft. We will talk." Grabbing his arm, he gave Dougie no choice but to go with him. Good. The boy needed to know that not everyone followed his rules. Vlad shut the door behind them, leaving Pandora alone with Dr. Steele and his dangerous notepad. Now she knew what he'd had hidden behind his back coming up the stairs earlier. He'd been planning this coup all along.

"You know why I'm here," he said after a few moments passed. Moments that felt like forever, each second inflating like a balloon full of anxiety.

"To extend this awful day?"

"That is not my intention."

"To torture me, then."

"Nor is that," he said, his voice calm. "Pandora, you and I need to talk. Just so you know, what I gather here will not be going into any records or files on you." She felt herself relax a smidgeon. "This assessment is for my own personal reassurance, and for your safety. I've told you before that I know what it's like to be in a dark place, and someday I will share that story with you. But right now I need to focus on you, and be sure that you are not in that dark place."

"But I am in a dark place."

She heard him inhale, a quick sharp sound that seemed to explode in the dim light, and oh, how gratifying it was to hear. "I see."

"And since you left your interrogation spotlight at home, could you turn that lamp on?" She pointed at the one on her desk.

"That wasn't funny, Pandora."

"I wasn't trying to be funny."

He rubbed a hand over the top of his head, then turned the lamp on. "Better?"

Of course. Now she could see his face, watch it for cues, know how to react to whatever curve ball he sent her way. Reading expressions and body language was how she survived, and it was getting too dark to do so properly. So she really hadn't been trying to be funny.

Well, maybe a little.

"Were you trying to kill yourself when you jumped off the Pine River Bridge?"

I don't know. That's what she wanted to say, to shout out loud, actually, but she couldn't take the risk. Too much was at stake to bandy with uncertainties, and again, she had made her deal with Vicki. She must hold up her end of the bargain.

"Wow, you like to *jump* right into things, doc," she said instead. A joke, but a necessary one. She needed a little time to figure out her strategy.

"This is very serious, Pandora." His expression was stern, his eyes focused unwaveringly on her. "Suicide is not a joke."

"I know that. But you have to admit that your approach was rather precipitous." She hoped she'd pronounced that last word correctly. It seemed there were a lot of words she said wrong, but Dr. Steele didn't correct her so she must have gotten it right. When it appeared that he wasn't going to admit to anything, she pretended to ponder the question for a few seconds. "I don't remember much of that day," she finally answered, "but I doubt killing myself was my intention. I'm not the kind of person who would commit suicide. I like myself too much."

It was true, and yet...

"Sometimes circumstances can change us, our way of thinking, even if only temporarily."

"Maybe," she hedged.

"There's no maybe about it, Pandora. Your father just died, and then your mother acted like it was your fault."

"So I wasn't imagining that!" Though she couldn't tell if it was a relief to know someone else had thought that, or not.

"I don't think you were. There've been other big changes in your life, too, haven't there? Me coming here, stirring things up with your friends. Sinclair's unusual behavior. Skippy leaving. Getting sent away."

"It's how things are around here. Never a dull moment."

"That must be exhausting for you."

She went on alert. Empathic statements are always a sign someone is trying to slip under your defenses. "What's exhausting? Besides this conversation?"

"Always feeling like you're in a boxing match."

"I don't feel like that," she protested. But that was exactly how she felt...*every day*. Yet even though she'd been fighting the good fight for far too long, she didn't think she'd survive without it. It was like air to her, like blood. Combat was in her veins. It kept her alive.

"You just threw a punch right there," he pointed out. "I was trying to empathize with you. You saw it as a threat and lashed out."

"I don't lash out, Dr. Steele. I make sure that I always connect."

"Okay. You swung at me, a nice upper cut, and I took it on the chin."

"Crikey, mate. Enough with the boxing analogies."

He smiled, and the sight did something to her heart, to her defenses. "Sorry. I was on a roll." His eyes flitted around. "I see you cleaned up your room."

She went on alert once more, quickly throwing her defenses back up. Damn that smile and its power over her. "It was starting to smell like something had died in here," she offered.

"Yes, I noticed that. In fact, I thought something had."

"Funny. Got a point you want to make?"

"I was curious. It seemed like interesting timing." Before she could answer, he went on, thwarting her counterattack, which was an extremely aggravating thing for him to do, and he no doubt knew that. "I went to the library to check out some books for you for your convalescence. Belatedly I realized that reading's probably not the best thing to do for someone with a concussion, but at the time I thought Ms. Net-terson would know what you'd like so I went to talk to her. She told me she checked out a stack for you only recently, but yesterday when I went to look in your room for the books I didn't find any."

So he'd gone to see Ms. Netterson, had he? Of course he had. What had they talked about? Her? As much as she wanted to believe that, Pandora seriously doubted they'd spent their time discussing a four-teen-year-old girl. She'd seen how they'd looked at each other when Dr. Steele had come to the library a few days ago to fetch her home—like stumbling across a desert and finding an oasis. Both were gorgeous, and single. They'd talk about themselves and their future babies, not some pathetic git who may or may not have tried to kill herself.

"Pandora?"

"What? Oh. Maybe an inmate stole them," she replied absently, won-dering where she had left them.

"Maybe. But I doubt it."

"Keep an eye out for them, will you? I don't have money to pay late fines, and definitely not for replacing lost books."

"I certainly will," he agreed, with a quirked eyebrow. He didn't be-lieve her, but thankfully he wasn't going to call her on it. The problem was, she honestly didn't know where the books were. Couldn't re-member what she'd done with them. There seemed to be a lot of holes in her memory, though why her father dying not long after she and Vicki had fought in front of him couldn't be one of them, she didn't know.

"Are we done here?" she asked, her head starting to ache.

"A few more questions. Are you thinking of hurting yourself?"

"Not at the moment, but if this goes on much longer, yes."

He sighed, made a note on his pad. "Is there anything that would keep you from hurting yourself?"

"Ending this conversation."

Another sigh. Another note. "I imagine that your sleep patterns and eating patterns have changed because of your concussion. How were they before that?"

Ah. This one she could answer without compromising herself. "Fine. I think. I remember not eating much because I had to stay out of sight so my grandmother and her goons wouldn't catch me. And Vicki doesn't keep much food stocked in our apartment. But I did manage to sneak down to the kitchen at some point and get some sustenance. So I wasn't starving."

"Did you want to eat?"

"Yes."

"How about now?"

"Since I hit my head, I feel sick to my stomach a lot, so no."

"Overall, how do you feel right now?"

"How do you think?"

"You need to tell me."

She felt out of patience, that's what she felt. And maybe a little scared. "I feel tired all the time, doc. I'm sad about my dad. I'm mad about Skippy being forced to leave. I'm a little weirded out that Dougie works here now. Oh, and someone tried to kidnap me for reasons unknown. My head hurts, and I just want to be left alone so I can get some rest. I already know I hit several points on the suicide watch list, Dr. Steele. That doesn't make me suicidal."

He studied her for several long moments and she stared right back. "All right. You've made your point. One last thing, then."

She groaned. "Out with it."

"I want you to make me a promise."

"I try not to do promises if I can help it. Less trouble for everyone that way."

"Just this once?"

He sounded so pathetic that she gave in. "What is it?"

"I know I let you down with your grandmother, but I won't make that mistake again. I let something that happened to me in the past interfere with my intuition, and I'm sorry." She didn't move so much as an eyeball, all her attention focused keenly on him. He couldn't be doing what she thought he was doing. "So, could you please come to me if you ever feel like you want to hurt yourself?"

He could. "You want to make a suicide contract with me?"

"You could call it that, yes."

"I could call it that because that's what it is, bub."

"Fine. That's what I want."

Damn him. "What do I get out of it?"

He looked surprised. "What?"

"A contract typically means both parties get something out of the deal. If I make this contract with you, what do I get out of it?"

A long minute passed as he seemed to consider her question. His face looked drawn, his lips tight, his eyes uncertain. "All right. If you do this for me for the next month, I will tell you about my past. About my Elizabeth."

She stared at him, stunned. She hadn't expected this at all. The existence of Dr. Steele's Elizabeth had surfaced during Pandora's search for Elizabeth Nepenthe, but he had never explained who she was or why she was such a big deal to him. "For realsies?"

That got a smile out of him. "For realsies."

She held out her hand, and he stood and took it in his own, a warm pocket of strength. She had to swallow the rise of pure emotion blocking her throat, which was coming from how comforted the simple gesture made her feel.

"Dr. Steele, you've got yourself a deal."

9

Shadow of Death

DR. STEELE LEFT her after that, looking a little less burdened once she'd made her deal with the devil (him being the devil). Before leaving he told her she could talk to him any time, day or night, about anything—like her dad dying, he threw in casually, then informed her that Dougie had stored leftovers from the party in the fridge and wished her a good night.

When he was gone, she lay in bed and thought about the enigma that was Dr. Steele. She still didn't know how she felt about him. One moment she despised him and everything he represented. The next, she saw him as the only person who could ever understand her. At this particular moment she really wanted to trust him, because he'd been accurate about one thing, a very important thing. It *was* exhausting always being on her guard. Sure such vigilance kept her alive—being on top of things both protected her and enlivened her—but still, it was so very tiring. And it felt like a kind of tired that wasn't ever going to go away.

She wondered about his dark moments. He'd once hinted that he might have been suicidal. Did it have to do with his Elizabeth and that song he liked to sing while walking on the beach, where a girl ends up dying? It was a very sad song. Maybe the same thing had happened to his Elizabeth. But who was this girl, or woman, and was she even alive? Poor Ms. Netterson might have to compete against a dead woman. But if anyone could win that battle it was old Nettie, with her flaming red lipstick and matching high heels. Pandora envied the librarian greatly, and if she didn't like the woman so much, would consider sabotaging the potentially budding relationship between her and Dr. Steele. In fact, she hadn't entirely ruled out the idea. What's a little sabotage between friends, eh?

At any rate, Pandora didn't think she'd have a problem sticking to her end of the bargain, but would Dr. Steele keep his promise? It was this question, along with where was her other pillow and third blanket, that accompanied her as she drifted off to sleep, thankfully before Dougie returned. She hadn't thought through exactly how he was going to tuck her in while she was in a bunk bed. Besides, being at her best around him right now wasn't easy, so she was glad for the reprieve.

The next day she didn't get out of bed. Dougie brought her aspirin for her head—not as effective as whatever she was getting in the hospital, but much safer—and meals on a tray, which were pretty good, being leftovers from the party. But she didn't react when he explained (but didn't apologize, of course) his reason for not returning in time to be there for her assessment, as he was discussing something important with Vlad. She wondered if it had anything to do with Lonnie and Ronnie and their strange conversation about choosing a master and picking out weaponry. It sounded exactly like something right up Vlad's alley.

She also didn't bother responding when he tried asking her questions concerning what had happened with Dr. Steele. She simply turned her back on him and plugged her ears. He acted like she wasn't ignoring him, which was rather annoying and took away from the impact of her less-than-subtle maneuver. But then, he was probably quite aware of that.

That afternoon, Vicki let herself into Pandora's room, without knocking, naturally, and told her about the professor's funeral, which was to be the following day at one in the afternoon, and would take place in the Nepenthe family graveyard. Pandora grunted an okay in response, and Vicki didn't push it, only adding, "I hope you're feeling better."

I hope you're feeling better. Five stupid little words that held very little meaning or depth overall, and yet they made Pandora want to cry like an abandoned baby. Instead, she pulled the covers over her head and went back to sleep. Not once had her mother even come close to apologizing about not making it to Pandora's homecoming party.

The next day—funeral day—she dragged herself out of bed and ate her lunch cold from the fridge before Dougie could deliver it, downing a Coke along with it, then went and took a long shower. The hot water hitting the back of her neck felt like heaven, if she believed in the concept, and for those twenty minutes before the hot water petered out, she did. Afterwards her head felt better than it had for a while, which was a huge relief. She needed to be at the top of her game for the funeral. Her emotions were so broken right now she felt like she could either end up howling at Reverend Richus, the asylum's pastor, for spewing his sentimental religious claptrap during the eulogy, or bawling her eyes out over that very same claptrap.

The day was rainy and dreary, and entirely fitting for the somber occasion. Still, she thought it would have been more fitting if it were a bright and sunny one, with a gentle breeze—Professor Robertson's favorite sort of day for bug collecting. Not that he would, or could, care anymore about the weather, but still. It would've been a nice nod to the old guy's memory.

Pandora pulled on a pair of black pants that felt a little snug around the waist and a black, long-sleeved shirt free of rebellious sayings or rock stars. She should probably be wearing something a little more formal, but she didn't own a dress, having sold the only one she owned (a gift/bribe from Dougie) to pay for a bike for Xavier for his sixteenth birthday last week. Xavier didn't know she was the one who'd paid for it, and she planned on it staying that way, but if he kept up this snub he seemed to be enacting against her, she might have to let the air out of his tires, and then out of the old windbag himself.

After tying her Doc Martens, she went to reach for her sporran, which was really just an old leather bag with tassels, but since it kind of looked like a sporran and she liked the word sporran better than bag, that's what she called it. She kept it hanging on the bedpost, but to her chagrin, she couldn't find it there. Nor was it anywhere in her room, not under her bed, in her desk, under a pillow. Where had she put it? She needed her sporran. She felt naked without it. Had it fallen off when she'd jumped in the river? Was it still at the hospital, or in Grandmother Belfry's car?

Seeing the time she gave up her search in disgust and headed downstairs to the lobby. Halfway down, she froze when she saw Vicki escorting a heavyset man with an ugly beard to the door. It was Hank "the Crank" Jackson, and he was a health and safety inspector. He and Mayor Daft were best buddies, fitting being that both were huge jerks. Every year Mr. Jackson threatened to close down the manor for some infraction or another. But somehow, every year, Vicki managed to rout him. This year, Dr. Steele and Dougie had met with him while Vicki was tending to Professor Robertson, and Dougie had sounded pleased with the outcome. So what had brought the evil fiend here this time?

Vicki closed the door on him, then leaned against it, looking exhausted. Pandora scurried down the remaining steps, and Vicki looked up at her approach. "What was the Crank doing here?" Pandora demanded, her heart racing. "We just had an inspection, and we passed. So what did he want?"

"He came to offer his condolences."

"Yeah, right. I can't wait to offer my condolences to his widow. Or, more like my congratulations. One less blight in the world."

Instead of agreeing, as she usually would, Vicki turned and headed toward her office. "Hang on a second, and then we'll go," she called over her shoulder, then popped inside and promptly returned with something in her hand. "Are you all right?"

"What?" Pandora lowered the hand that was rubbing her temple. No doubt the real reason Hank Jackson had shown up concerned something that would cost them money to fix. It was always money with this place. Or the lack thereof. "Oh. Yes. I'm fine." She pulled back her shoulders and stuck out her chin. "Just dandy, in fact."

"Well, thank goodness for that." Vicki was wearing a black dress and heels; her curly brown hair looked nice, if a bit flat on one side, as though she'd forgotten to brush it. Her green-brown eyes were a little bloodshot and she was as pale as the underbelly of a dead frog, but otherwise she looked all right. She held out one of the objects she'd fetched from her office. "I brought you an umbrella."

Pandora looked at it for a moment, wondering what the catch was, then took it. "Um, thanks."

"You're welcome," Vicki replied, ignoring Pandora's tone, which was healthily skeptical. Vicki didn't usually do things for Pandora. She claimed that leaving her to figure things out on her own and fending for herself built character and independence. Maybe she was right. Pandora had gotten along without anyone's help for a long time, and look at her now. She was doing just fine.

If she could only ignore what had happened this past week, and all the other times she'd gotten into trouble, she'd believe that.

"Who's all coming?" Pandora asked as they walked to the front door.

"It's a private funeral, so only family and a few friends. Afterwards, around two, we're holding a memorial service of sorts in the arts and crafts room. J.T. is setting it up." J.T. was their rec director, and he was as amazing at his job as he was over the top, which was nearly celestial. J.T. made Richard Simmons look like Queen Elizabeth II in a coma.

Pandora didn't know if she felt relieved to hear that the funeral guests had been limited to a few, or worried. The presence of lots of people could elicit either a good outcome or a bad one, depending. People could keep her in check just as easily as they could set her off. It was a toss-up, and Pandora didn't like those odds. She really didn't want to be disrespectful to her father's memory, plus she didn't want to add fuel to the suicide theories building up around her. Everyone already thought she was a jumper, so it was imperative she avoid doing anything to lend credence to that rumor. Dramatic outbursts at a funeral wouldn't help her case one bit.

Vicki opened the door and held it for Pandora, a gesture that Frank, their security guard, had done numerous times over the years. "Has Frank had his surgery?" Pandora asked. "Is he all right?"

"Frank? Oh, Mr. Steen. With everything going on, I hadn't thought to call. I'll have Bennington follow up on him tomorrow, if she comes in. Her mother has been sick." Bennington was Vicki's office manager, and she pretty much ran the place. She was of Korean descent, unmarried, and lived with her elderly mother. Vicki blew out a gust of air that lifted her bangs. "So many illnesses. Anyway, I think he went in for surgery today."

"Oh. Okay." Pandora didn't push it, mainly because the last person she'd known who'd gone into the hospital, other than herself, hadn't come out. She didn't think she could handle any more bad news right now.

Even though it was dark and drizzly outside, the outdoor light seemed too bright. All at once, everything was too much to take in, and she was tempted to spin around and run back inside.

"We'd better hurry," Vicki remarked, subduing Pandora's urge to flee. "It's almost one." She unfurled her umbrella with a snap, and Pandora followed suit, realizing as it whooshed open that it would make a good shield. From the light. From the stares. From the rain, too, she supposed.

Out of the corner of her eye, she spotted Ronny and Lonny walking down the drive. When they saw her, they veered off into the woods, as though trying to avoid her. A moment later, they each popped out from behind a tree. She pretended not to see them watching her, though she did wonder what the heck they were up to.

Vicki marched into the Nepenthe family cemetery, with Pandora lagging behind. About an acre in size, the graveyard was dotted with Victorian and modern tombstones, and surrounded by a cast iron fence with spikes. Every time Pandora saw the sharp black tips, she couldn't help wonder if they were there to keep people out, or to keep the zombified corpses in.

As they tromped toward the back of the graveyard, near the tree line, they passed a number of Nepenthe family tombstones, all of which Pandora knew quite well. She'd spent a lot of time wandering in and out amongst the stones, plus the posse used the graveyard as one of their meeting places when they needed to discuss anything they didn't want overheard. It was a favorite place of hers, for obvious reasons, but also because no one in the graveyard wanted anything from her. It made for a nice change.

Over the years a number of indigent inmates, with no family to claim them or money to spend on a burial site, had been buried in a back corner of the graveyard, which was where they were headed now. Since the Nepenthe family had moved away, close to a century ago, about thirty inmates had taken up residence within the fenced-in bit of land. Pandora imagined that if Mrs. Nepenthe, Elizabeth's mother, ever learned that a crazy person might be buried near her, they'd find her roaming the graveyard every full moon, voicing her displeasure. According to Elizabeth's diary, Mrs. Nepenthe, like Grandmother Belfry and Vicki, didn't believe mental illness was really a thing, that it was simply a lack of willpower or a run of bad luck (to be fair to Vicki, this was probably more her belief than the other part). Sad that things hadn't changed all that much in a century.

While living here, Pandora had witnessed a number of the inmates' funerals, even though technically she had not been invited to them. If spotted, she would have been summarily sent back to the manor to await punishment. Thank goodness for trees and binoculars. But it was different being on this side of the fence, trudging through the wet grass toward a gaping hole in the ground meant for her father. It seemed a harsh end for a harmless eccentric with a bug fetish.

As Pandora looked about her the whole scenario suddenly seemed very crisp and real, and not so fascinating anymore. She didn't think she'd ever stop being intrigued by death, but its allure for her would be different from here on out; the Grim Reaper had touched her with his icy fingers, and had snatched someone she cared about and pulled him under without remorse. Death, she realized, was far more interesting when it didn't hit so close to home.

She shivered and plodded on behind Vicki. She wondered if now was the time to ask her mother about what she'd said in the hospital about wanting to leave Nepenthe Manor. Right now, while she was being reasonably nice, and when she was especially vulnerable. To an outsider, the idea probably sounded cruel, but for Pandora it was survival. Knowledge was the only power she had; without it she would have joined the ranks of the manor long ago. She could also ask her mother about Dougie working here, about Vlad, too, and then seriously question her mother's grip on reality for hiring a weirdo stalker and a Russian thug, who had switched sides awfully easily.

But then Vicki, who seemed to sense Pandora's impending interrogation, started walking faster, leaving her and her questions in the proverbial dust. When Pandora got to the gravesite, Reverend Richus was already there. A lackey held an umbrella over the reverend's wild-haired head, because God forbid he get his fancy leather-bound, gold leaf fore-edged Bible wet; or his luscious locks, the white of which stood out against the black of the umbrella like snow on a mountaintop.

Gathered near the grave were Dr. Steele, Xavier, Carl (though no Nurse Devine), Cracker Jack, and Nurse Rackett, of all people. The Scandinavian ice queen was the head floor nurse for the inmates and managed them like a Viking—with a cold, firm hand, which always looked ready to snatch up an ax and wield it with authority. Pandora was pretty sure the nurse felt no attachment to the professor, but had probably heard that Dr. Steele was going to be at the funeral and had invited herself. At the moment she was leaning against Dr. Steele, apparently for 'support' as she wiped faux tears from her eyes. What a joke. Like the dried-up old virago ever cried or needed support. She was as strong as a polar bear and twice as mean. Grandmother and Grandfather Belfry were missing, but that was more a relief than a surprise.

Dr. Steele, struggling to stay upright under Nurse Rackett's weight, caught Pandora's eye, his expression sympathetic, but she looked away. He wasn't going to make her cry. No way.

As Vicki had promised, it wasn't a huge showing, but then there would be the memorial service afterward to compensate, and it was probably best to keep the inmates away from the cemetery anyway. Not only were they a morbid lot, attending ran the risk of setting some of them off...or giving them ideas.

The coffin was closed, and Pandora was both disappointed and grateful to see it that way. Dead people were intriguing to study, but this was a dead person she'd known and she didn't want to remember the professor as any way other than alive. To her the dead never looked at rest or peaceful. They looked empty, like a deserted house or a desiccated animal carcass. The stillness, the waxy skin, the sunken eye sockets. That is not how someone at peace looks. There's a wrongness that can't be unseen, and she knew this because she still dreamed of the dead creatures she'd seen over the years—several inmates, a drowned woman on the beach, a run over cat.

Her eyes fixed firmly on the ground, she went and took an empty spot between Cracker Jack and Vicki. She felt Xavier's nearby presence, but she didn't look at him. He was one of the people liable to set her off.

The reverend cleared his throat. "We are gathered here on this day to bid farewell to Peter Robertson, husband to Victoria Belfry and father to Xavier Carlisle and Pandora Belfry." Here the reverend's thin lips tightened into a sour moue. He and Pandora did not get along. In fact, just saying her name probably made him feel like he'd sinned. She noticed he hadn't used the word 'beloved' before husband and father and wondered if its absence was an oversight on his part or him being his usual hypocritical self, already passing judgment on them. "His life was short, and his way was hard," he went on, his voice a nice rich baritone, when it should have been more weaselly to match his personality. "If he had made different choices, he might have lived longer and been a more positive contributor to our little town, and perhaps his offspring could have learned from his example. But it was not to be, and so we should gain wisdom from his mistakes, many though they were."

Vicki sighed, and Pandora's fingers curled more tightly around the umbrella's wooden handle. "Get on with it," she mumbled under her breath. Vicki nudged her slightly, which only made Pandora madder. She had to bite her lip to keep from yelling at the reverend, dig her nails into her thigh to stop from launching herself at him and knocking him into the black hole behind him. She satisfied herself with glaring at the self-righteous prig as he was drawing in air to really get launched into his lecture. He ended up gulping back the words, probably because she was drawing a finger across her throat. No one could see her, because she had angled her umbrella just right, and his assistant was standing behind him. No, he was the only one to see the threat.

"I'll do it," she mouthed, slowly and clearly. "And I'll like it." She gave him a wicked smile, adding, "And I won't get caught."

He pulled back as though she had indeed launched herself at him, cleared his throat once more, and looked down at his Bible. "Ah, yes. And now I shall read from the 23rd Psalm."

Pandora nodded. She actually rather liked this one. Little did the reverend know that while his nemesis wasn't big on religion, and wasn't sure if she believed in God (she could never find a good explanation for why God let little children get raped and murdered, or allowed people to have mental illnesses, for that matter), she had read the Bible, and knew it quite well. The Old Testament was actually quite inspiring.

And now came her favorite part…

"'Yea, though I walk through the valley of the shadow of death,'" the reverend intoned, "'I will fear no evil; for Thou art with me; Thy rod and Thy staff, they comfort me. Thou preparest a table before me in the presence of mine enemies.'"

"Amen," the group chorused when he finished the psalm, Pandora loudest of all, hoping the last part—"'and I will dwell in the house of the Lord forever'"—was true, at least for her father. She was pretty sure this part didn't apply to her, nor did the mercy and goodness following her bit, but maybe it would apply to him.

The reverend went on for another twenty minutes, apparently enjoying the sound of his own voice as he expounded on the professor's life. Not that there was much to expound on. Vicki must not have shared much with the reverend, one of her smarter moves. But it did not deter the man, who used the time to preach about the evils of drugs and alcohol in such a way that made it difficult to call him on it.

At last he was finished, his expression full of the complacency of a man who believed he'd done his job for the Lord, and done it well. All that remained was to lower the casket into the ground. Pandora still had time to push the good reverend into the six-foot deep hole, but by use of restraint that even Jesus would consider miraculous, she held herself back. She did, however, mouth the word "hypocrite" at him, and his smug expression disappeared.

Carl and Cracker Jack worked the winch to lower the body into the ground, inch by agonizing inch. Pandora couldn't help imagining the metal cables snapping and the casket plummeting several feet, breaking open, creating havoc. But nothing of the sort happened, and they stepped away, their job finished. Vicki moved forward and took a handful of earth to toss into the grave. Xavier went next, then Pandora. When it was her turn, she peered down into the hole, the shiny black casket already desecrated by grit, then opened her fist and let the dirt slide out in a mere trickle. She really wanted to fling it down and start screaming and raging against an unfair world, but again she refrained from doing what she felt so driven to do. Maybe that's why her chest hurt and her throat ached so much right now. But she wasn't going to cry. Not in front of these people.

She went to stand by Xavier, but he retreated from her approach, stepping behind Carl. She frowned at him. Had he just blown her off? He most certainly had. Well, that was a mistake he would soon regret.

10

XAVIER WAS SHUNNING her, and also erroneously thinking he was going to get away with it. The small crowd began to disperse, and as it had stopped raining, umbrellas were furled and rain jacket hoods pulled down. Pandora didn't especially want to talk to any of them, so she trotted after Xavier, who was trying to sneak away unnoticed. Ah, the ignorance of the boy. As if he could give Pandora Belfry the slip.

She followed behind him for a ways, then called out, "Oi! Brother of mine."

He kept walking, completely ignoring her. Well, that changed things. She caught up to him, dropped her umbrella, and grabbed his arm. He tried to shake her off, but Pandora was well-trained in the art of detention. There'd been many a time she'd had to restrain one of the posse in the midst of an episode and knew what she was about. Like when Sinclair had an anxiety attack and nearly knocked himself out as he banged his head against the wall. Or Skippy in the middle of a manic phase, wanting to steal a car and drive to Texas. Or Birdy threatening to kill herself, or anyone within striking distance, with a pair of scissors a careless psych assistant had left lying around. Or Charles about to 'fly' from the attic window to rescue a cat in a tree he'd seen earlier in the day. Or Lucy lighting a chair on fire after finding a lighter that yet another careless psych assistant had left in the TV room.

To sum up, Xavier was not getting away.

"Would you let me go!" he cried when everything he tried to shake her, including swinging her into the cemetery gate, didn't work. This close up, she could smell the tang of the lemon drops he was always sucking on and the sweetly scented mousse he used to spike the top of his blond hair. She noticed that today's earring was a skull, appropriately enough, and his black suit was a size too small. His brown irises were surrounded by thready blood vessels and he had a fresh breakout of zits on his chin. He didn't look too hot.

"I'll let you go once you tell me why you're avoiding me," she panted, maintaining her grip through sheer determination. "The posse came to visit me in the hospital. Dougie came. Even Vicki. But not you. You didn't come to my welcome home party, either. There was fried chicken, Xavier. You love fried chicken."

"I do," he admitted, turning away, all attempts to break free ceasing. "But I was busy."

"What about now? Are you busy now, or can you take a moment out of your hectic schedule and welcome me back?"

He swung around, and at the furious expression on his face she dropped his arm. Not because she was afraid, but because she needed to get ready in case he started swinging. She'd heard that siblings often duked it out with each other, and she wanted to be in a good defensive position for when the fists started to fly.

"You need to stop raggin' on me," he growled.

"You need to answer my question."

"Listen to me, Pandora." He shook his fist in her face. "And listen good. I don't need this. All right?"

His bad guy pose didn't faze her. "Need what?"

"Another person in my life dying."

"But I didn't die."

"Not this time." He rubbed at the wrist he'd recently broken, as though it still bothered him even though it was healed.

"What's that supposed to mean?"

"What do you think it means?"

"I didn't jump on purpose, Xavier. I had a concussion. I wasn't thinking straight." Every time she gave this answer, it sounded more right. "I didn't want to die then, and I don't now."

He shook his head. "So that's your story? Seriously, Pandora. I thought you of all people would be brave enough to admit the truth."

"That *is* the truth." But it wasn't. Or it was. She couldn't remember.

"Like I can believe anything you say." He looked off toward the ocean. "Anyway, you have no right to be mad at me. You're the moron who tried to off herself."

Moron who tried to off herself? Had he really just said that? Of all the insensitive, boneheaded things to say. She stared at him in silent rage. Silent, because she couldn't make her mouth work, couldn't get the words to come out. She couldn't move, either. She wanted to scream at him, kick him in the balls, pull his hair. She wanted to hurt him like he'd hurt her, but she was frozen solid as an ice sculpture.

He shrugged. "Fine. Be that way. Don't talk to me. Just don't expect me to play your weird little reindeer games anymore." He was breathing heavily, like an angry bull. "By the way, your hair looks like crap." With that and a scowl, he stormed off, leaving her to stare at his retreating form.

"So does yours!" she shouted back, finally breaking through her strange paralysis. "Business in the front, party in the back, my ass! More like stupid in the front, stupid in the back!"

As far as insults went, this was not her finest, but it didn't matter. Xavier didn't react with a comeback, as she was hoping he would, simply kept walking toward the stables, hating her, wanting nothing to do with her.

Why did she care about him anyway? She hadn't liked him when he first arrived, and still didn't like his cockiness and arrogance or that stupid mullet he insisted on wearing. So she shouldn't give a crap what he thought.

I don't, she argued to herself. *Who needs him? Who needs anybody? Not me. I might as well get used to being alone anyway since Dr. Steele is intent on sending away all my friends, my mother is determined to make me leave the only home I've ever known, and Derek has yet to show his face. I simply need to remind myself that like Simon and Garfunkel sang,* I am a rock, I am an island.

End of story.

She picked up her umbrella and stomped toward the manor. Up the steps she raced and banged open the door, unsure what to do with the tempest raging inside her. Not seeing anyone to take it out on, she ran up to the apartment, two stairs at a time. Once in her room, she threw her umbrella onto the floor, climbed up into her bunk, and screamed into her pillow. "I hate him! I hate everyone!"

She punched the poor pillow too many times to count, until her head and ribs pounded in protest. Her breath came in short, quick pants and her mind whirled like a terrible storm.

"I hate the whole world," she sobbed as she rehashed all the wrongs done to her over her short, pitiful life. Her walk down memory lane fed into the sensation of drowning that was overtaking her, and with each transgression remembered, the feeling inside her grew worse and worse, like a body building up to vomit.

In one big swoop, all her emotions coalesced into a ball inside her chest, then shot outward like an explosion, setting off a sensation not unlike being on a rollercoaster when it plummets downward. The feeling spread through her body, weakening her, making her feel like everything around her was disintegrating.

Was this what it was like to go mad?

Even as she descended into a pit of despair, a tiny voice inside her head pointed out that maybe she was encouraging this downward spiral, and maybe that tiny voice, albeit overly preachy, was correct in its assessment. But it felt good to let herself fall apart, and it was so easy. She wouldn't stop. Didn't want to.

A loud knock on her bedroom door broke through her mind storm, dragging her back to the room, back to reality. "Go away, Dougie," she groaned.

"It's not Dougie Dolittle!" a lispy voice shouted back. The door swung open and banged against the wall. "Time to get up, pee-pee head!"

"It's *sleepy* head," Pandora couldn't help correcting.

Lucy waltzed into the room, followed by Charles and Sinclair. "I say what I mean, and I mean what I say!" She performed a little pirouette that ended with a dramatic bow. "Did you like how I made my entrance?" She straightened up and pulled a Strawberry Shortcake shirt down over her rounded tummy and behind.

"Amazing," Pandora muttered. "Now go away." She wanted to return to that lovely place, back to that mindless swirling sensation.

Lucy crossed her arms. "No."

"Go away," Pandora growled again.

"Not happening," Lucy retorted. "Not happening, not happening, not happening."

"I said, get out!" Pandora roared, sitting up and almost cracking her head on the ceiling. "I don't want you here. None of you. I just want to be left alone!"

Lucy giggled. "Sounds like someone's got a case of the Mondays."

Faster than a monkey, Pandora scooched along her bunk bed and was down the ladder in a flash, making her head spin with the effort. "It's not Monday, Lucy," she hissed, "and I don't have a case of anything except of being Fed-Up-With-You-All."

"You're breathing funny, Pandora," Charles noted. "You need to breathe *not* funny. Doesn't she, Sinclair?" Sinclair's anxious, rust-colored eyes found hers and he nodded vigorously. "See?" Charles said. "Breathe from your belly, not from your chest, and you will calm down and feel your best!" He demonstrated, his concave stomach pushing out like an inflating balloon as he pulled in a deep breath. He did this several more times. "See?" he repeated. "You need to do it!"

Pandora stared at him, still panting, and growing dizzier by the second. What was happening to her? She felt even more out of control than ever. "I don't need…your help or any…of that therapy crap," she rasped. "I just…need…you guys gone."

"Did someone get up on the wrong side of the bed today?" Birdy breezed in. "Oh, wait. I think that's you every day, Pandora."

"Breathe from your belly!" Charles cried, watching Pandora gasping for air as her rage demon threatened to take over. "Through your nose, down to your toes!"

Pandora took in his panicky blue eyes, his bluish lips. He was making himself sick. Damnit. If she didn't want to be attending another funeral, she had better do what he told her. But let it be noted that she was doing it for him, not for herself.

"You do it with me," she exhorted between breaths. "Show me how." He joined her, taking and releasing one breath after another, and slowly, slowly, Pandora felt less toxic, and the color of Charles's lips returned to a more normal shade.

"Your first panic attack?" Birdy noted casually. She was no longer wearing black, Pandora was glad to see, but was now channeling Brooke Shields—all big hair, big eyebrows, and big earrings, clean-cut and preppy in her pink blazer and red plaid skirt, pink lacy anklets and penny loafers. It was quite a turnaround.

Was that what that had been? How horrid. "No. Just a bad headache. It's from my double concussion, you know." And maybe it had been from that.

"Leave it to you to get a *double* concussion."

"I have a triple con-cushion," Lucy declared. "Got it from skydiving. So are you done acting like a wrecker of clues, Panic-dora? Cause we have to go celebrate the professor's death."

Despite her mood, Pandora had to ask, "What the heck is a wrecker of clues, Lucy?" Typically she could translate Lucy's malapropisms. Not this time.

"You know, a person who ruins everything."

"Huh?"

"Recluse," Sinclair asserted quietly, then began repeating the word over and over eleven more times.

"Oh." She wasn't sure she would ever have gotten that one. "I'm not a recluse, Lucy. I just needed some alone time." The inmates should understand that phrase. She'd used it on them often enough over the years.

Lucy threw her hands in the air. "Whatever you say, clue wrecker. Can we go celebrate the professor's death now?"

"You mean, celebrate his *life*."

Lucy scowled. "We can't celebrate his life, pudding butt. He's dead."

Pandora sighed and refrained from correcting her. "Fine. You go on your own. I'm staying here."

"So you're going to leave us alone with that girl?" Birdy demanded.

Pandora cocked her head. "What girl?"

"The new girl," Charles explained. "The one that's not very nice."

"She's in an attic," Lucy said. "Cause she does so many drugs and her brain is fried like bacon."

Attic. Addict. That one Pandora got. "I'm sure you guys can handle her."

"She's really mean," Charles persisted in a shaky voice. "She pushed me, Pandora, and I wanted to push her back, but I didn't want to hurt her, either." He hung his head. "That was brave of me, wasn't it, Pandora?" He snuck a glance at her.

She suppressed a sigh. The posse sure knew how to suck her back into their world, didn't they? In fact, they should have been awarded black hole status a long time ago.

"I'm supposed to be taking it easy."

"You can take it easy, just not on her." Birdy looked quite put out. Looking put out wasn't unusual for Birdy. What was unusual is that for once her ire didn't seem to be directed at Pandora. If Birdy was annoyed by someone enough to turn to Pandora for help, then the new inmate must be a tough case. She couldn't help but feeling a bit intrigued. But only a bit.

"I'll go talk to her, then I'm going back to bed. My head hurts." Though, funnily enough, it was starting to feel better. "Just give me a minute, all right?"

They eyed her warily, especially Sinclair, who'd pretty much been eyeing her warily the entire time, then shuffled out of the room. "We'll wait for you in the living room," Birdy called loudly, knowing Pandora's tricks.

"Fine. I'm just getting something for my head." They still had aspirin in the bathroom—she'd seen it when Dougie had cut her hair. Vicki must have forgotten about it, or truly didn't believe Pandora had tried to kill herself, otherwise, why leave something she could OD on out where she could reach it?

She shook two pills out of the bottle, swallowed them dry, then assessed her face. There were dark circles under her eyes, and a strange sort of vigor in her expression. She looked like she was getting ready for battle, and felt a tiny surge of anticipation in her gut. Having a target for her rage was exactly what the doctor would order. Well, Dr. Frankenstein, maybe. She quirked an eyebrow at herself, then spun around.

Time to sort out the new girl.

11

Sit and Spin

"YOU'RE TURNING INTO one of us, Pandora," Charles said worriedly when she joined them in the living room.

"What?"

"You're turning into a loony," Lucy clarified.

"I know what Charles meant," she said shortly. "I just want to know why he thinks that."

"Oh, we all think it," Birdy stated firmly. "First you try to kill yourself, then we find you flipping out. It was only a matter of time, you know. You can't live in a place like this and not be affected. *Duh.*"

"I did not try to kill myself, nor was I flipping out. I'm, well, my head hurts, and I'm, well..." She was struggling here. She couldn't share the real reasons for what they'd seen because she wasn't sure what those reasons were other than that her father was dead and her brother was avoiding her and her mother wanted to do something drastic and some mysterious stranger was trying to kidnap her. "Actually, I'm worried about Skippy," she finished triumphantly. Even with a concussion, she still had it.

"Oh, thank God," Birdy breathed. "I thought I was the only one."

"I'm worried, too," Charles admitted, and Sinclair nodded, but his expression told Pandora he didn't buy her story. Luckily, being practically a mute, he wouldn't pursue it. She felt a little annoyed, though, that she'd been able to distract the rest of the posse so easily. Didn't they care? Weren't they worried about her?

But she also felt relieved at escaping their scrutiny. She didn't want to discuss what had happened. Why should she expect they'd want to? Suicide was a taboo topic, and a scary one, and even just the idea of talking about it made her skin prickle.

"I'm not worried at all," Lucy declared. "Skippy can take care of his own damn, I mean, dang self."

"No, he can't!" Birdy cried. "He needs us to do that. He can't do anything alone. He can't even decide whether or not he has to go to the bathroom! He's a hopeless mess!" She broke down into sobs, which weren't really sobs, just fake ones. But a born actress, she did them well.

Pandora, relieved to be off the hook, took over. "We need something to take our minds off our troubles, don't we? Like when we explored the labyrinth. That was fun." Sinclair looked pained at the mention of the labyrinth. "But something different," she hastily amended. "Something indoors probably since I'm supposed to be taking it easy, on account of my terrible head injury."

Birdy fixed her with a disbelieving stare. "You have a concussion, not a spear through your head."

"Concussions can be really bad, you know."

"I've had six of them babies." Lucy crossed her eyes and stuck out her tongue. "I should probably get myself a football helmet."

"It's going to take more than a helmet to fix your head problems," Birdy muttered.

Lucy drew herself up like a rooster about to attack. "We need to think of something," Pandora quickly intervened. "Something we can do to get our mind off our worries." She was back on familiar territory, and it felt, if not good, normal. And she needed normal right now. "Let's brainstorm."

They stood in silence for several seconds until Lucy shouted, "I'm hungry! I didn't eat much lunch cause I was saving room."

Pandora sighed. "All right. Let's go downstairs and get some food, but keep thinking, all right, everyone?"

It was only a little after two and the arts and crafts room was already packed. Pandora wanted to believe it was because everyone had loved the professor so much, but as he didn't ever talk much to anyone besides her and Cracker Jack, and stuck bugs to his wall, and there was food here, she knew she'd only be fooling herself. Seeing the food, the posse headed straight for the long table at the back of the room and began helping themselves, proving her point. Though, to be fair, good food at Nepenthe Manor was in short supply. Whenever it looked at all edible (basically when Old Corker wasn't involved in its prep), people stocked up, like bears getting ready for hibernation. Besides, the posse knew the drill…don't be seen with Pandora or Vicki would find a way to keep them apart. Normally Pandora would rebel at this mandate, but today it was a relief to be away from them.

J.T., the rec director, short, paunchy, and fabulous, pranced around, greeting everyone like they'd just boarded the Love Boat. Vicki stood over in a corner, white Styrofoam cup in hand, watching the circus and frankly, looking not in the least mournful. She looked mad, actually, and Pandora wondered what had happened now. Dr. Steele was talking to a group of patients, two of whom Pandora didn't recognize. Must be the new arrivals Charles had mentioned. Vlad the Russian was sharing a laugh with Cracker Jack and his crude buddy, Jun Li. Dougie was stuck talking to Dr. Hannah, a therapist and an expert at getting people to cry.

But would she be able to make a robot cry? Stay tuned…

Spotting Pandora standing by herself, J.T. made a beeline for her. "Oh, you poor thing!" He attempted to envelop her in a hug, but it didn't connect because she did a neat duck and spin to escape it. "Oops! Missed you!"

When he came in for another attempt, she pointed to her head. "Have to take it easy, J.T. No physical contact. Doctor's orders."

His soft hands flew to his face. "Oh, dear. That sounds bad." He leaned forward and looked her in the eye. "And how are you holding up, hon? I heard about your, um, accident."

The room seemed to go quiet all of a sudden, and Pandora looked around to find people subtly, or not so subtly, watching and listening in. Good. Now was the time to give her story, and it looked like claiming it was an accident was the way to go.

"I got a concussion from playing basketball against the townies—we won, by the way." She waited for the clapping and hooting to stop before continuing, "And it made me sick to my stomach. So I was in my grandmother's car when I had to throw up. We were on the bridge, and I must have gotten dizzy and fallen off." She projected her voice so the whole room would hear her. "I still have temporary brain trauma, though, so I'll have to take it easy for a while." Temporary brain trauma. That sounded much better than a concussion squared. She'd call it TBT for short. Genius.

Standing close by, Mrs. Johnson, the resident sourpuss, and her crony, Mrs. Bodkin, gave her matching looks of disdain over their matching reading glasses (only Mrs. Johnson actually needed them). "Liar!" Mrs. Johnson hissed. "Liar!" Mrs. Bodkin echoed.

Pandora indicated them with a gesture. "Well, we all know why Mrs. Bodkin is here"—in addition to being a hypochondriac, she had the added bad habit of doing dangerous things to herself, like drinking bleach, for example, to make herself sick—"but what is it you're in here for again, Mrs. Johnson?" She paused a moment as the crank frowned at her. "Oh, that's right. Nothing." Mrs. Johnson had somehow managed to get a room at the manor when her husband was brought here, and after he died, she never left. So basically she was a freeloader (and one of the many reasons why Nepenthe Manor was always short on cash), with a lot of spare time on her hands and bile in her heart.

The old woman harrumphed and spun about on her fuzzy slippers, knitting bag clutched firmly in her age-spotted hand and Mrs. Bodkin in tow. Rather than leave the room, she made her way through the crowd like a linebacker, heading straight for the food table. The others, seeing that the entertainment was over, went back to eating and talking amongst themselves.

"Sorry about that," J.T. apologized.

"What for? You didn't do anything."

"Well, I should've at least said something. She had no right calling you a liar."

"She calls everyone a liar, J.T. She'd call the pope a liar if she ever met him."

J.T. giggled gleefully. "She probably would." He looked about. "Now, I didn't stop by just to bother you. There's someone here I want you to meet. I know your mother doesn't approve of you hanging out with the patients here, but this poor girl has cut herself off from everyone and I'm at my wit's end. Which doesn't take much doing!" he added with a self-deprecating smile. She wasn't fooled. J.T. was smarter than he looked, and benefited a great deal by playing the buffoon.

"Awesome," she mumbled, wishing she hadn't come. The last thing she wanted was to become someone's new buddy.

"Wait right here."

She was tempted to make a run for it, but the room was even more packed now, and any direction she went would lead her to someone she didn't want to be around. Dr. Steele, Vicki, Vlad, and Dougie stood near the two exits to the room like prison guards. At the moment, they were all engaged in conversation, but she had the distinct feeling that each and every one of them was watching her out of the corner of their eye. It was kind of creepy.

"Here she is!" J.T. cried, pushing a girl toward her. Pandora's first impression was one of revulsion. Not on her part, but on the girl's. She was practically digging her heels in as J.T. pushed her forward by the shoulders, as though Pandora was a big pile of feces. This must be Charles's problem girl. "Pandora, this is Rory Jones. She's eighteen, and new here."

Rory didn't look eighteen. She looked more like thirty; her brown face was gaunt, with fine lines around her mouth and sunken brown eyes. Her dyed blond hair, dark roots showing at least an inch, hung in strings, and she had a stud in her nose and tiny hoop earrings all down her right ear. The clothes she wore, a faded jean-jacket and ripped jeans, looked like someone's cast-offs, too big and stained with grease spots. Pandora wondered what her story was, then remembered what Charles had said about her. That she was mean. She looked mean.

"Hey," Pandora greeted, waiting for the pissy comeback.

Rory looked her up and down, then folded her arms. "Go to hell."

Right on cue. "Already here."

"Now, girls," J.T. gently, but nervously, scolded. He knew the beginning of a catfight when he saw one. "Let's be nice."

"Let's not," Rory shot back.

Pandora felt little flickers of anger in her chest, reminding her that she'd told the posse she'd deal with this little snot. "What's your problem?"

"Your ugly face."

"Oh, ho!" someone laughed from behind her. Birdy, of course. She and Lucy had joined them, plates in hand. Charles was still at the table, eating as much Jell-o as he could, and Sinclair was standing in a corner, looking morose and trapped, his eyes fixed on her like lasers. "That was a good one."

"What's it to you, fatty?" Rory snapped.

"Bust her balls, Pandora," Birdy ordered. Birdy was all for Pandora getting knocked down a few pegs, but she was not all for it happening to her.

"I'm really not in the mood for this, J.T.," Pandora said, her tone bored. "She obviously doesn't want to be around us, so why force it?"

"Because it's my job, Pandora!"

"You call herding a bunch of retards around a job?" Rory cracked.

There was a commotion by the food table and J.T. spun toward it. "Oh, Al. Not again!" He scurried off to stop Al the Addict from attempting to eat an entire loaf of bread. Togs, a patient and wannabe photographer, was pretending to take pictures.

Pandora was glad J.T. was gone. Now she could get down to business. A quick glance told her that her mother was busy talking to Dr. Malik. Perfect. She took a step forward, then another, until she was only a few inches from the newbie. The girl smelled of stale cigarette smoke and unwashed clothes, and there was a rust-red slit in her lower lip, probably from smoking.

"The only retard in this room is you," Pandora said in a low voice. "You're surrounded by people who are mentally unstable, and you're saying things that could set them off. Ever seen a bull fight? Because right now you're the red cape and everyone else is the bull."

Rory didn't even have the intelligence to look scared. "Like I give a shit. Run me over. Do what you want. At least it will get me out of this place." Wow. Xavier had been a smart ass when he'd first arrived, but this creature was so full of arrogance you could practically see it coming off her in waves.

Pandora felt a reluctant admiration. "Only temporarily. There aren't many places like this one left. You'll either get sent back here once you recuperate from all your nasty injuries, or go to jail."

"I'd rather go to jail. Safer there. Probably more freedom, too. I mean, look at you. You're like animals trapped in a cage, forced to do what you're told, not allowed to go anywhere."

"I'm not a patient here," Pandora felt driven to point out. This wasn't the first time she'd tried to distance herself from the inmates, and each time she did it she felt a guilty twinge. Maybe because she was more like them than she cared to admit, yet had escaped incarceration. She pushed that uncomfortable thought away.

Rory's upper lip curled into a sneer. "You could've fooled me. Now get out of my face before I deck you one." She brandished her fists at Pandora, giving her ample opportunity to read the girl's finger tattoos, which spelled DROP DEAD.

"Pandora can go where she wants and do what she wants!" Lucy hollered, and Pandora used the opportunity to take a step back, without looking like she was doing what the girl had ordered her to. Though from the smirk on Rory's face, she knew exactly what Pandora was doing.

The new girl looked at Lucy with vague amusement. "Oh, yeah? I've heard all about the places patients aren't allowed to go in this stupid place, you included, *princess*." She pointed a finger that ended with a chewed-up nail at Pandora. "I've heard things about you. None of them good."

"Yeah, well, consider the source."

"You saying the patients here are liars?"

"Nice try. I'm saying the staff members who told you about me are a bunch of tossers. But I'm touched that you found me intriguing enough to want to know more about me."

Rory's eyes narrowed, the only indication she'd been caught out. "I didn't ask. They just warned me off you. Now, if they're warning someone like me to keep away, what's that saying about you?"

"That you shouldn't get on my bad side?"

"That implies you have a good side."

"This is boring and stupid," Birdy complained, unsurprisingly annoyed that the attention wasn't focused on her. "Let's go, Pandora."

Pandora had never backed down from a fight in her life and wasn't about to start now. "I'm not finished here."

"Well, I am," Rory snapped, then turned to go.

Pandora grabbed her skinny arm. "Not so fast. You have an apology to make."

"The only apology I'll be making is with my fist."

"Name the place."

"Seriously?" she scoffed. "I just told you everything in this loony bin is off-limits."

"Are you scared, scaredy cat?" Lucy challenged, dancing on the tips of her toes.

"Not even close, moron."

"All right, then," Pandora spoke up, before Lucy could attack and get herself killed. "Meet me in the foyer, half past four." This was after all the inmates' therapy sessions had ended, and before the therapists bugged out and dinner was served. "I have an idea where we could go."

"This better not be a trap."

"I don't need to do traps. Besides, we'll have them with us." She threw her thumb at Birdy and Lucy. "It's a good cover."

"Fine." Rory cracked her knuckles. "I'm in the mood for a good ass kicking."

"Masochist, are you?"

"Funny. You're the one who's gonna be crying, Belfry."

"I don't think so, Rory."

"I go by Bones."

"Ah. Well, the name fits." She was certainly bony. But did she get the name and try to live up to it? Or was she bony in the first place, and got the name? A question for the ages.

Bones lifted her middle finger. "Sit and spin, Belfry. Sit and spin." Then she pushed her way out of the room.

It was a performance worthy of the bard, and Pandora felt a thrill go through her. It was show time.

"ARE YOU REALLY gonna fight Bones, Dora-Pan?" Lucy asked, watching the new girl strut off.

"She gave me no choice."

"I don't remember anyone sticking a gun to your head," Birdy pointed out.

"Who's got a gun?" Charles asked, joining them. His lips were actually a normal color for once, but only because he'd eaten a ton of cherry Jell-o. He pretended to shoot them all. "Pew, pew, pew!"

"Pandora's going to fight the new girl," Birdy explained.

"With a gun?" Charles looked more excited than he should about the possibility.

"With my fists," Pandora corrected. It felt good saying that. She was spoiling for a fight. Had been for some time now. Her head hurt, and fighting wasn't exactly taking it easy, but she needed this. An outlet for her feelings. What better way than to punch someone's lights out?

Sinclair was behind Charles and he looked nervous, shaking his head at Pandora's comment.

"Don't worry, Sinclair. It'll only take one punch."

He only continued to shake his head, either in disapproval, or disbelief that she could win. She didn't like either reaction and frowned at him. But she said nothing aloud, on account of his regression back to being a sorry mess. Though she wondered if anyone ever held back when *she* was fragile. She seriously doubted it.

Maybe because you never let on that you're hurting, a little voice inside her said. She knew that voice. It was rational, logical, and sensical. She hated that voice.

She looked around at the posse. "So I assume you're all going to show up?"

"Wouldn't miss it for the world," Birdy replied enthusiastically. "I win no matter which one of you does."

Lucy and Charles nodded, then Sinclair, his eyes on her watchful, nodded, too. Bunch of bloodthirsty little creatures, her posse. She knew they wouldn't let her down.

"Then I'll see you at 4:30 in the foyer. In the meantime, I'm going to my room. It's too loud in here. Later." She gave a salute and headed for the door.

The posse looked disappointed, but she wasn't giving in to their non-stop need for her presence. She was starting to feel bad again and she needed to rest up for the fight. Getting involved in a boxing match with a druggie probably wasn't the smartest thing to do when she had a concussion, but she'd meant what she'd said to Charles. Bones was so skinny she'd very likely go down with one punch.

As Pandora sidled out of the room, she avoided catching the eye of her four watchdogs, or anyone else. She needed to get out of there, and if they tried to keep her from leaving, she'd have to knock them flat. It wasn't an easy escape though, and she had to wonder why crowds couldn't part like the Red Sea when she approached. At last she managed to make it out the door, and hurried up the stairs, two at a time, to the apartment.

With the curtains drawn her room was cool and dark and she climbed up into her bed with a sigh of relief. Lying on her back, she stared at the watermark directly above her until her headache subsided and the anxious feeling in her chest loosened its grip. It was at this point she remembered her missing sporran. She also wondered what had happened to her basketball. She hoped she hadn't left it, or both items, at the park in town after the game. If so, surely someone had grabbed them for her. But who? And where was her stuff now?

I'll search for it in a bit.

That's the last thing she remembered thinking before startling awake. Her watch informed her that it was already five after four. Crap. She'd have to get moving if she wanted to find her sporran before heading down to the foyer. She needed a key from the key ring, which she always kept in her bag, to access the place where she planned to fight Bones.

She cautiously lifted her head. No pain. Good. She climbed down the ladder, not liking how shaky she felt. Maybe some food would remedy that. She grabbed a chicken leg from the fridge and ate it in a few bites. After two more legs and a cinnamon roll, she headed to the bathroom and took a look in the mirror, pleased at how her haircut made her appear sweet, but edgy, too. Screw Xavier's opinion. He was wrong. She didn't look stupid; she looked like an orphan. Orphanages often kept their wards well-shorn, and the buzz cuts turned them into desperados, a look she found appealing. But some institutions, like certain asylums, went too far, shaving half the patient's head so that if they escaped, they'd be easily identifiable. The idea was clever, but in a serial killer kind of way, and Pandora found she simply couldn't condone it.

Knowledge of such nefarious practices made her all the more grateful for her current status as a free citizen. But if she didn't watch herself she could lose that status. She had to be careful how she tread over the next few months. Perhaps picking a fight with one of the new admits hadn't been one of her brighter ideas. It had seemed like a good one at the time, but now it felt more like deciding to pick up a live grenade.

She couldn't back out now, though. Not without losing face, and the faith of the posse. She had to follow through. But she'd better get moving. She had about ten minutes to search for her sporran. She thought back to the day of the basketball game. She couldn't remember if she'd grabbed it after hitting her head, or if she'd left it behind at the court, or maybe it was in the Madmobile. Possibly someone else had picked it up and still had it. That could be any of the posse, even Dr. Steele or Xavier. Yet none of them had mentioned it to her. Jimbo or one of his crew could have taken it, which would be a disaster, as they'd probably already sold the bag and its contents to buy a pack of smokes and a forty dog.

She was starting to feel that jittery, bugs crawling on your skin, sensation that comes with stress overload, when she remembered something. The secret room.

She grabbed the large flashlight she kept in her closet and switched it on. Moving swiftly down the hidden passage, which led from her closet to the secret room, she made the trek in record time. When she tried the door, she found it unlocked and knew she was on to something. She never would have left the room unlocked unless she'd left the keys inside for safekeeping.

Once the door was closed behind her, she switched on the light. After blinking a few times, she looked around and immediately spotted her missing pillow and blanket on the couch, the library books, her basketball, and there, on the desk, was her sporran. She grinned and hurried over to it. In one swift movement, the strap was over her head and her bag settled onto her hip, just like old times. A quick search inside revealed her key ring lying at the bottom next to a small flashlight, along with a number of other essential items necessary for surviving in this place.

She looked around, brow furrowed in thought. She must have been planning to hide out from her grandmother after the basketball game, but after Derek's mom was found wandering about the manor, followed by Skippy's father coming to take him away, she'd been distracted from her initial scheme. Her theory made a lot of sense, but something about it niggled at her mind, something not quite right. A glance at her watch told her she had to get going, so she transferred the little niggle to another spot in her brain, to return to later. Grabbing the books, she dropped them off in her room, hoping to be able to read them some time soon.

Feeling better with her sporran back in its rightful place, she headed downstairs to the foyer, taking the steps slow and sure. She didn't want to trip and make everyone think she was trying to do herself in again, especially not with Bones in the audience. The last thing Pandora wanted to do was make that walking skeleton happy.

When she arrived in the foyer, she was glad to find it empty. The location they'd be going to for their fight was strictly off-limits, and not having witnesses to her impending rule breaking would be a nice treat for once.

A few minutes later she heard the sound of the posse approaching. Lucy arrived first, not even bothering to be quiet. Birdy, Charles, and Sinclair were more circumspect, though Birdy's heels were not. Each step sounded like a shotgun blast echoing through the vast open space of the lobby. Today, however, it seemed that she was exhibiting an unusually heightened awareness of the trouble she might be causing, glancing back over her shoulder every few seconds to see if anyone noticed. She seemed fidgety and on edge, but a pleased smile on her pale pink lips belied any sort of anxiety.

"We're here, we're queer, and we want some beer!" Lucy announced as she did a little wiggly walking dance toward Pandora. A male patient, who had long since been discharged, had hollered the phrase whenever he walked into a room, and Lucy had never forgotten it. He also liked to say, "I'm wildly gay, and I'm here to stay." Unfortunately, Lucy didn't know that the term gay could mean something other than happy (which her mother insisted it meant), same with the word queer (Mrs. Landry had naively told her daughter that it only meant someone who's a little different). So Lucy in her ignorance ran the risk of offending a good number of people, which, actually, was par for the course for her, and quite entertaining for Pandora. One time the girl had said to Mrs. Nelson, one of the do-gooder LoBAC ladies, who had come to drop off their monthly charitable donation, and who, herself, was quite aware of the alternative meaning to the word, "That hat makes you look like a queer." Followed by, "But it also makes you look really gay, too." The poor woman. On the other hand, if Mrs. Nelson was a queer gay, or a gay queer, knowing her hat might serve as a private signal to others indicating her alternative orientation could be a bonus.

"Shhh!" Pandora hissed at Lucy, who kept repeating herself, loudly.

"Keep your voice down." She glanced around. They couldn't linger here for long, so where the hell was Bones? Vicki's light was on in her office, either because Bennington was in there, or Vicki was. Bennington, Pandora could work her way around, but only after a sound scolding. Vicki, who was finally starting to act like a mother, was a wild card at this point. Whoever was in there, Pandora did not need a hassle from either one of them.

The outside door opened and Bones strutted into the foyer, looking quite pleased with herself. The smell of cigarette smoke and rain, along with Vlad, followed her inside. The Russian gave Pandora an assessing look. "You are not planning to go outside?" Only it wasn't a question.

Great. He had to say that right after she'd told Bones she could do whatever she wanted. "I told you I wouldn't. Besides, it's raining. Being so sweet and all, I'd probably melt." Bones smirked.

"Then what are you up to, hm?"

"We thought we'd play some hopscotch." She indicated the black and white tiles of the foyer. "Got a problem with that?"

"I have *got* a problem with your ability to tell stories and pass them off as truth."

"I thought that was the KGB's personal motto. You know...lie through your teeth, unless the truth serves your purpose better."

He lowered his head and gave her a "don't go there" look. She liked how touchy he was about the whole KGB thing. "I am going to go do my rounds now. When I get back, you had all better be gone." He pointed a finger at each and every one of them, though with Charles, he pretended to shoot. Charles grinned and clutched at his chest. "Be aware that I take no prisoners." With that, Vlad strode out of the foyer, down one of the numerous halls. Luckily it wasn't the one she needed to use.

She waited until his footsteps faded away, then looked around. The coast was clear. "All right, let's go. No talking"—she gave Lucy a stern look, and the insolent girl returned it—"walk very quietly"—this next one was directed at Birdy, who rolled her eyes—"and follow me." Bones got the look this time, but unfortunately she was chewing on a ratty fingernail and not paying Pandora any attention. She seemed bored, but Pandora knew her nonchalance was an act. If it wasn't, then it explained why the girl did drugs. Because she was dead inside.

With a signal, Pandora took off down a hall that led in the opposite direction of the TV room, the arts and crafts room, and all the therapists' offices. The lighting in the corridor was dim, various bulbs allowed to go unreplaced over the years as the passage was so little used. It was very quiet here, and even Birdy seemed to be making an effort to muffle her steps on the hardwood floor, though it made her slower than usual and put her last in line.

What many people did not know is that this particular hallway led to another wing of the building. It was a wing that was never used, and it had its own entrance from the outside, which was kept locked at all times. This area was completely off-limits, no exceptions. The story Vicki had spun for Pandora was that the wing was not safe, but Pandora had been inside it numerous times and had yet to see any signs of damage. Her explorations had been thorough and guided by a book she'd checked out from the library on all the things that could go wrong with a building's structure, from water damage to termites to bowing walls and cracks in the foundation. The area, although virtually abandoned, was fine, meaning Vicki had lied. Big shocker.

When they reached the door that served as the back entrance to the wing, Pandora stopped. She pulled out her flashlight and shined it into everyone's faces, one at a time, like a spotlight. "What I'm about to show you no one can discuss. It's like our, um, *other* project that we kept secret." She didn't want to say the word labyrinth because she didn't want Bones to know about it.

"You mean the labyrinth?" Lucy asked, all innocent eyes.

Pandora sighed. "Yes. Now I know you guys can keep your mouths shut, since no one has said anything about the labyrinth that I've heard. Not even Jun Li, and that guy knows everything." Lucy had been her biggest worry for tattling, but maybe there was a line that even Lucy knew she couldn't cross.

"Can we tell God about it?" Charles wanted to know.

"Yes," Pandora answered over Bones's snort of disbelief. Pandora might not be sure what she, herself, thought about the concept of God, but she wasn't about to mess with the posse's belief. Besides, she'd already tried to intervene a few years ago and the resulting shit-storm had been awful. When she'd declared her belief that maybe God didn't exist, Charles started shaking so hard she thought he was going to disintegrate right before her eyes. That was the exact moment she learned a particularly hard lesson, which is that when it comes to religion, everyone can believe whatever the hell they wanted to believe. Life is hard enough without someone taking away whatever it is you think you need to get through it.

"How about Dr. Steele?" Lucy demanded. "That man's so fine he can get anything out of me." She giggled wantonly. "And I'd like it."

Holy crap, Lucy. No more Dr. Ruth for you. "No way," Pandora stated emphatically, and Lucy giggled some more. Birdy said nothing, but she was still jittery, and Pandora gave her a searching look. Something was going on with that girl, and it was giving Pandora heartburn. "Are we agreed?"

"I could say yes and be lying," Bones answered. "I could report you."

"Yes, you could. But then I'd have to tell the Director that you broke into our apartment and stole some money." Or something like that, because in truth, Pandora didn't have any money to steal. And judging by the state of Vicki's wardrobe, neither did she. It occurred to Pandora that their state of poverty was further incentive for her mother wanting to leave Nepenthe Manor for a better job. She shoved that thought away.

"Have it your way," Bones agreed with a shrug. Pandora wasn't sure she could trust the juvenile delinquent not to talk, but then again, she couldn't really trust the posse, either. Except Sinclair. And only because he hardly ever talked. Her biggest problem was that the staff and the therapists had ways of tricking the posse into giving up information; it helped them head off future insurrections. The inmates didn't have Pandora's keen mind and absolute disdain for the integrity of the human race to pull them through such unfair cross-examinations, so she worried.

"All right. Here we go." She pulled her key ring out of her sporran and after some fumbling, inserted the proper key. The door creaked as she pushed it open. "Wait here." She stepped into the absolute blackness of the space, and using her flashlight, found the master switch to turn on the work lights. With all the flourish of Dr. Frankenstein, she lifted the breaker and light filled the room. "Come on," she gestured to the inmates peeking in.

They stepped inside, one by one, and looked around in awe. "This is the workshop," she explained. "The best part is this way." With a gesture, she headed toward the black curtain on the far side of the room, waited one moment to be sure the others had followed her, then pulled it to one side.

The posse, along with Bones, filed through the narrow space, and onto a black wood floor. Pandora watched them, pleased with their awed reactions. Even Bones looked impressed, if excessive eye squinting and a dubious scowl could be labeled as such.

Birdy's eyes shone under the scoop lighting fixtures that lit up the area, and she flung her arms wide. "My friends, this is where I was always meant to be."

"Welcome to Nepenthe Manor Theater," Pandora announced grandly, stepping out onto the bright and glorious stage.

13

Wet Paper Bag

IT WASN'T A huge theater, but it was amazing—a magical world unto itself where, with proper lighting and makeup, imagination became reality. Mr. Nepenthe, the man who had built the manor, and father to Elizabeth Nepenthe, had really known what he was doing. Too bad he'd decided to move out once Elizabeth had gone missing, never to return. Who knew what he might have accomplished if he'd stayed?

After the manor had sat empty for decades, some Nepenthe (perhaps Theodore, Mr. Nepenthe's son) had donated the building to the town of Bedlam, along with a large chunk of change to maintain it, to be used solely for the public good. It didn't sound like something the bratty brother Elizabeth had described in her diary would do, but stranger things have happened. After WWI, the manor served as a rest home to help house all the returning vets suffering from shell shock. It wasn't long, though, before the place transitioned into a sort of catch-all facility (aka a dumping ground) for the poor saps, typically the mentally ill or deficient, whose families didn't want them or know how to properly care for them.

The theater itself was a work of art. There were five hundred red plush seats, heavy red velvet curtains for the stage, an orchestra pit, its apron safely in place so no one could fall in (like Lucy), a catwalk, which the audience had no idea passed right over their heads, four opera boxes, two on each side, along with two nooks for spotlights, and a control booth at the back of the theater, just behind the seats. The small booth was a later addition some enterprising director had installed years ago, back when the manor actually still had some money to burn. The booth was pretty modern, and still functional, which Pandora knew because she'd taught herself how to run the light and sound boards. Playing around in that dark little room she'd felt like God, a powerful sensation one does not easily forget, or want to give up.

Over the years, she'd done her best to maintain the place without getting caught at it. Being that Frank, their ex-security guard, wasn't all that keen on doing unnecessary work, he'd made her job easy. Having Vlad around, however, might make coming and going a bit more challenging. She hadn't been in the theater for a few months, though, and the dust on the stage gave witness to that. After her fight with Bones, she'd have to give the floor a good sweeping.

Though maybe Lucy, who was spinning in circles around the stage, would do the job for her. Birdy was still holding out her arms, though every few seconds, her hands would draw in for kisses to be flung back out at the imaginary, obviously adoring, audience. Charles was hanging on a curtain rope, but the little dude was so light he couldn't move the curtains even a bit. He didn't seem to mind as he made Tarzan and monkey sounds while swinging back and forth. Sinclair was wandering around the stage, studying an old living room set still in place, taking note of the numerous specialized Fresnel lights overhead, then moving to the far wing, which housed the wardrobe, to assess all the costumes left behind. He didn't show his enthusiasm outwardly, but she sensed he was as taken in by this magical place as she was. Bones attempted to look bored, though she didn't quite succeed as her eyes darted around to all the piles of detritus lying here and there. Either that or she was looking for something to steal.

Pandora rubbed at her temples, feeling the beginnings of a headache coming on. Best to get this fight done and over with so she could go back to her room and sleep. Knowing she was being stupid, but also knowing she had made her bed, she needed this to be over, and soon. Not only had she brought the posse to a place they weren't supposed to be, exposing them all to getting in trouble (mainly her), and running the risk of someone (mainly Lucy) shooting off her mouth, she had also brought Bones, an unknown element, here to this sacred place. It was not her best decision.

But she had to get the new girl to back off the posse, and this seemed the only way to do it without having more grief heaped upon her weary shoulders. Though after Dr. Steele's use of the boxing match analogy to describe how she might be feeling, she had to grudgingly admit the irony inherent in her decision to fight Bones.

"So are you ready to go down?" she asked the skinny girl, who was now eyeing her with an obnoxious smirk on her cracked lips. Hmmm. Getting in trouble just might be worth erasing that smirk.

"I was about to ask you the same thing, *Bats*." Hearing the nickname the townies called her had the same effect as a large dose of pure irritation being injected directly into her veins. Pandora raised her fists. Out of the corner of her eye, she saw the posse gathering around.

"Let me know if you need my help," Charles volunteered, puffing out his fragile chest. "I could try out my mind powers on Bones."

Bones rolled her eyes. "First you have to have a mind, which I'm pretty sure you lost a long time ago."

Pandora felt her breathing rev up a notch. "Leave him alone."

Bones cocked her head. "Make me, Bats."

"Gladly." Pandora tossed aside her sporran, then strode forward until she and Bones stood only a few feet apart, smack dab in the center of the stage. She took in Bones's stance, assessed her strength, possible speed, and then factored in her own weakness—her growing headache. Pandora could take the girl, but she'd have to move quickly. There was something unpredictable in Bones's face, like this wasn't her first rodeo, and certainly wouldn't be her last. It would behoove Pandora not to underestimate the girl.

"Gonna fight, or just keep circling me like a buzzard, waiting for me to die of boredom?" Bones laughed at her own wit.

That's when Pandora made her move. She swung out at Bones, who ducked with a knowing smirk, but didn't see Pandora's left leg sweeping in an arc. Her foot connected with Bones's patella (otherwise known as the kneecap), causing the girl's leg to buckle. Bones went down on her knees, and Pandora ducked in with an elbow to the girl's ear, a hugely sensitive area, which would hurt badly, but not show too much damage. Bones fell back, clasping a hand to the side of her head.

Pandora was waiting for her to push herself to her feet to continue the fight when the sound of clapping echoed around the stage. She made the rookie mistake of spinning toward the offender, only to feel a sharp crack on the back of her head. She dropped like a brick and, quick as a lightning flash, Bones was on top of her like a wild animal. They rolled about for a bit, fighting for position, before Pandora managed to land a right hook that knocked Bones backward. Pandora shoved the girl off, and they both sat eyeing each other warily, Bones clutching her nose, Pandora the back of her head.

A shadow fell over Pandora and she looked up to see Dougie. "You were doing well until you turned your back on your opponent."

"Your stupid clapping threw me off."

"While in the midst of battle, one should never allow one's self to be distracted."

"Okay, Hannibal," she grumbled. "Now clear off so we can finish what we started."

"I see myself more like Sun Tzu or Alexander the Great, but Hannibal will do. As for my clearing off, that is not going to happen. As much as I enjoy watching you two fight for supremacy, I cannot allow this to continue."

"What the hell is going on here?" cried a new voice from the wings.

What was Xavier doing here? And was that Derek behind him? It was.

Why, Pandora moaned inwardly, *did I not lock the door?* She had been careless, and all because of her stupid TBT. She kneaded her neck vigorously in an attempt to rub away the pain. "How did you guys even know we were here?" She was pretty certain she'd checked to be sure they hadn't been followed. Hadn't she? She couldn't remember now.

"Hi, Dougie," Birdy greeted with a giggle and a flutter of her fingers.

Ah. It was all so clear now. She pushed herself to her feet. "Birdy Peacock, you big tattletale traitor!"

Birdy crossed her arms and gave Pandora an indignant look. "I am not a tattletale traitor! I was worried about you, and thought I'd better tell someone what you were up to. Dougie seemed the safest choice, right, Dougie?" She batted her eyelashes, and Pandora deduced that money had exchanged hands. Birdy was not the worrying type, and especially not when Pandora was involved.

"Are you his snitch now?"

"Color contacts aren't free, you know, and Daddy has become really tight-fisted these past few months. I know Mother tells him all the time to stop giving me money. She's such a bitch!"

"Can someone tell me what's going on here?" Xavier pushed his way back into the conversation. He was keeping the 'look like an idiot' theme alive, wearing a pair of blue shorts over gray sweatpants and a red headband, of all things. "I saw Dougie acting suspiciously and decided to follow him. Derek was with me in the lobby, so he tagged along."

"Pandora is teaching the new girl a lesson with her fists so she will stop being a bitch," Lucy explained self-importantly.

"I'm not a snitch!" Birdy talked over Lucy. "I'm a protector! I could be a psych assistant myself, you know. I certainly know enough about crazy people!"

All from personal experience.

"I'm hungry," Charles announced, somewhere in the middle of all that, sensing the growing tension and foolishly hoping to divert attention.

"Bitch, bitch, son-of-a-bitch!" Lucy sang off-key, while throwing in a little soft shoe.

Pandora sighed. This was not going how she'd planned. At all.

"Are you all right, Pandora?" Derek asked. She opened her eyes, not even realizing she'd closed them. Maybe she'd thought they'd all go away and leave her alone if she shut her eyes for a good long time. He was looking down at her from his height of 6'4", which is pretty gargantuan for a fourteen-year-old. His gray eyes showed concern; his dark hair was a mess, as though he'd sat with his fingers laced through it and his elbows on his knees, like someone does when they're very tired.

"I'm fine. Just haven't recovered from this yet." She pointed to her head, wondering how much he knew. What he knew. *If* he knew...

"I wanted to come visit you in the hospital," he said, his forehead wrinkled with frustration, "but my ma had a bad reaction to her medication and I couldn't leave her. And then I couldn't get a ride."

"Oh. Well, I was wondering why I hadn't seen you, but figured it had to do with your mom." She was glad she hadn't jumped to any conclusions about him not visiting. She'd misjudged him before; she wasn't about to make that mistake again. She thought about this for a moment. Not getting immediately pissed off at Derek and waiting to hear his side of the story was probably the most mature thing she'd ever done, and she felt both proud of herself and slightly disturbed by such blatantly abnormal behavior on her part.

"This is all very sweet," Dougie interrupted, his expression a study of distaste. "But it's meal-time and these young people need their sustenance. Come along, all of you." He motioned to them to follow. Pandora wondered why he was in such a big hurry.

"Not so fast," Xavier said, his voice harsh. His eyes fastened on Pandora and the look in them was full of fury. "You need to be stopped. You not only put yourself in danger, you put your friends in danger, too. This selfishness of yours has got to end here, and now, or someone is going to end up hurt. I'm not going to let that happen, not again."

"My *selfishness*? Are you kidding me? I was trying to help them, not hurt them. Bones here"—she waved toward the girl, who had managed to make herself almost invisible (which was a nice trick)—"was not being a good little patient. She was bullying them, Xavier, and I decided to put a stop to it."

"By bullying her back?" He crossed his arms and peered at her smugly. If only he could see his face in a mirror, how much it looked like everyone on the staff, up on their sanctimonious high horses. "Besides, it's not your job to look after the patients. Tell the staff and they'll take care of the situation."

"Oh, please. The staff couldn't punch their way out of a wet paper bag." Derek muffled a laugh, and she shot him a grateful glance. "And since when did you become such a wuss?"

"As much as I'd like to hear the answer to that," Dougie spoke up, his voice firm, "I need to escort the patients to the dining room. Pandora, I'll be up later to check on you."

"Don't bother, traitor," she hissed at him. Derek gave her an understandably questioning look, to which she could only shake her head and roll her eyes.

Dougie studied her for several long seconds, during which she could practically hear everyone breathing. "Whatever pleases you most, Pandora," he said at last, his voice calm, almost sweet sounding. Damn, she hated it when he said that particular phrase, and in that fraudulent tone.

"Anyway, I'm not leaving yet. New girl and I didn't finish our fight." She turned to Bones. "Well?"

Xavier stepped between them, and Pandora was tempted to turn on him. "There'll be no more fighting. Now everyone out." He began to herd the posse toward the workshop.

"Wait!" Pandora shouted, and everyone stopped and turned back, some faces curious, others not so much.

"Now what?" Xavier growled.

"We can't tell anyone we were in here. Not a soul. If Vicki finds out, she'll blow a gasket, and none of us will escape the fallout. She's walking a fine line right now, and she'll take us all down with her. I mean it. No one can know about this."

"I can stay quiet," Derek said, which was the perfect way of putting it.

"Me, too," Lucy agreed, smiling up at Derek.

Everyone else appeared to agree, even Bones, though she only nodded. Pandora didn't trust the conniving little wench, but could only hope she'd put the fear of God/Vicki/the apocalypse into the little deviant. Xavier turned to go again, and Bones trailed after him, her eyes focused intently on his back. Feeling a little relieved the fight wasn't going to continue, Pandora fetched her sporran and returned it to its proper place.

Derek joined her as she followed behind the strange little menagerie. "I'll take you to your room, Pandora," he said in a low voice. "I need to talk to you."

Dougie turned around to interrupt their little tête-à-tête, but Lucy grabbed his arm and pulled him forward, foiling his plan. "I can say bitch, can't I, Dougie? Jun-Li says I can because it's a female dog and you can call people female dogs."

"Jun-Li thinks it's funny having you say a bad word, Lucy. He doesn't stop to think that you could get into trouble because of it." *How diplomatic of you, Dougie*, Pandora noted. He played the game so well.

Lucy frowned. "So I shouldn't say it?"

"I think you should choose your times wisely."

She nodded knowingly. "I like your smartness. It serves me well."

He slowly pulled his arm away from her grasp. "I'm glad."

They left the theater the way they'd come in, and Xavier made a show of closing the door behind them. "Don't make me come rescue you again," he warned Pandora.

"You are so delusional, Carlisle. I was taking care of business and you and Dougie were dumb enough to get in the way of that. Besides, I thought you were done with me and my little reindeer games."

"I was only doing what I was told," he replied.

"What you were told?" she demanded, feeling a frisson of warning in her chest.

He gave a casual shrug. "Dr. Steele asked me to keep an eye on you. He's paying me, too. Cool, huh?" And with that, Xavier marched down the hallway, the posse trailing after him like obedient little duckies.

14

WHEN THE POSSE disappeared, Pandora locked the door, then grabbed Derek's huge hand and pulled him down the hall. "Come on. Before Dougie comes to check on me." His hand felt warm and strong, and she was amazed at her derring-do for taking it. She wasn't usually, or *ever*, this forward. This was Birdy's kind of behavior, but Pandora didn't let go. She needed his strength right now, especially after hearing that Dr. Steele was paying Xavier to babysit her.

Of all the *nerve*.

"I heard Dougie's working at the manor now," Derek said as they trudged up the steps to her apartment. "He's also staying here, in this building."

Pandora tripped, and Derek pulled her upright. She kept going, flustered. "I'd forgotten about that." She had, and she didn't like that she had. He was probably staying in one of the three tiny guest apartments on the other side of the building, close to the apartments used by the staff. The guest rooms weren't used very often, but sometimes a loved one needed a place to bed down, and Vicki had them use one of those rooms. They were small, dark, and cramped, probably to discourage prolonged stays, and they smelled of despair. If that's where Dougie was living now, he must be feeling the pain of separation from his spacious mansion and his butt-kissing butler, Bartles (try saying that five times fast). Knowing he was suffering, and the fact that he was a good distance away from her own apartment, made her feel a little better.

"I don't know much else," Derek went on. "He keeps away from me when I visit my ma."

"That's because you scare him."

"Not as much as he scares me." It was a blatant admission of weakness, but funnily enough, Pandora liked Derek the better for it. She also liked that he must know what she'd done, or attempted to do, when she'd jumped off the bridge, but still wanted to be around her.

Unlike that judger, Xavier.

Pandora opened the apartment door, but had to let go of Derek's hand to do so. After they went inside and she sat down on the smelly old couch, he sat next to her, taking her hand again. *The cheeky devil.* A wave of heat surged up inside her, and she thought she might spontaneously combust from it. But if she did, it'd be a hell of a way to go.

"So what did you want to tell me?" she finally got out. He was look-ing down at her hand, as though enraptured by it, and a funny feeling engulfed her body.

"Lots of stuff," he replied, keeping his eyes firmly fixed on her hand. "So much. I was worried about you, and I know how your ma can be."

"Not exactly motherly?"

"Right. So I thought about you being all alone in the hospital, with no one to hold this little hand of yours." He finally looked up at her and she felt an alien sensation, strong and startling, in her chest. "You shouldn't have been alone, Pandora. I did try to visit you one evening. Tried to hitchhike, but no one wants to pick up a guy who looks like Frankenstein."

"You don't look like Frankenstein. Well, not your face. Height and size-wise. Totally."

He gave her a lopsided smile. "I suppose so. But anyway, before I could talk to my pa about taking the truck, you came home. I wanted to be there for your party, too, but I didn't hear about it until after-ward."

"I thought as much."

"You did?"

"I'm pretty sure Dougie would rather cut off his balls than invite you."

He chuckled. "Probably." The humor on his face quickly evaporated. "Why do you hang around him, Pandora?"

She shrugged. "He hangs around me." Derek didn't respond, only looked troubled, so she changed the subject to one she was curious about. "So, is your mom going to be okay?"

He shook his head. "I don't know. But I do know her coming here was the right thing."

Pandora let out a breath she didn't know she was holding. She'd been so certain that Mrs. Choken needed to be at Nepenthe Manor, but now, well, she wasn't so sure of anything. If the woman had experi-enced a bad reaction to her meds, which could have killed her, it would be all Pandora's fault for thinking she knew everything, and maybe, just maybe, she didn't know everything. It was a humbling thought, and not at all welcome.

"Good," she said. "I'm glad." He squeezed her hand in response. "So I suppose you heard about my, um, accident?"

"Your accident?"

The sound of the knob turning startled them both, and their hands leapt apart as the door swung open and Vicki charged inside. "What's going on here?" She was still wearing her outfit from the funeral, and she looked utterly wiped out, and at the same time, full of furious energy. Derek abruptly stood, and Pandora joined him, not because she felt guilty, but because his towering height made her feel tiny, and perhaps a bit abandoned.

"It's a little thing called conversing, Vicki," she answered, a fake smile fixed firmly on her face, "otherwise known as socializing. I'm still allowed to do that, aren't I?"

Vicki wagged her finger at Pandora, like she was a naughty child. "Not alone in the apartment, you aren't."

"Then when? When I turn eighteen?"

"When you show me I can trust you."

"Do you hate me, Vicki? Or is it that you just don't want me to have friends?"

"Don't be ridiculous. You're overreacting as usual."

A throbbing started up behind Pandora's eyes and she rubbed her temples. It seemed that every time her emotions got involved, her head started to hurt. Must be a blood pressure thing. "I am not overreacting," she ground out. "I'm simply reacting to *you* overreacting."

"Listen, you need to rest," Vicki said in a calmer voice. "You're already overdoing it."

"And sitting on a couch talking to someone is overdoing it?" Pandora shook her head in disbelief. "So I can't talk to the staff, patients, or townies, and now Derek, who isn't any of those."

"His mother is a patient here," Vicki pointed out, her eyes flicking away from them as though she was quite aware she was the one being ridiculous. "It's a conflict of interest."

"Whose interest? Yours?"

"I'm not going to argue with you about this, Pandy." She turned to Derek, finally meeting his eyes. "I'm sorry to involve you in this, Derek, but I would really rather you didn't come up to the apartment unless I'm here."

"Which would be never," Pandora laid it out for him. "She's never here. It's always work, work, work."

"Well, that might be changing soon, and then it will be a case of be careful what you wish for." Vicki indicated the door. "Thank you for stopping by, Derek. Good night."

Derek, who looked like a wild animal caught in a trap, nodded. "Good night, ma'am." He gave Pandora a helpless shrug, then turned and left, barely fitting through the doorway. He shut the door behind him with a soft click.

"I cannot believe you had a boy up here."

"Dougie comes up here all the time."

"Dougie is staff now, and I trust him."

But not your own daughter? What was wrong with this woman? "You didn't before. What's changed?"

"My opinion of him has."

"Then you're a fool."

A muscle in Vicki's cheek began to throb. "This conversation is officially over, Pandy. Go to your room. Hopefully tomorrow you'll be in a better frame of mind so that you can see the sense of what I'm saying."

Pandora felt hot tingles all over her at the unfairness of it all. She hadn't been doing a single thing wrong and yet was being treated as though she'd tried to kill someone. "You know what I wish for, Vicki?"

"What?" Her mother sighed, her expression conveying that she knew she was about to get creamed on this one. She was right.

"I wish that Professor Robertson lived and you had died. At least then I'd have one parent who actually wanted to be around me."

Vicki glared at Pandora through narrowed eyes, her lips thin and pale. "Yes, well, in that you'd be wrong." Then she turned and left the apartment, slamming the door behind her.

Pandora dropped back down on the couch. What a thoroughly shitty day this had been. And she never did get to hear everything Derek had to tell her, hardly anything at all, actually. Her head fell back against the couch cushion and she closed her eyes.

Why did she bother? When she'd tried to help the posse she ended up getting scolded for her effort. Dr. Steele had the effrontery to pay her asshole half-brother to spy on her. Her mother thought Pandora was stupid enough to get pregnant at age fourteen. Vicki's worry would, of course, be warranted if Pandora were any other person, because lately she'd started to see the allure of having sex—if it had anything to do with the feelings she experienced whenever she was in close proximity to a male, it had to be totally amazing—but at the moment she wasn't convinced it would be, and the consequences of her curiosity were way too big to take the risk.

For now, anyway.

The doorknob clicked and her eyes flew open, thinking Derek had snuck back. But it was only Dougie.

"What do you want, snitch?"

He stood in the doorway, unmoved. "Your mother told you."

"My mother didn't say anything about you, though you've confirmed what I'd already guessed. You told her I was up here with Derek and she came a'running like your little puppet. What did you think you would accomplish by doing that, Dougie? Win my undying gratitude?"

His expression tightened slightly, the only indication of his irritation. "I was concerned. We know very little about Derek. He could be a womanizer." He crossed the room and kneeled down directly in front of her, his blue eyes running over her face, slowly and precisely. She felt a little thrill run through her, and she despised herself for it.

She found her voice. "Oh, please, Dougie. That's bullshit and you know it."

"Such vulgar language, Pandora."

"Vulgar language, my arse, Dougie. Derek is a nice guy, and you know it. You just don't want to admit it."

"People have two sides to them, Pandora. All it takes is a perilous event to trigger the dark side. Even the most well-meaning of people can do awful things if pushed to the brink."

She pressed her lips together. He had her there. "Well, that includes you, Dougie, so you'd better leave before your dark side shows itself. Oh, wait. Maybe it's your good side that has yet to appear, and what a scary thing that would be."

He ignored this. "I'm here to tuck you in, Pandora."

She crossed her arms. "I'm not in the mood for your perverted machinations right now, Dougie."

"You're mad at Dr. Steele and your mother, but you're taking it out on me. That's called displacement."

"I know what displacement is, and I'm not doing it!" she cried, her fists clenched. "I'm mad at *everyone* right now! I don't know a single person who hasn't let me down, including you." Vicki for being a crappy mom, Professor Robertson for being a crappy dad, Xavier for being a crappy brother, Dr. Steele for being a crappy doctor, even Derek, for being a crappy friend. He hadn't even stood up for her with Vicki, and last week he'd avoided her because his dad had told him to stay away. He might be a nice guy, but he was, she was realizing, somewhat lacking in the backbone department.

"Even Derek?" Dougie said slyly, somehow plucking that thought out of her mind like an evil magician.

"Shut up, Dougie."

"I wanted to ask your advice on what to do with your inmates," he said, wisely moving on. "They're acting out, and I'm not sure how to rein them in without resorting to tactics that some might consider inhumane."

"*My* inmates?" She groaned, loud and long. "Of course they're acting out. What'd you expect? Their friend, Skippy, was taken away against his will, and they're afraid they're next. They think I tried to kill myself, and if *I'm* crazy, then what chance do they stand? A patient recently died, reminding them that death is all too real. It's a lot to deal with all at once, for anyone, much less kids with mental issues. Plus, I haven't been around to keep them in line, and it doesn't take much for them to lose a grip."

"So tell me what to do to get them back in line. I can't imagine you would want them to suffer."

"Heaven forbid," she mumbled, then relented, not wanting to give Dougie any ideas. She was all for the strange and macabre, but she didn't want to encourage it in him. She had a feeling his idea of what's right didn't align with how most people thought, herself included. "They need to do something, Dougie."

"Could you be more specific?"

"You're the trained professional. Figure it out."

"Might I remind you that I need to keep this job, Pandora, to stop my father from closing this place down?"

She sighed. Blackmail at its finest. "I don't know what you expect me to do, Dougie. You know I can't leave the manor. You know I have a concussion and can't overdo it." Not that her past injuries had ever slowed her down, but Dr. Gara's words about only having one brain had left their intended impact on her. Well, a dent, anyway. "My brother has been paid to spy on me, and I'm not even supposed to be around the inmates anyway. What are my options here?"

"You've always figured it out before. You'll manage once more."

"But I don't want to manage. I'm tired, Dougie. I'm tired of everything and everyone."

"That's a result of having a brain injury."

"I'm not sure that's the only cause for my feeling this way," she spoke slowly, but clearly, wondering if he'd get the hint that all was not well in Pandora World.

"*I* am sure," he said firmly, his chin jutting forward. "It's quite obvious you are not the girl you were before you hit your head, and a concussion is the only sensible argument to explain why you've changed."

"Maybe I've changed because all other paths have been closed off to me."

"This change literally happened overnight," he went on, pretty much ignoring the intent of her statement. "It's a simple cause-effect relationship."

Nothing is simple, she thought, *and it didn't happen overnight.* She could remember snippets of how she'd felt before the professor died, moments when she thought she was losing her mind. It was very possible that this feeling wasn't temporary, that this was her new state of being. She shivered, as though Death had pulled her into one last embrace. She closed her eyes and hoped that when she opened them, her world would be back in its—if not normal—then usual place.

15

Done With Man

"YOU'RE TIRED," DOUGIE pointed out the obvious, while purposely and adeptly avoiding acknowledging her little cry for help. She felt him stand up. "Let me put you to bed."

Pandora opened her eyes, sensing that the world was still the same as it had been when she closed her eyes to it. "That's not at all creepy." She sighed and pushed herself to her feet, ignoring his outstretched hand. "I'm not going to bed, and you are leaving."

"Your mother asked me to keep an eye on you, and I plan to do that." He stopped and waited for his incendiary comment to catch fire.

She swallowed hard as she struggled not to show her fury. How like Vicki to hand off her responsibilities to someone else, and a sixteen-year-old psychopath, at that. "Tell her that I'm fine, Dougie."

"But you're not."

"You wouldn't want her to renege on her promise to let me stay here, would you? She can, and would, do that. She's broken her promises to me enough times for me to know that."

"What are you going to do, then?"

"What else? Do what you asked and figure out something for the posse to do before they hurt themselves. I've learned that being allowed to wallow is the worst possible thing for them."

"Let me help you. We can brainstorm together."

"If you want me to do this, Dougie, then you need to let me do it. Alone."

His nostrils flared slightly. "Now that I'm here, Pandora, you'll never have to be alone again."

"Being alone is safe, Dougie. Then I only have to worry about my own demons betraying me."

"I would never betray you. Everything I do is for you, even when it may not look like it."

Pandora cocked an eyebrow. Was it possible? Dougie actually sounded hurt. "I never asked you to do anything for me."

"No, you have not, nor do you ever, of anyone—at least, not without striking some sort of bargain first. Maybe that is why you're struggling."

With that and a clipped bow, he turned and left the apartment, closing the door quietly behind him. She was glad he hadn't turned back because then he'd have seen her staring after him, as wide-eyed and open-mouthed as a grounded fish. That had been the simplest Dougie expulsion she'd ever had. She wished she could duplicate it.

Feeling hungry again, she took a Coke and the last of the party leftovers from the fridge and plopped them on a plate. Several healthy squirts of ketchup—the condiment of champions—later, she went to her room to eat. She set her plate on her abnormally clean desk, then hung up her sporran, giving it an affectionate pat. Its return to her life reminded her of her theory about how it had ended up in the secret room. She still liked the idea that she'd left it there with the intention of using the place as a hideout from her grandmother, so why didn't it sit right? The other stuff she'd found there—a blanket and pillow, her books, some clothes—made sense, but why had she brought her basketball? It wasn't like she could practice in the secret room, not without alerting everyone in the mansion that there were secret passages following them down every hallway in the building. Maybe she simply hadn't wanted anyone to touch it. That was logical. She'd lost a number of items over the years to one patient or another. But really, the basketball's presence wasn't why she was feeling off about her hideout theory. Something else had triggered that impression, but what?

She shook her head and decided she was being paranoid. Wasn't that what concussions made you? She didn't exactly know, and right now, she wasn't sure she cared. She had other worries. Sitting down at her desk, she began to eat French fry after French fry, each liberally coated in ketchup, while ruminating about what she could do to help the posse.

It soon became obvious that her mind had nothing new to offer, other than the idea of putting them out of their misery, something Dougie might consider if she let the current state of affairs go on much longer. Speaking of Dougie, what exactly had he been accusing her of with his cryptic little statement? Had he not heard her cry for help, a cry that defied his belief that she *didn't ask for help*? For being such a genius, he certainly could be obtuse. Besides, every time she'd asked for help in the past, she'd been rejected. A person must either learn the lesson of self-sufficiency or keep getting burned, and if a person gets burned too often, after a while there isn't much left, only ash and bone.

A pad of paper on her desk beckoned and she began to doodle on it as she ate. Pictures of raving lunatics, spirals, skulls, snakes, all made an appearance. She wasn't very good at drawing, not like Charles, but the motion relaxed her mind, and soon her thought processes began to churn. Unfortunately, all the ideas she came up with involved either being outdoors or engaging in physical activity, neither of which she could do. She was tempted to go back on her promise to Vlad and Dr. Steele and do something outside. The posse needed her right now, and doesn't the end justify the means?

She kept trying, but found that time and time again her mind sabotaged the process as it drifted back to dwelling on all her most recent betrayals. Xavier, Dougie, and Derek topped the list today. Her brother had abandoned her in her time of need, Dougie had uncharacteristically chosen to follow the rules over making her happy, and Derek hadn't stood up for her against Vicki.

Stupid boys.

She set down her pen. "'I am done with man,'" she quoted the Creature from Mary Shelley's *Frankenstein*. The Creature was her favorite character in the book; a being of two worlds, he captured how she often felt. Victor Frankenstein's disregard for societal rules had always appealed to her, as well, but he reminded her a bit too much of Dougie, and she didn't like that. Plus, he'd treated the monster like everyone treated her, callously, as though she weren't a real person. She certainly didn't like that.

She fetched the book from a bookshelf and returned to her desk to thumb through it, skimming her favorite parts. The more she read, the calmer she felt, allowing an idea to germinate inside her mind. She knew what she needed to do...put on a play. It was the perfect idea. She would be indoors and hidden away, where the mysterious 'he' couldn't find her, and as a bonus, it would give the posse something to do. They all seemed to enjoy being in the theater, and putting together a play would occupy their time and keep them from thinking too much about all the bad things going on in their lives. And if she was lucky, maybe they could put on the play for the town, make some much-needed money, and send Hank Jackson back to the deep, dank pit from which he'd crawled.

All she had to do was write the play. Well, re-write it. Two years ago she'd translated the book into a play for one of her homeschooling projects, and it had turned out pretty amazing, if she did say so herself. She was sure Vicki hadn't even cracked it open to see what her daughter had done, even though she'd left a copy on her mother's desk, but Pandora hadn't cared about that. Writing the play had been a labor of love. All she had to do now was tweak it a bit.

Her personal copy was still where she'd left it...in the bottom drawer of her desk. She pulled it out, pushed her plate to one side, and began to read. An hour later she set the play down with a grin. Genius. Sheer genius! She'd stuck to the book quite faithfully, but there were elements from *Young Frankenstein* that she hadn't been able to resist adding, like an Igor, who'd never been in the original book. Lucy would make a perfect Igor. Birdy could be Elizabeth, Dr. Frankenstein's love interest (and yes, eerily so, *another* Elizabeth), and Pandora would play Justine, the poor girl who gets murdered. Charles should be able to handle a short stint as Dr. Frankenstein's hapless little brother, Willie Frankenstein. The Creature, well, the choice for that was obvious. Derek, of course. But who could she get to play Victor Frankenstein? Sinclair didn't speak, so he was out. Skippy was gone. Xavier wasn't talking to her. She might have to play the mad scientist herself; she could pull off two roles. She grinned. Perfect.

Feeling energized, she began her editing process, pouring all her slights and anxieties into the task. Hours later, her head began to bob and dip, until eventually it sunk to the desk, unable to hold itself aloft any longer.

Ψ

"Oh, no. Pandora. *No!*"

The sound of rapid footsteps approached, then someone grabbed her shoulders and shook her. Her consciousness worked desperately to pull itself from REM's dark abyss, and slowly she swam to the surface. Her head felt like someone had filled it with wet cement and her neck was stiff and sore.

"Why did you do it? Why?" What the hell was Dr. Steele talking about, and what was he doing in her room? Was she still dreaming? Why did he sound so freaked out? "You promised me, damnit! No, no, no…"

Pandora groaned and tried to pull away. "What is your problem, doc, and could you get off me?"

He pulled back and she saw his face light up. "Pandora? You're still alive."

"Of course I'm still alive. Crikey." She sat up and rubbed the back of her head. Her cheek felt strangely wet and she reached up and felt something slimy. She looked at her hand and saw a thick red substance covering her fingers. She wiped them on her pants. "Oh, crap. I slept on my plate."

Dr. Steele looked down at her desk. "That's…that's ketchup."

"What did you think it was?" She looked around, her neck protesting the movement. "I can't believe I fell asleep on my desk." She spotted her play and quickly began to gather it up. "I was writing," she explained, before shoving the whole mess into a drawer and slamming it shut. "For a home school assignment—where education never ends!"

She laughed, though it came out sounding a bit choked. She was so off her game it was ridiculous.

But Dr. Steele was equally off his, not appearing to notice her discomfiture. "Ketchup." He started to laugh. "Oh, thank God. I thought—"

Pandora's brain finally caught up to speed. "You thought I'd offed myself."

"I did. I, well, I…" He stopped, rubbed a hand over his face. "I would never have forgiven myself."

"Or Xavier. You did pay him to watch me, didn't you?"

"Pay him to watch you? No. I wouldn't do that to you." He paused, sighed. "I am paying him, though. I asked him to be on guard duty to keep an eye out for Baker and anyone else who looked suspicious. He's to be careful, and, of course, not engage if he sees someone lurking around."

Her eyes narrowed. "He told me you paid him to babysit me."

"Why would I do that?" He nodded when he saw her expression. "Okay, I can understand why you'd believe him, but he was yanking your chain. Brothers." He smiled. She didn't smile back. The smile dropped. "What can I say to convince you I'm telling the truth?"

"Pretty much nothing."

"All right, then." He held up his right hand. "I swear on Elizabeth's memory that I did not pay Xavier Carlisle to babysit you." The moment Dr. Steele uttered Elizabeth's name Pandora felt a strange sensation in her chest; basically he'd just admitted that Elizabeth was dead.

"All right, all right! I believe you." And she did believe him. Nobody who looked that serious was ever lying.

He relaxed a little. "I'm glad. I imagine Xavier stretched the truth because he's mad at you. I noticed it at the funeral. Do you have any idea why?"

She shrugged. "Because he's an unfeeling asshole?"

"Try again."

"Listen, doc. While guessing why Xavier has a stick up his butt sounds like a fun game, I need to wash this crap off my face and go get something to eat. I'm starving."

His eyes brightened. "You're hungry. That's a good sign."

"You betcha it is," she said, swinging her bent arm jovially. "I'm showing that I care about personal hygiene and my appetite appears to be returning. I'm not suicidal. Yahooie for me."

He smiled fondly at her, like she was his kid sister or something, and she wanted to kick him. "I've missed dueling with you, Pandora."

She didn't even bother responding to the old, 'make them feel like they're important so they won't want to kill themselves' ploy he was using. Granted, no one had ever tried that tactic on her, but she'd heard it used enough times over the years. Sometimes it was heartfelt; mostly it was not.

"I have a favor to ask of you, doc," she said, taking advantage of his current state of good will.

"Whatever you need."

"You don't even know what I'm asking."

"I'm a bit of a gambler."

She stifled a smile. "All right. I need you to give a note to Charles." Normally she'd put the note in their secret spot in the foyer, but with everyone being out of sorts, she couldn't rely on it being found in time. "And you have to do it when none of the other posse is around."

"I see him for a personal session today at two o'clock."

"Perfect. But when you give him the note, ask him to deliver it to Birdy and tell him it's top secret. He likes to be useful, and this should help him feel a little less anxious about things."

"He's worried?"

"He thinks everyone is going to leave Nepenthe Manor, and he'll be the only one left because his parents are dead and his grandma is useless, and that scares him."

Dr. Steele regarded her thoughtfully. "Ah."

"So you'll do it?"

"I already said I would."

She grinned. "Brave man. Just give me a sec." She pulled out a notebook, and when, after getting a pointed look from her, Dr. Steele backed away to go peer out the window through a crack in the curtains, she hastily jotted down her message.

~B~ Gather the posse and meet me in the foyer at 4:30 on Friday. Don't tell anyone, especially not DD, and that's the person, not your bra size. We need to keep this a secret. Trust me when I say you'll love it, and if you tell people, it can't happen. Ever. ~P~

She tore out the page and folded it in half three times, then sealed it shut with duct tape. "All right, I'm done." She held it out to Dr. Steele, who released the curtain and walked toward her. He took the note, demonstrating notable restraint in not asking about its contents, and tucked it into his jacket pocket. "You won't forget?"

"Well, as you've said before, I am rather geriatric, but I will do my best to remember."

"Thanks, old man."

"Any time. So what are you up to now?"

She fluttered her lashes, the epitome of innocence. "Why, I don't know what you mean."

"I meant, what are your plans for today?"

"Oh. Well, I want to finish my school assignment."

"Doesn't that bother your head?"

"A bit. But I'm almost done. When I'm finished maybe I'll go visit Shadow. She's probably going mad. She needs exercise or she starts chewing on her stall."

"You're going outside?"

Crud. "I forgot about that whole not going outside thing. Aren't the stables okay?"

He paused, thinking it over. "Can you let Vlad know when you go out?"

"I suppose I could," she not very graciously agreed.

"This is only temporary, Pandora," he reminded her, though his expression was dubious.

"But if we don't catch whoever wants to kidnap me, then it's not." Was this what it was like for the posse every day? Knowing they'd always be trapped here? It was a sobering thought.

"I suppose not. But let's not think that way." He went to the door. "I shall deliver your missive. Enjoy your day, Pandora, whatever direction it might take."

With that, and a rather odd look, he was gone.

AFTER WASHING UP and downing a couple aspirin, followed by a bowl of cold cereal and milk—wonder of wonders, Vicki had gone grocery shopping, basically for milk and cereal, but it was sustenance—Pandora spent the morning editing the play and deciding parts for everyone. When she was done, she made the changes on her computer and printed out copies for everyone, plus a few extras. She glanced through her character list and smiled as she read it.

Pandora Belfry	Director
Pandora Belfry	Screen Writer
Pandora Belfry	Victor Frankenstein
Pandora Belfry	Justine Moritz
Sinclair Prim	Assistant Director
Birdy Peacock	Elizabeth Lavenza
Derek Choken	The Creature
Lucy Landry	Igor
Charles Pippen	Willie Frankenstein

There. That should make everyone happy, Pandora thought, feeling quite pleased with the final product. Well, Derek probably wouldn't be too thrilled about being on stage, but he owed her for not standing up to Vicki, so she had no doubt he'd say yes. After lunch she'd track him down and, for principle's sake, 'ask' him to play the Creature. He wouldn't turn her down, though; he was made for the role.

Lunch was in full swing, so she was able to sneak into the kitchen to grab some chow on the go, pilfering two hot dogs, a napkin filled with tater tots, and a carton of milk, while Old Corker, the cook, was distracted with food prep.

Nourishment firmly gripped in her hot little hands, Pandora snuck outside and hid in a little nook next to the kitchen's back door, and where the Corker would go to sneak a smoke and a swig of whiskey. No one was about, and she downed the bland food as quickly as possible to avoid actually tasting anything, before tossing her trash in the outdoor waste bin.

Appetite satisfied for the moment, she sat on a rock that overlooked the ocean and thought about how to track down Derek. It was a misty, wild sort of day, and she was grateful for the darker skies. The sunlight made her head feel like it was splitting. She technically shouldn't be outside right now, but she needed the fresh air. Working on the play had made her eyes go fuzzy and her head throb. She hoped these symptoms would go away soon. She felt like a prisoner in her own head, and ached to be free of its tyrannical hold on her.

Inhaling the fresh, salty scent of the ocean, she squinted into the distance in an effort to relieve the tension behind her temples. All was quiet on the eastern front, no one stirring but the soaring seagulls and the pounding waves. She wasn't quite sure what she was looking for, and for the moment, it wasn't showing itself to her.

She sat there for some time, staring at nothing, and finally, feeling restless, decided to walk around the manor a few times. Her skin had gone itchy all of a sudden, her skull was tight and her senses on overload, and she hoped movement would help to disperse this sensation of being choked by her own body. Constantly feeling like an invalid was starting to piss her off.

When she rounded the corner and approached the front of the house, she saw the main door open to reveal Derek. He closed the door behind him and trotted down the stairs like a Clydesdale. What perfect timing, she mused, like it was meant to be.

"Hey, Frankenstein!" she called out.

He saw her and raised a giant hand in a wave of sorts. She caught up to him on the gravel driveway, joining him as he walked down it. "Just saw my ma," he told her. "She's doing better."

"I'm glad."

"Are you supposed to be out here, you know with that guy on the loose?" She heaved a frustrated sigh, hoping he'd get the point from the aggrieved sound that she didn't need another babysitter. She wondered who had filled him in on the whole Baker episode. Probably that tattletale Xavier, who deserved a good punch in the face. She felt like a prisoner, surrounded by wardens always watching her. She didn't like it. Not one bit.

"I'm with you, aren't I?" she deflected his question. "Besides, Dr. Steele said I could go to the stables." She was supposed to tell Vlad she was going out, but it was too late for that. *Oopsie doodle.* "My horse, Shadow, gets restless when she isn't exercised, so I'm going to take her around the paddock, then brush her down." She was talking too much, but his silence was a bit unnerving. This was why she liked using it as a weapon, and also why she hated it when it was used against her.

He stopped and turned to face her, and she was relieved not to have to walk anymore. He was a hard one to keep up with. "You should go back inside, Pandora. It's not safe for you out here."

She held up her hands, a teasing gesture. "All right, already. I know when I'm not wanted."

He relented. "My pa is expecting me home to help with…some stuff around the house."

"Oh. Right. Well, I won't keep you. I just wanted to ask you something. About the other night. When Vicki found us together."

He stiffened, like an animal knowing the attack was coming, but not quite sure where from. "You want to talk about the Director?"

She frowned. Now Vicki was the Director. Not even her 'ma.' "Yes, the *Director.* How come you didn't stand up for me?"

His eyes shifted away. "What do you mean?"

"You could've at least explained why you were there. That we were just talking. That nothing was happening. That it was all *innocent.*"

"I'm not coming between you and your ma, Pandora," he replied stubbornly.

"Even when she basically made it clear that you and I can't be friends?"

He frowned. "She didn't say that."

"You're a conflict of interest, remember?"

"Oh, that." He kicked a rock. "Well, maybe she's right."

"What?"

"I can't overstep my bounds, don't you see?"

"You're gonna have to help me out here."

His cheeks flushed and he looked away. "Your ma could kick my ma out, and my ma would have no one to help her, and she'd get sicker. Maybe she'd die."

"So you're saying Vicki would kick your mom out because you defied her and stayed my friend?" Pandora wasn't buying it. Vicki liked to see herself as a savior. Kicking Derek's mom out would make her the bad guy.

Derek looked at her again, a quick sidelong glance. "I'm saying it's a risk I can't take."

She stared at him, unable to process what she was hearing. He couldn't possibly be saying what she thought he was saying. "Then we'll have to be friends in secret," she stated firmly, refusing to acknowledge what he meant. "And to make amends for not standing up for me with Herr Diktator, you can help me out." He didn't respond, only stood mute, his hands in fists. "I'm putting on a play in the old theater, and I want you to be in it. Remember when you called yourself Frankenstein? Well, I want you to be *my* Frankenstein. Actually, you'll be the Crea-ture, because Frankenstein is the mad scientist who makes the Creature, but you know what I mean. What do you say? We can hang out, and nobody will know." She held out her hands in a pleading gesture, then quickly withdrew them when she realized what she was doing. Damned if she was going to beg.

Derek's gray eyes, filled with despair and pity, met hers, and she felt an uneasy pull in her gut. "I gotta go help my pa, Pandora. Sorry. Maybe I'll see you around," he mumbled, then rushed off, nearly knocking her down as he brushed by.

"Yeah, well, think about it," she called after him. "I could really use your help," she added in a desperate attempt to change his mind. But he didn't even slow down.

She kicked at a flattened pine cone as she watched him disappear down the driveway, hunched over, hands in his overalls pockets, boots rising and falling like a soldier's. *Another one gone, and another one gone*, she thought grimly. Then she turned and headed toward the stables, her feet dragging. *Another one bites the dust.*

It had never occurred to her that he'd say no, and now she was left without a Creature. But that wasn't what bothered her. What bothered her was that he was the only friend she could have had that didn't violate one of Vicki's rules, and he had passed on helping her out and now Vicki had won. Pandora's isolation was complete.

Well, not completely complete. There was Ronny sneaking down the driveway. When he saw her watching him, he tried to look like everything was perfectly normal, glancing around as though taking in the splendor of nature. But it's hard for someone who looks like a storybook character to blend in. He resembled a creeping crow, more than the merry tourist he was affecting. She had the distinct feeling he was spying on her, and she didn't like it.

When she stepped into the dimly lit building, she thought maybe she'd see Xavier there, but he, along with Carl, were nowhere about. Probably out working in the field, or fixing something in the barn. It was just as well. Either one was likely to set her off with their judgmental bullshit, and she didn't need that right now.

Shadow was in a snit, too, having been neglected for far too long. Pandora attached the lead to the jittery horse and guided her out to the paddock for a run. The naughty girl thrashed her head and nickered loudly, but eventually settled a little once she'd pulled a few laps. After a good long run, Pandora led Shadow back inside and brushed her down. The horse nipped at her several times, but after a bit the spoiled brat seemed to tire of her pout and ate the fresh grass and clover Pandora had picked for her.

"There you are," she heard a voice call out as she was starting to trim Shadow's hooves. She leaned out of the stall.

"Here I am," she acknowledged when she saw it was Dr. Steele. He entered the stables, his eyes taking in everything, and she turned back to her task.

When he reached the gate to Shadow's stall, instead of the lecture she thought he'd deliver about not telling anyone where she'd gone, he held out a handful of apple slices to Pandora. "Would she like these?"

Pandora straightened up, wiping an arm across her sweaty forehead. "I'm not sure she deserves them, but give them to her anyway."

After a few half-hearted nips, Shadow allowed Dr. Steele to feed her the apples, and Pandora was able to finish cutting her hooves and cleaning out the muck in them. That chore complete, she backed out of the stall and closed the gate while Dr. Steele pet the ornery horse and murmured sweet nothings into her pricked ears.

"Your face is pale. You're overdoing," he noted after she returned from putting away the tools. He patted Shadow on the rump, then left to meet Pandora halfway. Shadow nickered at him, but it was a surprisingly fond sound. She'd never made that noise for Pandora, ungrateful wretch.

"Carl is busy, and someone has to tend to Miss Picky." She didn't bother to mention that Xavier was scared of horses (even though the coward deserved to be outed), and so was useless to her. On so many levels, really.

"I could look after her until you're feeling better."

"Might as well just take her," Pandora said sulkily. "She seems to like you."

"She likes the apples I give her."

"Yeah, well, I give her apples and sugar cubes and tons of attention, and she only has abuse for me in return." Her complaining sounded an awful lot like whining and Pandora clamped her mouth shut. She was bordering on becoming maudlin, and it was time to change course. "So you're done with your sessions already?"

"Charles was my last patient for the day. I delivered the note to him, as requested." He gave her a little bow.

She nodded, frowning. "Good. At least one thing went right for me today."

His head tilted sideways, his blue eyes grew concerned. "Something happen, Pandora?"

It was only through sheer determination that she kept herself from bursting into tears. She'd never been so emotional in her life. Really, this stupid concussion was going to be the death of her, one way or another. It's hard to maintain your street cred when you're sobbing all the time. But even so…

"Only Vicki driving off yet another one of my friends."

"Derek?" he guessed.

She peered sideways at him. "How'd you know?"

He tapped his temple. "Professional skill. And she mentioned finding you two together up in your apartment. Alone."

How dare she share that? "I don't really want to talk about it."

"That's all right. I don't really want to listen." She gaped at him, and he laughed. "I'm kidding, Pandora."

"Oh. Good one." She smiled a little, surprised at his daring. It pleased her that he wasn't treating her like she was made of glass.

"Will it make you feel better if I tell you a bit about Elizabeth?"

Would it?! Holy crap, it would. Don't blow it, she warned herself. *Take it slowly.* "It might," she replied casually. "Though I've been having a hard time feeling better about anything lately." She hadn't meant to say that last part, but it had come out anyway.

"Yes, I know how that feels." She was about to correct him—that he *didn't* know how she felt because he wasn't going through what she was going through—when she remembered his past comments about dark times, how they'd taken all the joy from his life. So maybe he did know. He checked his watch. "I have a meeting in a few minutes, but I will tell you this." He leaned forward, as though about to confide the most secret of secrets.

"Go on," she urged. Finally she was going to learn about his precious Elizabeth, who she was perhaps a little jealous of. And she wouldn't even have to wait the month he'd bargained for.

"Elizabeth was my half-sister, and I wasn't allowed to see her for the first nine years of my life. Didn't even know she existed, actually. Like you and Xavier."

She stared at him, then swallowed a lump in her throat. "That's kinda weird."

"It's not the weirdest part."

"It's not?"

He shook his head. "Nope."

"So what is?"

"I'll tell you all about it, in a month."

"But—!" she sputtered. "You can't just leave me hanging like that, doc."

"Another time," he said firmly, checking his watch again. "I have to go now. And to be clear…I really do want to listen, Pandora. Always."

With a little wave, he left her.

17

Everyone Is a Suspect

PANDORA WATCHED DR. Steele's retreating figure with exasperation. Of all the lowdown tricks! How dare he offer her that little nugget, with promises of more to come, only to delay her gratification? She'd been outmaneuvered, and by an adult, of all things. It left a bitter taste in her mouth.

To remove it, she decided to track down some food and think of ways to get him to fess up sooner rather than later. She did not want to have to wait an entire month to learn about his Elizabeth. It was late afternoon, so she snuck a tray of food from the cafeteria before the dinner rush and brought it up to her room. She didn't want to deal with the noise of the dining room, or face all the curious eyes, or the whispering and pointing. She just couldn't.

After eating an early meal, she wandered around the apartment, unable to settle to anything. She couldn't scheme or read—both made her head hurt. Her room was already clean, so she couldn't occupy herself by pretending to clean it. There wasn't anything to do, or that she wanted to do.

She felt caught in a foreign land, where nothing made sense or felt right. Where everything was different, but in a way she couldn't define. Everything around her looked the same, smelled the same, sounded the same, and yet it was not the same. She was trapped in a sort of uncanny valley—a no man's land between being human and yet not, like a robot or a doll. That's how she felt right now, not fully human, merely humanoid. Could others see that in her? Her not rightness? People really don't like it when something looks human, but isn't, and do their best to avoid the offending creature. Pandora didn't want to become even more of an outcast than before, but she didn't know how to change things.

Not liking this feeling at all, she made up her mind to visit the theater. It needed a good cleaning, and doing something productive was better than obsessing or sulking or dwelling, all three of which were her usual methods of getting through a hard time. So she spent the next several hours sweeping and dusting and organizing, basically getting ready for their meeting tomorrow, then headed back to her room around nine o'clock to get some sleep. For some reason, sleeping on her desk the night before hadn't exactly been refreshing.

As she burrowed under the covers, she realized she hadn't seen Dougie all day. She stayed awake for half an hour to see if he would visit, but he didn't come. Either he was busy, or he was avoiding her. She wasn't sure how she felt about the latter. Relief? Annoyance? Curiosity? All three?

She fell asleep pondering this conundrum and awoke around eight. Her stomach hurt, sharp, shooting pains, and she thought she must be hungry. She showered, then dressed all in black. No one would even realize she was wearing mourning clothes, because she always wore black. But maybe the black beret would clue them in. It was a nod to Skippy and his love for hats, and to the professor, who liked it when she wore it. The beret looked good with her short haircut. *Not that I care about looking good*, she thought as she readjusted the angle. *Not at all.* She readjusted it again, then lowered her hands, finally satisfied.

She left the bathroom to seek out breakfast only to be faced with a shocking scene. Vicki. Still in the apartment, not dressed, not even her hair combed, sitting at the table, a cup of coffee at hand, and eating a pastry. Seeing it, Pandora's mouth started to water.

Vicki, perusing the newspaper, looked up. "Want one?" She pushed a plate of pastries toward Pandora.

Pandora approached her mother with caution, snagging a Bismarck and stepping back. For as long as Pandora could remember, Vicki had always gotten up early and headed down to work. Always. Even on weekends. "Thanks. Are you sick?"

Vicki didn't bother looking up, her eyes scanning the want ads. "Never better."

"Oh. Okay."

"You got a letter." She nodded at a square-ish envelope on the table. "Someone I know?"

Pandora shrugged. "Probably one of my many fans." She snatched it up and held it to her chest. It smelled like the pastry she was eating, and she knew immediately who it was from—Mrs. Hathaway, Pandora's pastry supplier and middle-aged confidante. Mrs. H., who Pandora wasn't even supposed to know, confined as she supposedly was to the manor's grounds. Mrs. H., a good woman and an amazing baker.

"Going to read it?"

"Later. I need to eat first."

"Hm. How's your head?"

"Oh. Um, better."

"Dr. Gara warned me that you need to take it really easy for the next couple weeks. I know Dr. Steele and Vlad have talked to you about that, as well as about you staying in the manor with that strange man still on the loose. You're going to do that, right?"

"The sun hurts my eyes," Pandora answered.

"Is that a yes?"

"More or less."

Vicki rolled her eyes, which quickly settled back on the newspaper. "I have a lot going on this next month, so I really need you to do your part."

"And that would be?"

"To stay out of trouble."

"I'm sorry my existence is such a hardship for you, Vicki."

"Me, too. Now go read your letter. I have things to do."

Pandora wanted to say something, anything, to pierce Vicki's indifference, but why bother? It never did her any good; never changed anything. She grabbed another pastry and scurried out the door, anxious to escape the toxicity in the apartment and to read her letter somewhere safe.

Down in the foyer, she slipped into a window nook hidden behind a curtain to read the letter in private. It was a little bright with the sun out, but her head seemed to tolerate the light better today. She tore open the envelope, pulled out the letter with sticky fingers, and began to read.

My dear, dear Pandora,

I heard all about your recent <u>accident</u> and I'm so worried about you, dear! How frightened you must have been! You wouldn't <u>believe</u> the stories I've heard about what happened. That you were pushed off the bridge by a homicidal maniac — after hearing that one I've started locking my doors, I'll have you know. That you jumped off the bridge because you'd been kidnapped by a stranger. Then there was the one about a high-speed car chase that ended with you crashing on the bridge and you flew out the window and into the river. I have no idea what to believe. It's all so <u>confusing</u> and <u>worrisome</u>!

I won't ask you for details, but if you could let me know how you're doing, I'd appreciate it, dear. I do worry so. I sent you a bag of pastries along with this letter—so that's where they'd come from. Damn that Vicki. Pandora had foolishly thought her mother had bought the pastries. Would she ever learn?— *to hopefully lift your spirits a little.* Success. *Please share them with your friends.* Oops.

I know you won't be able to come into the bakery any time soon, but don't you worry your head about that. That <u>lovely</u> boy Derek is helping me with the grease traps and keeping me up-to-date on the goings on at the manor, though he doesn't quite have your storytelling flair. Naturally. *He said he wasn't sure what had happened to you*—and seems strangely uncurious, Pandora realized—*but that doesn't matter. All that matters is that you're okay.*

I <u>miss</u> our little talks, and that's a fact, so I'll be <u>praying</u> to the Lord to heal you and bring you back to me. I never did tell you this, Pandora, but you're like the daughter I never had. You have brought joy into my life, and I have <u>always</u> looked forward to seeing you whenever you could come. I'd come visit you, you know I would, but I have a bad feeling this might cause a problem with your <u>mother</u>. That neglectful hussy, seemed to be the implication behind this particular underline.

I'm sorry, too, to hear about your father's passing. You are in my thoughts and prayers, <u>morning</u> and <u>night</u>. Take care of yourself, my dear. You've had a hard time of it, haven't you, you poor child.

Your loving friend,

Dolores Hathaway

Pandora brushed away an errant tear, then re-read the letter several times before carefully folding it and tucking it into her sporran. It was the nicest thing anyone had ever given her and she vowed to write Mrs. H. and tell her the truth, or at least the story she was telling everyone. At the very least, the little woman could rest easier knowing there wasn't some madman on the loose.

After scanning the foyer for people, Pandora exited the little nook and tiptoed across the floor to the forbidden hall. Once in the clear, she hurried down the corridor to the theater. She spent the next several hours relocating items so that they wouldn't clutter up the stage, making notes as she went about what they might need for the play and what they already had, and doing more cleaning.

The closer it got to 4:30, the more excited she grew for the posse's arrival. This play idea might just work! And if it did, she'd get to do something she'd always wanted to do...be on the stage. Who didn't crave the spotlight? Who didn't want attention in the form of adulation? Well, hermits, maybe, and people with social phobias, but other than that? Most people like to be noticed and acknowledged; it helps you believe you aren't invisible.

About a quarter after four, she headed to the foyer to wait for the posse to arrive. It was just her bad luck that Vlad happened to be doing his rounds at the same time, skipping lithely down the main stairs, a cigarette tucked behind one ear. Luckily he didn't see her until she was halfway across the floor.

"You have been staying out of trouble?" he called.

She froze, then turned to face him. "Vlad! You startled me."

"Is that possible?"

"It's the PTSD from my concussion, I guess."

He snorted. "Likely story." He looked her over. "What are you up to?"

"Who says I'm up to something?"

He patted his flat stomach. "My gut."

She indicated the backpack on her back. "I told some people I'd help them with a project." Strictly true.

"Oh, yes?"

"Oh, yes. I give 'til it hurts, you know." He lifted an eyebrow. "Well, I didn't say who it hurts."

He grinned, which made him look more threatening than ever, a compliment in her book. "You are a wily one, Pandora Belfry."

"As are you, Vlad Volkov, giving updates to my mother behind my back."

He shrugged. "It is my job as security guard to update the Director on everything of interest that is happening here at the manor. So, your mother... She is single?"

At the abrupt turn the conversation had taken, Pandora regarded him with renewed suspicion. "She is now. Professor Robertson was her husband, as I think you already knew."

"Some people would be lonely in her situation."

"She would be lonely if she weren't such a soulless automaton."

"Automaton?" he repeated the obviously unfamiliar word. Or maybe she'd said it wrong. She really needed to start looking up words more often.

She rubbed her brow. She didn't want to talk about Vicki anymore. "She isn't with anyone that I know of, and I would know because she hardly ever leaves this place. And this conversation is kind of gross."

"It is natural to have needs."

"Um, *ewww*. This is my mother you're talking about, and why do you care about her relationship status?"

"With a kidnapper on the loose, I need to assess everyone's vulnerabilities. I need to figure out who wants you gone and why."

He was investigating her kidnapping? How intriguing. "Wait. You don't think my mother was behind this?"

He tapped his head. "In my mind, everyone is a suspect."

"Good to know. I feel the same way. Every day."

His eyes narrowed. "That is a hard way to live life."

"It keeps me alive."

"Alive, but not living."

She pointed at him. "You're suspicious of everyone, too."

He shrugged. "I grew up in Russia. It is what we do."

"I grew up in an insane asylum. It's what *I* do."

"Touché."

"Right. So have you found anything out yet?"

He shook his head. "Nothing promising. But I will not give up."

She regarded him for a moment. "Let me get this straight. First you work for my grandmother to kidnap me, and now you want to find out who *else* wanted to kidnap me?"

He lifted an amused eyebrow. "Ironic, yes?"

"Indeed." The posse would be here any moment and she needed him gone. But her curiosity had been ignited. What was his stake in all this? What did he have to gain?

He tipped her a salute. "I will leave you to your giving now."

"I still don't understand why you care," she called after him.

"My pride has been pricked," came his disappointing answer. "And I like having you around." Now that was better. "Stay safe, Pandora Belfry."

"You, too, Vlad Volkov."

"I like the hat, by the way. It suits you." She touched it as he disappeared up the stairs. Did it really? Moments later the posse crept out from behind a corner, Birdy in the lead.

"We waited until the Ruskie left," Lucy said in far too loud a voice.

"Shhh," Pandora scolded. "We don't have much time before dinner and there's something I want to show you."

"This had better be good," Birdy threatened. "I'm missing *Hogan's Heroes*, and Colonel Hogan is not only really hot, he's very possibly my soul mate."

Pandora refrained from reminding her about Skippy. "Oh, it will be. Now come on."

With grins all around, they followed after her, down the dark hall, to their destiny.

I Want Top Billing

18

"WHAT ARE WE doing *here* again?" Lucy demanded, as Pandora used her key to unlock the door. "Xavier says it's like forbidden bananas, and we have to avoid it because it's poisonous and we could die a horrible, horrible death if we eat it." She pretended to gag as though poisoned.

"That's not what he said at all," Charles argued over the sound of Lucy's gagging.

She stuck out her tongue at him. "It is so! I heard him with my own eardrums."

"Your eardrums have holes in them, like your brain," Birdy growled. "So stick a cork in it, I want to hear what Pandora has to say."

There was a long moment of silence as everyone acknowledged this unorthodox statement. "Could you repeat that?" Pandora asked.

Birdy heaved a sigh. "You heard me just fine. Now let's get this show on the road."

"Funny you should put it like that." Pandora motioned them inside the theater after flicking on the lights. Before joining them, she turned and locked the door behind her this time, not wanting a repeat of the other day's fiasco. Never particularly patient, by the time she was done the posse was already making a beeline for the stage, Lucy skipping, Birdy sashaying, Charles pretending to fly, and Sinclair counting his steps, rushed though they might be.

Pandora hurried after them, motivated by her excitement to show them her plan, and by a concern that someone might break something. Someone named Lucy. When she reached the middle of the stage, she took off her backpack and pulled out the play. "I have something for you." This got their attention, luring them all toward her like dogs to a steak. When they reached her, she handed a copy to each of them.

Birdy frowned as she took one. "What's this crap? You know I don't like to read."

"We're going to put on a play," Pandora announced grandly.

"We're going to play!" Lucy cried, throwing her copy up in the air. Pandora was glad she'd bound the pages together, as the 50-page opus landed on the stage with a thunk. "Hurray!"

"You just made a rhyme," Charles pointed out with an appreciative smile.

"I'm a poet, didn't you know it? I could be a rapper, like Run-DMC. I'd be Run-DMLu-*cy*!"

"That's very clever, Lucy," Pandora acknowledged, because it was, "and you're right. We are going to play. At acting."

Birdy narrowed her eyes, then glanced down at the play. "*Frankenstein?* Are you serious?"

"Turn the page and see what role you're getting. You have a big one, Birdy, because you'll be Dr. Frankenstein's love interest, Elizabeth."

The frown eased a little. "Love interest. Now that I like. So who's my—oh, wait. Really? *You're* Dr. Frankenstein?" Her head fell back and her mouth gaped open in a show of disgust, then she returned her focus to Pandora. "I'm totally, completely into men, thank you very much, so keep your lesbo ideas to yourself."

"I'm not a *lesbo*, Birdy, and way to be accepting of people who are different."

"Oh, I can accept lesbos just fine. But I won't be kissing one, and certainly not you. I don't need another person falling in love with me."

As if… "I told you I'm not a lesbo, Birdy. We just don't have enough people for all the parts. Until we can find someone else I'll have to fill in."

"Fine. But I want top billing."

"What? Oh, all right." Lovely. Birdy was already playing the diva.

"What kind of roll am I going to be, Pankenstein?" Lucy asked sweetly. "Cinnamon? I like cinnamon rolls. Specially the frosting."

"Wrong kind of role, Lucy. You're going to pretend to be Igor, Dr. Frankenstein's assistant. It's an awesome part, and I'll work with you on your lines." Lucy couldn't read, though she pretended she could, making up stories as she went along, which were often filled with lots of fire and things burning. No book was safe. Not even Mrs. Johnson's *Holy Bible*, which the woman was dumb enough to leave unattended in the TV room.

"Igor? Isn't he a boy?"

"A girl can be an Igor. You'll be perfect."

"I will be," she admitted. "So I guess I'll do it. But only if I'm a girl Igor. I'll be Igirl." She grinned impishly, and Pandora had to smile. In some ways, Lucy was really very clever. But out in the real world, she would never be seen that way. *Just another retard*, that's what they'd think of her. But here, safe in Nepenthe Manor, she would be respected. It was her right to be respected, and also because treating her like a regular human being helped keep her from setting things on fire.

"Works for me, Lucy."

Sinclair tugged on her sleeve, then pointed to his name. He didn't look nearly as pleased as she thought he would at the prospect of being assistant director. "I know. Isn't that great?"

He shook his head.

She suppressed a groan. "What's wrong with being assistant director? That's a big responsibility, Sinclair." He made a circular motion with his hand. "You want to do more?" He nodded. "All right. You can do the curtains." He gave her a less than impressed look, followed by a dismissive shrug. He then pointed at her, the gesture quite obvious in its meaning. "No way, bubs. *I'm* the director, so be happy with what you got." He sighed and turned from her, his shoulders drooping pitifully as he began to shuffle away like an old man. Damn, he was a manipulative bastard. "All right, already! You can be…" An idea came to her. "You can be the stage manager." He spun back around, his eyes lit up like a child's at Christmas. She wasn't sure she'd ever seen him look like that. "That means you're in charge of making sure everything runs smoothly behind the scenes. Does that serve?" she asked sarcastically, though she had no idea how he was going to pull it off, being that he basically didn't talk. He nodded vigorously. "Good. That's settled. Everyone has a job."

Charles stepped forward. "What about me, Pandora? You forgot about me."

"No, I didn't." She pointed to the list. "See? You're going to be in the play. You're the boy that the monster kills. Awesome, huh?"

Charles didn't look particularly appeased, and she wondered if maybe she shouldn't have given the part of a character who dies to the boy who was always on the verge of death. Then again, they were all on the verge of death, weren't they? An aneurism can take a person faster than you can snap your fingers.

"I won't have to speak, will I?" he asked, blue eyes wide.

She breathed a sigh of relief; he hadn't noticed her faux pas. Another bullet dodged. "A few words, but they'll be easy."

"Who's going to be in charge of costumes?" Birdy demanded. "And who'll make the sets?"

"I haven't gotten that far. But we can all wield a hammer and paintbrush as well as the next person. Scratch that. I can wield the hammer. You better stick to a paintbrush."

"Very funny," Birdy, the queen of making violent threats using assorted weaponry, had the nerve to reply.

"I like to draw," Charles offered. "And I'm an awfully good sewer.

Dr. Steele said so when we made the new curtains for the foyer."

"We already have a lot of costumes, Charles, but maybe you can do some painting for the sets."

His lower lip plumped out. "A baby could do that, Pandora," he said mulishly, surprising her. He was usually so docile, but lately he'd gotten this bug up his butt about being treated like everyone else, when he wasn't like everyone else, not with his bad heart. "This is like the basketball game all over again," he went on, "where I had to stand on the sidelines and watch everyone else have all the fun."

She sighed. He was right, but she didn't know what else to do for the poor kid. She didn't want to be the person responsible for his death because she asked too much of him. She was his protector, not his assassin.

Sinclair plucked at her sleeve. "Producer," he croaked, then pointed at Charles. Pandora turned to Charles, who was watching her expectantly, eyes mournful as a dog begging for scraps. Sinclair began repeating the word producer, over and over, making it hard for her to think, to maneuver her way out of this. The theme song to *Charles in Charge* started going through her mind, and that didn't help, either.

"Sinclair can help me if I need it," Charles offered when he saw her hesitation, and Sinclair nodded his agreement. "But I think I can do it on my own, Pandora. I've got to be able to do it on my own…just in case."

Crap. This was going downhill fast. Producers are supposed to be rich and commanding, typically handling all the real stuff necessary to fund a play or movie. She didn't need to point out that Charles didn't exactly fit the producer bill. The boy thought he could fly, for pity's sake, and had also borrowed a fair amount of money from her over the years to buy Superman comics, so he was dead broke. But the perfect excuse that he would accept for why he shouldn't be the producer wasn't coming to her. Besides, using the phrase, *just in case*, meant he was scared about his future, and a scared Charles was a Charles in danger. What she wouldn't do for a Coke right about now.

She took in his wide blue eyes, his hopeful expression. *Crap squared.*

"All right. You can be the producer, Charles, and I'll change the list to include the new roles, giving you top billing, Birdy, since you have so many lines." Birdy preened. "You know this means you're going to be in charge of a lot of stuff, Charles. It can be overwhelming."

"Not if I have one of those." He pointed to her clipboard, the gleam in his eyes covetous.

"Maybe," she hedged, even though she knew it would take a hell of a lot more than a clipboard to do the job. Plus, she liked her clipboard. "All right," she gave in. "There's an extra one in Vicki's office. You can have this one." She removed her list from the clip, leaving behind the pen and stack of notepaper for him to take notes, then held out the board to him.

He took it eagerly, his whole face aglow. "Thanks, Pandora! You won't regret this. I'm really good at this sort of stuff."

"Promise me that if you get stuck you ask me or Sinclair for help. This is a team effort, big guy."

He puffed out his chest. "You can count on me."

She wasn't sure what she could count on him for. To ask for help? To get the job done? To buckle under the pressure and leave her to clean up the mess? If she were a betting woman, she'd pick option number three. Since she was already playing two roles and directing and probably running the lights and sound, too, she needed him to do his job without her always helping him.

But really, when she thought about it, what exactly does a producer do? Their biggest job was to find money, and this play obviously didn't need any funding. What harm could he do? Besides, he had gotten a fair amount of money out of her over the years, and just recently her clipboard. Charles could be Sinclair's mouthpiece, too, telling other people what to do. He'd like that, plus he was quite good at knowing what Sinclair was saying without Sinclair actually having to say it. She nodded. This might just work.

"You guys will have to leave now to go eat," Pandora told them after glancing at her watch. "But I'll put your copies of the play in our drop-off nook in the foyer, and you can pick them up there. Just make sure no one sees you doing it. There are spies everywhere." Everyone nodded their agreement, except Lucy who had wandered away.

In fact, nobody seemed particularly eager to leave. Birdy was perusing the play, searching for all her lines, which were plenty, and speaking them out loud. Lucy was trying on costumes, and Charles went to join her, picking up all the discarded ones. Sinclair was running an eye over the entire stage and nodding thoughtfully.

"Do you want a clipboard, too?" she asked him. He shook his head, then tapped his temple. "You're sure you don't want to write things down? There's lots to remember." He shook his head again. "Okay. If you change your mind, let me know."

She rather liked having a clipboard, actually; it made her feel powerful, and she suspected Charles wanted one for that very same reason. Sinclair, however, seemed quite confident he could keep it all in his head. Pandora hoped he was right.

She gave them fifteen minutes to do their thing, then called them over. "We'll meet again tomorrow, in the morning, around nine. It's not Visitor's Day this weekend, so we should all be free. Just come to the lobby. Oh, and I'll take your plays." She already had Lucy's, from where she'd discarded it earlier. Sinclair gave her his copy, then Charles, who shook his clipboard at her with glee. "Maybe leave that here, all right?" He frowned. "I agree. But you know what the Hessian can be like. She'll take it from you and sell it on the black market." Knowing the Hessian's dark ways quite well, he reluctantly set it down on the stage.

When it was Birdy's turn, she slapped her copy down on the pile in Pandora's hands. "Find me a legit Dr. Frankenstein and I'm in."

Pandora stared dully at Birdy's retreating back. She was asking the impossible. They were already short on people to fill roles. Derek hadn't committed to being the Creature, and Xavier was being a jerk to her and would say no if she asked. But maybe she'd have to swallow her pride—which she knew without a doubt would taste unbearably bitter—and ask him if he'd join them.

The very idea made her want to gag. But show business is a demanding mistress, and the show must go on, mustn't it? Too bad she couldn't sacrifice a goat and be done with it. But noooo. Once again she had to sacrifice herself.

And would anyone care?

Not in this world.

19

Taking a Psycho Break

BEFORE HEADING UPSTAIRS, Pandora dropped off the plays in their hiding spot, then went to snag a clipboard from the empty office. If Bennington had come to work today, she'd left early. And if Vicki had interrupted her donut eating and want ads perusing long enough to go to work, she was no longer at it. The office was locked, something Pandora quickly remedied with her key, and it was dark, so it was good she always kept a flashlight in her sporran.

As Pandora locked the door behind her on her way out, she realized Vicki wasn't kidding when she'd warned her daughter to be careful what she wished for, because if she wasn't working there was a good chance she was in the apartment. Pandora had often complained to Vicki that she was never around, and now here she was, which was the last thing Pandora wanted tonight. She was feeling pleased about the play, and still riding that high. She didn't need Vicki ruining her good vibes right now.

Lots of drug references going on there, Pandora, she noted to herself. But it was probably because she actually felt kind of good. Not so depressed and overwhelmed, anyway, and she didn't want that feeling to end.

So where could she go, if not to the apartment? She wasn't supposed to go outside, and the secret room seemed awfully isolated at the moment. Plus, she was starving. She'd actually forgotten to eat lunch, and was basically running on donut fumes.

There was no help for it. She'd have to eat in the cafeteria. She slid the clipboard into her backpack, and tucked the bag behind a curtain to be picked up tomorrow. She was halfway across the lobby floor when the door that led to the second floor opened and out stepped the Hessian. A smile crossed Pandora's face when she spotted her nemesis. Time for a little payback.

"Hello, Hessian," she greeted, and the big lug of a girl froze. She hadn't seen Pandora yet, and the look of uneasiness on her face was rather comical. When her close-set eyes landed on Pandora, her expression soured into a frown. "I heard you ratting me out to my grandmother the other day. Is that your new job? Being a rat?"

"I ain't got nothing to say to you, Miss Smartypants."

"Oh, really? So you deny telling my grandmother where I was?"

"She asked, I told. Ain't worth my job to not do as I'm told."

"She gave you money for it."

"The cheapskate gave me a dollar."

"You sold your soul for a dollar?"

"I didn't sell nothing," the Hessian said slowly. "I see where you got your bad ways from. Your gran's a real piece of work, ain't she?"

"Then you should've known better than to get involved with her."

The Hessian waved a thick finger in Pandora's face. "Now you listen here! I got eight little brothers and sisters at home, and I can't lose this job. So leave me alone. I was hoping to eat something, then head up to my room and get some sleep, but instead I gotta go cook supper for the lot of them. My dad took off again, and my mom's got a late shift tonight." Because the Hessian lived at Nepenthe Manor, she would have to walk home and walk back. It was getting late, so she'd be out after dark. Pandora felt a slight twinge of something resembling sympathy, but ignored it. A person can't survive on being sympathetic. She hardened herself. This had to be taken care of, and now.

"There are eight more of you?" she sneered. "That's quite a collection of trolls your parents produced."

The already low brow lowered even more. "Who you calling a troll?"

"Um, you and your siblings? I wasn't trying to be subtle."

"We ain't trolls. You're a troll, Pandora, with your ugly mug and your ugly personality. I know I ain't perfect, but I got my reasons. Good ones, too. What've you got? All this." She waved her arm around the lobby. "And you ain't got no idea, do you? You're more spoiled than a coon's carcass left out in the sun too long, and I feel bad for the Director having to be your mom."

"You have no idea what my mother is like behind closed doors, Hessian. No idea. So don't go turning her into some kind of hero."

"At least she doesn't judge me by how I look."

"That's what you think. Now here's the deal," Pandora hissed, tiring of this stupid conversation, which was making her feel strangely uncomfortable. "Stop spying on me. Don't talk to my grandmother. Don't rat me out. It's that simple."

"And I told you, Belfry. I have to do as I'm told. It's how I keep my job. Now go bully someone else for a change. I've got a long night ahead of me."

Having said her piece, the Hessian pushed past Pandora and trudged out the door, her square shoulders set. Pandora watched her go, still a bit uneasy about the whole scenario. But why should she feel sorry for the Hessian? The girl had done her wrong, and she was going to pay

for it. Otherwise she'd keep doing it—cause *she* was the real bully—
and Pandora would be the one paying the price for not standing up to
her.

Determined not to show weakness, Pandora marched into the cafeteria, head held high. She soon spotted Dougie and Dr. Steele at the staff
table, then the posse, talking and laughing at theirs. Sinclair was silent,
of course, as he watched her walk by, his expression intense. Her nose
wrinkled in annoyance. What was with him, staring at her like that all
the time? It was starting to feel like he was assessing his prey.

She picked up her tray and went down the line, getting a piece of pie
from Gladys, who didn't say a word or meet Pandora's eye as she
slipped it onto her tray. When Dr. Steele had first arrived, the cafeteria
worker had transferred her affections to him, giving him Pandora's pie,
but it appeared that when people thought you'd tried to kill yourself,
they treated you nicer. It seemed a messed up way to get attention.
Definitely not a healthy strategy, but Pandora wasn't going to turn
down Gladys's apple pie. It was like a little slice of heaven.

The other inmates in the dining room watched her as she walked past
them, trying mightily to look like they were not watching her, and failing. But nobody said anything mean or threw anything at her, and she
was pathetically grateful for their restraint. They could be a mercurial
bunch, these inmates; one never knew which way they'd jump (ha). But
it seemed this time, they had decided to leave her be. Even Bones, who
was sitting by herself—big surprise—only gave her a knowing smirk as
Pandora passed by.

On her way out, she didn't need to look at Dougie and Dr. Steele to
know both of them were watching her. She picked up her pace, and
felt relieved when she was out the door. Even though everyone was
behaving nicely, she didn't want to stay, for several reasons, one being
that the mood could change very quickly. She decided she'd go back to
the theater and eat there. That should be a safe place.

When neither Dr. Steele nor Dougie had called to her, she at first felt
gratitude, followed by annoyance. What were they up to, getting all
cozy with each other like that? She hoped Dr. Steele wasn't sharing
anything with Dougie. Just because he was staff now didn't mean he
was privy to information about her. He was only an intern, after all.
There must be different rules for them. Though she had a feeling it
wouldn't matter if there were. She made a mental note to follow up on
this with Dr. Steele.

Back in the theater, she sat out in the audience on a cushy, red seat
and ate her supper at a leisurely pace, enjoying the apple pie immensely.

When she was finished eating, she decided to go through the costumes to see if any would work for the play. She found several pieces, but nothing that would fit a giant. Derek would have to wear his own clothes, and if he had some that were a bit too small on him that would be awesome. Birdy would certainly like that, and Pandora had to admit, in one hidden corner of her mind, that she might like that, too.

By the time she returned to the apartment, her head was throbbing. Vicki was nowhere to be seen, but her bedroom door was shut, meaning she was inside. How strange a scenario this was. Vicki home. It was unheard of. Perhaps she'd been inhabited by an alien. It seemed a more logical explanation than anything else.

After taking some aspirin, Pandora fell into bed and slept the sleep of the dead.

Ψ

The next morning, she awoke feeling enlivened. Apparently the posse weren't the only ones who needed a project. Vicki's door was still shut when Pandora crept out of the apartment, meaning Vicki was actually sleeping in. The theory that an alien had taken over her body was sounding more and more plausible. Luckily it was a Saturday, so it wasn't like she'd get in trouble for not going to work.

In the lobby, Pandora met up with the posse, all of whom looked as excited as she felt. Even Sinclair. This was the magic of the theater doing its work. They had to wait a few minutes, pretending a nonchalance none of them felt, as a nurse escorted one of the new patients—Gloria, the schizophrenic—from the cafeteria to the TV room. Gloria was mumbling to herself, but she was aware enough to notice Pandora, giving her a long look from beneath lowered lashes. When the interlopers were gone, Pandora fetched her backpack, then she and the posse booked it to the theater passage, breathless with the thrill of nearly getting caught.

As soon as they arrived, they got to work. Birdy practiced her lines, Pandora and Sinclair mapped out the sets, and Charles proved quite adept at turning their ideas into images. She always knew he could draw—he loved copying the superheroes from his comic books—but she hadn't realized how well he could draw free-hand. She envied him his skill.

"You're very good, Charles," she told him at one point, and he grinned happily.

Lucy stayed busy figuring out her costume as Igirl, and they were all reluctant to leave for lunch. When they returned, furtively and happily, they set to work once more, Sinclair making mental notes on what they'd need to build the sets versus what they already had. Charles re-did his set sketches to accommodate changes, and Pandora ran through Lucy's lines with her. A natural ham, the girl took to the role like a duck to water. When she got tired of memorizing, Pandora dismissed her to go help Charles while she herself went and assessed what they had for materials in the workshop.

Everything was going so well, until it wasn't.

"So this is where the little miceys come to play," a familiar voice stated snidely.

Pandora swung around. There, standing in the doorway of the shop, was Bones, the proverbial cat. "What are you doing here?"

"I might ask the same. You're not supposed to be in here, you know."

"I'm not a prisoner. I can do what I want."

"Really?"

Pandora groaned inwardly. She didn't have time for this. "All right. Maybe not. So what do you want from me, Bones? Money? I don't have any. Favors? You already know the staff doesn't like me here. Pills? Nurse Rackett would murder me if she caught me, but only after she tortured me to find out who they were for, and I'd give you up in a heartbeat."

"I don't want any of that. I was bored. Figured I'd see what you losers were up to."

Pandora regarded her warily. "Then you're not going to tell on us?"

"Do I look like a tattletale to you?"

"Not really," Pandora decided to be honest.

Bones looked slightly surprised, as if expecting to be thought the worst of. "Yeah, well, I'm not a tattletale. Not my thing."

"Then what do you want? Come to finish our fight?"

"I just want to hang out here. Better aura than that cesspool." She threw a nail-bitten thumb over her shoulder. "And I'm less likely to cause you trouble if I'm not out there."

Pandora sighed. "Fine, stay." She didn't want Bones here at all, but it was better than her sabotaging them. "But you've got to keep your snide remarks to yourself. We're working here."

Bones hooked her thumbs through two belt loops. "What're you working on?"

"A play," Pandora replied defensively.

Bones clasped her hands together, and if you can flutter your eye-lashes sarcastically, she did it. "Like *Romeo and Juliet*?"

"Like *Frankenstein*."

Bones actually looked interested. "Not bad. Getting that giant to play

Frankenstein?"

"The character is actually known as the Creature. The scientist is Victor Frankenstein, and while I refer to him as Dr. Frankenstein because it sounds good, he's not really a doctor. Both are common misconceptions."

Bones rolled her eyes. "Whatever you say, *Professor.*" Pandora wondered if that was a pointed remark in reference to her father, or a lucky shot. "So are you getting him or not?"

"I'm working on it."

"What about the other one?"

Pandora frowned. "Which one?"

"The one with the earring."

"Xavier? You saw how mad he was at me. So no."

"We all saw it, and we were all shocked. So who's gonna be Dr. Frankenstein?"

"I don't know. Right now it's me. Charles is Willie Frankenstein, Lucy is Igor, and Birdy is Elizabeth, his fiancée."

One eyebrow shot up. "So you and the bird girl are lesbos?"

Pandora sighed. "We're not lesbos. We just don't have enough people. People that we can trust anyway."

"Hm. Well, I ain't doing it."

"I didn't ask you to."

"Pandora!" Lucy called. "Why you talking to yourself? Are you taking a psycho break?"

"It's calling having a psychotic break," Pandora muttered under her breath, "and I'm on the verge of one." She pushed the curtain aside and stepped onto the stage.

Bones followed after her. "Did you miss me?" she announced, her skinny arms spread wide.

Seeing her, the posse froze, except Birdy, who pointed her play at Bones, like it was a hatchet. "How'd you get in here?"

Pandora turned to Bones. "Yeah, how did you get in here?"

She held up a lock pick. "I let myself in."

"That's what Xavier can do!" Lucy cried. "All I can pick is my nose. And my underwear. It's always riding up my crack."

Bones gave an amused snort, and if Pandora wasn't mistaken, she'd say it was a genuine laugh she'd heard. "He a thief?"

"I don't know," Pandora replied. "I don't think so. I don't know all that much about him really. He's my half-brother."

"You don't say." Pandora didn't like the look on Bones's face. It spelled trouble.

"Stay here," Pandora ordered, then motioned to the posse to join her as she crossed to the other side of the stage. When they gathered around her, she said her piece, "Bones promised she wouldn't rat us out, so I told her she could stay."

"No way," Birdy declared vehemently. "If she stays, I go!"

"Then she'll tell on us, Birdy, and there won't be a play."

"You said she promised she wouldn't rat us out."

"Does she look like someone who'd let a little thing like a promise keep her from exacting revenge?"

Birdy looked over at Bones, who was watching them with her ever-present smirk. "No."

"Then we're stuck with her. Maybe I can put her to work, sweeping or something."

"I don't like it, Pandora."

"Me, either," Lucy agreed. "Bones is one mean mother-fu—"

"Lucy!" Charles gasped, his face turning blue. "That's a really bad swear!"

"I was only going to say mother-fudger."

"You were not," Birdy scolded.

"Was too," Lucy argued, then gave Birdy a raspberry.

"Gross, Lucy!" Birdy raised a fist.

Lucy made a face and waggled her fingers. "Can't touch me, can't touch me!"

"Listen, guys." Pandora stepped between them before a brawl broke out. "I can't kick Bones out or she'll tell. So just ignore her, and she'll get bored and stop coming. All right?" They nodded reluctantly, though Birdy still looked thunderous. Pandora turned back to Bones. "All right. You can stay."

Bones didn't even bother to look up from contemplating her bitten nails. "Like I needed your permission."

It took all Pandora's strength not to punch the little she-devil right off the stage.

20

THE LITTLE SHE-DEVIL, however, remained surprisingly quiet as they went about their work. After sitting in the front row for several minutes, her torn, off-brand sneakers propped on stage, Bones got bored and began to wander around the theater. They all kept a side eye on her, but she didn't do much of interest—trailed her fingers along a few stage props, glanced up at the lights, then suddenly turned and sprinted up the stairs to the light and sound booth, as if that were her destination all along.

Half an hour later, the stage lights began to turn on and off. Lucy soon found Pandora in the workshop and tattled on Bones. "Tell her to stop, or I'm gonna have a little Caesar!"

"A seizure, and no you're not."

"Am so."

Lucy looked on the verge of losing it, and at that moment actually kind of resembled a little Caesar having a seizure, so Pandora put down her hammer and headed toward the middle of the stage. As soon as she stopped and faced the booth, a Fresnel lamp popped on over her head, literally placing her in the spotlight.

"Having fun?" she called up to the booth, her hand shading her eyes. The light felt like it was burning her eyeballs.

For an answer, the spotlight went out, then three other lights flashed on and off around her in a sort of Morse code pattern.

"Don't break anything up there," Pandora tried again, squinting. "Cause I'll be the one paying for it." Too late she realized her words could be seen as more of an incentive than a threat.

The stage went dark. Lucy screamed and Charles whimpered. Birdy swore and Sinclair tapped his foot, loud and fast as a woodpecker. Just as quickly, the lights flashed back on, and an array of colors shone overhead.

Bones had somehow figured out which switches represented which lights, and a genius idea occurred to Pandora. "Say, you want to do light and sound for our play?" She was inviting the devil into her home, but what else could she do? She needed someone to do the job, or it would fall on her shoulders, and she had enough to do as it was. Plus it might keep Bones out of trouble.

The lights went out, then back on. Twice. Then a disembodied voice echoed through the room. "Yes."

Lucy laughed and clapped her hands. "Do the flickering again!" she ordered, then began to do *The Bus Stop*, a crazy disco move J.T. had taught them. Bones complied and Lucy really broke it down, gyrating all over the stage. Birdy looked mildly amused, Charles thrilled, and Sinclair appalled. Pandora wondered briefly what her own expression might show, then figured it was probably a cross between stupefaction and amazement. That girl could out disco John Travolta.

After several minutes, Lucy fell to the floor and lay on her back, panting loudly. "I'm pooped!"

"Good, because it's time to go eat."

Lucy sat up. "I don't want to!"

"We have to eat to keep up our strength."

"True." She started smacking her lips. "I am hungry."

"You guys go on ahead. I'll lock up."

Birdy shrugged and slid her play down the front of her shirt. Charles's eyes widened in amazement, and maybe just a little bit of curiosity. The boy might have a dicky heart, but apparently not a dicky dick. Pandora nodded in appreciation of her own wit.

Charles tore his eyes away, but only after Birdy finished situating the play. "Can I bring my drawings with me?"

"Yeah, all right. Just don't let on it's for the play."

"I don't need my play," Lucy said, tossing aside her copy. "It's all up here." She tapped her temple.

Bones had come down to join them. "I'll take it."

Lucy narrowed her eyes. "All right. But only because you lighted up my life."

Bones smirked. "You're a funny kid."

Lucy jumped to her feet and brandished a fist. "I'm not a kid!"

"Easy, cowboy." Bones held up her hands. "You're a funny little shit. Is that better?"

Lucy cocked her head to one side, considering. "Yes."

Bones shook her head, then rolled up the play and stuck it into the back pocket of her jeans. "Later, losers," she said with a salute, then stalked off.

"I don't trust her," Birdy declared.

"Yeah, well, join the club. I don't think she'll tell on us, though."

"Why not?" Charles asked.

"Because she likes being here, and if she tells, she'll ruin that."

"You'd better be right," Birdy threatened. "If I ever want to leave this place, I can't afford to get any black marks on my record." Pandora lifted an eyebrow. "Well, any more black marks."

Poor, delusional Birdy. To the average person, she looked reasonably normal, and she could pass for normal, too. But only for a while, and only in a world where everything went smoothly. But when problems happened, and they would, nobody in the real world was going to watch over her, make sure she took her medication (which she didn't like to take because she claimed it made her boring), or protect others from her explosive temper. Even on meds, the girl was a force of nature. But without them, Pandora had seen what that looked like and it wasn't pretty. Of course, that had been a long time ago. Years. But still…the beast inside never died, did it? Pandora knew it was still there, lurking, and if Birdy was ever loosed upon the world without proper supervision, well, woe be to those who crossed her the moment she stopped taking her medication.

It wasn't fair. It wasn't right. But it was a reality.

Nonetheless, Pandora kept her mouth shut. Today she didn't have the energy to serve as the ill-fated messenger. "I hope I'm right, too," was all she said. "Now make sure you check around before you leave the theater, and especially before you leave the hall and go into the lobby. Sinclair, can you lead the way?" His nod was as serious as a heart attack.

The posse seemed content to follow him out, and she watched them go before turning to her task. She had decided to make sure everything was in order before leaving the theater—no messes, no damage, no obvious signs they'd been here—and so she spent the next half hour or so giving the whole place a thorough going over. Everything looked good, and she left the theater feeling like maybe things were looking up. Her head hadn't ached too badly today, even with the light show Bones had put on, although a faint throbbing had started up in her temples. Even so, she was getting better, she felt sure of it.

After locking the door, she went to fetch her dinner, nearly running over the last of the new patients, whose name she'd discovered was Tobias, and who was strangely by himself. "Sorry," she said quickly, grabbing his arm to keep him from falling. He was rather tottery, his bloated belly under a royal blue robe throwing him off balance, though he carried himself with dignity.

"No need to apologize," he replied graciously, his voice rich and deep. "I might be a king, but I know how to be fair."

"I can see that, your Highness," Pandora quickly improvised. She always went along with a patient's delusions. It seemed cruel not to, and besides, in the past whenever she'd tried to challenge their seemingly irrational beliefs it left them befuddled and out of sorts. So she stopped doing it. They were happier in their world anyway. Vicki, on the other hand, still tried to convince them of the error of their ways and it always went wrong, which showed how entrenched her beliefs about mental illness were—even when she caused damage she refused to give up on her skewed worldview.

"What is your name, child?" Tobias enquired politely, clasping his hands behind his back.

"Pandora."

"Are you one of my subjects, Mistress Pandora?"

"I'm actually your chief advisor. But you likely have so many people to do your bidding, it can be hard to keep track of us all."

"Ah, yes. You're very likely correct in your surmise. So what do you advise me on?"

"Foreign policy, proper etiquette, and what to do with prisoners."

"Oh, prisoners!" He looked both troubled and a little excited. "And what shall I do with them, pray tell?"

"Throw them in the oubliette without delay," she advised. "But only if you're absolutely positive they're guilty."

"I see, I see." He nodded and rubbed his patchy white beard. "You are very wise. I shall consider your advice. Yes, I shall."

She swept him a bow. "I will leave you to your duties, King Tobias."

"Very good, very good." He left her to continue roaming the halls, his slippers making a scuffing noise as he shuffled away, and when the nurse came hurrying out of a nearby passage, Pandora simply pointed in the direction he'd gone.

Once in the cafeteria, she was glad to see that most everyone had already come and left, and she carried her tray up to the apartment with the feeling that she'd gotten away with something. She had spotted Vicki's light in her office, so she knew she'd be able to eat in her room without having to interact with her. But as Pandora passed by their kitchen table, her relief turned to anxiety. The top was covered almost entirely with notes, resumes, and newspapers opened to the want ads. Vicki was really doing it. She was looking for a new job.

And just like that, Pandora's mood soured and her appetite withered away. As much as this place could feel like a prison, as much as the inmates drove her up a wall, as much as she wanted to get away, the idea of leaving horrified her. It occurred to her that the inmates weren't the only ones who might not be able to cope with the 'real' world. Maybe she couldn't, either. Not that she wanted to. Much.

Maybe a little. It would be cool to see some of the places she'd read about, do some of the things she'd seen on TV. It would be nice to make her own money and have her own place, too. How freeing it would be to be in charge of her life and not have to answer to anyone or to carry the responsibility of so many people on her shoulders.

But even if she and Vicki moved out, she wouldn't get that. Vicki wasn't exactly a "let's go do something fun!" kind of gal, and Pandora wouldn't be able to do much with her life without a college degree or an invention that made her a lot of money. She was only fourteen, after all, and homeschooled herself. She couldn't even drive. Her options were severely limited. So if push came to shove, she'd rather stay here in this maddening place than try her luck out in the real world. At least here she knew the devil quite intimately. Out there, she could only guess who he, or she, was.

And what would happen to the posse if she left them? Dr. Steele would push them out of the nest, and they wouldn't be ready to fly, and they'd plummet to the earth and smash their soft skulls and break their fragile little necks. And then what? Who won that game?

No one.

But what could she do? Much as it pained her to admit, Vicki was her mother, and what she said was law. Pandora had no rights, no input, no power. It was galling. So even if she wanted to stay, Vicki wouldn't let her.

Pandora sighed and picked at her food, sculpting the meat and potatoes into a monster, an excellent likeness that reminded her of the Creature. Poor, pitiful thing. He could never fit in anywhere. Just like her. She was a poor, pitiful thing, too. A familiar sharp pain grabbed at her stomach and tears pricked her eyes. Once again, she felt an urge to let herself go, to embrace a helpless spiral into the darkness.

But then a succession of images flickered through her mind—of Lucy dancing onstage and Birdy concentrating on her lines, of Charles's glow as he worked on his drawings, and even Sinclair seemed lighter and less watchful. She couldn't let them down, and could only hope—that pernicious enemy of all logical persons—that Vicki didn't find a job before they'd finished their work on the play.

But then what? It's not like they'd be able to perform for anyone—Vicki wouldn't let them—which would be both disappointing and a shame. Because the play was good, if she did say so herself, and the inmates would benefit from a night of entertainment, of doing something different from their same old humdrum routine, and if they were able to sell tickets to the townspeople, they might make a little money at it, too. But, like Birdy, she was dreaming if she thought any of that could happen. As far as Vicki was concerned, the theater was a death trap. How she got that idea, Pandora wasn't sure, but if she knew her mother, she knew the woman wouldn't budge on this. Plus, letting them do the play would be yet another burden to deal with, and Vicki wouldn't want that.

So Pandora was right back at square one. Well, mostly. They could still do the play for the fun of it, for the process rather than simply the end game. Xavier had once scolded her for being too outcome-oriented. She supposed he meant that she rushed toward the goal and missed the fun along the way. But what did he know? He was just a stupid boy who blamed her for making his life a little harder. Well, boo hoo. Excuse her for wanting to have an end product, for wanting to find that treasure at the end of the hunt. Why not? Yes, maybe she could enjoy the ride along the way a little more, but still, she wanted to actually put on the play for other people. What was the harm in that?

As she got ready for bed, Pandora tried to concoct a scheme for how she might make it happen, but she was in a rush, expecting Vicki to walk through the front door at any minute, and she couldn't think. It was probably a wee bit irrational, but she had this feeling that if she could avoid Vicki, she could avoid having to move. She couldn't even tell Pandora they were moving. It was kind of like the magical thinking everyone does when they imagine all the bad things that could happen to them, believing that if they imagine it, it won't happen. This coping mechanism doesn't actually work, of course, other than to alert you to be on the lookout, but it certainly helped a person function. Otherwise nobody would get out of bed in the morning.

Finished with her ablutions, Pandora climbed into her bunk and settled onto her back. She realized as she pulled the covers up to her chin that she hadn't spoken to Dougie for a while. What was he up to now, with this giving her the cold shoulder approach? Because of course he was up to something. It likely had to do with her reminding him that she'd never asked him to do anything for her. Because the best explanation—that his feelings were hurt—didn't fit Dougie. She wasn't even sure he experienced real feelings beyond those related to revenge and his, *gag*, urges. Whatever was going on with him, he wasn't happy with her and was making it quite clear by avoiding her.

Once she saw him again, she'd be sure to say, *Real mature, Dougers*. But then she'd be guilty of hypocrisy, wouldn't she? Because in a round-about way, that's what she was doing with Vicki, and perhaps had done all her life.

Not that she'd ever admit that to him…or anyone.

21

Gravitas of the Moment

SUNDAY STARTED OFF as a great day. Pandora and the posse got a couple hours of work in before lunch, then met up again afterward. Once inside the theater, everyone went their separate ways, and Bones headed back up to the control booth, Lucy's copy of the play in hand, to continue working out the lighting and sound effects.

After an hour or so of working, Pandora, not hearing Lucy for some time, decided she had better go check on the girl. She found her sitting in the audience staring up at Birdy. Apparently she'd gotten bored of watching Charles draw and had moved on to listening to Birdy read her lines.

Pandora sat down next to her. "How's she doing?"

Lucy shrugged. "She's not as good as me."

"No one could be that good."

Lucy threw her pudgy hands in the air and wiggled them back and forth. "You know it."

"Oh, Victor!" Birdy emoted. "Of course you want to marry me, and you shall soon have your wish. Our love is like a fire that burns within us both. But you're always so busy with your scientist duties, when you should be getting busy with me, and that troubles me, my love. I don't want anything to come between us. Not even my Calvin Kleins."

"That sounds like one of Birdy's Harlem Romance books," Lucy whispered loudly. Birdy didn't entirely hate reading, and often read out loud to Lucy from cheap romance novels, which might explain a few things about Lucy's recent interest in all things carnal.

"It's *Harlequin* Romance," Pandora corrected her, while shooting Birdy a dirty look.

"That's what I said."

"Whatever, and no it doesn't." That wasn't entirely true. The lines did sound like they came from a tawdry romance novel, but that was a necessary evil. Elizabeth wasn't the most interesting of creatures, and Pandora had known that she'd have to jazz up the role or Birdy wouldn't do it. But still…there was no need for making things up. "Birdy, stop adlibbing. You're taking away from the gravitas of the moment. It's not *getting* busy, and they didn't have Calvin Kleins back then."

"I'm trying to spice things up a bit."

"Well, at least make it fit with the time period, and be sure you run any changes by me. We don't want people laughing when they should be crying."

A thoughtful look crossed Birdy's face, as though she were contemplating which would be better. "Well, we certainly don't want them falling asleep."

Pandora couldn't argue with that. "I agree. But you have to keep in mind the message of the play. People like to laugh. But they remember you when you make them cry."

"I like that," Lucy declared. "Making people cry so they remember me."

"It only works when you do it with dramatic words," Pandora hastened to amend, probably uselessly. "Not with fists or mean words or *fire*."

Lucy gave her a big wink. "Whatever you say, boss." Pandora sighed and shook her head.

"What does it matter, anyway?" Birdy complained. "It's not like anyone's going to watch us."

Pandora couldn't let that slide. "Maybe I can convince Vicki to let us put on a show for the inmates. Maybe even for the whole town."

Birdy's eyes lit up. "Really?"

Before Pandora could respond, *sure, when hell freezes over*, a loud noise rolled through the theater, followed by lights flashing on and off.

"Woo-hoo!" Lucy shouted and clapped her hands. "It's storming inside!"

Bones was obviously trying out a few tricks. A number of sound effects had already been programmed into the board, so it was a simple matter of pressing a button to make it thunder, followed by some knob sliding for the brilliant flashes of lightning. The effect was great, and would be perfect for the play. If only people could come, they would love it.

"What is going on here?" Vicki's voice cried out from stage right, followed by an echoing boom of thunder. It was quite the dramatic entrance, and Pandora wondered if her mother knew any other way to make an appearance.

The lights stopped flickering and the thunder faded away, leaving the theater silent. Vicki stood center stage with her hands on her hips and a menacing scowl on her face. The side curtains parted and Xavier appeared, followed by Dougie. They both took up positions near Vicki, but not too near. Furious, Pandora jumped to her feet and ran up onto the stage just as Dr. Steele and Vlad stepped through the gap in the curtains. But there they stopped, keeping a good distance back as though mere observers. Wusses.

"Answer me, Pandy," her mother demanded, her cheeks flushed and nostrils flared. "What are you doing in this place? And with the patients? You know you're not allowed to socialize with them."

"I told you not to come in here again, Pandora," Xavier couldn't help throwing in like a fool. Dougie was wise enough to keep his mouth shut.

Vicki turned on Xavier. "You knew about this?"

He shrunk a little. "Well, yes. But I told her she needed to stay out of here or she'd get in trouble."

"And you didn't think you should tell me what she was up to?"

"I didn't want to bother you, Director Belfry. Not with all that's been going on for you. You've got too much on your plate as it is." Oh, very smooth, Xavier.

Vicki regarded him for a moment, then turned her attention back to Pandora. "I'm not going to ask again."

"I wrote a play and we wanted to act it out. What better place than our very own theater? It's safe, and I'd be inside. I thought maybe we could even perform for the staff and patients," she rushed on. "That would be for free, of course. But we could sell tickets in town to anyone who wants to come, and make some money for—"

"I knew you were up to something," Vicki interrupted, as though Pandora hadn't spoken a word. "Because you're *always* up to something."

"Maybe because I'm *always* losing my mind from boredom." *What an interesting, and perhaps ironic, way to put it,* a part of Pandora mused. "I need to do something, Vicki," she said aloud. "Living here, I feel like my whole world is closing in on me."

"Yeah, well, welcome to my world twenty-four/seven for the last fourteen years."

"So you should understand what I'm going through," Pandora tried, even though she knew her plea wouldn't get her anywhere. But she wanted it on record that she'd made an attempt to speak calmly and rationally to her mother and had been rejected. Sometimes all you had going for you was public opinion.

"What I understand," Vicki ground out, "is that I told you to stay out of this place. It's dangerous, and someone could have been killed. Can you imagine the lawsuit? We're skating on thin ice as it is."

Pandora swept her arm around the stage and toward the seats. "Does it look dangerous to you? I checked everything over, and I didn't find anything wrong. No leaks, no weird cracks in the walls or foundation, nothing broken or worn. I did my homework, Vicki. I even wrote a report about my assessment for one of my home school assignments. Just to see if you actually read my work. Apparently that was hoping for too much." Actually, what was too much—in terms of drama, anyway—was that last line, but in for a penny, in for a pound, as the Brits like to say.

Vicki's skin turned a shade of puce that should be impossible for human skin to achieve. "Don't you try to pin this on me. You broke the rules, and I've let you get away with that far too often. Not anymore. I'm done with looking the other way. What's it gotten me? Nothing but trouble."

"What's changed, Vicki?" Pandora asked, actually quite curious to know, and maybe a little nervous, too. Vicki was not behaving according to script, which typically went *bluster, bluster, bluster,* then forget all about it. Or, give Pandora a light slap on the wrist because Vicki was too busy to do anything else. Her mother was like an actor who'd forgotten her lines and had decided to throw all caution to the winds and make stuff up, and that stuff threw everything off track.

"I've changed." She snapped her fingers and pointed to the exit. "Now get out of my sight before I really lose my temper."

Dr. Steele stepped forward. "Director, may I have a word?"

"No, you may not!"

He didn't even flinch, and Pandora revised her opinion of him as a wuss. "Too bad. You're going to get one." The revision continued. Score one for the doc. Vicki glared at him, outrage evident in every line of her tense body. Dr. Steele put out his hands, looking very much like someone trying to placate a mad bull. "Listen, I know you're hurting inside. It's been a long week and you just lost someone you loved. I know you're also worried about your daughter…"

"You have no idea what I'm feeling," Vicki snarled. Pandora had never seen her so feral. Something must have happened to her. Something bad.

"I know you're furious, and I know you feel betrayed."

At his words, Vicki visibly pulled back, maybe even flinched. "Betrayed?" Her eyes widened and she looked like she wanted to run. "What makes you think that?"

Vlad stepped forward, cutting off her escape. "Director, I think this playacting might be a good thing for your daughter. It keeps her inside and out of trouble. Few people know about this spot, and it will be safer for her to be here. I will even look the place over myself."

"I can spend time here after my sessions," Dr. Steele volunteered. "To serve as a sort of chaperone."

"And I will check on them many times throughout the day," Vlad added.

"I can serve as the staff monitor for the patients," Dougie offered, though he didn't once look at Pandora. "You have my word, Director, that there will be no lawsuits on my watch."

Vicki looked around at all of them, her wounded eyes and bowed stance conveying exactly how she felt…as though she were surrounded by enemies. It was a stance Pandora knew quite well. "Fine," she said in a dead voice. "Do what you want. I don't care anymore."

Pandora had won, but it felt a hollow victory. She was used to Vicki giving in, to not putting up much of a fight. But this time, she'd seemed much more invested in winning…and then to suddenly give up? It didn't seem right, in fact, seemed to be a sign of something foreboding, like a vague warning of an impending explosion, set to go off at some future, unknown time.

"Come with me, Director," Vlad coaxed, taking her arm. Vicki blinked at him a few times, as though she didn't recognize him, then allowed him to lead her off the stage and through the parted curtains.

An eerie quiet descended over those remaining. They were quite used to outbursts, along with fights and screams and crying from the inmates, all par for the course. But when a member of the staff, and the Director at that, flaked out, well, it called for a moment of silence.

"Is she gone?" a voice asked from the darkness of the house.

Pandora made out Bones creeping down the steps. "She's gone."

"Does that mean we can't do this anymore?" She looked as upset about the idea as someone without a soul can look.

"She's not going to stop us."

"So we really could put on our play for other people!" Birdy squealed excitedly, clapping her hands.

"Let's not get ahead of ourselves," Dr. Steele spoke up. "The Director doesn't even want us in here, so I'm not sure she'll want anyone else."

"We'll worry about that later, doc," Pandora said, though she wasn't hopeful of a positive outcome. "What I want to know is how she found out about us." She turned her eyes on Xavier. "Care to explain yourself, brother of mine?"

He held up his hands. "I didn't say a word! I only saw your mom marching across the foyer looking furious. So I followed her, and when I saw her heading toward the hall that led to the theater, I knew something big was going to happen. To you."

"I followed Xavier," Dougie added. "Because I don't trust him." Xavier rolled his eyes.

"And Vlad and I followed Douglas," Dr. Steele offered. "I think we both sensed something was wrong."

"But how did Vicki even know we were here?" Pandora asked. Of course nobody answered her. So maybe the better question was, who had something to gain by telling on her? Xavier, of course. She remembered seeing the Hessian, too, and both the new patients, not long after or before she'd been in the hall leading to the theater. The Hessian seemed the most likely candidate for telling on her, having a personal vendetta, but the new patients, King Tobias and Gloria, could be guilty, too, acting as spies for the mystery man. While they'd seemed harmless, they could have been acting. Stranger things had happened. Bones didn't like her, either, but she'd been in the theater at the same time Vicki had showed up, and had seemed disappointed when she'd thought they might have to stop coming. Still…she couldn't be ruled out. Nobody could, actually. Not Dr. Steele or Vlad or any of the other patients or the posse. The informer could be anyone.

Anyone at all.

PANDORA TURNED TO Dr. Steele. As much as he intrigued her, she wasn't all that keen on having a watchdog breathing down her neck all day long. "You really don't need to babysit us, doc. You're a busy man, and we'll be fine on our own."

"Oh, I don't mind. I've always loved the theater." He opened his arms wide. "It's a magical place."

She frowned. "It is. But it's going to be less magical if you think you have to act as our nanny. You just have to *be*, doc. No doing."

He gave her a proud smile. "How existentialist of you."

"Stop deflecting. This is serious. If you're going to stay, you'll have to let go of all your rule following and repressive ways. Vicki never said that you had to be here, so if we're going to allow you to stay you have to promise you'll behave. And by behave, I mean leave all your adult crap at the door."

He took this in. "All right, as long as I can intervene if I think someone's life is in danger." Luckily he didn't look directly at her as he said this or she'd have to kick him in the nads.

Pandora pondered his proposal, then turned to the posse, including Bones in her question. "What do you guys think?"

Birdy gaped at her. "You're asking our opinion?"

Pandora suppressed an urge to snipe back. "Yeah, well, maybe I have to leave some things at the door, too."

"You've changed," Birdy noted smugly, obviously pleased with her own insight. "I think it's for the better, of course, but it's kind of freaking me out, too."

"It's my TBT," Pandora said dryly. "I'm not in my right mind."

Bones gave a coughing sort of laugh. "I can second that."

Pandora turned to the girl, choosing to take the high road. "So what do you think? You're one of us now. Can the doc stay, and only intervene if someone is about to die?"

Bones gave Pandora a long look and Pandora wondered what she was thinking. "I don't give a crap what he does," she finally answered, "as long as he stays out of my way."

"Fair enough," Pandora agreed. She felt a grudging respect for Bones's answer, and that bothered her. She didn't want to like the girl. She was kind of the enemy.

"I want him!" Lucy cried lustily.

"To stay?" Pandora clarified.

"Yeah, sure. That, too." Lucy snickered.

"Me, too," Charles agreed, giggling along with Lucy, though Pandora doubted he understood the ribald nature of Lucy's giggles. Then again, after catching him checking out Birdy's cleavage, maybe she was underestimating the kid.

She turned to Dr. Steele. "I guess you're in."

He actually looked happy, and she kind of felt like a hero. It was a powerful feeling.

"Am I to be voted on?" Dougie spoke up.

Pandora turned to the group. "Well?"

Everyone shrugged, not committing one way or the other, except for Birdy. "He can stay." She wrinkled her nose at him flirtatiously.

Birdy's flirting gave Pandora a great idea. "All right, Dougie, you can stay. But then you have to be in the play."

"What's the play?" he asked, his expression and voice bland, as though he couldn't care less. But she knew he did. She could tell by the way his left hand curled into a fist. She had found his tell. Curled left fist equaled interest.

"It's *Frankenstein*, and you get to be Dr. Frankenstein."

Birdy whooped and clapped her hands in approval.

"You want me to play the role of a mad scientist?"

"Shouldn't be much of a stretch. But you're going to have to learn to speak louder. Unless we can find a way to put a microphone on you." She looked at Bones, who nodded, indicating she thought it could be done. "Agreed?"

"I accept." He gave her a detached little bow, but she caught the intrigued gleam in his cool eyes. He might have been giving her the cold shoulder earlier, but he couldn't resist the allure of the stage. No one could.

"Count me out," Xavier felt compelled to say, quite loudly.

"Oh, okay. I mean, I need someone to build the sets, but whatever. I guess I'll have to figure out all those power tools by myself."

He took a step closer. "Power tools?"

"They're pretty intimidating, I know, but I think I can handle them. Who needs all their fingers, right?"

Xavier puffed out his chest, as though he thought looking bigger and stronger would make him better at running a tool. Pandora could work those babies blindfolded, but he didn't need to know that. "Dr. Steele,

I think I'd better take over the set building. I've had a few shop classes, so I know what I'm doing."

"If you don't mind, I'd love to help with that," Dr. Steele responded, his own eyes bright. "I built sets for the drama department in high school."

"Oh, please," Birdy scoffed. "With your looks, you must have been the star of the play."

"Back then I didn't exactly look like I do now, and I certainly didn't have that sort of confidence." Like Birdy, Pandora wanted to cry bull-pucky, but decided to keep her mouth shut until she could get a hold of some photographic proof. There was no way this guy had ever looked bad. "I prefer behind-the-scenes work, anyway, and would rather leave the acting to the experts."

Birdy preened. "The ability to act is a gift so few have been given." She turned to Dougie, her voice becoming business-like. "I hope you've got it."

He blinked at her, slow and steady, as he was wont to do. "I will manage."

"Good. I don't want you bringing me down. Luckily we won't have to fake the amazing chemistry between us." She batted her fake lashes at him.

"I agree." Oh, yes, thought Pandora, Dougie would play his role just fine.

"I'm going to be Igirl," Lucy spoke up. She'd been rolling around on the floor throughout their conversation, but had apparently decided now was a good time to join in. "It's really Igor, but that's a stupid name. So I changed it to Igirl, because I'm a girl, and I'm not stupid. I'll be the hottest Igirl ever."

Dr. Steele nodded, somehow managing to keep his face straight. "I think you'll be a great Igirl, Lucy."

"Oh, I know I will. I was made for the role."

"I'm going to be the producer!" Charles said excitedly. "It's my job to get money for the play." His blue eyes settled on Dougie, and Pandora had to smother a laugh. Why that clever little sneak! He'd gone right to the source. "For all the stuff *Pandora* might need," he added, waggling his eyebrows at Pandora. Sweet, innocent Charles. Wow. She had not seen that one coming. He knew Dougie liked Pandora and was not afraid to take advantage of that. Or maybe Sinclair had given him some pointers, because this kind of deviousness was very un-Charles-like.

"What will you be doing, Pandora?" Dougie asked, all polite interest.

"I'm the director, of course, and I'm playing Justine."

"Wasn't she in love with Dr. Frankenstein?" She was, and it just now occurred to Pandora that playing both Justine and Dr. Frankenstein wouldn't have worked at all. Stupid TBT.

"I'm not sure I would say she was in love."

"Idol worship, then?"

She inhaled deeply, looking for patience. "Give it up, Daft." His eyes focused on her, so intensely she turned away.

"So when can we get started?" Xavier wanted to know.

Pandora checked her watch. "Well, we still have a few hours until meal-time. Charles has drawn all the sketches for the sets. You and Dr. Steele can talk to him. Hang on a second." She ran and fetched her extra copies of the play from her backpack, amazed at her prescience. She had somehow known she'd need them. She handed a copy to Dr. Steele, Xavier, and Dougie. "Look it over, see what else we need. Dougie, you and Birdy can work on your lines together."

"You're going to put our names on here, right?" Xavier asked, holding up the script.

"Yeah, Pandora!" Birdy added her worthless two cents. "You said I get top billing."

"There are several things I have to change, you two divas, but I've been a bit distracted by my head injury. I can't do everything, you know."

"Wanting proper acknowledgement for my skills and expertise is not being a diva," Xavier lectured, ignoring her pointed reminder about her struggles.

"Not in the least," she replied sarcastically. "Anyway, I'm not changing anything until we find someone to play the Creature."

"Have Cracker Jack do it," Xavier suggested, his condescending tone summoning up images of the wise professor—all-knowing, but basically full of crap. "He's pretty tall."

"What a great idea, Xavier!" she gushed, and he preened like an idiot. "I'm sure he'll be fine during the resurrection scene."

"Why shouldn't he be?"

"Well, you know what happens then, right? Thunder and lightning, very, very frightening? Especially for someone with shell shock."

Xavier had the good grace to look chagrined. "Oh, yeah."

"I was thinking we could get Derek to do it." She lowered head slowly, dramatically, and added softly, "But he won't."

"Did you ask him?"

Her head swung up. "Of course I did, you nimrod."

"Pandora," Dr. Steele cautioned. "Name calling doesn't help."

She turned on him. "You're not allowed to do that here. Remember?"

He held up his hands in surrender. "Right. Sorry."

"Only Nepenthe Manor staff and residents should be allowed," Dougie stated coolly.

"You don't get a say in this," Pandora snapped, "and anyway, he said no. I'm sure that will make you happy."

A reptilian smile spread across his face. "As far as I can be made happy, yes."

"Well, without a Creature, there's no play," she challenged. "So you're going to have to pick your poison."

"I'm sure we'll find someone," Dr. Steele couldn't stop himself from intervening, though secretly she was glad, since the inmates were starting to look a little rebellious. "Don't you, Pandora?"

"I'm sure we will," she pushed out, reluctantly. She sounded like that obnoxious Pollyanna chick, but it was a necessary evil to keep the posse from out and out losing it. "Now let's get to work."

After a moment's pause, Xavier, Dr. Steele, Sinclair, and Charles, followed by a singing, dancing Lucy, headed to the workshop. Bones bounded up the stairs, two at a time, to continue working on light and sound. Birdy picked up her script, where she'd dropped it after Pandora had threatened there would be no play, and started to read aloud.

Dougie took Pandora's arm and pulled her away, depositing her by the curtains. "You must not bring him here."

No need to ask who 'him' was. "Why not? We need a Creature, and he'd make a great one."

"Don't waste your energy on someone who will only end up letting you down."

"Derek hasn't let me down," she argued, then remembered that he had. More than once. But had any of those times actually been his fault? She could argue both ways.

"I would never say no to you, Pandora," Dougie persisted, his gaze almost fanatical as he looked down at her.

"Good. Can I have your Lamborghini?"

"Of course."

"You're so full of crap, Daft."

"I'd give you anything you desire, Pandora."

From center stage Birdy yawned loudly. When that didn't get her the attention she so desired, she stomped her foot. "Hello? Can we get this show on the road?"

Dougie turned toward her. "One more moment, Birdy, and then we can commence." He faced Pandora again. "Anything."

"Save the acting for the play, Dougie."

"You're the only person to whom I show my true self, Pandora. I ask that you not give me cause to regret doing so." Then he spun on his heel and left her staring after him. Cripes. The guy gets a lead role, and already he's acting the diva.

Waltzes In and Drags Him Away

AT FIVE O'CLOCK, Dr. Steele, Xavier, and Dougie escorted the inmates to supper. As they filed out of the theater, all of them were talking excitedly about which sets to build first or discussing their favorite lines or what their costumes would look like. Pandora watched them go with mixed feelings. She wanted to join in, at the very least maybe get some kudos for coming up with the idea of doing a play in the first place. But she had a headache, and besides, she needed to make sure all was well before locking up. Now that Vicki had given permission for them to be here, Pandora knew she had to stay on her best behavior to keep the privilege. Her mother was like a ticking time bomb right now, and one wrong move could set her off, ruining everything.

Funny how she kept equating her mother to a bomb about to go off.

The plan was to meet tomorrow after lunch to continue their work, with Dr. Steele coming when he was done with his therapy sessions for the day. Xavier was beaming when he left, and while Pandora was still mad at him for being such a jerk to her, she was also kind of pleased to see him looking so enthusiastic, which wasn't like her at all. Maybe she was losing her hard-earned edge, or maybe her TBT was weakening her. She picked the second theory.

Her head injury was turning out to be a good fall guy, and she was going to be sad when the day came and she could no longer use it as an excuse for any unusual behavior on her part. But she figured she could wring at least a few more months out of it. She'd seen the Bodkin at work and had learned to fake it from the best. For the moment, however, she didn't have to pretend. She still felt more than a bit wobbly, and her headache was not helping any.

She trotted up the steps to check over the light and sound booth. Inside she found scribbled notes all over the place, evidence of Bones's activity. Pandora peeked at a few of the notes and was surprised at the creativity and thoroughness in the little directives, spouting phrases like "selective visibility" and "mood and focus" and "composition and projection." Bones seemed to know her stuff. While Pandora felt a bit jealous at the girl's obvious expertise in an area Pandora considered to be one of her own, she was able, for once, just to be grateful she didn't have to do this job in addition to all her other ones. She was finding that being the director was a lot of work.

On her way back down, she spotted Dougie standing on the stage waiting for her. "Is something wrong?" she called as she took the small steps to the stage at a dangerous speed.

He crossed over to meet her. "I came to escort you to dinner." He held out his hand.

She ignored it. "I can escort myself, thank you very much. Besides, I still have work to do here."

"I'll help you," he said firmly, "then we'll go eat."

"I've got it," she bristled. "I'm just checking to be sure everything's in order before I go. I don't want to give Vicki any ammunition to shut down the play."

"She was very angry with you today."

"Oh, you noticed?" She shrugged. "That's nothing new. I think she's been angry with me since the day I was born."

"I would rejoice in your birth."

"Yeah, well, your birth wasn't responsible for turning your mother's true love into a zombie."

"Neither was yours." Dougie hesitated, as though pondering whether to share something else. "Your father was drinking, yes?"

"That's the story. I was born a little after noon, so he must have been hitting the sauce quite early. He was at a birthday celebration, I guess."

"That seems odd. To be drunk so early in the day," he added when she didn't say anything. The thought had occurred to her, of course, but alcoholics can be drunk at nine in the morning, so why not?

"What are you saying?"

He hesitated. "You carry around a lot of baggage, Pandora, and it gets in the way of your progress."

"Baggage? Me? I don't think so." She straightened out the curtains, then grabbed a broom. She'd swept the stage not that long ago, but some dust had fallen from the lights, and besides, she needed something to do with Dougie standing so close to her, saying things she wasn't sure she wanted to deal with right now. Or ever.

He reached for the broom. "Let me do that."

"So you can get blisters and ruin your hand modeling career? I don't think so."

He held out his hands, palms up. The skin was calloused, and there were even a few white scars marring the pale surface. "I moved on from those a long time ago."

She clutched the broom. "I'm fine. I want to do it." She began to sweep—short, brisk strokes.

"This play is very important to you," Dougie noted as he watched her work.

"Not really," she lied.

"What will happen if you can't find someone to play the Creature?"

"What do you think? He's kind of the main event."

"Who are our other options?"

"Other than Derek and Xavier, who is mad at me right now, Cracker Jack is our best choice. But his PTSD rules him out. Outside the posse, he's the only inmate here who could actually focus long enough to learn his lines. Too bad Skippy's gone. He could've done it."

"I heard his father took him away."

The broom flew back and forth. "That crook doesn't deserve that term. For years he hasn't shown any interest in Skippy, and then he just waltzes in and drags him away, like he has a right to. Now no one knows where Skippy is or how he's doing. It's a travesty! He's one of us, but Vicki didn't do anything to help him. No one did. I've always believed you can't rely on adults for anything, and the bastards just keep proving me right."

"Adulthood in our society does not necessarily reflect an age, but serves as an institution, one that ensures humans conform to rules and regulations. I find that repellant, but not surprising."

She stopped sweeping. "So what can we do? A perk of being part of the adult institution is power."

"You can have power and not be an adult. I point to myself as an example of this."

"That's because you're rich, Dougie. Money gives you power, even if that money comes from your parents. I don't have that luxury. Vicki is allowing me to stay at Nepenthe Manor as long as I don't mess up. One wrong move and off I go. Short of running away and taking to the streets, I don't have any other recourse. She used to let me get away with murder, but not anymore. I thought maybe this play would make things right for everyone, but my idea only served to piss her off even more." She banged the broom on the floor. "What does it matter, anyway? We won't be able to do the play without the Creature."

Dougie stared at her long and hard, and she began to sweep again, if only to avoid that probing gaze. "We will find your Creature," he promised after a few moments had passed. "I will make it happen."

She sighed. "I don't see how."

"You are feeling hopeless."

"Because I'm *helpless*, Dougie!" She shook the broom handle at him.

"And don't pull that therapy reflection crap on me. I know what you're doing, and it's annoying."

"I'm trying to connect with you."

"You're trying to control me."

He blinked slowly. "I don't think anyone can control you, Pandora."

"Except my mother."

"Not even her."

"Whatever. Listen, I've got to finish this up. You should get back to the posse. As you know, mealtimes can turn bad very quickly. Lucy once started a food fight that took two days to clean up. They had to scrub mashed potatoes out of the light fixtures with toothbrushes." It had been magnificent.

"I don't want you to worry about finding someone to play the Creature, Pandora. As I said, I will make it happen."

She shrugged, feeling increasingly morose. "Either way. I'm not sure why I even care. Vicki will find some way to ruin things. She always does, one way or another." A wave of emotion surged through her body like an electric shock, and she turned away from Dougie. To keep herself from bursting into tears she started sweeping fiercely. Sweet Mary, she was a mess.

Dougie strode over and grabbed her arm, pulling her round to face him squarely. She readied the broom to whack him one, but refrained when he leaned in closely. "I told you I would do anything for you, Pandora. So do one thing for me."

She peered at him suspiciously. "I'm not going on another date with you."

"While that is something I want, that is not the one thing I need from you right now."

"What do you *need?*" *A kick in the ass?* she almost added, but bit back the words, seeing the serious expression on his face.

"Your trust."

He squeezed her arm, as though driving home his point, then let go and walked away. She watched him disappear though the curtains, then rolled her eyes. Like she would ever trust him. That would be like trusting the devil. But still…she did rather enjoy the show he'd put on for her just now. And she did feel a bit better for it. Less hopeless and helpless, anyway.

She swept up the small pile of debris into a dustpan and dumped it in the trashcan in the workshop. As she was turning about, she heard the back door to the shop open. Dougie again.

She readied the broom to strike, but it was only Vlad. "What are you doing here?"

"What do you think?" She liked that he didn't feel the need to exchange pleasantries with her. It saved so much time.

"Checking up on me?"

"Close, but no cigarette. I am checking over the theater. I promised your mother I would do so, and that I would report back to her on what I found."

"You won't find anything wrong."

"If I do, I will have to tell her. I work for her now."

"Is that how Russians do things?"

"Do things?"

"You know, change loyalties. First you were my grandmother's lackey." Then Dougie's, and maybe still Dougie's. "Now you're my mother's."

He regarded her through slitted eyes. Had she gone too far? She hoped so. As an employee working for her mother, he now acted as Vicki's representative. And as Vicki's representative, he was fair game.

He smiled. "I am loyal to my family and myself first, and I am no-body's lackey."

"Nice dodge, cowboy."

He gave her a two-fingered salute. "To further correct you, I never changed loyalties. Your mother wants what your grandmother wants... to keep you safe."

Pandora gave a derisive guffaw. "You think my grandmother wants to keep me safe? Wrong answer. She wants to keep the Belfry dynasty safe. I'm the only grandchild. So if I fail, the family fails, which means she failed. And my grandmother doesn't do failure."

"And you do?"

"I can't afford to fail, but not because of some stupid name. Because too many people rely on me."

"I think, Pandora, that you carry a burden of your own making. How wearisome that must be."

Dr. Gara had said something similar...that Pandora was basically the source of her own problems. Which made both of them idiots. She had found a way to survive in a hostile environment. She had found that way as a child, and it had saved her. She had saved herself. Her defiance, her resilience, her ingenuity...all these traits had kept her from going mad.

Until...*possibly*...now.

"And I think, Vlad, that you've already been brainwashed by my mother."

For the first time since she'd met him, he looked almost uncertain before making his expression go blank. "Leave the Director out of this," he said in a hard voice.

Pandora stared at him. "So you no longer think she's a suspect?"

"I do not think she is the source of your trouble."

"Shows what you know." She indicated the theater with a sweep of her arm. "Better get on with your job. I think you'll find everything is in working order. I've had to do some maintenance over the years, but nothing major."

"I am sure you have done your best."

"That's not at all condescending."

"You are not an architect, engineer, or inspector, so forgive me if I am skeptical. No one can be all things, Pandora."

She regarded him steadily. "The whole phrase is, 'no one can be all things to all men,' or people, and I agree. I can't be all things to all people, because not all people are intelligent enough to get how amazing I am."

Vlad gave a raspy chuckle. "Perhaps you are right. Now go eat. You are looking, how do you say it?" He frowned, then snapped his fingers. "Peaky! You are looking peaky." He grinned, pleased with himself. He really was quite good with the language. Such skill made Pandora suspicious. Didn't spies typically have a good facility with languages? And there was that comment he'd made about prison. What exactly had Vlad done in his previous life? Been a super villain? "I will close up when I am done."

She leaned the broom against the wall, an idea taking hold of her. "Vlad?"

"Yes?"

"How much does it cost to take out a life insurance policy?"

He frowned in thought. "If you are healthy, not terribly much, I do not think. Though it depends on how big a payout you want."

"And can you take one out on yourself?"

He squinted at her. "These are strange questions, Pandora."

"Just answer."

"I think you can do so. Why are you asking?"

"No reason." She gave him a regal nod. "Now if you will excuse me, I'm going to my room." She turned and left him, feeling his changeable eyes boring into her back.

That should learn him.

HER QUESTIONS ABOUT life insurance followed Pandora upstairs to her room. She felt too tired to brave the cafeteria, and she'd eaten all the leftovers from the party, but she was starving. If they had any money, she'd order a pizza. But that was the problem, wasn't it? They didn't have money. They never had money.

But if she could find a way to get some, then maybe she could save this place and stay here for as long as she was needed. What if they really could sell tickets to the play? What if they invited the whole town to come? Wouldn't that get Hank off their back? Convince Vicki to stay on?

She hadn't really been serious about the life insurance idea. Even if it were only ten dollars a month, she still couldn't afford it. But if she could…well, that led to all sorts of other questions, didn't it?

So back she went to her previous problem. They didn't have a Creature, and even if they did, Vicki would never let them put on a play for the town. She was very protective of the inmates and this place. She let the LoBAC women come once a month, but she limited their visit to the lobby or her office. Visitor's Day was held every other Saturday, but again, kept to the arts and crafts room. So to open the manor's doors to the entire town? Never.

Pandora sighed despondently, and her stomach growled in harmony, followed by zaps of pain in her lower abdomen. Her temples pulsed, and her mind whirled. This must be what it felt like to get caught in quicksand. Slowly sinking deeper and deeper, and knowing that no matter what you do you're not getting out. Escape is impossible, no matter how hard you fight. In fact, the more you fight the faster you'll meet your fate. Your destiny is to choke to death on dust and bits of glass.

It made one want to give up.

Hungry and tired, she plopped down on the couch in the living room and stared at nothing, her fingers tapping restlessly on the worn couch cushion. Where was Vicki? Gone off on another inmate rescue mission? Not likely. Not if she was looking for a new job—she would consider her responsibility to the mentally ill over. After their showdown in the theater, she was probably hiding out in her office. Old habits die hard.

There was a knock on the apartment door, startling her. "Come in," she called, leaning forward.

The door opened and a tray, followed by Dr. Steele, entered the room. "Thought you could use something to eat."

She gaped at him. "You brought me supper?"

"Directors are famous for neglecting their own needs when in the midst of making magic." He grinned and set the tray on her lap. The meal didn't look very appetizing—it never did—but the *two* pieces of apple pie certainly did. "May I sit down?"

"I won't stop you." Had he come to tell her about his Elizabeth? She felt herself perking up.

He sat down, his weight on the cushion pulling her toward him. Startled, she scooted away. Then regretted doing so, but she couldn't undo her action without looking like an idiot. "I wanted to thank you, Pandora."

"Thank me?"

He gazed up at the ceiling, a smile lighting up his face. "I don't remember the last time I've felt like this. Being in the theater today was, well, it made me feel like I was young again and the world full of possibilities. It's been very therapeutic, and I have you to thank for that."

She blinked at him, not at all sure how to respond. "But I didn't really do anything."

He glanced sideways at her. "Pandora Belfry being modest?"

"I'm not being modest. I just don't know how I could do anything for someone like you."

"Someone like me, huh? And what would that be?"

"I don't know." She felt her cheeks warm. Was she blushing? "Perfect," she mumbled.

He laughed out loud. "Perfect? Au, contraire, ma chérie. I am far from that. But that's okay. Perfect people are boring."

"Because they're predictable."

"Exactly. And no one wants that."

She stabbed a bean with her fork. "Absolutely not."

"I hope you don't think I'm perfect because I'm predictable? That would be a fate worse than death, wouldn't it?" He winked at her.

"Most definitely. But no, that's not why I think you're perfect. I guess it's because you never have a hair out of place, or a single blemish, and you always seem so calm and in control."

"You know what they say…perception is the key to success."

"In other words, the old 'fake it 'til you make it' ploy."

He pointed at her. "Got it in one."

"Speaking of faking it, you aren't sharing things about me with Dougie, are you? He's not really staff, you know. Not like he should be."

"I would never share anything of a sensitive nature with Douglas, especially nothing concerning you." He saw her dubious expression, one she did nothing to hide. "I know you think I've been taken in by him, but I assure you I am quite careful with what I say and what I do around Douglas Daft. That being said, the Director hired him to work here, as staff, albeit as an unpaid intern, so I'm obligated to share certain things with him. But never anything personal about you. I promise you that." He placed a hand on his heart.

She believed he meant what he was saying, but she didn't like how he kept qualifying his words. "Never share anything *of a sensitive nature…*" and "*Never anything personal* about you…" It meant he shared some things about her. Plus, she wasn't sure she could trust his definition of those words.

"I don't think Vicki should've taken him on," she grumbled.

He shifted on the couch, then leaned back. "Listen, Pandora, I've only known your mother for a short time, and I know she's in mourning, but I feel like something else is going on with her."

"Yeah, me too," Pandora grudgingly admitted. She wondered how much she could share with the good doctor. Oh, what the hell. She'd take the plunge. At this point, what did she have to lose? "I think she's looking for a new job."

"What?" He looked startled. "Now?"

"I'm pretty sure she only stayed this long to look after the professor. Now that he's gone, well…she feels it's time to move on."

"Did she say this to you?"

Pandora gave a bitter laugh. "You think Vicki would share something like that with me?" She shook her head. "No, she's only hinted. Plus she's been looking at want ads, and not going down to work like she always does. She's acting flaky, too. You've seen her. She wants out."

"Taking you with her."

She nodded, unable to respond because of the sudden lump in her throat. The words, spoken aloud, were hard to hear. "I know you think it would be good for me to leave here, but I don't want to," she finally managed to get out. "This place is all I've ever known, and I'm not ready to go." Crap. She was sharing too much. But again, what did she have to lose? Her whole world was falling apart around her. This was her SOS, or SMS…Save *My* Soul.

"Of course you aren't ready. You're only fourteen."

She squinted at him suspiciously. "But you want the posse to leave.

You've said this place isn't good for them, or *me*."

"You know what I want, Pandora?"

"A raise?"

He smiled. "Sure. Why not? But I also want everyone here to be happy. It's a lofty goal, I know, but wouldn't it be great if we could achieve that? No matter what it took?"

"Everyone here happy? Not going to happen, doc. Just getting Mrs. Johnson to smile would require an act of divine intervention. A brain transplant, at the very least. Or lots of alcohol."

"Okay, okay. I get the picture. Well, then maybe we'll start with just some of us."

As if she couldn't guess where this was going. "Like the posse?"

"And you. You're all still young. You have your whole lives ahead of you."

"So we're back to you wanting us to leave this place," she said dryly. At this point, she would have crossed her arms grumpily, but she wasn't going to let go of her tray and end up dumping her pie on the floor. She wasn't sure of the last time anyone had swept it.

"I am thinking of that, and eventually you will leave. But only when you're ready."

"And what if we're never ready?"

"You will be ready. Sooner than you think."

"How can you know that?"

He pushed himself to his feet and stood looking down at her, blocking the ceiling light just right so that it cast a glow around his head like he was some sort of divine creature. "Because I have faith." He smiled, patted her head like a father would, then turned to go. At the door he turned back. "Eat your dinner, then get some sleep. We need you healthy, Director." With a smile, he left her, shutting the door quietly behind him.

After eating her pie, Pandora did as she was told. But she did it with a lighter heart, even though she realized he hadn't told her anything more about his Elizabeth, the sneak. Only moments ago she'd thought her whole life was the equivalent of a quicksand pit leading to a long, drawn out death. And now? Well, she didn't feel hope exactly. That would be idiotic. But she did feel like she had something to work toward.

For the moment, anyway. Which, for the moment, would have to be enough.

She had a play to put on.

Ψ

The following morning the posse, led by Dougie and Xavier, entered the workshop, unexpectedly early. "Dr. Steele got us out of our other activities!" Charles hurried in to tell her. "Even therapy! He said this would be better for us right now. That it would make us happy."

Pandora suppressed a smile. Well, the guy was certainly true to his word. "Cool."

Charles sidled closer and whispered, "And I got Dougie to put up some money for us."

Dougie was trying to pry Lucy off his arm at the moment, unaware he was the topic of discussion. "How much?"

"Five hundred dollars," he breathed, and his breath smelled sweet, like applesauce.

Five *hundred* dollars? "Well, he was very generous."

"So what should I spend it on?"

"I don't know. Use your imagination."

His eyes sparkled. "I will! Now I have to go try my costume on." He spun away, pulled Lucy off Dougie, and together they skipped toward the costumes, where Sinclair was waiting for them, his eyes remaining fixed on Pandora until they arrived.

Birdy swiftly commandeered Dougie to run lines. Xavier started organizing a pile of wood, mumbling to himself, and Bones, who was watching him, only left when she realized Pandora was watching her watching him.

An hour later, Pandora was up on a giant wooden ladder helping Bones with light positioning when she saw someone walk onto the stage.

"Derek?"

He shaded his eyes as he looked up at her. "Can we talk?"

She temporarily tightened the clamp she was adjusting and scrambled down the ladder. When she reached the floor, she yelled up to the booth, "I'm taking five."

Bones turned off all the lights, then flipped them back on, either showing she'd heard or expressing her disapproval. Probably the latter. Pandora gave her a thumbs-up.

She hurried over to Derek, feeling slightly winded. That ladder was tall. It had nothing to do with the fact that he looked really good. His dark hair was tousled from the wind, his cheeks slightly red against his tanned skin. His hands were shoved into the pockets of his pants—regular ones this time, not his typical overalls.

"What's up?" she asked, all casual-like. Though it came out "Wzup?" like she was drunk.

"I, well, I did some thinking about what you asked me. You know, about being the monster for the play."

"Yeah?" she prompted when he didn't continue, his eyes scanning the theater.

"Well, I suppose I could help. If you still need me."

"Seriously?"

"Yep."

"What does your dad think about it?"

"He doesn't know," Derek replied stubbornly, "and I don't plan on him knowing."

"Of course. So," she quickly changed the subject. "Have you ever acted before?"

"No. Acting's not really my thing."

"Oh. Well, can you memorize lines?"

"I'll do my best."

She suppressed a sigh. A reluctant actor with some pretty significant lines. But still...she eyed him up and down...in terms of a physical specimen he was perfect.

"Choken!" Pandora turned to see Dougie stalking toward them. It was the loudest word she'd ever heard him utter. As he approached, he jabbed at Derek's chest. "This place is off-limits to you." Derek stood his ground, eyeing Dougie with barely concealed contempt.

"Back off, Dougie!" Pandora yelled. "He's the monster."

"Yet another reason why he shouldn't be allowed in here."

"Very funny. My problem is solved. He's going to be the Creature."

Dougie scowled. "Have you run this by Director Belfry?"

"Since when did you become a card carrying member of the bourgeoisie, you old stick-in-the-mud geezer? I thought rules were only meant for the peasants of the world?"

"They are, and he's the peasant." He pointed at Derek. "Now, shall you escort him out, or shall I?"

Pandora drew herself up. "He's not leaving, Dougie. I need him here...for the play, that is. If you have a problem with that, then you're the one who needs to leave. I'll find someone else to play Dr. Frankenstein."

"Oh, no, you won't, Pandora!" Birdy interjected, looping her arm through Dougie's. He flinched, but didn't disengage, much as it looked like he wanted to. "If he goes, I go."

Pandora rubbed her forehead. Actors are so damn dramatic. "I don't want anyone to go, but we need a Creature, and Derek is perfect for the role. Just look at him!"

Birdy happily did so, licking her glossy lips as she scanned him up and down. She let go of Dougie's arm and sidled up to Pandora. "I wonder if he's muscular *all over*," she said in a loud whisper, which, judging by Derek's reddening cheeks, he'd heard.

It was a thought, Pandora regretfully admitted, that she had wondered herself, but that didn't stop her from reprimanding Birdy. Standards needed to be maintained. "Get your mind out of the gutter, girl. He's a human being, not a piece of meat."

"It's an honest question, Pandora, and enquiring minds want to know."

"Yeah," Lucy called. "My enquiring mind wants to know."

Luckily Lucy hadn't heard Birdy's original comment. "Fine. We're talking about Fermat's last theorem, which says that no three positive integers can fit the equation—"

Lucy held up her hand. "Stop talking, Pandemonium." She beamed up at Derek. "Hi, giant guy. I'm Igirl, and I'm going to be the one who fetches your brain."

"He could certainly use one," Dougie said snidely. Dougie being catty? How human of him, and yet another chink in his armor. It appeared that Derek was Dougie's kryptonite.

"So it's settled," Pandora announced. "We have our Creature. Welcome, Derek!"

He gave her a small smile. Dougie turned on his heel and marched toward Sinclair, indicating his opinion on the matter.

At that moment, the sound of thunder filled the theater. Pandora wasn't sure if the ominous rumbling was simply Bones testing something out, or a portentous sign of a storm brewing...

25

The Old Gaslighting Game

THE NEXT MONTH flew by. Nothing too out of the ordinary happened to Pandora during this time, no attacks or threats made, no sightings of stalkers lurking about. Except for Ronny and Lonny. Being that they had the subtlety of giant walking sticks whilst trailing after her whenever she went outside, they didn't really count.

Not long after Vlad did his inspection of the theater, he gave them the go ahead to continue with the play, neglecting to apologize for doubting Pandora's word, of course. He stopped in quite often, giving advice while watching Pandora out of the corner of his eye.

Thankfully, the mystery man seemed to have given up on the idea of taking her. Her grandmother kept her distance, too, no doubt embarrassed by what Pandora had done. Having discovered her granddaughter was flawed, she apparently no longer wanted Pandora with her. It was a huge relief. Frank was still in the hospital recovering from his surgery, so Vlad remained at his post as security guard. Apparently there'd been complications, but no one was very forthcoming about the details. Probably because of what had happened to the professor— went in alive, came out dead.

Her head and ribs were almost normal again, but she still felt out of sorts, weepy and cranky at the turn of a screw, with the occasional pain attack hitting her gut like an electric jolt. Sometimes she felt like she'd swallowed a python and it was strangling her insides. Luckily those times didn't last long.

She wasn't sure what was happening to her, and as the threat of being thought crazy hung over her head like an anvil, she didn't say anything to anyone. It would pass. It must, because she wasn't sure how much longer she could handle this crap. She wasn't sleeping well, and despite not eating the best—the theater is a demanding mistress—her clothes continued to grow tighter. The dark circles under her eyes looked cool, but the belly bulge over her favorite jeans definitely did not. The idea that she might have a tumor dogged her thoughts on a daily basis.

As though rubbing it in, the posse was full of energy and bonhomie. They were blossoming in their new roles, and in their freedom from the daily drudgery of the asylum's monotonous routine. In fact, they seemed better off without their therapy sessions, and Pandora wasn't sure what to make of that.

She snuck out to take care of Shadow as often as she could, soon realizing that someone else was looking after her, too. Dr. Steele? Probably. She didn't mind as much as she thought she would. Mucking out the stall and dealing with the ornery horse could be tiring, and it was nice to have some help. She thought about recruiting Ronny and Lonny, but didn't want to burst their bubble. They always looked so pleased with themselves, thinking they were being so sneaky. Though it was annoying how they always seemed to know when she was coming.

She wrote a thank-you note to Mrs. H., along with an explanation about what had really happened regarding the kidnapping. Mrs. H. had written back, expressing her relief, and also how much she missed Pandora. She said she <u>wished</u> she could come visit, but the summer season was in full swing and she was short on staff. But hopefully <u>soon</u>... Pandora wasn't holding her breath. She was pretty sure the manor and its inhabitants kind of scared Mrs. H.

There'd been no word on Skippy, and no one talked about him, either. Either the posse had repressed their feelings about him being gone, or he had already been forgotten. Repression was understandable, if a bit depressing, but if the others had already forgotten about him, well, that was kind of horrible. Pandora didn't want to forget about Skippy, and she certainly didn't want anyone forgetting about her if she ever had to leave. Being remembered by other people was her only way, so far, of achieving immortality.

Derek and Dougie assiduously avoided one another, except when running lines. The dislike between them was obvious and uncomfortable, like a bad smell in the room, but luckily their rancor actually enhanced their performances. Derek wasn't the best actor in the world, but as he was the Creature, his stiffness could be interpreted as natural for someone who'd been sewn back together, piece by piece. For his part, Dougie had learned to speak louder than a hissing snake, and at times had even shown emotion. He really was a good actor.

Derek kind of avoided her, too, actually. She thought his joining the play had meant he'd gotten over whatever snit he'd been in, but it seemed she was wrong. He did rehearsals, then cleared out, claiming he had to go help his pa or visit his ma, probably go see Laura Ingalls, too. Pandora wanted to find out what was going on with him, ask him what he'd wanted to tell her before Vicki kicked him out of their apartment, but she simply didn't have the time or energy to pursue it. Maybe once the play was finished.

Every day, after everyone left for the evening, Dougie insisted on meeting with her to rehearse their lines as Dr. Frankenstein and Justine. There weren't many of them. Justine wasn't exactly a lead character, and really, her best moment was when a villager, thinking she had killed little Willie Frankenstein, grabs her and carts her off, to throw her to her death over a stone wall, where she would land on a nice soft port-a-pit beneath the trap door camouflaged by a piece of scenery. The best part was that Dr. Steele had agreed to play the role of the angry villager, so she got to be picked up by him over and over, struggling and screaming like a wild animal. And as director she got to say when she thought they'd nailed the scene. Just before perfection happened, she'd add something new to try, and they'd have to rehearse it, over and over.

It's good to be the king.

During their time together, she had to work at keeping Dougie on task. Unlike Derek, he seemed to have forgotten he was mad at Pandora, and used their rehearsal more as an opportunity to discuss Nietzsche and Machiavelli while plying her with ice cold Cokes than to practice. Or he'd speculate about what they would do together when the play was over—go on a real date, play one-on-one basketball, visit a museum devoted to medical freaks, run an experiment on the inmates together. He didn't bring up tucking her in anymore—big relief—but he also refused to discuss what he'd said about finding a god, and she finally decided he'd said it simply to needle her.

Once a week, he would ask for updates on Vicki, whether she was still looking for a job or not. Pandora tried asking him about Ronny and Lonny, what they were up to, but he'd only shrug. "The fewer people who know, the better." If he'd wanted to drive her around the bend, he couldn't have picked a better way. She told him that, and he only blinked slowly at her before saying, "You're stronger than that, Pandora." It was infuriating, and she despised how he was constantly testing her.

But playing Justine, when she could pretend to be someone else and not have to be in charge of anything, made up for Dougie's annoyances. It occurred to her that this must be how Vicki felt all the time—always having to be in charge, without ever getting a break from it—and she quickly pushed the realization away. Feeling sorry for her mother wasn't going to help anyone. Still, persistent little demon that it was, the thought popped up quite often, typically when things were going bad on the set. Spilled paint, tantrums, missed lines, blown fuses, all were par for the course, and happened way too often not to be some sort of lesson. She longed to escape the constant stress and chaos, if only for a few brief shining moments, and playing Justine helped. So she put up with Dougie's possessive behavior, deflected his questions about their future together, and generally kept her mouth shut. Two could play at the old gaslighting game.

Thankfully, Vicki had returned to her old work habits, and Pandora was immensely grateful. For the moment it looked as though nothing was going to change. Her mother had merely been in mourning, and maybe wanted to put the fear of God in Pandora, too (if that was even possible), to get her to straighten out and forget about what had put her in the hospital. Vicki's pretending to want to leave had worked its intended magic; Pandora was keeping busy and staying out of trouble.

Vlad seemed to be doing his part to keep Vicki out of their hair, as well. On her way to the theater, Pandora often spotted him in Vicki's office, discussing something with her. Something quite important, judging by their serious expressions. Probably Pandora's earlier threat to purchase life insurance. Or the rising price of gasoline. Adults were painfully dull like that.

Her mother's stand-down, along with Pandora's heavy workload, led to a growing laxness in her vigilance. Granted, she'd seen the new patients a few times in the foyer, and one time she'd found King Tobias on the stairs leading up to their apartment. But he claimed to be looking for his crown because someone had stolen it. He seemed quite sincere. Pandora had watched him closely after that, but he made no effort to kidnap her, and she found herself relaxing once more. She was so busy she simply didn't have the energy to be on the alert all the time. When day after day passed and nothing happened, she slowly began to forget she was in danger. It was a relief to forget.

Sinclair, Charles, and Dougie spent a strangely large amount of time with each other, especially when Pandora was busy running lines with Lucy, Derek, and Birdy. She figured they were up to something, but every time she approached their little group, she heard only vague comments on costumes or altering stage directions, even what was for lunch. What they were up to, she couldn't ferret out. Dougie wasn't talking, and believe it, she'd tried, and so she finally let it go. As long as it didn't involve her demise, she couldn't be bothered.

Xavier and Dr. Steele spent hours together sawing wood, painting the background scenery, and laughing. Pandora envied them their job, and truth be told, their growing connection, which Xavier seemed intent on showing off whenever she was around. He was still mad at her, obviously, and this was his way of getting back at her. What a sadist. The worst of it was that she'd sometimes catch Bones with them, not just watching, but helping out, talking and laughing with them. Kind of flirting, actually. It was all rather disgusting.

Xavier and Dr. Steele's latest project involved building a platform that would raise Derek into the air during the resurrection scene. She wondered where the money had come from to fund all the necessary equipment for the complicated machine, but judging by Charles's self-satisfied expression whenever he saw it, and Dougie's proprietorial air over it, the cash had come from the Daft coffers. Above and beyond the five hundred bucks. Charles was turning out to be far savvier than she'd given him credit for.

The sets were turning out really great, too. There was a village scene, a room inside the castle, the laboratory, which was amazingly realistic, a prison room, and an outdoor set, with fake trees and the like. Sometimes, after everyone had left the theater, she would stand in front of one of the scenes and imagine she was really there, really part of the story. She savored those times, and wished she could simply stay where she was, in a sort of dreamland, with no pressure or responsibilities.

Once in a while she'd remember what Dougie had hinted about the professor, about how it was odd him being drunk so early in the day. At the time she hadn't caught on that he might be trying to tell her something. But maybe he hadn't been, and she was making something out of nothing. Her uncertainty bothered her, like a cavity that flared up on occasion, but not enough to do anything about. She simply didn't have the time. Nor did she have time to track down Dr. Steele and demand he tell her about Elizabeth. Like her, he was burning the candle at both ends, doing his day job, plus spending hours and hours at the theater, building, painting, and acting. He looked happy, though, so she figured she'd leave him be for now. The agreed upon month was almost up, and once the play was done, *BAM!*, she'd be all over him to spill the beans.

Word had finally gotten out amongst the inmates that some of the patients were doing a play, and a bunch of them wanted in on it. To appease them Vicki agreed, reluctantly, to let them watch a performance, which was to occur one week from now. Just the thought of it made Pandora's blood pressure soar. There was still so much to do, including printing up the programs, which she'd had to edit several times to appease everyone's egos in regards to title, order of presentation, and actor bios.

On top of all that, Lucy continually muffed her lines, and, Pandora was beginning to suspect, on purpose, to get attention. Charles had grown increasingly fidgety, Sinclair kept popping up in strange places, startling her, and Bones was being very secretive and proprietorial about the sound and lighting. Pandora wanted to do some practice runs with all the effects, but Bones kept putting her off, saying she still had more wiring to do and some last-minute touch-ups to make. *Come dress rehearsal, you'll be thrilled with my genius*, or so she'd written. Most of their communication was through notes, and she kept the door to the booth locked to avoid distractions (another note), so Pandora was never able to get her way. It was annoying, but she let it go.

Instead, she worked on keeping things together by the skin of her teeth, and sometimes by actual skin. While sanding a set piece, she'd taken off a layer on her knuckles and bled like a stuck pig. But show business isn't for the weak. And the bandages got her a bit of attention from everyone, which was like a caffeine jolt to her tired system, and it, along with real caffeine, kept her going.

And then they were down to two days.

And now, only one. Today was the dress rehearsal.

And Derek had gone missing.

The Part Where You're Naked

26

WELL, NOT MISSING, per se. More like Derek had yet to show up for dress rehearsal, which was due to begin in half an hour. Pandora had distinctly told him to come early so she could apply his make-up. She'd come super early herself to get ready. Her costume was a Victorian-era dress, which looked awesome, but was quite annoying in its amazingly adept ability to make even the simplest movement difficult. Birdy had opted for wearing a corset under her gown, and was struggling to get into it, with Lucy's help, at that very moment. Which would explain all the caterwauling going on in the dressing room.

"Where is he?" Pandora demanded for the fifth time as she stomped across the stage. She turned on Xavier, who was putting some last minute touches on one of the laboratory set pieces. "You're going to have to stand in for him."

He laughed. "Not happening."

"Can't act?"

"Not a lick," he admitted unashamedly. Damn him.

"Without the Creature, there is no play. You know that, right? I knew he was going to do this to me."

"Calm down. He'll be here."

"Don't tell me the monster let you down?" Dougie said quietly from behind her.

She spun around. "Don't you start." She scanned him up and down. She had to admit his Victorian outfit of a red waistcoat, dark jacket, and snowy white cravat was a good look for him—if only he could rid himself of that supercilious expression he so often wore. Though, admittedly, it made for a perfect mad scientist look. Mad scientists were all so arrogant, weren't they?

"You look amazing," he told her. "Like a femme fatale."

"I'm going to be a femme fatale if that boy doesn't show up soon!"

"He'll show," Xavier repeated as he painted. "Derek won't let you down."

"He has before," she mumbled.

"And he will again," Dougie felt inclined to point out.

"Don't you have some lines to practice?"

"I would never let you down, Pandora."

"That's because I have no expectations of you."

He didn't even wince. "You need to take a deep breath and relax. I'd hate to see you reverting to your earlier, erratic behavior."

"Oh, cram it up your—"

"Cram it up your what?" Lucy asked, tugging on Pandora's sleeve. Thankfully she was already in costume, a hodgepodge of colorful pieces she'd selected herself, ranging from a purple headscarf to an orange gypsy skirt and pink ballet flats. She was certainly a unique Igor.

Pandora pulled in a deep breath, just as Dougie had suggested she do, damn him and his good ideas. "You look great, Lucy."

She twirled around. "I know! I picked everything out. Dr. Steele says I have a good eye for color." He was right. Although Lucy was pretty much wearing every color of the rainbow, she had placed the pieces together in a complementary fashion, so that their differences brought out the best in each other. One might almost imagine it was her commentary on their motley and diverse cast and crew.

"You could be a designer," Pandora acknowledged, and a strange feeling of pleasure surged through her, like Lucy was her kid or something, and she was proud of her. This was getting weird.

"I could," Lucy declared. "I can be anything I want."

"Well, not *anything*."

"I can so, Pansy Butt!"

"Probably not a professional basketball player."

Lucy tilted her head to one side. "Maybe not that one. But everything else, definitely."

Pandora gave up. "Definitely."

"Where's Derek the Giant?" she demanded.

Pandora was about to answer when she heard a rush of footsteps behind her. "Right here," he panted.

Dougie lifted his eyes to the ceiling in disgust, yet another very human gesture. Was it possible he was becoming more like the rest of humankind? She snorted inwardly. Not in this lifetime.

She spun about to face Derek, who was breathing hard, as though he'd run all the way from town. "I knew you'd make it in time," she lied smoothly. "Now come on." It was Xavier's turn to roll his eyes, but he refrained from mentioning her crisis of faith.

"You're late, Choken," Dougie pointed out, his expression almost angry. No, not almost. He was definitely angry. Furious. Like he hadn't wanted Derek to show and was mad that he had. Which meant he'd rather be proven right than the show succeeding. Pandora felt inclined to electrocute the traitor, but unfortunately, nothing on the set could actually perform the task. The static electricity balls, paid for by Dougie's money, only looked like they could.

"I wonder why," Derek aimed his words at Dougie, then turned to Pandora. "Sorry. Something came up."

She peered into his eyes. "Is everything all right?" She leaned forward. "With your mom?"

He nodded, then looked over her head, very likely at Dougie, since his gray eyes, normally so calm, had narrowed to angry slits. "She's fine. We'd better hurry."

"We won't have to do the whole effect. Just your costume should be fine."

They headed toward a fitting room and Pandora waited outside for Derek to change. He'd brought in some old clothes for his costume, and she and Birdy and Lucy had enjoyed transforming the pieces into artfully torn rags. Birdy had wanted him to go without a shirt...*and* pants. Pandora had nixed that idea, but only because she knew Vicki wouldn't allow it.

"My mother would have allowed it," Birdy had argued.

"Your mother wore a hooker dress to church," Pandora had argued back.

"True. Man, I wish I'd been there to see that. The church ladies would have had a cow." Birdy shook her head. "All right, if we can't go pantless and shirtless, then let's take off as much material as we can get away with."

That had been the fun part. But based on how long it was taking Derek to come out, Pandora wondered if maybe they'd gone a little too far.

Finally the door opened and Derek poked his head out. "I look like an idiot."

"Let me be the judge of that." Pandora motioned him out. Behind her stood Lucy, watching avidly, and a second later Birdy's door swung open as though she'd been waiting for him to make an appearance. Her outfit, with its low-cut bodice and tons of lace, was way over-the-top, but it made an impact, and wasn't that what theater was all about? Too bad if it wasn't, because Birdy was not budging, nor was her cleavage.

Derek slowly emerged from the changing room, and for a few seconds, all was silent in the theater. Then Lucy whooped and clapped her hands excitedly, and Birdy started fanning herself. "Land's sake, that boy is hot enough to boil water!"

Pandora didn't know whether to continue staring or look away or what. The costume revealed more than it covered, and what it revealed was a lot of muscles. The boy was so ripped that his muscles had muscles. His eyes met hers. "This isn't going to work."

"You look great!" she said heartily, or tried to. Her voice came out sounding a little funny, but it wasn't every day you come face to face with an actual god. "Perfect. For the role, I mean. You make the perfect Creature."

"I could just cover you in frosting and eat you up!" Lucy cried, and that was probably the most accurate statement any of them could make at that point.

Derek's cheeks went pink, then he held out his hands imploringly. "Nothing fits right, Pandora. Everyone's going to laugh at me."

"I can guarantee you no one's going to be laughing, big guy," Birdy said, then licked her lips.

"Birdy's right," Pandora rushed in to say. "Nobody's going to laugh at you."

He shook his head. "It doesn't feel right."

"Not for you, but it's right for the Creature, and at this moment that is who you are."

"I don't think I can do this."

"But I took out the part where you're naked. You know, in the resurrection scene."

He gaped at her. "Naked?"

"Yeah," she said, recovering her aplomb. "So be grateful."

"Pandora, please don't make me do this," he begged.

"Yes, Pandora," Dougie interjected, then pursed his lips in spinsterish disapproval. "Don't make him do this. It's obscene."

Pandora clapped her hands. "Way to go, Dougie. You not only look like Mrs. Johnson right now, you sound like her."

"Maintaining a certain decorum is necessary, so that we can actually put on this play."

"Oh, please. By the time anyone sees Derek, nobody will want to stop anything. He'll be a sensation!"

Derek stepped forward. "I don't want to be a sensation, Pandora. I'm only doing this—" He stopped, looked down at his massive feet.

"You're only doing this for what?"

"Nothing. Let's just do the rehearsal."

Pandora frowned. Something was up. "What were you going to say, Derek?"

"He obviously doesn't have anything of importance to say," Dougie interjected, tapping his watch, "and we're running out of time."

She glanced back and forth between the two of them. Derek refused to meet her eye and Dougie met it with a cool gaze. But Dougie was right. They had to get moving. Dr. Steele was going to arrive in the middle of the play, do his thing, then leave again to attend a staff meeting. Timing was crucial.

"Fine," she sighed. "Let's do this."

Ψ

The dress rehearsal was a nightmare. As feared, Lucy muffed her lines. Birdy overacted and Dougie kept shooting eye darts at Derek and missing his cues, which was totally unlike him. Plus, he spoke too quietly. Derek was so self-conscious that she could barely hear him, and he kept crossing his arms tightly over his chest, which completely ruined the effect. Dr. Steele was late, and when he threw her over the wall she nearly landed on the floor because someone (Lucy) had knocked the port-a-pit out of place. Charles was a trembling, nervous wreck, and Sinclair looked about as pale as she'd ever seen him. As you might imagine, having to deal with all these troubles messed with Pandora's own performance. Her timing was off, and her voice sounded high-pitched and frantic even to her own ears.

It was awful.

From the wings, Xavier kept repeating the old adage, "bad dress rehearsal, good show," which didn't help her feel any better, nor did seeing his dubious expression whenever he said it. Each issue on its own was fixable, but as a whole, entirely insurmountable. They were screwed. The only thing that went well was the lighting and sound. For being such a brain-fried malfeasant, Bones had done a brilliant job. But she was the *only* success amidst a rancid stew of failures.

They were going to flop and everyone was going to laugh at her and Vicki would say 'I told you so' and they'd have to move just to escape the humiliation and Pandora really would go mad. It was too much.

After everyone, uncharacteristically quiet, changed out of their costumes, Derek practically sprinted out of the theater, as though the hounds of hell were chasing him, and Dougie and Xavier led the posse and Bones to go eat. When the theater was empty, Pandora plopped down in a chair in the front row. After making sure she was truly alone, she lowered her head to her hands and started to cry—big, messy, jagged sobs of pain. She just couldn't keep it in anymore.

As though mocking her, the sounds echoed back, and she knew that this was it. She couldn't go on. The Muses had won. Pandora Belfry had failed, and this time, she wasn't making a comeback.

27

Burn Me in Effigy

PANDORA WAS NOT a big crier. Lately she'd let loose once or twice, like when the professor died, but typically she wouldn't let herself travel down the dreaded road to Wimpville. But she had never before felt like such a failure. Sure she'd failed plenty of times, as did all the greats of the world, but she'd never given up or felt like quitting. She did now.

Though she had to admit the crying helped her feel better, even if it made her head ache and her eyes puffy. No one had seen her bawling her eyes out anyway, so she needn't feel so feeble for succumbing to the drip side. It was a small, small comfort.

She pushed her tired body up from her seat and dragged herself to a changing room. Several handfuls of cold water later, she wiped off her face with a few vigorous swipes of a hand towel that smelled like Birdy's perfume. After cleaning up her mess and hanging the towel to dry, she left the theater with slow, plodding steps.

As she left the theater and entered the corridor, she nearly had a heart attack. Up ahead two shadowy figures stood very still and very close to one another. One was definitely Tobias—she could tell from the outline of his paper crown—but she didn't know who the other person was.

What were they doing in *this* hallway? Where were the psych assistants in charge of looking after them? Pandora pulled in a deep breath and marched toward them.

"Hey!" she called. "What are you two doing here?"

They jumped apart, guiltily. "I am the king," Tobias announced grandly, recovering his composure. "I'm allowed to go wherever I please."

She marched past the two figures and motioned them to follow her. "Come on out of there. It's, um, not a safe place for members of the royal family," she adlibbed.

The two lurkers stepped out into the foyer, blinking in the bright light, and she realized the other person was the new patient, Gloria.

"But I am the king!" Tobias repeated insistently. "I can do anything!"

"Of course you can, King Tobias." She lowered her voice. "But as I said, this is not a safe place for a king. There are spies." She pointed down the corridor. "Just waiting to get you."

His eyes narrowed as he considered this. "I see. Have you met my queen?" He gestured to Gloria.

Pandora shook her head. "I've not had the pleasure, your majesty."

"Queen Gloria, this is one of my advisors, Miss, um... Oh, dear. I'm not good with names, especially those of my underlings."

Taking no offense, she nodded at Gloria. "Your majesty."

Gloria returned the nod, quite majestically, and with a mischievous sparkle in her brown, somewhat hazy looking, eyes.

"There you are!" an irritated voice filled the foyer with the force of its amplitude, and the Hessian came bustling out from the cafeteria hall. "I thought I told you two to stay put!"

"I was showing the queen around," King Tobias explained to the Hessian, looking not at all flustered or apologetic. He made an excellent king. Too bad he couldn't be in the play. He'd probably do quite well in any of the roles.

The Hessian shook her blunt finger at them. An orange stain marred her white uniform, and her face was red from her exertions. "And I told you to stay in the cafeteria while I cleaned up the mess you made." King Tobias and Queen Gloria exchanged a crafty look, as though maybe they'd planned the little contretemps as a distraction.

"Ah, yes," he acknowledged. "So you did. I quite forgot."

The Hessian glared at Pandora. "Count on you to be around when there's trouble."

"I'm not the one who left them unattended."

"I was just fine until one of your lot started throwing things. They're out of control, you know, and they make everyone's job harder. But you wouldn't understand what it's like to have to work for a living, being the Director's daughter and all, would you? Must be nice not to have any real responsibilities."

Pandora knew she shouldn't take the bait, but she was in a weak state, and she couldn't stop herself. "I have real responsibilities!"

"Is that so? And what might those be? Causing trouble? Sneaking into town? Stirring up the patients with your dumb ideas?"

"I keep the posse in line, Hessian, and you know it. Without me they'd be a lot worse, and so would your job. And anyway, I can't work for a living because I'm still a kid."

The sneer on the Hessian's face ratcheted up another notch. "You've got no idea how good you got it, Belfry. Your own bedroom, plenty to eat, a horse to ride whenever you please. So stop trying to make it look like you got it bad." She turned to Tobias and Gloria, who were trying to sneak away. "Not happening." She snapped her fingers at them.

"Back to the cafeteria you go."

The two rebels turned right and headed toward the cafeteria, but they made it look as though they had decided to change course entirely of their own inclination. No way were they doing it because someone told them to. Pandora had to admire that. Though she still wondered why they'd picked this particular hallway to hide in. It seemed rather suspicious.

The Hessian turned back to Pandora. "Word's out that you and your mom are leaving. Good. Then maybe you'll see what real life is like. Maybe you'll see how lucky you were."

"Who told you we're leaving?" Pandora demanded, despite herself, once again.

The Hessian smiled, pleased she'd hit her target, and Pandora cursed her impulsive mouth and weakened disposition. "It was in *The Bedlam Bulletin.* Trudy Goodly wrote that she heard your mom was looking for a new job. And this week, word's out that a job opening was in the want ads." The Hessian chuckled. "I'd say it was nice knowing you, but that'd be a lie, and unlike some people in this place, I ain't no liar."

With that bombshell, the girl turned on her ugly wedge nurse shoes and stomped off to the cafeteria.

"You just admitted you *are* a liar!" Pandora yelled after her, but the Hessian, having no concept that a double negative turns a statement into a positive, only shrugged as she disappeared down the hall. "She's lying," Pandora muttered to herself. "She has to be."

She took the stairs to their apartment two at a time. Once inside, she searched for the newspapers Vicki typically left on the coffee table, but there were none to be seen. Not the *Akmore Express News, The Bedlam Bulletin,* or even the library newsletter. She plopped down on the couch. It was true. If it weren't, why would Vicki go to the trouble of hiding all the papers? She obviously didn't want Pandora to know what she was up to, so she could sabotage her mother's efforts. Because she would sabotage her efforts.

So her nightmare had become reality. They were going to leave Nepenthe Manor. What was she going to do? About that, about the play? If they were going to move, she should cancel the play now. It would be a good excuse. Sorry, can't direct, have to pack. That way nobody would get to see how much they all sucked.

She stood up. Time to bite the bullet and admit defeat. She'd tell Vicki that the play was off, and demand to know when moving day was taking place.

She marched back down the stairs to Vicki's office, determined to play it cool, determined to not be affected by this news, news her mother hadn't even bothered to share with her. She was the stone-faced girl, free of emotion, hard as a rock, untouchable.

She grasped the doorknob and realized her hand was shaking. *So much for being the untouchable rock.* But as she twisted the knob, she realized it was locked. Vicki's light was on, but after peering through the glass side panels, Pandora realized her mother wasn't there. At least not at her desk. Maybe she was back in Bennington's office, making copies. Bennington's mother was doing a bit better lately, but Bennington still hadn't been able to come in as often. So maybe Vicki was doing her job for her. Maybe this is why she'd returned to working, because no one else was doing anything.

Pandora knocked on the door. Then again, louder. No one was home. Fine. She'd let herself in and wait, and maybe use the time to search for the missing newspapers. Perhaps they were in the secret hi-dey-hole in Vicki's desk.

After using her key, Pandora slid inside and hurried straight for the desk, the ever-present scent of coffee greeting her. Who knew when Vicki would be back? She was probably out getting food, or using the bathroom, and would return soon. Pandora leaned down to open a drawer when she heard the doorknob click. She scurried out from behind the desk, banging her hip on the corner of it. The door opened and Pandora hurriedly leaned against the front of the desk, an innocent smile on her face and her eyes wide with anticipation.

But it wasn't Vicki.

"Dr. Steele?" This man was everywhere. "What are you doing here?"

He stepped inside, then closed the door behind him. "I'm sure I could ask the same of you. But why bother? I doubt I'll hear the real reason."

"Very funny. I came to ransack Vicki's desk. You?"

"I'm not sure if I should laugh at that or accept it as the truth."

"Just accept it. So what can I do for you, doc?" Now that she'd made up her mind about the play, she felt almost reckless, like she had nothing to lose. It occurred to her that maybe that wasn't a good place to be in. But what the hell.

The doctor studied her for a moment, maybe picking up on her puffy eyes, her new c'est la vie attitude. "Nothing, actually. I had a few things I wanted to discuss with the Director. Do you know when your mother will be back?"

"You do know she doesn't keep me informed as to her whereabouts, right?"

"But she left the office unlocked?"

"That is open for debate."

"I'm going to pretend I didn't hear that." He paused, looked her over. "You've been crying."

"I have not! It was...an allergy attack. All that dust in the theater. Probably got stirred up during rehearsal."

"I see. And it has nothing to do with how awful things went."

Her shoulders dropped. "You thought it was awful, too?"

"That's how dress rehearsals go. It means our first night will be great."

"You don't look like you believe a word you're saying."

He gave her a half smile. "I'm trying to be positive."

"Well, you're failing." She pushed away from the desk. "I'm canceling the performance."

"What?" She was surprised at how he sounded...as though he were upset. "You can't do that, Pandora," he told her, his voice quite firm.

"I'm the director, so I can do what I want," she replied, just as firmly. "Besides, you saw what happened today. Actually you didn't even see most of it. It was a nightmare, Dr. Steele. There were so many problems I don't even know where to begin to fix them all."

"You've already crossed the proverbial Rubicon, Pandora. You can't go back on this one."

"Watch me." Seeing his disapproving expression she threw up her hands. "It's one performance, Dr. Steele! No one will even care."

"A lot of people will care. Your friends, the patients who've been talking about nothing else since they heard about the play, and me. I happen to care a lot about this."

"Enough to finally tell me about Elizabeth?"

A muscle in his cheek twitched. "Are you trying to blackmail me?"

"Don't pretend you're surprised, and actually, no, I'm not. Because we're not doing the play. Trust me, doc. You'll thank me on this one."

"So you're giving up? I've never taken you for a quitter, Pandora."

"I'm not a quitter," she bristled. "I'm a realist."

"You're quitting because you're afraid of failure."

"So what if I am? That doesn't make me a bad person. I've had enough failures in life as it is. I don't want another one. Not this big. Not with so many *witnesses*."

He sighed, rubbed a hand over his face. "All right. I wasn't going to tell you this, because it was supposed to be a surprise, but I think you need to know..."

When he didn't say anything for a moment, she prodded, "Tell me what?"

"Your friends came up with a plan, and I decided to go along with it." He shifted uneasily. "At the time it seemed like a great idea. A solution to a lot of problems."

"I'm not going to like this, am I?"

"Well, not right at this moment. But actually, it was your idea."

"My idea? Nice. So I'll get the blame?"

He shook his head. "I'll take the blame."

"And get fired? No way. Cause guess who'll get blamed for that? People around here love you, and if you get fired over the play, I'll be the scapegoat. They'll burn me in effigy." She paused, briefly imagining the scene. "No, they'll burn me for real."

He eyed her. "Can I just tell you what it is?"

She sighed. "Might as well. Better to know what's coming then get rammed from behind."

"We're going to put on the play for the whole town. The day after tomorrow, actually. So Thursday's performance will be for the patients, and Friday's is for the town."

She literally felt all the blood leave her head, and leaned hard against the desk to steady herself. "Oh, crap."

"Yes, well, it should be interesting."

"If I thought it was bad before—" She stopped herself from saying any more.

"Go on."

"Oh, nothing." She gave a shrug, though she felt sick inside. Sicker than she'd ever felt. She was doomed.

"It's not nothing, Pandora. What were you going to say?"

"Does Vicki know?" she asked, accelerating away from his inquiry like the Roadrunner.

"She does."

Pandora gaped at him. "How did you get her to agree?"

"I didn't."

"Then who did?" She paused, then answered her own question. "Dougie. He made some sort of deal with her, didn't he?"

"I have no idea what he did, but the word miracle comes to mind."

"I'd say that with Dougie witchcraft is the more appropriate term."

"So you're in?" he asked, the hopeless fool.

She crossed her arms. "No way."

"But we're sold out."

"*Sold out?*"

He smiled. "Your Ms. Netterson has been a real warrior. She advertised the play, put up posters, and pretty much didn't take no for an answer. She sold every last ticket. That woman could sell ice to an Eskimo."

"But people paid money? *Real* money?" Her mouth was dry, her heart a hammer in her chest. "And *every* seat is going to be filled?"

He was watching her closely. "That's generally how being sold out works. Nettie said it actually didn't take all that much convincing. People wanted to come."

"I'm sure they did." Pandora's head started to pound and she pressed her hands to her temples, trying to make the pain go away. "So not only am I going to fail in front of all the patients and staff at Nepenthe Manor, I'm going to fail in front of the entire town of Bedlam?"

"You're not the only person putting yourself out there, Pandora," he said dryly. "We're all taking a risk."

"But I'm the only person who'll be blamed! Don't you see?" She bit back a sob. "The staff here, they're always looking for ways to bring me down. This will be like handing them grenades to throw at me!" Her chest rose up and down like bellows and she blinked furiously to hold back the tears threatening to erupt. "And there are these kids in town, the ones we played basketball against. They've called me Bats Belfry since I was a kid, and they hate me, and when this play fails, cause it will, they'll have their revenge on me. For beating them at basketball, for standing up to them. I'll never be able to move beyond it. Never." She held out her hands to him. "They'll have won, don't you see, Dr. Steele? All those years of fighting back against them and their nasty ways, of fighting the staff to show them I'm not just another head case they can treat like crap. All for nothing!" She slammed her hand on the desk, causing a pile of papers to fall.

When she saw the newspapers spilled across the floor, she leaned down to pick one up. It was *The Bedlam Bulletin*, and the headline was: *New Position Opens Up at Asylum*.

That's when she fainted.

28

"SHE ONLY FAINTED, Director." Pandora came around to Dr. Steele's voice. She was lying on something long and soft and lumpy—their apartment couch. He seemed to be sitting right next to her; she could feel his leg pressing into her side. But she kept her eyes closed, sensing she was about to hear things. Important things. "She was a little upset at how the dress rehearsal went, and when I told her the whole town is going to be watching the play, well, she went down like a rock. I think she needs food. I wager she didn't eat all day." Dr. Steele was right—she hadn't. Maybe that's why her head hurt so much. "Do you have anything to give her?"

There was an annoyed sigh. "Probably not. I need to go shopping again. That girl eats like a horse." Another sigh. "I knew this idea was going to cause trouble. But the money will be nice, and Vlad did say the theater is in good shape. I'd swear the previous director told me it was dangerous in there. I wonder what the problem was." A few seconds of silence passed. "So now she's freaking out about the fallout from getting her way, huh?" Vicki had the nerve to chuckle. "I guess this is a case of be careful what you wish for." That's twice the sadist had said that. Not that Pandora was counting.

"I think Pandora was only trying to do the right thing."

Vicki's laugh had an edge to it. "Pandora was only trying to do the Pandora thing."

"I'm going to have to disagree with you on that one." Dr. Steele's voice was firm, almost heroic.

"You're saying she's doing this for others?" There was amusement in Vicki's voice, and Pandora felt like someone was sticking needles in her eyes.

"I am, and she's scared of failing because she thinks everyone is going to come after her."

"Oh, please. She's being paranoid."

"I don't think she is."

"Trust me. I know my child. She loves the attention."

"If that's true, then I wonder why? I mean, what makes her go to such extremes to get that attention?"

"Nice try, *doctor*," Vicki replied in a tight voice. "But you're not pinning this one on me. I have a job. It puts food on the table. I've pretty much been a single mom for fourteen years, and I do the best I can. Pandora has a nice life here. I get that she might be a little bored at times, but all kids get bored. Boredom is better than what's out there. I've done everything I can to protect her—limiting her exposure to the patients and to the townspeople—who can be real shits, you know— but she defies me at every turn and in doing so, she pays the price."

"I think she's just really lonely."

Pandora felt herself tear up and had to bite her tongue.

"Maybe. But I'm keeping her safe. It's for her own good."

"Well, I hope you're right." No response. "Say, maybe you could go get something for her to eat? I'll try to see if I can bring her around."

"Should I fetch the nurse?"

"If I can't get Pandora to wake up, I'll go get Nurse Devine myself."

"All right. I'll see what I can do. I do try to keep up with things around here, but I'm not very good at it. Obviously." Vicki admitting weakness? That seemed scarier than anything she'd done so far.

The sound of the door shutting came first followed by another stretch of silence. Pandora couldn't help it, she opened an eye...to see Dr. Steele looking down at her. "Nice nap?"

"Very refreshing."

"I'll tell you what...I feel a bit guilty about springing the news on you like that. So I'm going to make it up to you."

She widened her eyes, but said nothing. If he wanted to believe he was the culpable one, let him. But it had been that headline, glaring and irrefutable, that had done her in. Vicki had found a new job. Why else would there be an opening?

"Up for a story?"

"I guess so," she said in a weak voice, but on the inside a frisson of excitement jolted her wide awake. She knew what was coming.

"It's about my Elizabeth." He paused, seemed to gather himself, though his face was pale and he was blinking too fast. "You're sure you're ready to hear my story?"

"I was born ready, doc. Are you sure you're ready to tell it?" She asked the question reluctantly. She didn't want him backing out, but he didn't look too good.

"I think so." He pulled in a deep breath. "All right. The thing is, well... here's the weird part I started to tell you about. My Elizabeth actually lived here at Nepenthe Manor."

"Wait. You mean, Elizabeth Nepenthe was your Elizabeth?" That didn't seem right.

He shook his head. "Wrong Elizabeth. My Elizabeth was Elizabeth Hanigan, and she stayed here at the asylum."

"You mean, her family lived here. Like Vicki and I do."

"No." He shook his head ruefully. "Elizabeth was a patient here. I believe she was possibly manic-depressive, maybe schizophrenic. Maybe both. The first time I came to see her here was the first time we met. I was nine, and she was fourteen. Before that, I didn't even know about her. My mother kept it from me in case she couldn't find her, and I think she felt ashamed, too. It was only later that I learned a lot of what I'm about to tell you."

"Let me get this clear…your sister was a patient *here*?" Pandora was having a hard time wrapping her head around this.

He smiled. "Yes, she was. But I didn't see her as a patient, or even sick. We had an instant connection, and in a short time we became very close. She was fun and interesting, always coming up with ways to beat the establishment, or simply a fun game for us to play. She didn't treat me like a little brother; she treated me like a friend. For three years, I visited her almost every weekend and some weekdays, and she actually seemed to be getting better during that time. We even talked about what we would do when she got out, cause of course she'd get out. She wasn't truly sick! She was as normal as you and me. That's what we told ourselves, anyway. We had ideas, big, grandiose schemes that would probably never happen, but they were a lot of fun to think about."

He stopped, stared down at his hands, gripping each other tightly. "But then something happened."

"What happened?" Pandora breathed when the silence dragged on far too long. She could be hugely patient when need be, but this was too much.

"First a little back story." Pandora suppressed a frustrated sigh. "I know, but it's necessary." She made a circling motion for him to continue. "My mother once dated an American named Henry Hanigan, who'd come to Ireland claiming to be looking into his ancestry. The real reason he'd come was to escape some sort of scandal he was involved in at college, but of course he didn't tell my mother that. He could be very charming, and things grew serious between them. In a short time my mother got pregnant. Not surprisingly, Henry didn't want anything to do with a baby, and he took off back to America. He was a rich, spoiled only child, and had no interest in getting married or being a father. But my mother had his address, and wrote to him there, begging him to come back. He never returned to his home, so his parents read the letter. They were older, and knowing their son's ways—

that he might never settle down and have a family—they decided they wanted the child. My mother said no, so they threatened her, said they knew powerful people in Ireland and they'd have her put into an institution if she didn't comply. They were lying, but she was young, without a job or an education, and no family support. She didn't know what to do. As far as her family was concerned, she'd made her bed. So, hoping this was for the best, she gave up her child to Henry's parents, who'd flown over with a team of lawyers, and she never heard from them again. She tried to contact them, but they didn't answer her letters. Fast forward to a few years later, she met another man, my father. He was an American, too, so as you can imagine it took a lot of time and effort to get her to trust him. Eventually she did, and they dated, then they got married and had me."

"Were they happy together?" Pandora dared to ask, surreptitiously crossing her fingers. She wasn't expecting much, but for some reason she wanted them to be happy.

Dr. Steele nodded. "For the short time they were together, they were very happy. My father was a good man, and he loved us both very much. But he died in a car accident when I was six. When my father died my parents had already been planning on moving to America to be close to his family. My mother needed to find work, which was limited in Ireland, so she went ahead with the plan. She wanted a better life for me, and she wanted to track down Elizabeth."

He rubbed his face tiredly. "It took three years and an article in the paper to find her. Elizabeth had tried to kill herself by jumping off the same bridge you did, Pandora. That sort of thing makes the paper, rich family or not."

A shiver, as though someone were walking over her grave, shook Pandora. "You have to be joking." She said it like a wish, not a challenge.

"I wish I were. That bridge has been used before for that very reason, but it's not the best way to go if you really want to die because it isn't very high. I know all about it, because I grew up near here. My mother knew where Elizabeth's father had gone to college, Akmore University, so she moved us to Akmore, figuring he hadn't gone far away from where he grew up. Unfortunately, after some questioning, my mother learned that he'd never returned home. Even worse, during those three years my mother never heard about or found an Elizabeth Hanigan. I'm pretty sure that's because her grandparents kept her hidden, hiring tutors to teach her, keeping her out of the public eye. They were paranoid that my mother would come back and take her."

His expression darkened. "This was their idea of protecting her, but they only succeeded in passing along their warped version of the world. My sister was a mess inside, and it was their fault. She thought it was hers, though, and I'd spend hours trying to convince her it wasn't. My mother tried, too, but Elizabeth didn't want anything to do with her. Her grandparents, you see, had told Elizabeth that her mother had abandoned her. And since my mother felt that this was the truth, she didn't have the strength or confidence to convince Elizabeth otherwise."

He straightened up. "But Elizabeth would see me, which helped my mother feel a little better. I wish you'd met my sister, Pandora. You two are very much alike, though you don't have long-term mental illness. I'd say what you went through was situational depression, which many people go through, and comes about from going through a difficult experience, and not clinical depression, which is more severe and comes and goes throughout your entire life."

Are you sure about that? Pandora wanted desperately to ask. *Because I'm not.* "You said something happened?"

"After three years of going undiscovered—which shows you how little anyone visited Elizabeth—her grandparents finally learned that I existed. Elizabeth told them, actually. She was in a manic phase, and it all spilled out. She told them everything, even though she promised she wouldn't ever tell anyone about us. I didn't blame her... Well, I don't now. I probably did back then. I was only twelve. But I do blame her grandparents. They bribed the Director, and he told me I could no longer visit my sister. A year later she killed herself. She was only eighteen. *Eighteen!* There was a scandal, and the Director quit not long after that. I didn't know it, but later I found out that your mother took over the job. Actually, she must have been pregnant with you at the time."

Pandora wrapped her arms around herself as she did the math. "So at the time I...well, you know, came into being..." Why couldn't she just say the word 'conceived' like a normal person? "Well, was that around when Elizabeth died?"

He lifted an eyebrow. "I would say it was pretty close."

"Huh." Was it just her, or was this a weird coincidence? Elizabeth dies and Pandora Belfry appears on the scene. How crazy is that?

"So now you understand why I can't support the idea of keeping patients in this place when they shouldn't be here."

Pandora blinked at him, then realized what he was saying. "But if your sister was schizophrenic or manic-depressive, and she couldn't go back to her grandparents or her dad or mom, where would she go?"

"She was eighteen when she died. An adult. She could live on her own, and I would stay with her and help her." His expression was stubborn.

"You were only thirteen when she died, Dr. Steele. How were you going to keep her alive? Pay the bills? Deal with her meds?"

"I would've done it. You and I aren't all that different, Pandora. When we're determined to do something, we make sure it gets done."

She took a brief moment to preen at the compliment. "But I don't treat the patients here. I don't give them medication or monitor their medical issues or talk to them the way the therapists do." She couldn't believe she was saying these words, pretty much the opposite of what she'd been espousing for years—that the staff here was useless. But while a good number of them were inept, some were not, and those few kept a lot of the patients alive.

"You feel guilty, don't you?" she surmised. "That your sister died and you lived, and got to go on with your life." She girded herself to say this next part—the ugly truth. "You had a whole year to do something before she died, and you did nothing, am I right?"

Dr. Steele's face went pale and his hands curled into fists. "I did try, Pandora," he ground out through clenched teeth. "I did! But nobody would listen to me...a kid. I had no power, no say, and soon the guards wouldn't even let me past the gate. I did try to save her!"

"Of course you did," she said calmly, even though she didn't feel calm in the least. This was big, and she was going to say things that couldn't be unsaid. Dr. Steele might end up hating her, but it had to be done. "But as you know, perception is stronger than reality. You believe you didn't try hard enough, that you're the reason your sister died, and you've been beating yourself up over it ever since."

His eyes darted around the room. "It's why I became a psychologist. So I could make sure what happened to Elizabeth wouldn't happen again."

"So after you got your degree," she deduced, "you returned to the scene of the crime, hoping to re-enact an incident that happened years ago, but this time around you would change the ending."

His eyes met hers. "Perhaps."

"But you can't change the ending, Dr. Steele."

"Not for Elizabeth," he admitted, sounding defeated.

"She's dead and gone."

"But maybe I can change the ending for someone else," he added quietly.

Did he mean her? Much as she wanted to ask that question, she couldn't, because as much as she wanted it to be about her, it wasn't. So she asked another question. "Where did she...do it?"

He looked down at his hands. "Are you sure you want to know?" She nodded. "She did it in the theater. She hung herself from a light bar."

29

One Organ at a Time

"HOLY CRAP."

A reluctant laugh ejected from Dr. Steele. "Yes. Holy crap."

"Right over the stage? Really?"

"Elizabeth had a friend at the manor, and he told me what happened. He was the one who found her, actually."

"But you seem like you're so happy there. And I refuse to believe it's because of Xavier."

He laughed again, stronger this time. "I like Xavier, he's a good kid. But the big reason I enjoy the theater so much is that Elizabeth and I would sneak away and hang out there. I have very good memories of the place, and I feel like she's still there. It's comforting."

"But knowing she killed herself there…doesn't that creep you out?"

"Strangely, not one bit."

She had to respect that. "So how did her dad handle it when he heard about her death?"

Dr. Steele's face grew angry. "I don't know. He didn't go to the funeral. His parents died a year later and the house was sold. As far as I know, he hasn't been seen since he left my mother in Ireland. I've heard rumors that he changed his name. I've never been able to confirm anything, though."

"And your mom? She must have been a mess."

"Actually, after Elizabeth died, she was a rock. I went through a long, dark period, and I think she thought I'd inherited Elizabeth's mental illness. But thanks to her, I pulled through. Unfortunately, the better I got, the worse she did. Depression runs in the family, and she was able to fight it while looking after me. But after I recovered, she sunk into a deep one. She blamed herself worse than I did."

"She didn't off herself, too?" Pandora asked worriedly.

"No." His tone was dry, and maybe a little amused, too. "She didn't 'off herself.' She got better when I went to college and did well for myself. She's in Florida now, and owns a little business selling handmade Irish souvenirs. It keeps her busy. I think all that sun helps, too."

"Do you worry that your depression could come back?"

"I do, but only sometimes. I used to worry all the time about it, and that maybe I'd end up schizophrenic, too, but then I realized worrying wasn't very healthy, so I mostly let it go."

"How?"

"By telling myself that if I got depressed again, I'd deal with it then."

She stared at him. "You make it sound so easy."

"It wasn't. It isn't. But every day I don't think about it, the forgetting gets easier. Though I admit there are still bad days, when it's harder to let it go."

"Have you had a lot of bad days since coming here?"

"I've had some pretty rough days, but also some of my best." That was a compliment, wasn't it? But was it being paid to her? Wouldn't that be something?

Not that this was about her.

"Do you think the previous director told Vicki the theater wasn't safe because it was the place where Elizabeth died? Because he didn't want anyone snooping around?"

"I wouldn't rule it out. No one ever noticed her missing when I went to visit her. She was suicidal, and yet no one kept tabs on her. Elizabeth left a note, which was luckily found by that friend of hers I told you about. He memorized it, and wrote it down for me."

"What did it say?" she asked, but in a quiet voice so as to not seem too unfeeling.

"She addressed it to me, and wrote that she was sorry she had to do this. Being so isolated had been too hard for her. She missed me, but she didn't blame me. She claimed her dad, who I'm pretty sure never once visited her, and her grandparents were the ones who killed her by cutting off all contact with her. I believe her grandparents stopped visiting altogether after finding out about me—they were punishing her, I expect. Teaching her a lesson. So basically that last year she was all alone. I still have nightmares about that."

A few pieces clicked. "That's why you let Skippy go...and me, too."

He looked away. "Do you ever make a choice to do something, and at the time think it's for the best, then afterwards wonder why you did what you did?"

"Never."

"Pandora."

She smirked. "Okay, fine. Yeah, I guess so. And sometimes I don't know why I chose to do something, or...well, sometimes I don't remember why I did."

"So when someone says, 'well, you made a choice,' is it actually a choice? Because you're making it based on limited knowledge."

"Exactly," she replied, feeling relieved. "Like choosing to eat six donuts in one sitting. Only afterwards, when you feel sicker than a dog, do you realize how stupid that was."

He arched an eyebrow. "Personal experience?"

"I'm not at liberty to say."

"Nice dodge."

She shrugged. "It's what I do."

He smiled. It was good to see him smile. He seemed so much younger and lighter and happier. And she liked seeing him this way. When he looked so serious, as he had when telling his story, it was like something inside him was eating him up, one organ at a time.

"I have a picture of her. Do you want to see it?"

"Um, sure," she replied as nonchalantly as she could, because she really, really did.

He reached into his inside coat pocket and retrieved a small book. Opening it, he pulled out a photograph. Pandora looked up at him, then took the picture from him, carefully and reverently, as though she were handling an ancient book. She looked the photo over. Elizabeth was very pretty, dark hair pulled back into a ponytail, with piercing blue eyes, just like Dr. Steele. But there was something else about her. Something familiar. Pandora couldn't place what it was, though it was probably some other resemblance to Dr. Steele. She turned the photograph over to find a poem.

"Read it," Dr. Steele prompted. "It was her favorite."

"*They Are Not Long* by Ernest Dowson." She looked up at him. "The next bit's in Latin."

"I'll read it for you. '*Vitae summa brevis spem nos vetat incohare longam.*' It means that the brevity of life stops us from having long hopes. Not false hope, but long hopes," he clarified when she opened her mouth. "Two different things. Now you read the rest."

She frowned, then looked down at the poem, quickly reading it through. It was good. She took a deep breath and began to read out loud in her best theater voice:

They are not long, the weeping and the laughter,
Love and desire and hate;
I think they have no portion in us after
We pass the gate.

They are not long, the days of wine and roses,
Out of a misty dream
Our path emerges for a while, then closes
Within a dream.

Pandora read it again, then again, and each time had to struggle to keep herself from crying. It was just so perfect.

"Elizabeth liked the part about the gate, since Nepenthe Manor has a gate. She liked the connection."

"I like that, too."

"I only wish she could've understood the whole meaning of the poem. Life is short. Don't hang onto old grudges, and make the most of the good times."

"Maybe she couldn't let go of old grudges. It's very hard, you know."

"Maybe. We have that in common, I suppose."

"We could learn from her, you know."

Dr. Steele's eyes fastened on hers. "Do you think so?"

She shrugged, not committing. "A person could certainly try."

"Fair enough."

Pandora pulled in a long breath. This was getting awfully deep. "I wonder where Vicki is. I'm starving."

"Me, too, actually."

Like an answer to a prayer, there was a bang on the door. Dr. Steele stood and hurried toward it. He flung it open and Vicki staggered in, carrying three boxes of pizza, a big bottle of Coke, and what looked suspiciously like a bag from Mrs. Hathaway's bakery.

She dropped everything onto the table. "I couldn't handle the cafeteria food, so I went out and got us something edible."

Pandora sprang up and raced toward the table. "You bought food?"

"Yeah, well, someone had to."

"Why don't you get plates, and I'll get the glasses?" Dr. Steele suggested, right before Pandora had a chance to interrogate Vicki about her motives. Because this was extremely suspicious behavior, and could only mean Vicki was going to deliver bad news or try to get Pandora to do something she didn't want to do.

Clamping her mouth shut, she did as she was told, showing him where the glasses were. She pulled out silverware and napkins, too, because they weren't animals, and set the table as best she could with all the food piled on it. Vicki was sitting at the table already, opening the boxes to reveal a glorious array of choices—cheese, pepperoni, and tomato and mushroom. Warm dough, tomato sauce, and Italian spices filled the air. It smelled heavenly.

Pandora decided now was not the time to look a gift pizza in the mouth, so she pulled out a chair, grabbed a slice, and began to eat like there was no tomorrow. The three of them dined in silence, until at last their hunger was sated.

"I am so full," Vicki announced, wiping her mouth with a napkin.

"I can't believe we ate all three boxes," Pandora groaned, holding her stomach.

"Me, either," Dr. Steele agreed, falling back in his chair.

"But we still have donuts!" Vicki held up the bag.

Everyone perked up, ready to take on dessert. Pandora passed around the Coke bottle, finishing it off, then grabbed a glazed donut. "This is the life," she sighed after a few bites.

"You look like you're feeling better," Vicki noted.

"I am. Too bad they are not long, the days of pizza and donuts."

Dr. Steele chuckled. "Though I have a feeling a portion of them will still be with us after we leave the table."

Vicki looked back and forth between them. "Did I miss something?"

"It's from a poem."

"Ah. So Pandy…" Brief pause. "You know about the play now?"

Pandora felt all the pleasure of the meal fly away, and she pushed away her plate. "Thanks for reminding me."

"Sorry. I'm getting quite good at being the 'ghost at the feast' these days, aren't I?" It was an apt quote, but Pandora couldn't tell if Vicki was legitimately sorry for ruining their meal by bringing up the play, or she was being sarcastic.

"Pandora feels like there's a lot of pressure on her," Dr. Steele explained.

"Unlike the rest of us?" Vicki stated calmly, though her grip on her glass was turning her fingers white. "This was your idea, anyway, wasn't it?"

I only wanted to do something that would make things better, Vicki! I thought a play would help all of us. It kept me inside so that I could heal and not get kidnapped, it gave the posse something special to do, and it gave the inmates something to look forward to. While it's been really hard, I feel like I learned a lot from the process. But I don't want to undo all that by exposing us, me, to humiliation. I don't want to be a bigger target than I already am. I just wanted to do something good, and leave it at that.

That's what she wanted to say. Instead she resorted to being snarky. "You can always get a new job. I can't get a new life."

"What's that supposed to mean? Are you trying to manipulate me by threatening to harm yourself?"

"What? No!" *I am not Birdy!* "I only meant I can't undo the damage this is going to do to me." That's all she meant. Of course, that's all she meant. Right?

"I'm sure your ego is strong enough to handle a few criticisms."

"You overestimate my strength, Vicki."

Her mother looked at her, long and hard. "All I know is that you're stronger than I've ever been." She shoved back her chair. "Now if you two could clean up, I have something I have to attend to."

She was out the door before Pandora could say another word. Dr. Steele stood up and began to clear the table.

"Did she just give me a compliment? I mean, there wasn't an underlying insult in there that I missed, right?"

Dr. Steele started the water running. "I think she truly meant it as a compliment."

"Is she dying?"

"I don't think so."

"Then what is she up to?"

"I don't believe she's up to anything. But you know what's sad?"

"What?" Pandora asked, immediately suspicious.

"That your mother gives you a compliment and you act like this is a huge anomaly, and then wonder what's the catch."

Pandora bristled. "I'm not being dramatic, Dr. Steele, if that's what you're implying."

"That's not what I'm implying. What I'm trying to say is that it shouldn't be that way."

"Oh." She dumped the plates into the sink full of soapy water. "Well, I agree."

"So what do you want to do about the play?"

She sighed. "I don't win no matter what I decide, do I? If I cancel it, I'm the bad guy. If the show goes on, and fails, I'm the bad guy."

"And if it succeeds?"

She gave him a look. "Having delusions again?"

"I think we're all going to be great."

"They have medications for that," she persisted.

He glanced sideways at her. "I mean it, Pandora. And besides, I'd like to do this for Elizabeth. As a sort of memorial to her."

Pandora bit her lip. How could she say no to that? "Oh, great. Use emotional blackmail." She grabbed the washcloth and began to scrub a plate. "All right. I'll do it. The show must go on, mustn't it?"

"Thank you, Pandora."

"Thank Elizabeth. No way am I getting on the bad side of a ghost." She set the plate in the drying rack. "Oh, crap! We don't even have programs. I should probably whip something up tonight, then I'll have to print them out. Seating capacity is five hundred!" She sighed wearily. "This is going to take forever."

"Charles and I took care of all that."

She nearly dropped a plate. "You did?"

"He did the artwork for the cover, then used the money Dougie donated to pay for the printing costs. I simply did drop-off and pick-up. They look great."

Pandora shook her head in disbelief. "You did that for me?"

"As hard as it is to believe, Pandora, we're all in this together. You're not alone. Not anymore."

Not alone anymore? She didn't even know what that meant.

"Should I pretend not to know about the town performance?"

Dr. Steele considered this. "Well, I'm typically not big on deception, but I think in this case, pretending is the way to go. Charles is really psyched about surprising you."

She smiled ruefully. "Wouldn't want him dropping dead from disappointment, would we?"

"Nope. And nice alliteration."

She grinned. "That was good, wasn't it?"

They finished up the dishes in silence, then Dr. Steele hung up the dish towel. "Go get some sleep," he told her. "Tomorrow's a big day."

He headed toward the door, and just before he disappeared, she called to him. "Dr. Steele?"

"Yes, Pandora?"

"I'm sorry about your sister. I'm going to do my best tomorrow to make her proud."

"I think, Pandora, that she would be proud of you no matter how things turn out tomorrow." With a smile, he turned and left her, and she felt maybe just a little bit less like she was going to attend her own funeral.

30

PANDORA WATCHED FROM a tiny gap through the curtains as the inmates and staff filed into the theater. They were talking and laughing, but mainly looking eager, as though they couldn't wait to witness her downfall. It wouldn't be a full house, but it would feel like one.

Seeing them all together, especially the staff—the frowning Hessian and the sour-faced Nurse Rackett, a fidgety Vicki standing next to an alert Vlad, a strangely spiffed up Carl with his arm around Nurse Devine's shoulders, even a jolly J.T.—made Pandora's stomach roil.

Her rebellious eyes kept searching for the professor, even though each time she realized what she was doing she'd scold herself for being an idiot. She felt a little sad that her dad wouldn't get to enjoy their performance. He liked watching TV, the more terrible and dramatic the better. So he'd probably really like their play. She sighed and felt even worse.

On the plus side, Charles's programs had turned out totally awesome. The cover page featured a lifelike drawing of the Creature, high up on a platform, forks of lightning shooting in through an open skylight, with an evil looking Dr. Frankenstein staring upward in triumph, and Igirl, hand on an electric switch, laughing with delight. It was perfect. Charles had even gotten the names right, along with giving Birdy top billing. Birdy had been very happy about that. And someone had remembered to dedicate the play to the professor. When she'd read the dedication, "For Peter Robertson, amateur entomologist and much missed dad…" she'd almost started crying, but she'd managed to bite her lip hard enough to avoid that disaster.

She rubbed her forehead, which hadn't stopped aching since Dr. Steele had told her about the entire town coming to see the play, and let the curtain fall shut. Much as she wanted to get off this ride, it wasn't happening. The show was going on whether she wanted it to or not. She headed toward the dressing room, mumbling to herself.

"Hurry up, Birdy," she hissed through the door. "The show starts in ten minutes."

"I'm coming," Birdy hollered. Then began doing voice exercises. "Me, me, me, meeee!"

"You, you, you, youuuu!" Lucy, who was standing nearby, mocked her.

"Shut up, Lucy. A star is about to be born."

"Yeah, me, thunder thighs."

"I don't have thunder thighs!"

"Guys!" Pandora yelled. "Knock it off."

"We're just letting off some self-esteem," Lucy told her importantly.

Why could she say self-esteem here, and not when that's what she really meant to say? "That's steam, and do it quietly."

Lucy made a show of looking around. "Where's Derek?"

"He's around here somewhere. I did his make-up earlier." It hadn't been easy standing that close to him. Her hand shook the whole time and she kept getting hot flashes. But she'd done her job like the professional that she was, needing to start over only once.

She glanced about. He'd better still be here. The last thing she needed was him getting cold feet and ducking out. She sighed and rubbed her temples. Why bother worrying? This was going to go horribly anyway. Might as well not get all stressed about it. Though maybe she could walk out now, and keep walking and walking and…

"There he is!"

Derek emerged from the orchestra pit, but he was dressed all wrong, wearing a regular shirt and pants, and not his actual costume. The cuffs on both pants and shirt were tattered, but that was about the extent of wear they had, and they covered way too much body.

"What happened to your costume?"

He shrugged. "I couldn't find it."

She gave him a disbelieving glare. "Yeah, right."

He held up his hands. "I left it in the dressing room yesterday, and now it's not there. I looked around a bit and found some of my other old clothes and put them on. They should do."

Pandora thought quickly. This could still be salvaged. "I have scissors."

"Can't we leave them as they are? My ma's going to be in the audience."

"She is?" Pandora sighed, then wondered why exactly she was so disappointed. "Oh, fine. This is going to be a disaster anyway. I was just hoping your muscles could serve as a distraction from all that."

Even under the make-up she could tell he was blushing. "I don't think my costume changes anything one way or the other."

"Yeah, well, apparently you haven't looked at yourself in the mirror lately."

He stared at her, but was saved from answering by Dougie's appearance. Dougie was fiddling with something on his jacket, and when he

saw her watching him, he smiled smugly, like he thought she was checking him out. Fat chance. "It's a microphone. I told Bones that I didn't
need one, but she wouldn't listen. She's as bad as you."

Pandora frowned. "Just try to keep your breathing at a normal level
and it should be fine. Yesterday I could barely understand you, and
since you're the main character, we need to be able to hear your lines."

"Ahem!" Birdy interrupted, emerging from the dressing room that she'd
commandeered for her own use. "I believe *I'm* the main character."

"The play's called *Frankenstein*, not *Elizabeth*."

"About that…"

"We're not changing the name of the play, Birdy. Now, where's
Charles?"

"Over here!" He bounded out from behind a set. He was dressed as a
young child, which wasn't much of a stretch, and behind him came Dr.
Steele, in full Victorian laborer regalia—white shirt, sleeves rolled up to
show his muscular forearms, black suspenders holding up loose fitting
dark gray pants, black leather boots and a flat cap. He hadn't dressed
for rehearsal yesterday because of his meeting, so she'd yet to see him
in costume. He looked magnificently tough and strong, and even more
magnificent now that she knew some of his back story and felt kind of
connected to him.

"Woo-yee!" Birdy exclaimed, fanning herself with an old-fashioned
lace fan. "Did the temperature just rise in here?"

"Dr. Steele, you're looking mighty fine!" Lucy called out between
cupped hands.

"Um, thanks, Lucy. You're looking fine yourself."

"You mean hot. I look hot."

Pandora decided now was the time to derail this conversation, even
though she wouldn't have minded saying something herself, mainly so
Dr. Steele would have to compliment her in return. But she was the
director and had to be above all that. Being in charge is so hard.

She clapped her hands. "All right, everyone, listen up." The whole
gang, including Xavier and Sinclair, gathered around her. Bones was up
in the booth, doing her thing, but her presence wasn't necessary right
now, because she was the only one yesterday who'd done what she was
supposed to do. "I'm not going to mince words. Yesterday's performance sucked." Birdy gasped and clasped a bejeweled hand to her chest.
Lucy kicked out at Pandora's ankle. Charles looked on the verge of
tears. "So if we don't want to end up being the butt of everyone's joke
for the next five years, we'd better get our shit together and do this
right!"

"She said shit," Lucy whispered to Charles.

"I know," he whispered back.

"All I'm asking is that you stay focused on what we're doing here, and set aside your own personal wants and needs. And that you don't let me down."

"Can we say a prayer, Pandora?" Charles begged.

She paused. Prayer was not her thing. "Oh, why not?" she gave in, but only because he looked so hopeful. "At this point, I'm willing to try all avenues."

Charles beamed, then bowed his head and closed his eyes. Everyone followed his lead, and Pandora sighed and did the same. "Dear God, please let us not suck today. We've all been working really, really hard, especially Pandora"—Birdy snorted—"and if we fail, she might jump again. So fill us with your power and maybe let Jesus walk beside us. Okay, thanks. And amen."

"I'm not going to jump, Charles!" Pandora exclaimed when he opened his eyes. "All right?"

"Yeah, sure." He gave her a fake smile.

Holy crap, he was patronizing her. "I'm not," she repeated firmly.

"Not if Jesus is holding your hand."

Oh, sweet Mary. His damn grandmother must be sending him religious 'miracle' tracts again—the ones that fed into his delusion that he could pretty much walk on water and fly through the air like Jesus. Usually Skippy was able to talk Charles down after he'd read the stories, but he wasn't here.

She caught Dr. Steele watching her and she drew in a deep breath. "If it makes you feel better to think Jesus is holding my hand, then by all means, imagine away." Charles nodded and smiled happily. "Great. Now, can we get to our places, please?"

For once everyone did as they were told, and without arguing. She found her headset and turned it on. She typically wore it to talk to Bones, but she didn't want to actually put it on her head in case she forgot to take it off when she had to appear on stage. She moved over to the curtain and parted it slightly. The natives were getting restless. She glanced at her watch, then lifted the headset mic to her mouth, and one headphone to her ear.

"Hey, Bones, we're coming up on seven o'clock. Dim the houselights, please."

"Your wish is my command," came the snarky reply. The houselights went low, then back up to full illumination, then dimmed again to a count of three before returning to full. The audience started talking excitedly, and a few screeches were heard. Little Gustav shouted out a few harmless profanities, "shiznit buttwinkle ninnyhammer!" but stopped when several voices, in near perfect harmony, told him to shut up.

"All right, take down the house lights."

Bones lowered the lights, and the crowd noise dimmed along with them, until both extinguished at the same time, like magic. So far, so good. Pandora quickly took her spot, then Xavier and Sinclair parted the curtains, and the lights on stage slowly went up.

The play had begun.

Holding her breath, sometimes a bit too long, Pandora followed along with every scene, hoping that Sinclair on the other side of the stage would keep Lucy and Charles and the rest of the crew on track with their entrances and exits.

One of her favorite scenes was coming up and she watched avidly as Dougie addressed the audience in a soliloquy. She had taken the words directly from the book and had him speak them aloud.

"'I collected bones from charnel houses,'" Dougie's voice vibrated with an eerie tone, the effect heightened by the microphone, "'and disturbed, with profane fingers, the tremendous secrets of the human frame. The dissecting room and the slaughter-house furnished many of my materials; and often did my human nature turn with loathing from my occupation, whilst, still urged on by an eagerness which perpetually increased, I brought my work near to a conclusion.'"

The audience loved it; they loved Dougie, loved hating him, anyway. And he seemed to relish their strong reaction to him.

The resurrection scene went over well, too, and no one freaked out about the thunder sounds and lightning flashes, at least not that she could tell. When Derek made his debut as the Creature, there were quite a few delighted shrieks (she was pretty sure several came from J.T.). The audience would be even more delighted if Derek had been wearing his other costume, but what can you do? At first, he was a bit stiff in his presentation, but he soon relaxed and seemed to become the Creature more and more with each word he spoke.

The scene where he killed Little Willie, for being so horrible, actually turned out to be surprisingly touching. Well, after Willie had died, that is. Let's face it, the kid is kind of a brat. Upon being seized by the Creature, Charles delivered his lines perfectly, "'Let me go, monster! ugly wretch! you wish to eat me, and tear me to pieces—You are an ogre—Let me go, or I will tell my papa.'"

Based on the boos following Charles's speech, the audience sounded like they were more on the Creature's side than Little Willie's. The bloodthirsty lot actually cheered when Derek strangled Charles until he was lifeless, a pose which he managed to display almost a little too well, and Pandora was glad when she saw his shadowy form exiting the stage once the scene was over. The touching part came when Derek gently laid Willie down on the floor and closed his eyes with two fingers before placing in Willie's outstretched hand the damning locket he'd found. The scene had been perfectly executed, though Pandora felt sure the symbolic duality behind the juxtaposition of such terrible violence next to such gentility was lost on the audience.

Pandora's best scenes were coming up next, if only she could get them right. She'd survived the earlier ones shockingly well, but now she was in prison for Willie's murder—her own locket, which the Creature had placed in Little Willie's dead hand, being the smoking gun pointing directly at her. She sat down on the bed, adjusted her skirt, and waited for the lights to rise. When they did, Birdy and Dougie entered from stage left, her cue to begin her speech. From the start, the words flowed from her mouth, and she never felt more alive. For her part, Birdy was a bit over the top in her delivery, but the audience ate it up like starving dogs.

" 'In these last moments,' " Pandora spoke with real emotion, which nearly made her tear up, " 'I feel the sincerest gratitude towards those who think of me with kindness. How sweet is the affection of others to such a wretch as I am! It removes more than half my misfortune; and I feel as if I could die in peace, now that my innocence is acknowledged by you, dear lady, and your cousin.' " She held out her hand to indicate Birdy and Dougie, each in turn. Dougie held out his hand as though to take hers, then slowly allowed it to drop when she turned away.

" 'I wish that I were to die with you,' " Birdy emoted, clapping her hands to her chest. " 'I cannot live in this world of misery.' "

"Probably not, but you must," Pandora adlibbed, before returning to script. " 'Farewell, sweet lady, dearest Elizabeth, my beloved and only friend; may heaven in its bounty bless and preserve you; may this be the last misfortune that you will ever suffer. Live, and be happy, and make others so.' "

" 'The innocent suffers,' " Birdy said to Dougie in an aside, " 'but she whom I thought amiable and good has not betrayed the trust I reposed in her, and I am consoled.' "

Dougie and Birdy made their exit, and when they were gone, Pandora fell back, as though in a faint. The stage went dark. She'd done it. Now for the best scene of all—Justine's death, where Dr. Steele snatches her

and carries her away to throw her off a cliff. She'd used some poetic
license and made this part up, since the book really hadn't shown anything happening to Justine. She couldn't in good conscience accept
that. Death scenes were the bread and butter of good entertainment.

The audience roared with approval as Dr. Steele tossed her over the
wall with quite a bit of enthusiasm, and Pandora had the distinct sensation that despite his claims of preferring behind-the-scenes work, he
was loving every moment of his time on stage. Luckily, she still hit the
port-a-pit closely enough to take the edge off the fall, and was able to
head back upstairs to direct the rest of the play with only a small bruise
on her tailbone.

Things were, knock on wood—she rapped her knuckles on the
nearby wall—going really well. Xavier was right…bad dress rehearsal,
good opening night!

They were coming up on the end now. The Creature had demanded
that Dr. Frankenstein create another being like him so that he may
have a companion, but Dr. Frankenstein wasn't having it.

" 'You purpose to kill me,' " Derek spoke with surprising fervor. " 'How
dare you sport thus with life? Do your duty towards me, and I will do
mine towards you and the rest of mankind. If you will comply with my
conditions, I will leave them and you at peace; but if you refuse, I will
glut the maw of death, until it be satiated with the blood of your remaining friends.' "

The audience hooted and hollered their approval.

" ' 'Abhorred monster!' " Dougie cried, with equally surprising fervor.
" 'Fiend that thou art! the tortures of hell are too mild a vengeance for
thy crimes. Wretched devil! you reproach me with your creation;
come on, then, that I may extinguish the spark which I so negligently
bestowed.' "

The two circled each other like warriors in battle.

" 'We may not part until you have promised to comply with my requi-
sition. I am alone, and miserable; man will not associate with me; but
one as deformed and horrible as myself would not deny herself to me.
My companion must be of the same species, and have the same de-
fects. This being you must create.' "

There was more verbal sparring, but finally Dr. Frankenstein gives in.

" 'I consent to your demand, on your solemn oath to quit Europe for
ever, and every other place in the neighbourhood of man, as soon as I
shall deliver into your hands a female who will accompany you in your
exile.' "

The scene ends and Dr. Frankenstein goes off and tries to create another creature, but in a moment of moral crisis, he undoes what he has done. When they meet again, the Creature is royally p-o'ed, an emotion Derek portrayed quite well.

"'You have destroyed the work which you began; what is it that you intend? Do you dare to break your promise? I have endured toil and misery. I have endured incalculable fatigue, and cold, and hunger; do you dare destroy my hopes?'"

"'Begone!'" Dr. Frankenstein cried. "'I do break my promise; never will I create another like yourself, equal in deformity and wickedness.'"

"'Remember that I have power; you believe yourself miserable, but I can make you so wretched that the light of day will be hateful to you. You are my creator, but I am your master;—obey!'" Derek seemed to relish speaking this last bit particularly.

"'Your threats cannot move me to do an act of wickedness; but they confirm me in a determination of not creating you a companion in vice. Shall I, in cool blood, set loose upon the earth a demon, whose delight is in death and wretchedness? Begone! I am firm, and your words will only exasperate my rage.'"

"'I go;'" the Creature finally concedes, "'but remember, I shall be with you on your wedding-night.'"

"'Villain! before you sign my death-warrant, be sure that you are yourself safe.'" Here Dougie gave Derek a glare of such loathing that the audience went silent. It was beautifully done, though almost a little too realistic.

Birdy's favorite scene followed, where the Creature chokes her to death, and she gets to enjoy rubbing her body against Derek's while he kills her. "He is so hot," she had confided to Pandora numerous times over the past month. "Too bad you'll never get to do that with him."

"Writhe under him as he strangles me?" she'd once answered, her tone heavily sarcastic. "Yes, I'm really missing out."

The chase scene ensued, followed by the Creature's death scene, and then the play ended far too soon and the clapping went on forever and Pandora never wanted it to end.

They were stars!

31

Fooled You!

THE CONGRATULATIONS SEEMED to go on forever, and then, all too soon, it was over. Even Vicki had been somewhat complimentary, saying, albeit a bit succinctly, "I'm impressed."

Vlad, standing close to the Director as though playing bodyguard, had clapped Pandora on the back like a proud papa. "Well played," he joked.

Despite the bad joke, Pandora smiled at him. "It's what I do."

"You do it well." He winked at her before maneuvering Vicki past the crew and out the side entrance. Pandora watched them go with a strange feeling in her gut. He looked like he was either trying to protect Vicki from Pandora, or protect Pandora from Vicki. Either way seemed weird.

As the last of the staff and inmates filed out, the cast, with the exception of Derek, who had left to escort his mom to her room, gathered around on the stage, laughing and talking excitedly. Pandora felt like she could lie down and go to sleep right there, she was so exhausted, yet at the same time fly to the moon. It was the best feeling in the world.

"What you did with the lights was awesome!" Xavier called to Bones as she climbed the stage steps to join them.

"Thanks," she mumbled, and Pandora tried not to stare too obviously as she watched a slow blush descend over the girl's sharp features.

"Yeah," she chimed in, looking for a way to compliment Bones without going overboard. She didn't want to scare the girl off. "You could do this for a living."

Bones snorted disdainfully, but Pandora caught a small flicker of interest in her eyes, right before she turned away. "Nobody sane would hire someone like me."

"Lucky for you people in the entertainment industry are kind of crazy."

"Not that crazy," Bones grumbled.

Pandora let it go. "So this is it, guys. I guess tomorrow we clean up." Charles started doing an excited little tap dance, and Lucy joined him, clapping her hands to create a Latin-type rhythm. Birdy looked smug, while Sinclair and Dougie watched her closely. Bones pretended nonchalance, but even she seemed interested in Pandora's reaction. Pandora frowned as she looked around at all of them. "What's going on? Why are you all staring at me?"

"Surprise!" Charles yelled, echoed by Lucy's "Supwise!"

"But it's not my birthday…"

"I know it's not your birthday, silly! That's not the surprise," Charles pushed out in one breath. He quickly inhaled and began again. "We're doing the performance for the town tomorrow, and they had to buy tickets to come, and we're all sold out, and it's going to be great!"

"Whoa, whoa! Hold on, Tiger." Pandora focused on Dougie. "What's this about?"

He gave her a look that conveyed he knew she knew, and was pleased she'd figured it out. She hadn't, but she wasn't about to burst his weird bubble. "Charles and Sinclair and I took your idea to put on the show for the town, and sell tickets to help raise money for the asylum, and we made it a reality."

"What?" She didn't have any trouble feigning breathlessness, because that's how she felt. Yes, she had already told Dr. Steele she'd do it, but she couldn't forget the potential consequences. They *had* rocked tonight's performance, however, so maybe she was worrying about nothing. And maybe she'd also grow wings and fly out of here. "How'd you get Vicki to agree? And wouldn't Hank Jackson have to sign off on something like that?"

"After I explained what doing this play would mean for the asylum and for the community," Dougie replied, "they both agreed. Mr. Jackson will actually be attending tomorrow. He said he was looking forward to it." Hank Jackson rooting for them? Had hell frozen over?

"Vicki gave in? Just like that?"

"Of course."

"Wow." She turned to Charles and Sinclair and made herself smile. "The entire town. I can't believe it. I didn't see this coming. You totally got me guys."

Charles wiggled with pleasure, but Sinclair only continued to watch her closely, like he'd been doing for an entire month. It was getting annoying.

"We've been planning it forever!" Charles cried. "Are you surprised, Pandora? Does this make you happy?"

"Completely gobsmacked, my friend. And yes, I'm really happy that you did this." He held up his hand for a high-five and she complied. "You guys are awesome. So did everyone know about this but me?"

Charles giggled gleefully. "Yes! You were the only one! Even Derek knows!"

"We fooled you, we fooled you!" Lucy chanted. "I didn't say a word, did I, Dr. Steele?" She held out her hand. "Now where's my five bucks?"

"Right here." Dr. Steele took a bill from his pocket and laid it across her outstretched hand. "You did great."

She mimed a swipe across her forehead. "Boy, am I glad that's over. Hardest five buckeroos I ever earned."

"All right, guys," Dr. Steele said, giving Lucy a fond smile. "I know I'm not supposed to play the adult card in here, but I think it's time for bed. We have to do this all over again tomorrow and we need to be at our best."

"I'm always at my best," Birdy stated, then gave a big yawn. "But I do need my beauty sleep. It's really hard being the star of the show. I feel like I always have to be on."

Pandora bit her tongue. Hard.

"Will you escort them to their rooms, Dr. Steele?" Dougie asked politely. "I'd like to stay and help Pandora put everything to rights."

He nodded. "No problem."

They left in pairs, Lucy dancing and Charles saying something to her about how prayers really do work, Xavier talking quite earnestly to a surprisingly attentive Bones, Birdy regaling Dr. Steele with the best scenes she performed, with only Sinclair going solo, and glancing back at Pandora every few steps.

When they were gone, Pandora turned to Dougie. "Why'd you do it?"

"Because I could."

"I'm sure there was more to it than your ego, and for the record, I don't think it's a good idea."

"It was your idea."

"I know that, but it wasn't my best. Now Hank Jackson is going to be in the audience, and if we mess this up in a way I know only the posse is capable of doing, and in front of witnesses, he's got a good excuse to shut us down." She refused to state her real reason for not wanting to do the play in front of the town.

"I took care of everything, and trust me when I say he's not going to shut us down." Did he just include himself as part of the *us*?

Weirdness all around her.

"How can you be so sure about that?"

"His daughter is in love with me." As he said this, his expression didn't alter one bit, though he was very likely preening on the inside.

"What?"

He gave his slow blink. "You find that hard to believe?"

"Um, *yeah*. Does she have any idea what kind of person you are?"

"Oh, yes. We've known each other since we were children. Our parents are good friends. It's always been a sort of expectation that Debra and I would marry."

Pandora took a moment to absorb that last word. "Marry?"

"When we're older, of course."

"Why have I never heard of this girl before now?" she demanded, feeling a bit peculiar inside and not sure why.

"Because I have never felt the need to share that information with you before now."

"So is she your girlfriend?" It was a question she'd never thought she'd ask Dougie, or even care to ask Dougie.

"She is not."

"But you just said you're going to get married and—"

He was beginning to look put out. "I said nothing of the sort. Our parents think Debra and I will marry. Debra believes she and I will marry. I, however, am not of the same opinion, nor will I ever be."

She swallowed, wondering why she felt almost *relieved*. "I see. Poor Debbie."

"*Debra* is a force in her own right. She doesn't need your misguided sympathy."

Something clicked in Pandora's mind, something that should have been obvious a month ago, when she'd found out Dougie had gotten a job at Nepenthe Manor. "You made a deal."

"I made several deals. One was with your mother. I told her if she gave me a job here, I would get Hank Jackson off her back."

"And you got Hank Jackson off her back by agreeing to do his daughter."

"That sounds far more tawdry than the reality. I merely agreed to take her on a date."

"And did you?"

"I did."

Her skin started tingling. "Was it fun?"

"Define fun."

"Did you have fun or not, Dougie?"

"I made the best of a problematic situation."

She clamped down on the satisfaction she felt. "You're a real prince."

"But now she wants a second date."

"Are you going to give it to her?"

"That remains to be seen."

Her satisfaction fled, and she drew herself up, determined not to show her discomfiture. "So you bribed Vicki and Hank, and you told your father you would spy for him if he let you work here. Aren't you enterprising?"

"Nobody 'let' me do anything, Pandora. I simply wanted to make sure everything went smoothly."

"Have you told your father anything yet?"

"Nothing relevant."

This was beginning to look like a dead-end conversation. "I still don't like the idea of putting on a play for the town."

"You were amazing tonight, Pandora. You will be amazing tomorrow night. You can never not be amazing."

"*Gag.* I hope you've never said anything like that to Debbie."

"Debra."

"Potato, pot-ah-to."

"Are you jealous?"

"Of Debbie?" She snorted. "Hardly. Now I have to get to work. Everything's out of sorts, and I nearly missed the port-a-pit tonight." She rubbed her sore hip. "I think Lucy moved it again."

"You're hurt." Dougie's jaw tightened. "That is unacceptable."

"I thought you'd be into that sort of thing." She started picking up various stage props and returning them to their proper places. Dougie followed her.

"Only when applied to my enemies."

"Like Derek?"

"I hardly consider such a weak adversary to be my enemy."

"Derek? He's about as weak as a rhino."

"I'm referring to his mental capacity."

"His mental capacity isn't anything to sneeze at, either."

Both Dougie's hands curled into fists. Another tell, communicating something subtle like, *you're starting to antagonize me.* "I don't understand why you like him."

"And I don't understand why you don't. So I guess that makes us even."

"You understand perfectly well why I don't like him, you simply don't want to acknowledge it."

"Acknowledge what?"

"That the two of us are rivals for your affection."

"For my affection?" She shook her head, amazed at his obtuseness. "You just made the mistake of thinking I have affection to give, which

I don't. I'm too damn busy cleaning up messes to deal with that sort of crap."

"So you wouldn't go on a date with Derek?"

She paused in her housekeeping, knowing she had him. "I never said that."

"So you would."

"Why not? You went on a date with Debbie."

"I was fulfilling my half of a bargain."

"And you intend to go on another date with her."

"If necessary. I'm still deliberating on that. She might prove useful, and I do not want to miss out on the opportunity to make the most of her feelings toward me."

"How delightful you are," she drawled like a Southern princess. "I understand now what she sees in you." She headed out to the seats to pick up programs. There were several that had been left behind, which could be reused.

He followed after her. "I make the most of every interaction I have, Pandora. You should do the same."

"Oh, I will. And if that means dating Derek, so be it."

He crunched a program in his hands, and it gave a menacing crackle. "I won't allow it."

"It's not your choice. And stop ruining the programs. We can reuse them."

"I don't give a damn about the programs."

"You should. You paid for them."

"Tell me you won't date Derek, and I'll let it go."

"Let what go?"

His cool blue eyes slid deceptively to the side. "This topic."

That's not what he'd meant. "I'm not telling you anything of the sort because it's not your business."

"Everything you do is my business."

She pointed a rolled-up program at him. "What are you up to, Douglas Daft?"

"I'm saving you, that's what."

"And what if I don't want, or *need*, to be saved? I'm not an endangered species."

"You have no idea what you want or need, Pandora." He dropped his programs on the floor and walked away, back stiff.

Was it her imagination, or did he get weirder by the day?

And was it her imagination, or did she actually like that about him?

32

PANDORA TRIED NOT to let her last interaction with Dougie keep her awake. But in trying not to think about him, and how for a brief moment of madness she had found him somewhat appealing, other thoughts invaded. Problems, to be more precise.

Problem one was that they'd need ticket takers for tomorrow. With the townsfolk coming to gawk, Nepenthe Manor had to look somewhat professional. She'd probably ask Jun Li and Cracker Jack to do it, since they were the most manageable inmates, which wasn't saying much. Cracker Jack should be all right. Jun Li, who was very good at being vulgar, on the other hand...

Problem two was that she had a feeling Derek wasn't going to like what she'd done to his costume after she'd finished cleaning up the theater. She'd searched for the one that had gone missing, but it didn't surface. After some thought, she formulated a pretty good theory about what had happened to it. It involved Dougie, lighter fluid, and a match.

The last problem was more complicated. Plots and schemes were brewing right under her nose and she'd missed them. She'd blissfully hid herself away in the theater, but life was still going on, things were still happening, and she'd had no idea. This seemed to be occurring more and more often lately. She was becoming both irrelevant and underprepared.

Her biggest worry concerned what Dougie was up to. He had a plan, and was playing it out like a well-orchestrated concerto, and she felt like she was only seeing the tip of the iceberg. Like maybe he had recruited everyone around her. Like maybe the whole world was in on it. Question was: What was *it*?

She pressed her hands to her temples. She had to stop thinking. Everything had gone really well today. Tomorrow would be fine. It had to be.

Ψ

It was Friday evening and the theater was packed. Had everyone come to see the girl who'd jumped? The girl who'd almost been kidnapped? Pandora scanned the audience through a gap in the curtain and both wanted to take it all in and throw up. She could see Hank the Crank in the front row, talking to a sour woman next to him—probably Mrs.

Crank. To his right sat Mayor Daft and Mrs. Daft, both looking like someone nearby had farted. A woman in a low-cut dress grabbed an aisle seat by the exit, and it took Pandora a moment to realize it was Nurse Abrams from the hospital, here to watch Dr. Steele, no doubt. Lordy, Pandora could smell the woman's desperation from here. She didn't see her grandmother or grandfather anywhere, one thing in her favor.

Toward the back she spotted Jimbo and his moronic friends screwing around, none of whom seemed to know the proper way to sit in a chair. He was showing off to a big-haired girl, the same one at the basketball game who'd kept score and who couldn't spell. Sadly, but not surprisingly, she seemed to be falling for his antics. Dum…as…dert, that girl.

There were some allies out there, as well. Ms. Netterson, fabulous in a little black dress. Mrs. H. amongst a gaggle of friends, holding court. The LoBAC women. Lucy's mom, Mrs. Landry, and all her kids, but no Mr. Landry, big shocker. The Peacocks, including Birdy's goth wannabe sister Jessica, sat dead center. Mrs. Peacock was regaling everyone around her, as Jessica scowled at the program in front of her. The Prims had come, as well, but she wished they hadn't, for Sinclair's sake. He never seemed very happy when they were around. No Grandma Pippen, thank goodness, but then Pandora hadn't expected Charles's grandma to come. The recluse hadn't left her house for over a decade.

To record the whole potential fiasco was a tiny woman standing near the exit, a camera hanging on a strap around her neck and a notepad in hand. That must be Trudy Goodly, ancestor to Gertrude Goodly, the society writer from Elizabeth Nepenthe's time. Apparently Trudy had followed in good old Gertrude's footsteps.

Everyone backstage was in a positive mood, ready to put on a great show. Only Derek looked unhappy after finding his costume altered. But he didn't say a word, giving Pandora a mournful look before returning to the dressing room to don it. She probably shouldn't have done it, but he looked really good, and Lucy had given her a thumb's up in agreement. Seeing the change, Dougie's brow had lowered thunderously, and Pandora hoped he'd keep it together and not find some way to get back at Derek and ruin the play.

The house lights dimmed for the last time and the curtains parted. The play was about to begin. The performance started out relatively smoothly. Dougie delivered his lines with even more intensity than yesterday's performance, and the audience was rapt.

"'I had worked hard for nearly two years,'" he intoned, "'for the sole purpose of infusing life into an inanimate body.

"'As the minuteness of the parts formed a great hindrance to my speed, I resolved, contrary to my first intention, to make the being of a gigantic stature; that is to say, about eight feet in height, and proportionably large. After having formed this determination, and having spent some months in successfully collecting and arranging my materials, I began.'"

The play continued, building suspense as the resurrection scene approached. Derek lay unmoving on the platform as it rose into the air. Thunder cracked and lightning flashed. "Live, my son!" Dougie cried out, the mic amplifying his voice to great effect. "*Live!*"

Lucy dramatically threw a switch and the platform returned to the floor. Dougie leaned over Derek's inert form. "No!" he cried upon finding no signs of life. "You must live!" He pounded Derek's chest, a bit too realistically, and Pandora grew nervous. "Live!"

Derek's arm jerked out and his hand wrapped around Dougie's throat. Crap. That wasn't part of the play. Derek pushed Dougie away and sat up, then released him with a little shove. Dougie staggered back, holding his throat, then quickly recovered. "It's alive!" he crowed hoarsely. Then stronger, "It's alive!"

Derek pushed himself off the platform and stood upright. The crowd gasped with both fear and pleasure.

And then all hell broke loose.

The lights blinked out and darkness filled the theater like an inky flood. This was definitely not part of the play. Had they lost electricity? Pandora's question was answered when the sound of voices began. Recorded voices.

"Abandon hope all ye who enter this place," one entreated, its tone high-pitched and wobbly.

"I'm not crazy!" cried another, echoed by a "Shut up!" and a slapping sound.

Screams started up, then moans. Sighs of pain, shouts. A buzzing noise, like an electric switch being thrown. Or was that a saw?

Lights started flashing all around the theater, and the voices grew louder and more frenzied.

"Welcome to the asylum, new recruits," another voice, louder than the others, broke through. "The doors are locked. Your hands are tied. You're all alone."

A pause followed by a maniacal laugh. "And you can't get out. You can't get out!" More maniacal laughter, echoing loudly all around the theater.

The audience, realizing something wasn't quite right—that maybe this wasn't actually part of the play—started to stir nervously. Pandora could sense they were on the verge of a panic. Dougie tried to take back the stage, yelling something out to the audience, but his microphone was off and he couldn't be heard over the recorded voices.

People were standing up now, some started pushing toward the exit. Pandemonium broke out as their panic grew and the lights flickered. Shoving, shouting, more people up, moving, struggling to escape…

"What is all this noise?" a voice bellowed from the stage. The Creature. The audience froze.

"Make it stop!" he bellowed again, and the recorded voices died away.

People slowly retreated back to their seats, sat down quickly, sheepishly. Some nervous giggles broke out. A few titters and pokes at those who'd panicked and tried to flee.

The ones who stayed are the stupid ones, Pandora thought to herself. But for once she was glad for their stupidity.

The stage lights stopped flickering and slowly came back on, and there Derek stood, in all his glory. Nearly shirtless, towering over Dougie, his hands held out in entreaty. He looked amazing, and Pandora couldn't take her eyes off him.

"I have made it stop, my son," Dougie spoke soothingly, and Pandora was relieved to hear his voice. His mic was back on. "All is well now."

And the show went on.

At intermission, Pandora left the riled-up crew and raced up to the booth. She turned the knob, and surprised to find it unlocked, opened the door. But when she heard voices, she froze, the door cracked just a bit.

"That was the best you could do?" The voice was familiar, but she couldn't place it.

"What do you expect?" Bones retorted, her voice defiant. "It's not like I can come and go as I please."

"I'm paying you to do a job, and you didn't do it."

"Maybe I'd do better at it if I saw some more of that money you promised me."

"Don't make me laugh. I give you any more and you'd get yourself high and be useless to me. I'm not sure what I was thinking hiring a loser like you. I've a mind to hire someone else."

"Don't do that," Bones begged, her voice almost frightened. "I'll figure something out."

"You have the rest of the play to do that. One more screw-up like I just saw and you'll rot in this place. Do I make myself clear?"

"Crystal."

Pandora let the door click shut and stepped back around the corner. The door opened soon after and out came Hank Jackson. Hank the Crank? What was he doing talking to Bones? And what was he planning?

A dim light shone down on his features as he pulled the door closed behind him and in that moment Pandora saw something. A resemblance. To someone she knew. But who?

There wasn't time to figure it out. Pandora slipped away and back down the stairs. She told the posse, who was fast growing overexcited, that Bones, being a bit of a troublemaker, had simply been trying something new to shake things up, and good job to Dougie and Derek for going along with it. Both Dr. Steele and Dougie regarded her skeptically, but for once chose not to intervene. The posse accepted her explanation, and quickly calmed down enough to ready themselves for the next act.

Soon the dimming of the houselights began, signaling that intermission was nearly over. But Pandora was really worried now. What was Bones going to do next? And when? She'd fooled Pandora well and good, pretending to want to fight, pretending to not want Vicki to shut down the play. Due to her head injury Pandora hadn't seen through the big faker, and that bothered her to no end.

Should she go up there again? Confront the girl? She wanted to, but her big scenes were coming up, and it was likely Bones had locked the door…standard procedure once the play began.

So what could she do?

Nothing. The show must go on.

Despite her worries, she managed to perform her scenes quite well. Strangely, thinking the whole time that Bones was going to target her actually made her better. And this time, she hit the port-a-pit squarely. Today was not her day to die.

When Derek launched into one of his speeches to Dr. Frankenstein, not a sound came from the audience as they listened raptly, almost guiltily. It was one of Pandora's favorite parts, and now she realized why. It was as if Mary Shelley was talking about her, about anyone who has been shunned for being different. It was the lament of every single inmate who had passed through Nepenthe Manor. It was the shout of the freak, the cry of the mentally ill. It was a speech that Derek, and the whole posse, including Pandora and Dougie, understood all too well.

"'Hateful day when I received life!'" Derek shook his fist at the sky. "'Cursed creator! Why did you form a monster so hideous that even you turned from me in disgust? God, in pity, made man beautiful and alluring, after his own image; but my form is a filthy type of yours, more horrid from its very resemblance. Satan had his companions, fellow-devils, to admire and encourage him; but I am solitary and detested.'"

We appear mostly human, until you look a little closer, Pandora thought. *Then you see the fissures, and all the way through the cracks to reveal what's inside us. Non-conforming limbs, abnormal brain, weird soul, different beliefs, an offbeat heart.*

The play rolled onward, without a sign of trouble. Pandora had tried contacting Bones several times through the headset, but there was no answer. Derek delivered his final words with dignity…

"'But soon I shall die, and what I now feel be no longer felt. Soon these burning miseries will be extinct. I shall ascend my funeral pile triumphantly, and exult in the agony of the torturing flames. The light of that conflagration will fade away; my ashes will be swept into the sea by the winds. My spirit will sleep in peace; or if it thinks, it will not surely think thus. Farewell.'"

Numerous sobs met this speech, then Dougie finished off the play with his soliloquy, and the play ended successfully.

Or had it?

33

Cesspit of Despair

THE APPLAUSE WAS wild, the audience on their feet. But Pandora couldn't enjoy any of it. As the people clapped and cheered, something nagged at her. What would Hank Jackson get out of sabotaging the play? Even though she claimed he could shut down the manor, she wasn't sure he could make that happen solely on the basis of something going wrong in a play.

Unfortunately she didn't have time to figure it out; she had to join Charles, Dr. Steele, and Lucy onstage for their acknowledgement bow.

It wasn't until a large hand covered her mouth and jerked her backwards that everything became clear in her mind. Of course, all too late. She was caught, and caught good. She fought and clawed at the sweaty palm cutting off her air, but her attacker was strong and handled everything she threw at him as he dragged her down into the orchestra pit. Her odd fitting dress didn't help, making every move awkward and pathetic. She was trapped, with no way to free herself.

Everyone, caught up in the fervor of the moment, failed to see what was happening right under their very noses, as per usual, even though she once managed to get a short yip out when her attacker's hand shifted to get a better hold.

The pit was dark and cool, with only a small light from the stage to guide them along. When it was too dark to go any further, they stopped moving, and the hand covering her mouth left it to grasp her free arm in a tight grip. She kept fighting, but his hands were like vises and she couldn't shake him.

"Stay still!" Henry Hanigan hissed in her ear. "You and I need to have a little talk, and just so you know, you can make all the noise you want, no one's going to hear you over that racket."

She swallowed hard and stopped trying to get away. He was right. The applause was loud, even all the way down here. Her only hope of escape was if someone came looking for her. She was supposed to be onstage right now, but the others probably thought she was up to something and had no wish to lose their moment in the spotlight to track her down.

"I know what you want," she asserted, "but there's no way you're going to get it. I'm not leaving."

"Oh, yes, you are, missy. You and your mother have made my life a headache for years, but I put up with you both because I didn't think you'd ever learn my secret. But then *he* showed up and the risk became too great. So I need you gone."

"You hired Baker to kidnap me, didn't you?"

"And what a waste of time and money that was. Should've stuck to my creed...if you want something done right, do it yourself."

She couldn't argue with that, being that it was her own creed. "So where's Baker now?"

"Double-crossing bastard ran off with my money and is probably living the high life now. If I ever catch him he'll hope he'd never met me. But here's the good part for you. If you leave, and don't say a word about this conversation, then I'll see that your mother gets a new job she'll actually like. She'll be happy. Think of it, Pandora. Your mother will finally be happy."

"Vicki's already happy," she replied, though not as firmly as she'd have liked. It was hard talking to someone she couldn't see, who was holding her captive with a grip that cut into her skin like rubber bands, and who seemed hugely unstable. The air was cold, it was incredibly dark, and she was entirely on her own. This felt very, very wrong, but she didn't know how to make it right.

"Oh, please," Henry sneered. "Who could be happy in this place? It's a cesspit of despair; it smells of hopelessness and bedpans. This is hell on earth, and you and I both know it."

"Then why didn't you do something to change things here? You have money. You could have done something."

"Let's just say something happened to prevent me."

"Yeah. Greed. Selfishness."

The grip tightened. "I'm not here to negotiate with you. You promise to not say a word, and your mother gets her dream job."

"What makes you think I know anything?" It was a dumb question, but Pandora needed to delay him. At least until the clapping died down, which didn't seem to be happening very quickly. Her only chance was to scream her bloody head off and hope someone would hear and come rescue her.

"Even if you don't, I know your type. You won't stop until you ferret out every last secret. Whatever you know or don't know, I want you gone. Lucky for you I'm not entirely coldblooded, or you'd be dead." The word seemed to echo in the small space. "Though it was too bad your little stunt at the bridge didn't work out like you'd planned." Sheesh. Even Henry Hanigan thought she wanted to kill herself. "That would've made my life so much simpler."

"Sorry I lived."

"Me, too."

"But are you sorry about what happened?" She was alluding to his daughter's suicide, of course. And in doing so, giving away that she was quite aware of what his secret was, part of it anyway. But again, she needed more time. The clapping overhead went on and on, with no end in sight. Any other time, she would have basked in it. At the moment, it was the worst sound in the world.

"I learned a long time ago that being sorry is a waste of time. Now, do we have a bargain?"

"I suppose we do," Pandora replied slowly. It was time to change tactics. She wasn't really sure he wouldn't kill her if push came to shove. After all, no one would guess he'd done it, because no one knew who he really was. When it came right down to it, killing her was his best bet for keeping what he'd done secret. "I'll do it."

"You will?" He sounded surprised, and for a brief moment his grip relaxed, just as she knew it would. All those tussles with the staff over the years had taught her a few tricks. With a violent wrench she pulled out of his grasp, and tore off into the dark.

"Get back here, you interfering bitch, or you'll regret it!" Yes, he was definitely capable of killing her. Maybe today was her day to die. She ran faster.

The sound of his footsteps getting closer filled her ears. For being on the portly side, he was surprisingly quick. His hand grabbed her shoulder, startling her, and she ducked low, shaking it off. She kept running, pumping her arms as fast as they would go. At the last second, she veered to the right.

"What the hell?" he howled as he smashed into the port-a-pit straight on. She could hear him hit the floor, but knew he wouldn't stay down long. He couldn't afford to let her get away. She sprinted down the remainder of the corridor and came out on the other side, into the light. Her head was pounding, her breath came hard, and she wasn't sure how long she could keep this up. She was so horribly out of shape.

Nearly stumbling, she slipped off the stage and raced up the house steps to the control booth as the audience continued their zealous clapping. But they wouldn't continue clapping for much longer—probably because now she needed them to keep at it so they wouldn't leave. She had to do something to stop them from going. A few of the audience members, including Nurse Abrams, gaped at her as she sprinted past.

"Making an announcement," she gasped. "Stay tuned!"

"Stop her!" Henry shouted. She glanced back. Damnit, that man was hard to shake.

She made it to the booth door only to find it locked. She pounded on it. "Open up, Bones!" she gasped, barely able to breathe. "It's me, Pandora, and I'm in danger!"

No answer.

She pounded again. "I'm going to denounce that jerk, but I can't do that if you don't open up."

The door swung open, a hand popped out, and yanked her inside, just as her pursuer rounded the corner. Bones locked the door, and spun to face her. "I didn't want to do it."

"Yeah, sure."

Bones laughed over the sound of a fist pounding on the door. "Okay, yeah, I did. At first. I was the one who ratted you out to Vicki."

Pandora didn't give away that she'd had no idea until today. "But it didn't work."

"No, and I'm glad. You're not as awful as he made you sound, and then you kind of acted like I wasn't a piece of gum on the bottom of your shoe, so tonight I tried to do the least awful thing I could do. I still did it, though." Her tone was defiant, but underneath it Pandora heard a slight quiver.

Pandora regarded her nemesis. "You did. But he threatened you. I heard it. Said he'd force you to stay here if you didn't do something else before the end of the play. But you didn't do anything else."

More pounding, followed by several swear words and threats to kill them.

Bones looked away. "I've screwed up my whole life. Just for once I didn't want to be that person."

"Good. Then give me the mic for the house. I've got something to say." She ran over to the window that looked out over the audience. The stage curtain was closing and the audience was standing and stretching, some were already leaving. "Quickly!"

Bones gestured to it. "You're on. Make it good, though."

Pandora picked up the microphone and pressed the button. "Hello, Bedlamites!" The mic hissed and squawked with feedback and she pulled back a little. "Please don't leave yet." People paused and looked around, then someone saw Pandora up in the booth and pointed. She leaned over and slid the window open. "Please, just give me two minutes. I've got something to say."

"It's Bats Belfry!" Jimbo cried out. "The looniest girl in the whole town."

She glared down at him. He was going to ruin things. Nobody was going to listen to her if they thought she wasn't a reliable source. She had to think quick, but it was hard with her head pounding and the pounding on the door working against her.

"Hello, Jimbo," she said loudly. "Still reeling from getting beat in basketball by a bunch of kids who live in an asylum?"

"You know it!" she heard Lucy shout out from the stage. She always made sure she stayed in front of the curtains when they closed so she could wave to the people leaving, and for once, Pandora was glad the little rebel didn't listen to her. "Big baby actually cried!" Lucy added, followed by a scornful laugh. The crying couldn't be confirmed, but far be it from Pandora to refute Lucy's claim.

Jimbo scowled, opened his mouth like a dying fish, then shut it again. "I thought as much." She scanned the audience. "My real name is Pandora Belfry, as you all know, and recently I was nearly kidnapped by someone because he feared what I knew. There's a man here, right now, pounding on the control booth door"—the pounding stopped abruptly—"and he's after me because I figured out that he did a terrible thing."

Now the entire audience was staring up at her, as was the crew onstage, the curtains rapidly parting to reveal them all. She focused on Dr. Steele, because he was the one who most needed to hear this. The banging on the door had stopped, though Pandora thought she heard something tapping against the door handle, like maybe Mr. Hanigan was trying to pick the lock. She didn't have much time.

"For the last several years the whole town has known this man as Hank Jackson, Bedlam's health and safety inspector." A stunned hush fell over the audience as they tried to process this information. Pandora had never liked the guy, but apparently he'd done a good job of presenting himself as Mr. Upstanding Citizen to everyone else. So it hadn't been King Tobias or his paramour Gloria, or the Hessian, or Ronny and Lonny. Not Vicki, either. Or even the enigmatic Vlad. No, it had been a respected member of the establishment. Someone from the outside. Someone supposedly sane.

"Around here we know him as Hank the Crank"—Bones snorted in amusement—"and he's been trying to get this place closed down for as long as he's been on the job." Why he hadn't succeeded was a mystery; Vicki had always managed to outsmart him. It was rather an impressive feat, Pandora had to admit. "Some of you might agree with him on that, but might I remind you that if the inmates—I mean, patients—

aren't in here, they're going to be out there amongst you. So pick your poison."

Bones rolled her eyes and made a circular motion with her finger. *Get on with it*, she mouthed.

"Anyway, Hank Jackson wants this place closed down for a very particular reason that has nothing to do with saving you money or helping the patients here. No. Mr. Jackson has a dirty, little secret, and just now he tried to blackmail me into keeping that secret. But I got away, and now I'm going to tell you what that secret it."

Bones leaned forward, interest piqued.

"Hank Jackson is not his real name. He's really Henry Hanigan." A gasp went up from the crowd, though mostly from the older cronies. They remembered the Hanigans. "Yep, those Hanigans. The same rich old farts who once lorded it over Bedlam, and whose granddaughter, Hank's daughter, ended up killing herself in this very place. Hank Jackson abandoned her as a baby, and abandoned her again when she got sick and had to come to Nepenthe Manor for treatment. She was left all alone, and she couldn't handle it and she killed herself. All because he was too selfish to take care of his own child."

The door swung open and Pandora spun about. "Lies!" Hank shouted as he rushed inside. He reached for the microphone. "Give me that!"

Pandora held it out of reach from him. "Help!" she cried into it.

After a short struggle, he managed to grab the mic and yank it out of her hand, then knock her backward with a violent swing of his arm. She fell to the floor clutching her eye where his fist had connected, the other hand holding her head where it had hit the wall. "This girl is clearly delusional. We all know she tried to kill herself only a month ago."

"I did not!" she protested feebly. "That was an accident!"

"She obviously isn't to be trusted," he went on as if she hadn't spoken. "Besides, I'm pretty sure *Bats* Belfry's reputation precedes her. Not the most believable person, is she?" All the way up here Pandora could hear murmurs of agreement.

Pandora wanted to launch herself at him, but her head was doing funny things. Her eyes found Bones, and she made a pleading expression. A long moment passed, then the girl stood up, her typically inscrutable expression a study in fury. She regarded Hank's smug expression as he looked out over the audience, an audience that was taking his side. Without warning her right hand darted out and punched Hank right in the solar plexus. He bent in half and she grabbed the mic, smacked him on the head with it, and he dropped to his knees as though in supplication.

"He paid me to sabotage this play," Bones said coolly into the microphone. "I have the money in my room. He also threatened me that if I didn't do it, I'd never see the outside of this place again. That he had the power to keep me here." She leaned out the window and pointed at them all. "He said he could do it to each and every one of you, too. That his power was supreme, and he could do what he wanted."

It was the perfect thing to say. The townsfolk might not care what Hank did to other people, but when he threatened to use his power on them, that's where they drew the line. Pandora gave Bones a thumbs-up as an angry uproar poured through the window.

Bones set down the microphone. "Are we even?"

"I'd say so."

"Good." She walked over to the door and opened it just as Dr. Steele, followed by Ms. Netterson, rushed inside.

"You bastard!" Dr. Steele cried, grabbing Hank by the shirt and hauling him to his feet. "You killed my sister!"

"I knew you were trouble from the moment I saw you," Hank sneered at him. "I recognized you, you self-righteous ass—the brother who abandoned his sister. That's right. Where were *you* when she needed you?"

Dr. Steele pulled back and punched Hank right across the jaw. Hank's eyes rolled and he crumpled. Dismayed, Dr. Steele let go and stepped back. "Did I kill him?"

"I certainly hope so," Pandora mumbled, rubbing her head. "But probably not. He's still breathing."

"If you hadn't done it, Andrew, I would have." Ms. Netterson took his arm and guided him away. "But now we need to leave." She fastened her beautiful eyes on Pandora, her expression confident. "You'll come up with a story, won't you?"

"We can't leave her," Dr. Steele protested, and something warm inside Pandora flared into life. "She's hurt."

Pandora wanted to hear more, but time was of the essence. "Nettie's right, doc. You need to get out of here. You avenged your sister, now go before you end up in jail."

"I don't care about that," he declared, looking like the hero in every movie she'd ever seen.

"You have important work to do helping people, Dr. Steele," she reminded him. "That's how you're going to make things right for your sister. You can't do that from jail."

Reality hit him, and he reluctantly nodded. "All right. But I'll be back in a few minutes."

"A few minutes," she repeated, then gave him a salute as Nettie pulled him out of the booth.

Thirty seconds later, the Chief of Police, Captain Red Banty, pushed into the booth, gun drawn. "Don't move, Jackson, or I'll shoot!"

Pandora held up her hands. "Put that thing down, Banty. I already took care of the ass. That'll teach him to try to kidnap me, then assault me, then malign my name."

The captain, whose nickname came from his red hair, was a Southern transplant who walked the line between being a rule follower and a renegade. He lowered his gun and waved it carelessly at Hank. "Y'all did this to him?"

She curled her hands into fists and held them up. "With a little help from Truth"—she brandished her right fist, then looked to her left—"and Justice."

"Well, then I've just about seen it all, haven't I, young lady?"

"I think you have, Captain. I think you have."

BALDING, AND WITH a slight paunch, Captain Banty didn't exactly run the tightest ship, but he wasn't totally incompetent, either. He used his walkie-talkie to call an ambulance and then ordered a couple officers to escort it to the hospital once it arrived.

"No one's escaping on my watch!" he declared with a flourish of his gun. It seemed the drama bug was infectious.

Dr. Steele, Nettie, and Vicki had tried to come in several times, but he shooed them away, saying it wouldn't take long to do what needed to be done.

When Hank, still out of it, had been carried away on a stretcher, the captain settled in to take Pandora's statement. He was in uniform, yet Pandora thought, to have arrived so quickly he had to have been in the theater watching the performance when all this was going down. Didn't he have any other clothes?

"So this is the man who tried to kidnap you last month?"

"He's the man who paid someone named Baker to kidnap me." He wrote this down.

"Do you have proof he did?"

"I asked him if he hired Baker and he said yes." More or less.

"Where's this Baker fella?"

"I believe he fled the country."

"That's a shame."

"Well, he grabbed me off the stage earlier and threatened me, so he's guilty of that, too."

"Not much to hold him on," he surmised.

"Attempted kidnapping? Assault?"

He shrugged. "You're still alive, aren't you? And he's got money. I have a feeling he'll be out in six months to a year. Your word against his, you know."

"That's total bullcrap."

"You said it." He paused, looked her over. "But I'll do my best to see he gets what he deserves."

"Really?" She couldn't help sounding a wee bit sarcastic.

He placed a hand over his heart. "I promised to uphold the law, and if, after some very thorough digging, we happen to find more dirt on him, all the better."

"He did change his name," she pointed out. "I think he disguised himself, too, by growing that ugly beard. And maybe he gained weight. That's probably why no one recognized him as Henry Hanigan. I'll bet there's something there. Some reason why."

"I reckon you're right."

She snapped her fingers. "There was a scandal. Something he did in college."

"I'll definitely look into that." He pushed himself to his feet, his knees cracking with the effort. "Best get you to the infirmary. There's one here, right?"

She nodded. "And you'll do everything you can?"

He tipped his hat. "Sure will, little lady. It's the least I could do. You lot here don't get your fair share of breaks, do you? Besides," he headed for the door, "I sure did like your play. Reminded me of how I felt growing up as the little fat kid nobody liked. Figured I'd come in an official capacity as a sort of back-up." Well, that explained the uniform. "To make sure everything went okay for y'all, and I ended up enjoying the heck out of myself."

Pandora was nearly speechless. Was this really 'the man' she was talking to? His show of support didn't jive at all with her impression of people in power. It had to be an anomaly, but damned if she wouldn't give credit where credit was due. "Well, I'm glad you were here, Captain Banty."

He grinned, and she could almost imagine the piece of grass clamped firmly between his teeth. "Me, too, sugar."

"Even though one of your officers is in the mayor's back pocket and you allow it." She couldn't resist stirring the pot, could she?

His blue eyes twinkled. "Ah, yes. Officer Riley." He paused, eyed her steadily. "Now are you sure he's all he seems to be?" She stared at him. Could it be that Officer Riley, the man who let Dougie get away with speeding and no doubt numerous other infractions, was a double agent? How intriguing, and wouldn't it just kill Dougie to know that? Not that she'd let on. For the moment anyway. "Now go get yourself looked at. Heard you've had your fair share of accidents lately. Wouldn't want any of that sticking, now would we?"

"We would not," she agreed. She gave him a salute. "See you around, Captain."

He grinned. "Not if I see you first!" Then he slipped out the door, chuckling to himself.

Knowing now that the man was a bit smarter than he looked, Pandora was glad Bones had bailed before he'd arrived, for her own sake, and for the sake of their story. A former drug addict wouldn't be considered the most reliable witness. But where would she go now? What would she do? Could she even leave the manor without the proper paperwork?

The door had barely shut before it opened again and Dr. Steele and Nettie rushed in. "Where's Vicki?" Pandora asked, then shut her mouth. Why did she care?

"She felt she'd better deal with all the townspeople," Dr. Steele explained. "They had a lot of questions. As do I."

Nettie placed a hand on his shoulder. "All of which can wait. Right now we need to get Pandora to the infirmary." Seeing the intimate gesture, Pandora looked away, feeling a little sick. She'd seen this coming, but had hoped she'd been wrong. Dr. Steele was hers, and she didn't want to share him.

There. She'd said it. She wanted him all to herself. Maybe not as a boyfriend. He was a bit old for her. At the moment, anyway. But maybe as a friend. A mentor.

Or a father.

She pushed that provoking thought away. "I'm fine, Nettie," she said brusquely. "You two go do what you need to do. I have work to do, too. Lots of clean-up."

"The others and I can manage all that," Dr. Steele offered. "Besides, I think we'll be doing this all again tomorrow."

"Tomorrow?"

"And maybe a matinee on Sunday."

"A matinee on Sunday?" She clamped her mouth shut; she sounded like an idiot parrot.

"People loved the play. A lot of them want to come back, actually, and word is spreading. You up for it?"

Loved the play? Had she died and gone to some sort of heaven? "Of course I am." But could they do it without Bones? She didn't think they could.

"Good, because you missed your curtain call tonight."

"I was a little busy," she responded, deciding not to share what all had happened with Hank. He'd tell Vicki, and Pandora would never get to do anything again.

He studied her for a moment, then held out his hand to her. "Come on." She couldn't help glancing up at Nettie, who nodded and gave her a mischievous wink. Pandora took hold of Dr. Steele's warm, dry hand, slightly calloused from his work on the sets, and he pulled her to her feet. She swayed a moment, then righted herself against the wall.

Sensing their concern, she stated firmly, "I don't have another con-cussion, if that's what you're worried about." She felt the back of her head. "Just a bump."

"And a black eye," Nettie noted, looking her over.

"Nothing a little stage make-up can't fix," Pandora said firmly. She was not about to be sidelined, though she liked that Nettie had noticed the black eye. It felt good to be bathed in attention from one of the beautiful people, those gods that walk amongst us. It was like a benediction.

"Let's go join the others." Dr. Steele motioned for her to go ahead, and grabbed the door when she opened it to hold it for her. Exactly like a dad would do.

Stop that! she admonished herself.

As she carefully descended the steps, she noted that the theater had cleared out, and the crew was cleaning up and organizing without her having to say a word. If any of their families had talked to them after the play, it appeared they hadn't caused too much damage.

Xavier nodded as she stepped onto the stage. "Heard the good news about the play?"

He was speaking to her? "We're doing two more shows. Not sure I'd call that good news."

"But you're a hit."

She looked around at everyone working, spotting Bones helping Derek move the Arctic tundra scene. So she hadn't bugged out. Not yet, anyway. "*We're* a hit."

He gave her a disbelieving look. "Pandora Belfry sharing the spot-light?"

She returned his disbelieving look with a dry one. "Stranger things have happened."

"Stranger things always seem to happen to you. Like that guy. Did he really do all that?" He fixated on her eye. "And that?"

"He did," she replied, pleased to note that her brother actually looked angry. It was also a little odd to have someone related to her being so protective, and she wasn't sure exactly how to handle that.

Luckily Dr. Steele joined them at that moment, but without Ms. Net-terson. "Where's Nettie going?" she asked. She'd wanted to talk to her about something she needed her to do. Looks like she'd have to call her tomorrow morning.

He turned to watch the librarian walking away, her hourglass figure swaying back and forth, a bemused smile on his face. He was totally hot for the woman. Well, at least now Pandora didn't have to worry about him getting it on with Vicki. That could have turned into an Oedipus redux of massive proportions.

"She's off to get more tickets to sell and to print out more programs." When she disappeared out the door, he turned to face Pandora. Xavier had rushed over to help Derek and Bones with the platform, which had been wobbling, leaving the two of them alone. Dr. Steele was frowning in thought. "How on earth did you know all that about Hank?"

"A bit of brilliant deduction actually. It was the picture you showed me of Elizabeth. She looked familiar, but I thought it was because she looked like you. And then, when I saw Hank, aka Henry Hanigan, under a light, I got that feeling again—that there was some sort of connection I needed to be making. It was only right as he grabbed me that I figured it out. Elizabeth's father is Hank Jackson. That stupid beard of his threw me for a while. Apparently, when you came here, it got him nervous, because of course he knew who you were. That meeting you had with him while Vicki was in the hospital with the professor? Hank was so agreeable, which he never is, because he didn't want you focusing too much attention on him." She smiled to herself. And here Dougie had thought it was because of his keen intellect and manipulative abilities.

"I never saw it," he said regretfully. "The resemblance."

"That's because you don't have my awesome observational skills." He raised a challenging eyebrow. "How do you think I survived this place so long?"

"True," he said, conceding the point. "But I should've known."

"Why would you want someone you loved to resemble someone who's creepy as all get out?"

He laughed. "He is creepy as all get out, isn't he? But you could be right. The mind works in mysterious ways."

"That it does."

His expression softened and she steeled herself, suspecting he was about to say something terribly sentimental. "I'm glad I told you about Elizabeth, Pandora."

"Because it helped me nail Hank?" she asked, affecting nonchalance.

"That, and because afterward I felt so much lighter. A burden shared is a burden halved." Ah, there it was, the proverbial platitude, and even drippier than she'd been expecting. "I hope someday to be able to do the same for you."

Pandora felt a chill run down her spine as she remembered herself thinking of Dr. Steele as a father figure. Had he read her mind? "I'm afraid my burdens are rather tricky, doc, and dislike being halved." She flailed around for another topic. "Um... Nettie, I mean, Ms. Netterson, is nice." Crap. She hadn't meant to go down that road. But he'd thrown her with his drippy offer, and she wasn't firing on all cylinders.

He paused a moment, regarding her with those knowing blue eyes of his. "She is."

"I suppose you guys will probably go out on a date." Her tone was grudging, but she couldn't help herself. "I mean, if you're interested in her. Cause she's great, and you're not half-bad yourself."

He grinned. "Are you giving us your blessing?"

"I can't imagine how you could proceed without it," she quipped. "Cause, well, I kind of feel like you and I are, I don't know"—she looked away—"family now, after all we've been through." She let out a long breath as she stared down at the tips of her old-fashioned shoes. She'd said it out loud, and she couldn't take it back, and she didn't want to. *Now who's being drippy?* she scolded herself, but she didn't apologize.

When the silence had stretched to breaking, Pandora looked up, preparing herself for the disgust she felt sure she was about to see. But it wasn't disgust. Dr. Steele was wiping at his eyes, and nodding. "I'm honored you think of me as family, Pandora. I feel the same way about you." He slung an arm around her shoulders, and she didn't feel all tingly, like before. She just felt kind of safe, and protected.

"Now, now," she said. "No need to get all emotional."

He laughed and pulled away. "Sorry. Emotion is kind of my thing."

"I've noticed that, Dr. Drip." Not wanting her own emotions to get any ideas, she quickly indicated the others, working hard, without her having to direct them once. She still couldn't quite get over the miracle of it. "Should we go help out before you dissolve into a useless pool of tears?"

He laughed. "Okay, okay. One more thing, though..."

"If you're going to ask if you can ride Shadow, then you're pushing your luck."

He grinned. "I wouldn't dare. Actually, I thought maybe after the matinee you could come with me to the graveyard. I visit Elizabeth's grave every Sunday afternoon." Elizabeth's grave was at Nepenthe Manor? She mentally reviewed all the headstones, but didn't remember an Elizabeth Hanigan. "We could visit the professor's, too."

She'd been avoiding the graveyard ever since the professor's funeral. *I have to wash my hair,* was what she wanted to tell Dr. Steele. Cause she didn't want to go, and if she ever did, she certainly didn't want to go when there were witnesses. She'd been feeling so weepy lately, she was certain she'd break down sobbing, and she didn't want Dr. Steele seeing that. He'd go all doctory on her, and no way was she feeding that beast.

"Thanks, but some other time," she finally managed to get out.

"Of course. When you're ready."

She gave him a fake smile and scurried away to call Nettie. That was the problem with letting down your defenses. Once lowered, people found a way to get inside, and when they got in, they'd see things. And the things Dr. Steele would see in her, well they'd likely send him running all the way to Mexico. That was not something she could let happen.

35

Off My Meds

SATURDAY'S PERFORMANCE HAD been jam-packed, the front row filled with screaming girls who were there not just to see Derek, but Dougie, too. It looked like their Sunday matinee was going to be more of the same. An hour before the curtains were to go up and already the front row was filled with giggling, simpering females. Pandora viewed the girls sourly. She was the one who'd written the screenplay, organized the posse, directed and acted, and had basically made all this happen. And did she have any fans screaming her name?

They didn't even *know* her name.

Since the Hank incident, she'd managed to steer clear of Dougie and Derek, not feeling up to talking to either one of them right now. They'd want to know details about Hank, which the posse kept badgering her to give all day Saturday, and she really didn't want to go into it, having had to relive the incident in her dreams. Besides, a weird tension existed between them all, and it made Pandora wary. Something was off, but she didn't have the time or energy to figure it out. But as soon as the play was over, she'd fix things with both of them. If only for her sanity, which, come to think of it, was a rather ironic way to put it.

Bones had stuck around, thank goodness, and had 'sabotaged' the play once more, though this time Derek and Dougie knew exactly what to do when she turned out the lights and started the recording. But why had she stayed on? And did she plan on staying indefinitely?

Twenty minutes before the play was to start she cornered Bones up in the control booth, expertly picking the lock and letting herself into the room. She needed some answers. She sniffed at the air, which smelled like lemons. Was Xavier up here? Looking around, she ascertained he wasn't, but then she realized Bones was sucking on something as she fiddled with the sound board. A lemon drop, perhaps?

"You're still here."

"Way to state the obvious." Bones's response was belligerent, her mouth set into two stubborn lines. When Pandora didn't answer, she went on, "I've got a job to do, don't I?"

"Wait. So you're *staying* at Nepenthe Manor?"

Bones looked at her like she'd just sprung another head out of her neck. "Staying here? Hell, no. As soon as the play is over, I'm outta this hellhole. Dougie's taking care of the paperwork for me. I wasn't meant to be here anyway. I might be a druggie, but I'm not crazy."

"You're clean now, though, aren't you?"

Bones peered down at her bare arms. They looked relatively smooth and mark-free. "For now."

"Do you have a place to stay? You'll go back to using if you're around your old friends."

"You think I don't know that?" Bones barked, then shrugged. "I was thinking of going to Kensington, maybe see if I can get into a theater company there."

"You'll need money for the bus, for a place to stay, for food."

"I have what Mr. Jackson gave me. It's not much, but it's a start."

"I'd give you some money, but I'm dead broke. Though maybe I can sell something of mine." She mentally scoped out her room.

"That eager to get rid of me?"

Pandora nodded vigorously. "Uh, *yeah*."

Bones chuckled. "I still don't like you, Belfry, but you're funny, I'll give you that."

Pandora had to force the next words out because she really didn't want to say them. "Well, if the city doesn't work out, you can always come back here."

Bones gave her a look. "I'd rather slit my throat."

"No, you wouldn't, drama queen."

"Yeah, maybe not. Bit messy." Bones looked out at the house, and her whole body went stiff, as though preparing to get hit. A few seconds passed before she spoke again, her voice low. "So, um, thanks, all right?"

Pandora felt her own self going all rigid. "For what?"

"For giving me something to do."

"Oh, that." She relaxed. "You were doing me a favor. You've seen this lot. It's like herding cats." Bones nodded in agreement. "Also, you took out Hank. I meant what I said before, we're totally even."

Bones continued staring outward at the gathering crowd. "I like even," she said quietly.

"Good." Pandora went to the door. The play would be starting soon.

"Hey, Belfry?" Her hand on the knob, Pandora turned back around. "You and Xavier. Whatever your problem is, you need to get over it. You're lucky to have a brother like him, you know."

"Says the girl who doesn't have to deal with his ego on a daily basis."

Bones snorted. "Says the girl whose ego is bigger than this planet."

Pandora decided not to touch that one. "You like him, don't you?"

"So what if I do? He's been a good friend. It's not often a person stands up for someone like me." She must be referring to their fight, when Xavier had intervened and saved her from getting a beating. Pandora was pretty sure he hadn't done it for Bones's sake, but she decided not to share that bit of information. Which was very noble of her.

"Did you tell him you like him?" Interesting question coming from someone who would rather cut off her own arm and eat it than admit something like that to anyone.

Bones refused to look at her. "He deserves better than a junkie, you idiot."

"You're not a junkie. Not anymore."

"Shows what you know. Once a junkie, always a junkie."

"Okay, fine. But it's not all you are, you know. You're also, um, good at knocking people to the floor, and doing this." She indicated the booth. "You're good at this. Very good."

Silence.

She turned the doorknob. "Break a leg, all right?" She laughed, rapping her knuckles on the door. "Normally I'd have meant that literally. But not today." A slight dip to Bones's head and a faint smile showed she'd heard. It would have to do.

The play began, and their final performance turned out *mostly* disaster-free. Lucy, having let fame go to her head, had decided she liked improvising and making people laugh. She was a hit, and she didn't screw things up too badly—and luckily Dougie handled her antics well. The audience clapped especially hard when she gave her last bow at the end of the show, so Pandora put it in the win column.

The stage after the performance quickly filled with fans, and Xavier didn't even bother closing the curtains. A gaggle of girls, and even a few guys, surrounded him as he expounded on his set-building expertise, and he looked quite pleased with himself. The control booth, when she looked up at it, was dark, and Pandora sensed that they'd seen the last of Bones for some time. Maybe forever. She actually felt kind of weirdly sorry about that.

Finally the girls left, with autographs and giggles and longing looks at the boys, and several at Dr. Steele, who'd had to convince them that their depression, now that the play was over, was not serious, and that coming to Nepenthe Manor for a stay definitely wasn't the way to cure it. Dougie left with one of the girls, and Pandora wondered if it was the infamous Debbie. She was very pretty, but looked wildly distraught, tears running down her perfect face. It just now occurred to Pandora that with the downfall of Hank came the downfall of his whole family, Debbie included. She wasn't sure whether to feel triumphant or what. The sour twisting in her gut was quite clear on the subject, and Pandora scowled. She did *not* want to feel sorry for Debbie Jackson.

When they were gone, a lone figure stepped out from the shadows. He was tall and wearing a hat and Pandora felt a rush of happiness inside her when she saw him.

"Skippy!" Lucy cheered, then raced toward him. Charles followed, and Birdy screeched and knocked them out of the way to envelop the poor boy in a massive hug. Everyone gathered around, all asking questions at once.

"Wasn't I great?" Birdy cried, clutching him tightly.

"Are you back for good?" Charles asked the more important question.

"Where the hell you been?" Lucy demanded, another good one.

Sinclair kept looking back and forth between her and Skippy and nodding, as if reaffirming something. She didn't like that look.

Finally Birdy released Skippy, and he was able to talk. "I'm definitely back for good," he announced with a grin. "My dad dropped me off this afternoon, just before the play. The Director let me come watch. It was really awesome, by the way." Everyone clapped and hollered in agreement.

"He just dropped you off?" Pandora queried, suspicious. She needed this to be permanent, not temporary.

"Turns out all I had to do was make his life miserable. Sadly, it didn't take much." His toe tapped the stage anxiously. "I went off my meds, and he couldn't handle it."

She pulled a dismayed face. "You went off your meds? Are you back on them now?"

"Oh, I went back on them pretty quickly when I realized that I could just act crazy, and that would be enough."

Pandora suppressed a sigh of relief. Skippy off his meds was not a pretty sight. "Well, I for one am really glad you're back." The posse chorused their agreement, punctuated by a "Woo-hoo!" from Lucy.

He beamed. "Me, too. It was awesome being on the outside, out there using my wits to survive in the real world, but I missed you guys. We did some really cool things, though! I can't wait to tell you all about them." Judging by the avid expressions on the posse's faces, Skippy was going to dine out on this experience for the next year. "Did I miss much here?"

Everyone started laughing and talking at him, catching him up on all that had happened. Pandora gestured to Sinclair, and he separated from the others. When he saw her expression, he shrunk a little, knowing exactly what was coming.

"What gives, Sinclair? Why have you been watching me like a hawk all month, and why do you keep looking at Skippy like you're the one who brought him home?"

Sinclair paused, then reached into his pocket and pulled out a much worn note. Clearly he'd been expecting her to ask this question for some time now. After giving him an assessing look, she opened it and read it.

I stopped repeating myself and terrible things happened. The Professor died, Skippy got taken away, and you jumped off a bridge. When I started up again, good things happened. I should have known better. I got selfish and tried to make a life for myself, but I'm over that now. I will not fail you again.

She read the neatly written note once more while composing her thoughts. When she knew what she wanted to say, she called out, "Everyone? Get over here. We need to clear something up." Sensing a developing drama, they stopped their talking and scurried over to surround her and Sinclair. Dr. Steele stopped what he was doing and joined them. Derek stuck to the edges, as though he wished he were somewhere else. Sinclair, for his part, looked ill. "So here's the deal. Sinclair has gotten it into his head that he's the reason for what happened to me and the professor and Skippy."

"But he had nothing to do with it," Skippy protested. "It was my dad who took me."

"Did you hear that, Sinclair?" Of course he'd heard it, but judging by his mulish expression, he wasn't buying it. "You don't have control over our lives, and it's actually kind of arrogant to think that you do. You didn't hurt us, and you didn't save us. If that were possible, the world would either be a much better place, or a much worse one."

"My world couldn't get any better," Birdy stated dramatically, her arm firmly wrapped around Skippy. "I finally know what I want to do when I get out of here—be an actress, of course—and I have my man back."

Pandora could easily have dissected everything Birdy had said, but why bother? What would it accomplish? Besides, she'd literally just told Sinclair he was arrogant because he thought he could control everything. And maybe, just maybe, this was a little bit of the pot calling the kettle black.

Maybe.

"You have to go back to doing whatever it is you were doing before the bad things happened, Sinclair." She couldn't let on that Derek had told her what that was—cleaning up the labyrinth. She'd promised. "Whatever you were doing, it made you happy." He shook his head stubbornly. "All right, fine. What if we were to do it with you? So you could keep an eye on us?" His brow wrinkled as he thought this over. Slowly he began to nod. It was a start. "Good. You'll probably have to tell us what it was, and then we'll go do it when we have the theater all set to rights."

He nodded again, and the posse cheered. Their life was orderly once more, with a project ahead of them to look forward to. For them, life was good. For Pandora, several issues remained to be fixed.

One of Them

36

"XAVIER," SHE CALLED out as he started walking toward the workshop. "We need to talk."

He stopped, turned. Slowly. Then he waited for the others to move farther away before he spoke. She noticed he was looking better these days, other than that stupid mullet he insisted on keeping.

"I thought you didn't like talking about things."

"I'm standing up for myself, and that's different." *Clearly.* "So why are you mad at me?"

His expression went blank. "I thought I made that clear."

"Oh, please. I don't think my jumping off a bridge is the real reason you're mad at me."

He regarded her warily. "What makes you think that?"

"Because the last time I talked to you before I fell I said we should go to the town-wide yard sale next weekend. Someone who wants to kill herself doesn't plan for the future."

He fiddled with his earring. "You could've been trying to mislead me."

"Why bother? Besides, if I had wanted to die, I'd be dead, and there wouldn't have been any conversation about it. I'm not like Birdy, constantly threatening with words and half-assed attempts to get attention. I would never play that game. Other games, yes. But not that one."

"Okay, fine," he said mulishly. "So you didn't want to die. That's just great."

She stared at him. "It kind of is *great.*"

"But I wasn't there."

"Of course you weren't. I was in my grandmother's car."

His mouth screwed up. "You don't get it. I didn't even know your grandmother was taking you away. And even if I had known, I wouldn't have known what to do about it. I couldn't save my mom or the professor or you because I didn't know how. And I hate that, this feeling of not having any control, like watching an accident happen and there's nothing you can do to stop it."

"Well, I don't like it, either, you idiot. Nobody does."

"You still don't get it." He looked down at his scuffed high-tops. "You can't die, Pandora." His voice shook, but he pushed on. "You're the only family I've got left. Well, you and my grandma, but she's completely evil, so she doesn't count. You're only partly evil." He peeked over at her. "I'm more mad at myself, really, for not doing something, but I took it out on you because you make it so easy." He sniffed and gave her a little grin.

"Thanks. That's very touching." Actually, it had been, especially when his voice had gone all wobbly. "But just so you know, Dr. Steele and Vlad didn't do anything to help me, either, and they *did* know. I'm not going anywhere, Xavier. We still have to hit some yard sales. You can use all that money you made off Dr. Steele from *babysitting* me, even though you failed miserably at your job." He had the grace to look a little embarrassed. "We missed the big one, but usually you can find a few every weekend all summer long. Besides, you need to learn to drive so you can give me rides and scare the hell out of me cause you suck so bad."

"For your information, I'm an excellent driver. Dr. Steele took me out a few times this month, and I was pretty awesome."

She made a disbelieving face. "Awesome at sucking, maybe."

"Just plain awesome." He paused for a moment, stared over her head at something in the distance. "Do you miss him?"

She didn't have to ask to know he meant the professor. "I suppose I do. A bit. I miss more what could have been."

"At least you got some time with him."

"Yeah, well, at least he loved your mom more than mine."

His eyes fastened on hers. "He what?"

"I heard him say it, right before he went into the hospital. He was sort of rambling, but he said he loved your mom best, and that he should've stuck by her no matter how bad your grandma was, and that he was going to her. Vicki doesn't know he said this," she warned. "It'd probably push her over the edge if she did, so don't say anything."

Xavier turned away, but not before she caught the gleam of tears in his eyes. She bit her lip so the same wouldn't happen to her. "You're not making that up?" he asked, his voice all wobbly again.

She held up her hand, even though he couldn't see it. "I swear on the professor's freshly dug grave."

All the air seemed to whoosh out of Xavier, then he made some swiping motions across his face before turning back around. "Well, that's crappy for you and your mom, but thanks for telling me."

"Yeah, well, it'll be one more sucky experience to add to my memoir."

"It's probably going to be a long memoir."

"You know it."

He pulled in a deep breath, and let it out with real force, as though clearing himself of bad mojo. "Speaking of sucky experiences, do you know what's going on with Derek?"

"You think something's wrong with him, too?"

"Oh, yeah. Definitely. Even though his mom's doing better he's gotten more distant. Cagey, even. Not like him at all. Something's up."

She sighed. "Something is always up with that guy."

"Go talk to him."

"Why me?"

"You know why, idiot."

"Bones likes you," she blurted out, not wanting to deal with the implication behind Xavier's words. Because if he'd noticed Derek's 'feelings' toward her, then maybe others had, and maybe they'd seen hers toward him. Talk about being in a spotlight she didn't want shining on her.

He shifted uncomfortably. "Huh. Well, she's cool, but she's not really my type."

"Because she's a junkie?"

"Well, I'd be lying if I said that didn't matter. But no. That's not it."

"Too Stygian?"

"No, she's not too dark. And that's STI-jee-an. Not sty-GEE-en."

Damnit. Another word she'd gotten wrong. "Because she's Hispanic, then?"

"What? Are you crazy? No! She's just not my type," he repeated stubbornly. "All right?"

"All right, all right. Message received. Though, for the record, some people are prejudiced against Hispanics, so it was a legit question. I don't get it myself. With the exception of Bones, they always seem so full of life."

Xavier shook his head, then pointed toward the seats. "Derek's out there picking up programs. Better catch him now when Dougie's not around to ruin things."

"He does wreak havoc, doesn't he?"

"I think that's why you let him stick around."

"Maybe," she conceded. "I do rather like havoc." *The more chaos, the better*, was her motto, after all.

Xavier shoved her toward the house. "Go."

"Fine. Maybe we can get Dr. Steele to drive us if there are any yard sales next weekend?"

Xavier smiled. "I'll check my calendar."

"The one with nothing written on it?"

He shoved her again. "Stop stalling."

She was stalling. But damn his eyes, Xavier was right, this had to be done. And now. She couldn't stand any more of the drama. She left the stage, and started picking up programs, slowly making her way toward Derek. When he saw her he stopped and straightened up. He was still in his costume, or what was left of it, and Pandora found herself suddenly, and absolutely, speechless.

"Hey," he greeted, almost shyly.

"Hey. You, um, did a really great job as the Creature. People loved you."

He gave her a wry smile. "Let's just say I'm glad I won't have to wear this anymore." He indicated his barely there costume.

"It's a good look for you." She couldn't believe she'd just said that. But, boy, did she mean it.

Luckily he ignored the compliment. "What happened to your eye?"

"Hank Jackson did it." She'd covered it with stage make-up, but apparently this close up it could still be seen.

His face went red. "You mean it?" She nodded, and he started breathing hard. "That jerk! If he were here, I'd punch him into next week, picking on a defenseless girl like that."

"Defenseless girl?"

His eyes widened. "I didn't mean it like that, Pandora. I just meant he's twice as big as you, and you've been under a lot of pressure. You're not defenseless, and you're definitely not a girl."

Not a girl? Did that mean what she thought it meant? That he thought of her as a woman? She promptly decided to put him out of his misery. "Mellow out, man. I forgive you."

He grinned sheepishly, and the blush faded. "Thanks." He paused, cleared his throat. "I wanted to thank you for something else, too."

"For what?"

He started rolling up the stack of programs in his hands. "For giving me this part. I know I didn't want to do it at first, but it fits me. Like that Mary Shelley lady knew exactly how I felt, like she knew what I lived with every day."

"I feel the same way whenever I read the book. Being different isn't easy, is it?"

He nodded, then looked down. "Especially when you can't hide it."

"Exactly."

"The funny thing is," he said thoughtfully as he rolled the programs into an impossibly small tube. "It seems to me you go out of your way to *not* fit in."

"I do not!" He pointed the tube at her spiky hair. "Oh, well. That was a protest. I didn't do it for me, I did it for everyone who's oppressed."

His lips twitched. "Well, we thank you."

"Are you teasing me?"

"I'm glad you're still around to be teased."

"About that." She paused, took a deep breath. "I don't think I was trying to kill myself."

"I know."

She stared at him. "You do?"

"I was there."

"That day? But—" And then it all came together, what he meant to say to her in the apartment. Why Dougie refused to tell her who her rescuer was. "You saved me."

"I pulled you out of the river and did mouth-to-mouth. You were dead, Pandora, and then you gagged and spit out a bunch of water and came back to life." That last part didn't sound nearly as romantic as the first bit, and she decided to be sure to delete it from future fantasies. "You spoke to me. You asked if it worked. Your plan." Her *plan*. Could it be? "You said you did it so you could become an inmate and stay at Nepenthe Manor."

"I said that?" Now that sounded more like her, and explained why she'd moved all her stuff to the secret room. So she could hang out there whenever she needed to get away from the other inmates, since there was no way her mother would let her stay in her bedroom if she was a suicide risk. Not with the unbarred windows, the mirror that could be turned into a hundred sharp blades, the access to cleaning supplies, the actual sharp blades in the silverware drawer. It would show preferential treatment, which Vicki wouldn't allow. So it appeared that Pandora had made sure that once she was an inmate, she wouldn't actually have to live like one. Classic.

"So I knew you didn't want to die, and because my ma *did* want to die, I had to stay by her side and not spend time with you like I wanted to. Her new medication made her feel like that. She's better now, though."

"I'm glad for that, Derek. I really am." And she was—she liked Derek's mom—but she was still confused about a few things. "How did you get to me in time?"

"I was walking over to visit my ma—I took the road cause it was high tide—and that's when I saw you pass by in your grandma's car. I saw the determined expression on your face."

"You're sure I didn't want to die, though? I can't remember any of it." Not even the mouth-to-mouth, which would have served as a great way to occupy her mind while in the hospital, and probably for the next six months. Hell, for the rest of her life. Minus the choking and spitting, of course.

"I'm sure. I've never run so fast in my life. Good thing the driver was so slow."

"Yeah, Jenkins drives like a turtle. It's because he's, like, a hundred and twenty years old."

Derek smiled, though it didn't quite reach his eyes. He looked at the rolled up programs in his hands, then set them down on the floor, like he was stalling. "I'm glad you're doing so well now, Pandora, because now I know I can leave and you're gonna be all right."

"Leave? Right now?"

He gave her a strange look. "Yes. For a good long while. You know, when we move."

"Move?" She felt suddenly breathless. "Tell me you're kidding."

He looked pained. "I wouldn't kid about something like that, Pandora."

"But why?" A wordless shrug. "Your dad's making you do this, isn't he?"

"If I don't do what I'm told, Pandora, someone gets hurt. My friends, my family. Me, sometimes. I don't want to go, but if I don't, we could lose everything. My ma will get sick again, and my pa will give up on everything again. I can't let that happen. It's bad enough he's already given up his pride, selling our place to a Daft. I can't make it worse by fighting him on this."

What he was saying finally clicked. "Don't tell me you're selling to Mayor Daft!"

"Mayor Daft?" He regarded her closely. "Um, no. Wrong Daft."

"Then who—" Obviously not Mrs. Daft, which left only one Daft. "*Dougie.*" That skeeze. She'd kill him…slowly.

Derek leaned closer, his forehead furrowed, as he tried to read her face. "I thought you knew."

She found herself leaning toward him. He had that effect on her, like a big, muscley magnet. "How would I know that?"

"I figured Dougie had bragged about it. How could he not? Especially to you. I thought you knew all along. That's why I was kind of mad at you before, and why I didn't want to do the play."

She felt sick. "I'd never have supported this, Derek. *Never.*" She shivered a little, feeling something precious slipping from her grasp. "You can't go."

He sighed. "I know it don't—it doesn't—always look it, but my ma and pa have done right by me. So I have to do right by them. That means being there for my ma, and doing what my pa asks of me."

"But you shouldn't have to ruin your life for them."

"My pa never did anything bad to me, though it might've looked that way at the basketball game. He wouldn't've hit me, though. He never has once. He just gets scared sometimes and it comes out in anger. Right then, I was where he could direct it. And my ma, she was better, back when I was younger. We were close, and we did stuff together as a family. But then she started getting sick more and more often, and my pa started watching me, thinking I'd turn, like she did. Sometimes I thought I'd turn just cause he was watching me so much." Pandora could understand that. "But it was just his way. It's all he knew how to do."

"All he could control."

"Right."

"Where will you go?" she asked briskly, tears threatening. She could not break down. Not here, not now. She couldn't do that to him. She wouldn't add her weight to his already much too heavy burden. Plus she was still wearing stage make-up, and it would run, and his last image of her would be her face melting.

Which actually might be kind of cool.

But no, she must stay strong.

"To the next town over. My uncle has a farm there and a small cabin on his property. We'd live there and help out with the work."

"But when would I ever see you?"

"That's just it, Pandora." He looked miserable. "Probably not much. Maybe when I come visit my ma. But I've got a feeling that won't happen as often as I'd like. The money just ain't there."

So much for my happy ending. No wonder I decided to jump. Pandora's hand flew to her mouth. *Oh!*

So now she knew. She was one of them. There was no plan. She'd truly wanted to die. But did that make her forever crazy, like the posse?

"But I still owe you for the Coke you gave me," she pushed out. "I still owe you."

"You don't owe me nothing. I mean anything, Pandora." He held out his hand. "Can we part as friends?" She reached out, slowly, then cautiously took hold of his hand. It was warm and strong, like always, and it swallowed hers whole, like always.

Just when it was starting to get a little awkward—like what was supposed to happen next?—he pulled her to him, and before she knew it her cheek was pressed against his bare chest, and they were hugging so hard.

She could have stayed there forever.

37

Quite Enamored

OF COURSE, DOUGIE had to ruin it. "Pandora, we need to talk," he called across the theater. He was using his mic, so she heard him quite clearly.

She didn't move, hoping he'd go away, like all the way to the moon. She was not in the mood to talk to that manipulative bastard.

"Now."

She sighed. "Hang on a sec, Derek." She pulled away just a bit and leaned around him. "Can't you see I'm busy?"

Dougie didn't so much as twitch. "Derek's mother is asking for him."

"How do you know that? You weren't in the patients ward."

He held up a walkie-talkie. "How else?"

Derek stepped back and she felt his warmth leaving her. "We won't be moving for another month or so, Pandora. We'll talk again, all right?"

"It better be soon, or I'm coming to your place, pa or not."

He grinned. "I think you scare him."

She laughed and pressed a hand to her chest. "Little ol' defenseless me?"

"You're about as defenseless as a mama bear with a hatchet."

She laughed. "Well, he should be scared. I don't like that he's doing this to you."

"I don't think he has much choice, either. When my mom got sick he couldn't work like he used to, had to take odd jobs. Then the taxes on our property went way up, it being on the ocean and all." She remembered overhearing Vicki complaining about the tax increase to Bennington a while back. "We just couldn't swing it anymore."

She suddenly deflated. It seemed lately that lots of people had the same problem—no choice. Not a real one anyway. "All right. Go. Say hi to your mom for me. I'll see you soon. Maybe we can go share a Coke at the Chowder Shack. I might have some allowance coming my way, and it would be my treat."

He smiled. "I'd like that."

"Pandora…" Dougie called, his impatience amplified via the microphone, which might just find itself getting broken in two.

"I'm coming, you troll!" She looked up at Derek. "Soon."

"Soon." With a smile, he headed to the dressing room to change.

She sighed despondently. No choice. No control. No life. She looked up to see Dougie heading toward her. "What do you want?"

"He told you what I did." Lucky for the microphone, Dougie had turned it off.

"He thought I already knew."

"Ah. Well, it was the only way to get him to do the play."

"What?"

"I told him that if he didn't cooperate there was a chance his mother would get kicked out because they couldn't pay."

"You tricked him into doing the play?" The pain in her gut flared to life, making her want to gag. No wonder there was such animosity between them. How could Derek have even stood to be around her, thinking she'd known everything Dougie had done? And not once had Derek told on Dougie, even afterwards, he'd never said a thing. "But there are programs that could cover her stay. SSI, Medicaid. Something."

"Ah, yes. I forgot about those."

"No, you didn't. You manipulated him." And then tried to manipulate her by intimating that he'd 'let it go,' it being his threat against Mrs. Choken, if Pandora agreed to drop Derek.

He blinked even more slowly than usual, and she had to wonder if this was another tell. "I told you I would take care of things, and I did."

"But not like that! You forced him to do it."

"And it ended up being a good thing for him."

"The end justifies the means…"

"Exactly," he said softly. "I knew you'd understand."

"I understand the saying, Dougie. That doesn't mean I agree with it. What you did was just plain gross." He'd acted mad when Derek had volunteered for the play, when all along he'd known he was going to do it. Because he'd tricked him into doing it. And then he'd tried to make sure Derek didn't show up for dress rehearsal, probably using the same threat, to make Derek look bad in her eyes. She was appalled by Dougie's subterfuge, though her darker side couldn't help but be impressed with its complexity.

He frowned. "Your head injury really set you back, didn't it?"

"Set me back? How about I set you back?" She brandished her fist, furious. "Like into a wall?"

He gave her a small smile. "I'd like to see you try."

"You're such a shit, Dougie. I was actually starting to tolerate you, but now I see my brain injury was screwing up my thought processes more than I realized. I'm glad I'm finally coming to my senses."

"I was trying to help you, Pandora. And I did. I fail to see how I went wrong."

"So buying Derek's home out from under him doesn't count as assholery?"

"That's not a word, and once again, vulgarity does not suit you." He adjusted his cravat. "So that's what he told you about. Because he's leaving. How unfortunate." *For who?* she wondered. "I bought the Choken property to ensure that my father would never get his hands on Nepenthe Manor. I bought out the neighbors on the other side, as well."

"With what?"

"When I turned sixteen I came into my inheritance, given to me by my grandparents. Father tried to keep that bit of information from me, but Bartles found out about it ages ago. He heard Father talking to Hank Jackson about it once—how the money would allow them to buy all the land around the manor so they could shut this place down."

"But neither of them is going to get what they want." How satisfying that felt, and she owed that feeling to Dougie, which was mortifying.

"For the moment anyway. My father does not give up easily. Luckily for you, neither do I. Though I am rather upset with myself for not guessing who Hank Jackson was. I always knew he was a loathsome toady, but I didn't realize he was residing under an alias. I should have seen that. Now I understand why he pushed Debra toward me. He must have lost any money he inherited, and quite quickly, too. Hence the reason he took the lowly job of an inspector." And hence the reason he'd said to her in the orchestra pit, when she asked why he hadn't done anything to improve conditions at the manor, 'Let's just say something happened to prevent me,' meaning he'd lost all his money. She was quite sure, though, that if he hadn't lost it all, he still wouldn't have done anything. "My father more than likely made sure he got the position, so he'd have someone to do his bidding. But now, because of his friendship with Hank, my father will need to do damage control, which should keep him off my back for a while."

"So poor Debbie has lost you?"

"She never had me." Strangely gratifying to hear. "I'm quite rich now, Pandora, and I have used some of that newfound wealth to help you, as I said I would. I keep my promises."

"Oh, please. You bought the Choken property to get rid of Derek."

His expression didn't change, though she could almost feel the waves of satisfaction coming off him. "That was merely a bonus."

"So what else has your money done for you? Is Vlad still under your pay? Did you buy Ronny and Lonny too? Were they part of your weird plot?"

"The twins? Oh, no. I merely asked them to keep an eye on you and to monitor the comings and goings of visitors to Nepenthe Manor. In exchange, I introduced them to *Dungeons and Dragons*." Well, that explained their stalkerish ways, and also their strange conversation with Dougie about choosing their master. "It's a role-playing game. They are quite enamored of it."

"I know what D&D is, and I can't believe you got them into it." She closed her eyes, then opened them again. "Because they aren't cut off from reality as it is, Dougie! You used them, and you exploited their biggest vulnerability to get what you wanted."

"They are none the worse for it, I can guarantee you that. I have found them likeminded friends in town, who are quite willing to play the game with them. They have a social life now, which is not something they had before. Before they merely existed to open and close the gate and drive the Madmobile. Now they have something to look forward to."

It sounded great, for them anyway. But Pandora knew these sorts of 'favors' came with a cost. "All thanks to your generosity."

"I don't do generosity, Pandora. Everything they have now is merely a byproduct of my dedication to your safety. I was not put on this earth to make it better for others, but if that happens as a result of what I do for you, then so be it."

"So this is all my fault?"

"Your only fault is that you are sometimes blind to your place in this world."

"And that place is at your side?"

"In a manner of speaking."

"That's not happening, Dougie." She shivered at the thought. "So was Dr. Steele on your payroll?"

"Dr. Steele is far too noble for that."

"But did he talk about me?"

Dougie's normally bland expression shifted slightly. "Only in very vague terms."

She took some comfort in that. "He's lucky. Now if you'll excuse me, I need to go see Vicki." She had to make sure Derek's mother got financial help to stay here for as long as she needed. It was the least she could do to make it up to Derek for what Dougie had done. For *her*.

Gak.

"Let her know that the proceeds of the play will cover the cost of repairing the sinkhole in the driveway, and take care of another issue she was concerned about."

"Is this your subtle way of reminding me that you're the person responsible for staving off financial ruin for Nepenthe Manor for another year, and that I now owe you?" She paused. "And what is the other issue you mentioned?"

"I'm not at liberty to say, and I didn't have anything to do with saving Nepenthe Manor. It was your idea to sell tickets. I merely made that happen."

She shook her head. Typical Dougie. Slippery as an eel. "This isn't over."

"I certainly hope not." He took a step closer to her. "You have made my continued existence worth pursuing, Pandora. Life around you is never dull, and I find myself wondering what you'll do next. It's worth every sacrifice I make."

"And how do *you* make sacrifices, Richie Rich?"

"For starters, I live in this place and do things I find repulsive simply to be closer to you."

"That which does not kill you only makes you stronger, Dougie," she sing-songed. "So it's not a sacrifice, it's the making of you."

He wrinkled his nose. "I'll remember that the next time I'm cleaning up vomit."

She laughed. "This is what it's going to be like for as long as I live here, Dougie."

"Which, of course, may not be long."

"Right. Because Vicki wants to leave."

"Does she?"

She narrowed her eyes. "Last I heard."

"Do you want to leave, Pandora?"

"Someday."

"But not yet."

"Not yet," she agreed, feeling like she was being lured into a trap.

"Because I would follow you wherever you went. I can. I'm going to file for emancipation from my parents. It might take some time to achieve, but it will happen, and I'll soon be free from their controlling ways. For the time being, I have seen to it that Nepenthe Manor will remain an asylum. You will be safe, and your *friends* will be safe."

"And if I leave here?"

He shrugged. "Then Nepenthe Manor is no longer my problem. I will sell my properties and follow you."

"Then you've given me no choice, Dougie. I can't ever leave."

"Of course you can." He sounded almost miffed, which she liked being the cause of. "This place is not your responsibility."

"Then whose is it? Who will fight for the inmates here?"

"Other people. Adults. The government. I don't care. Just not you."

"You really don't get me, do you, Dougie?"

"I understand you very well, Pandora, and that's why you can't stay here. At Nepenthe Manor your skills will go unnoticed, and with every year that passes you will lose more and more of your divineness until eventually you'll become as flat and dull as everyone around you. You will become a nothing, a nobody. I will not stand by and watch that happen."

Her divineness? Was she the 'god' he'd found? Because that wasn't at all disturbing, not to mention a bit challenging to live up to.

"Then you should leave, because I won't let the inmates down by abandoning them. I'll fight for this place with everything I've got."

His jaw pulsed. "Then you've just signed the death warrant of every person in this place."

And the trap door closes…

Her hackles literally now stood at full attention. "What are you saying?"

"That I've changed my mission."

"To what?"

"My new goal is to ensure that what has happened to the vast majority of the other large psychiatric facilities in the country happens to Nepenthe Manor. It will be shut down, and boarded up, and eventually become that haunted building everyone avoids all year until Halloween comes along."

"You wouldn't dare."

"I would, if it were the only way to save you." Then he turned on his heel and left her.

He was getting very good at getting in the last word, wasn't he?

It Was All Rather Revolting

38

PANDORA WATCHED DOUGIE go with a queasy feeling in her gut. The queasiness quickly turned to discomfort, and she felt a throbbing in her lower region that had nothing to do with longing. The pain was worse than usual, and she knew she'd better go take something for it. But first she had to talk to Vicki and make sure Mrs. Choken was going to be okay. She also needed to clear up matters between them ASAP. She had to know what her future was going to be, because if Dougie really meant what he said, it affected the lives of everyone in this building.

Knowing—well, hoping—Dr. Steele and Xavier would look after the posse, she went to find her mother. She wasn't in her office, but she might be in their apartment, which would be convenient because Pandora really needed some aspirin.

Her mother was sitting at the dining table, head in her hands. Seeing her like that stirred up all of Pandora's fears, and she knew her worries about Mrs. Choken had to be put on hold. She needed to know once and for all what was going on.

"You have to tell me. Are we leaving?"

Vicki looked up. "Well, if I could get a job, I'd be out of this place in a heartbeat, but it seems someone has put out the word that I'm untouchable."

"But I read in the paper about a new position opening up here."

"Oh, that. It's not for my position. I can't even get an interview."

"That's kind of weird, don't you think? Because you're good at what you do." It was true, which is why Pandora could deduce that someone had interfered with Vicki's job-hunting process. Someone whose name rhymed with buggy, sluggy, and druggie.

Vicki frowned. "Is that a compliment?"

"I do give them on occasion." Should she tell Vicki about Dougie and his devious machinations? Including his insane scheme to shut down the asylum?

"Well, I needed it. It's been a long month, and finding out that Hank Jackson has been such an ass all these years because he was hiding his own incompetence as a father was the last straw. That jerk even encouraged me to find a new job, because I was so *good* at what I did, and he thought I deserved better than Nepenthe Manor. And I, being an idiot, fell for it." Her mother dropped her head into her hands once more and her shoulders started shaking. Pandora noticed she wasn't wearing the oversized leather wristwatch she'd always worn—the one Pandora sensed had been the professor's before his accident.

Pandora was appalled. "Are you crying?"

Vicki's head swung up. "Crying? Hell, no. I'm furious!" She paused, bit her lip hard, very possibly puncturing it, and Pandora froze, knowing she was on the verge of witnessing something historical. Vicki was about to confide in her, but she didn't want to. "I'm *furious*, and you want to know why?" Pandora gave a stunned nod. "Because I've spent the last fourteen years of my life running this place, even though everything and everyone seemed to be conspiring against my success, and I did it to look after a man who didn't love me. He loved someone else and I was completely, stupidly blind to it. My entire adult life has been a waste!"

So this was why Vicki felt betrayed. Because of Professor Robertson. When Dr. Steele had said that day in the theater, "I know you feel betrayed," he'd been talking about Pandora's actions. But Vicki had thought, if only for a brief moment, that he knew about the professor picking Xavier's mom over her. Pandora had kept her mouth shut all this time, thinking her mother didn't know, but she did.

"But why do you think the professor didn't love you?" she half-whispered.

"I *know* he didn't love me," her mother spit out, "because he wouldn't shut up about it at the hospital! He kept going on and on about how he'd done Judy wrong. How he'd made a mistake marrying me." She smacked her palm on the table. "*Fourteen years!* And now I can't find another job and my mother is going to literally make me eat crow and my daughter is screwed up because I forced her to live in this hellhole."

"You think I'm screwed up?"

"What?" Vicki ran her hands through her hair, messing it up even further. "No. I mean, you doing that jumping thing." She swirled her finger in the air. "That was screwed up."

"Maybe," Pandora conceded, though she still wasn't quite sure why she'd done it. As a plan to stay here? As a viable alternative to living with her grandmother? Because she was concussed? Or because, half-mad with anger and grief, she was miserable and had truly wanted to die? If only for that brief moment in time?

In the end, though, did the *why* matter? She'd done something dangerous, and had almost paid the ultimate price for it. Maybe that made her crazy, but it would be crazier not to learn something from all this. Though what that lesson was, she wasn't sure.

"You didn't really want to kill yourself, did you?" Vicki asked in a quiet voice.

Pandora shrugged. "I'm actually not sure." Vicki looked horrified, and Pandora took some comfort in that, which was probably a little weird.

"I didn't really believe you'd meant to. I thought you were only bargaining with me, you know, playing me like you're so good at. Otherwise... Well, I'd like to think I would've done something for you."

"I'd like to think that, too," Pandora said honestly.

Vicki rubbed her face. "Maybe I didn't say or do anything more because I couldn't face the possibility. It scared me too much."

Pandora considered this, and decided to accept it as a sort of apology. "Well, I dealt with it, and I'm okay now. So no harm done, I guess."

"You shouldn't have had to do it alone," Vicki said in a tired voice. "But I had a good reason for pushing you to be independent, Pandy. This world is a horrid place full of horrid people who will only let you down, and you needed to learn that before you got burned so badly you wouldn't recover." *Like if you killed yourself*, she didn't need to add.

"Aren't other people supposed to be teaching me that lesson? People who are *not* my family? Your family is supposed to have your back, isn't it?"

Vicki peered at her grimly. "Did your concussion give you amnesia, too?" *Um, yeah.* "You know quite well that your family can be your worst enemy. They know best how to hurt you. You've seen it with the people here. Hell, my mother scares me more than the most hardened criminal because she knows exactly where to aim her poisoned darts without leaving any visible scars. The apple doesn't fall far from the tree, does it?"

"You're not nearly as bad as Grandmother," Pandora admitted, stumbling a little on the word nearly.

Vicki's smile was wry. "I suppose that's something to hold close to my heart late at night when I'm wondering what I'm still doing in this hellhole." She gestured wildly. "Don't you get it, Pandy? I'm worse for you than anyone. That's why I stay away from you, why I ask other people to keep an eye on you, why I didn't come to your welcome home party. I'm my mother's child, after all, and no amount of therapy is going to change the fact that I'm bad for you. I mean, you nearly killed yourself, and I didn't do anything to help you."

Pandora decided to address the one point she felt safest managing. "I don't think this place is a hellhole. I like it here."

"Are you trying to prove my point?" Vicki asked dryly, then heaved a sigh. "I don't know why you like it here. For me, running this place is like being in a war. There's constant pandemonium, and we're always leaking money and under threat of getting shut down. Not to mention I'm dealing with a population that is, to be nice about it, extremely challenging. I stayed here to be with the man I thought I loved, and whom I thought loved me. And what did my sacrifice get me? *Nowhere*, that's where it got me."

Maybe Dr. Gara had been right about Vicki—that she did have a lot on her plate, and that motherhood can be a terrible burden—and maybe just this once, Pandora would give her a pass. She pulled in a deep breath, readying herself to take on the hardest role she ever had to play: a kind person. "You're wrong, you know. The professor loved you."

"Oh, please, Pandy." Eye roll. "You're only trying to make me feel better."

"When have I ever done that?"

Vicki tilted her head to one side. "Good point. Go on."

"I know he loved you because he talked about you when I'd go visit him. And it was you he talked about, not Judy. He said your name, and he went on and on about your gorgeous auburn hair and amazing green eyes and your kind soul." Pandora made a face. "Frankly, it was all rather revolting."

"You're lying." But Vicki was leaning forward, listening.

"If I were lying, it would be to your detriment. You know that. I'm telling you this for the professor, not for you." Her mother acknowledged this with a shrug, and Pandora went on. "I think he loved you both, in different ways, and I think that ate him up inside. I think some of his issues were from the accident, and some were from the guilt." Pandora was making this last part up as she went, but it sounded right somehow. The professor had talked about some strange things, and only now she wondered if this love triangle dilemma was at the root of his ramblings. "I sat with him when he talked. I think it helped him not feel so confused. He might have been talking about Judy at the end, but most of the time, it was you."

Vicki shook her head, not daring to believe. "If you're making this up…"

"He called you his honeybunch." It was the one bit of truth she was absolutely certain of, because it always annoyed her when he did it.

Her mother gasped. "From our song."

"I guess. Whatever the reason, it was kind of sickening." She clasped her hands together and fluttered her eyelashes. "Oh, my honeybunch! My sugar pie! *Ew.*"

"He did love me," Vicki said, half to herself.

"Just don't let on to Xavier. He's been through enough."

"I'm pretty sure I can hold back," Vicki replied, back to her normal sarcastic self.

A pain gripped Pandora's gut. "Oh, man," she groaned, unable to hold it back.

Vicki re-focused on her. "What's wrong?"

"My stomach hurts."

"Gas?"

"I don't think so."

"You aren't trying to change the topic, are you?"

"I wish. It's been happening all month, and I just don't feel right." She clutched at her stomach, then her eyes widened as she felt something hot gush out between her legs. "I need to go!" She jumped up, raced to the bathroom, and whipped down her pants. There, on her pale blue underwear, was a swath of red blood. She was bleeding. She was... *Oh, crap. No, no, no. Not this!*

Birdy was always complaining about it being that time of the month, or that Aunt Flo had come to visit, or she was on the rag—well, it felt like always, but could only be a few days a month. Pandora had hoped, and perhaps had performed a few odd rituals in the dead of night, to never be faced with this dreaded thing. But here it was. And it was awful.

Vicki knocked on the door. "Pandy? Are you all right?"

"I'll be all right. I'm just... It's just..." Oh, dear Lord, this was the worst. "I, um, need something for something that just happened involving blood."

There was a pause, then it clicked. "Oh, hell. So that's what's been going on with you. I mean, you're no angel, but you've been acting really weird lately. Cutting your hair, jumping off a bridge, acting super touchy. I went through the same thing when I was your age. It was awful. This is why I shouldn't be a mother. I didn't even warn you about the nightmare coming your way. Lord help me, I didn't even have "the talk" with you."

"Oh, I learned all that stuff from Birdy." A groan made its way through the door. "And Dr. Weisenhammer." A snort of laughter, and Pandora felt a surge of something positive go through her. "So I'm not going crazy? Birdy gets grumpy when she's, um, having this problem, but she doesn't act like she's losing her mind." Maybe because she'd already lost it, so it was hard to tell the difference. "Not like I felt like I was doing anyway."

"If you haven't gone crazy after living in this place for fourteen years, Pandy, I think you're going to be all right. Unfortunately for you, you've inherited my first-period woes." Pandora winced. She did not want that word coming up between them ever again.

"I need something to put on."

"Oh, yeah. Under the sink."

Pandora dabbed at the stain on her underwear with some toilet paper, then rooted around until she found the bag of pads. She pulled one out. "Holy crap! Do we have anything smaller than this diaper?"

"I'll pick something up for you tomorrow. And maybe get you a book, or something, about these things. I'm not sure Birdy is the best source on it. Or me, for that matter."

"I agree." Pandora attached the giant thing to her underwear, then stared at it forlornly. "So this is it, huh? This is my life from now on?"

"Yep. You can't stop the puberty train."

"Am I going to feel this way every month?"

"Maybe the first couple times, but it will level out soon enough. Then there'll just be cramps, leakage, bloating, and insomnia."

"I hate this."

"You and the rest of sisterhood."

Pandora flushed the toilet and opened the door, feeling all hot and prickly and embarrassed. But Vicki wasn't there. She was already back in the kitchen, pouring something into a cup. "What's that?"

"I'm fixing you a drink."

"Like a hot toddy?"

"No, you lush. Hot chocolate."

"Oh, that sounds good." Pandora's stomach rumbled. "Any toast?"

"I'll see what I can do."

In the end, Vicki made herself some hot chocolate, too, and a plate of toast to share. They sat together, eating and drinking in a companionable silence, almost as though they were a real mother and daughter. It was kind of nice.

"This moment we're sharing?" Vicki paused. "Well, maybe we could do more of these. Once in awhile. When neither of us is, you know, riding the crimson tide."

"Ew!" Pandora gagged. "Yeah, maybe. But let's not overdo it, all right?"

"Agreed." Vicki sipped at her hot chocolate. "So what do you think of that Russian guy, Vlad?"

"Well, now that I know he isn't part of the conspiracy to kidnap me, I think I can safely say he's all right."

"High praise, indeed."

"Why do you ask?"

"That opening you read about? It's for a new security officer. Turns out that while Frank's going to recover, he needs a lot of physical therapy, and he won't be coming back. I'm thinking of giving the job to Vlad. Full-time." She took a quick drink of hot chocolate.

"Okay. Whatever. What's gonna happen to Beetle?"

"Believe it or not he actually got himself a job. A real one. They're renting an apartment in Akmore and he's going to support his dad." Good for Frank, and for that loser, Beetle, finally doing something useful for once. Bad for Birdy, though. She was going to lose her make-up and contact lens supplier. That was going to cause a stink. "We took up a fund to raise a deposit on the place, and I'm hoping there's enough left over from the play to add to the pot, too." So that was the 'other issue' Dougie had been referring to.

"Dougie said to tell you there's enough for the sinkhole and for the fund."

"Oh, good." Vicki looked relieved. "All thanks to you." Pandora felt warm all over, and barely managed to avoid grinning like a fool. "And Andrew, I mean, Dr. Steele, also contributed a nice chunk of change for the fund. He's too nice, that man."

"Naïve is the word I'd use."

Vicki laughed. "Yeah, me too. Surprised he's survived this long."

Pandora was of the same mind. "So Vlad is our permanent security guard, and we're staying here for a while longer."

"You're okay with that?"

"Anything not to stay with Grandmother Belfry."

"Yeah, sorry about that." Vicki really did look sorry. "I was feeling pretty crappy about a lot of things, and I directed all of that crap at you. And I really was worried about you and wanted to get you away from here to protect you. I'm not a good mother, maybe, but I'm not a monster, either."

"Well, for what it's worth, I don't wish that you'd died instead of the professor. Cause as much as you neglect me, I think Professor Robertson would have been worse."

"I will cherish those words always." Vicki smiled, the look almost fond. Pandora took a mental snapshot of it and stored it away. "I think what you did with the play was a good thing, and I'm glad you were strong enough to keep at it even though I was being such a bitch to you."

"Are you high?" Pandora couldn't stop the words from coming out. "Sorry. This is just not like you."

Vicki leaned back in her chair. "No, it's not. But maybe while I can't stop being my mother's daughter, maybe I can be more like my daughter."

"That's a stretch. I'm awesome incarnate." Pandora grinned.

"You get that arrogance from your father, you know."

"Probably. You should've seen him when he caught an elusive bug. You'd think the man had just captured Bigfoot. So does this mean we aren't going to fight anymore?"

"Now who's high?"

Pandora smirked. "Yeah, okay." She picked up another piece of toast. "So, um, Derek Choken is moving."

"I heard that."

"But his mom…what's she going to do? I know they don't have the money to keep her here."

"Oh, she's all set. She won't have to go."

Pandora sat up. "What?"

"Someone was on the ball and sent in her application for benefits, and she qualifies. I asked around, but no one copped to it. Not even Dr. Steele, our resident light touch. I got the paperwork in the mail on Friday."

No one copped to it.

Was it Dougie?

Who else? Damn that boy. Just when she thought that she'd worked him out of her blood, he found a way back in. Even so, he was still plotting the downfall of Nepenthe Manor, and she couldn't forget that.

"I'm glad she can stay. She's kind of a mess."

"Nothing a little time can't fix." Typical Vicki. "You know who's going to be a mess after this?"

Pandora leaned forward eagerly. "Who?"

"My mother. It's going to kill her that I'm not leaving the manor." Vicki's smile was gloating and triumphant as she set her empty mug on the table.

"One more thing…" Vicki froze a little. "Why did you let Dougie come work here?"

"Oh, that." Vicki relaxed. "To help keep an eye on you. Why else?" Ah. That actually made sense.

"Oh. Are you going to let him keep working here?"

"Well, he's doing an excellent job, doesn't cost the manor any money, and his father hates every moment of it. What do you think?"

Pandora thought Dougie wasn't going anywhere any time soon.

Vicki stood up. "Why don't you finish up the toast? If we're staying I'm going to have to figure out some stuff. Thank goodness Bennington's mother is doing better. I'm drowning in paperwork."

As she headed toward the door, Pandora noticed there was a spring in her step. Her hand on the knob, Vicki stopped and faced Pandora. "Are you going to be okay?" Pandora nodded, barely able to keep from tearing up. She'd wanted Vicki to show she cared, even if just a little, but now that she was doing it, she was making it very hard for Pandora to keep her composure. "You know, Pandy... Whatever happens after this, I'm glad we had this moment. Remember it, all right? I'm not sure what's coming for us, but it probably won't be a bed of roses, will it?"

Pandora rallied. "Probably not."

"You'll stay out of trouble for at least a little bit now? Let things settle down?"

"But Trouble is my middle name."

Her mother cocked an eyebrow. "Funny. It's mine, too."

Then she was gone.

39

Such Different Fathers

PANDORA FINISHED UP the toast and her hot chocolate, then washed the dishes. Her conversation with Vicki had been really weird, in a good way. She wouldn't regret it, but she probably would forget it in a week or so when trouble started up again between them. It was just their way...to spar over every little thing. Dysfunctional, but theirs. Funny how that gave her a warm feeling all over.

She headed downstairs, waddling a little because of the diaper she was wearing, but feeling better than she had in weeks. As she crossed the foyer, she heard talking and peeked into Vicki's office. Vlad was leaning against her mother's desk and they were both laughing. Pandora had a funny feeling seeing them like that. She knew why, but didn't want to acknowledge it. Not yet. Maybe not ever.

She headed outside and spotted the Hessian trudging up the steps, a gym bag slung over her shoulder. "Is it too much to hope you're moving out?" Pandora asked as they grew close to one another.

The Hessian looked up. "You wish, Belfry."

"I do. But then, if you left, who would I heckle?"

The Hessian frowned. "What do you want?"

"I saw you and your family at the play today."

Caught off guard, the Hessian actually smiled. "Yeah. We won some kind of raffle." A raffle? So that's how Nettie had managed to get them the free tickets. "I was real glad, cause I couldn't go before. Had to stay with Mr. Crump cause he was having fits. But anyway that librarian lady called my mom to tell her we won and she delivered the tickets herself. Right to our house! There was even an extra one so my aunt could go." Her eyes went a little moony. "Now there's a good lady." She looked down her broad nose at Pandora. "Unlike yourself, that is."

"Well, I'm glad your family won the tickets."

"You are?" Suspicion made the Hessian's voice harder than usual, and it was probably warranted after all the scuffles they'd been through over the years.

"Your brothers and sisters, and especially your mom, they all looked like they had a good time."

"They did." More suspicion. "Best part was when you got thrown off that cliff."

"That was my favorite part, too." Pandora paused. Sometimes it was hard to say things that might be true, but went against one's very nature, and also undermined a feud one had carefully cultivated for years. "They seem like good kids."

The Hessian reared back, as though Pandora had lunged at her. "What's your angle, Belfry?"

Pandora batted her eyes innocently. "Angle?"

"You're being nice."

Pandora laughed. "Ah, well. Must be my brain injury. Well, I'm off to visit my dad's grave. Have a nice day, Hessian."

Okay, that was the closest she was going to get to apologizing for being so mean to the Hessian earlier, and to her aunt, Nurse Neanderthal, at the hospital. She'd stepped over a line with them, and even though she'd kind of been doing that for years, she didn't like to think of herself as completely evil, like Xavier's grandmother, or her own, for that matter. It didn't feel very good.

But still… She wasn't about to let the Hessian entirely off the hook. Pandora had a rep to maintain, and the Hessian could be a real monster herself sometimes.

"You're up to something, Belfry," the Hessian called after her. "I don't like it!"

Pandora tossed her a wave, and was gratified to hear a disgruntled snort. She was back, baby! Maybe Cracker Jack was right. She would make it through this.

Taking her time, she headed toward the cemetery, making a few adjustments to her diaper. This thing was awful. When she finally looked up, she saw the sun was getting low and the trees cast shadows over the graveyard. Dr. Steele was easy to spot, being the only living human in the place. Of course, he stood out no matter what he did. He was just that kind of a guy.

Hands in his pockets, he was positioned in front of a gravestone not all that far from the professor's. Apparently Hank hadn't even bothered to give his daughter a decent burial in town—she'd been buried along with all the other inmates over the years who'd had nowhere else to go and no one left to care what happened to them.

Fresh roses stuck out from a vase that sat on the grave. She recognized the plain stone right away, noticeable because of its brevity. It contained three letters—E.A.H.—and nothing else. No birth date. No death date. No epitaph. Just Elizabeth's initials. It was something Pandora had always found rather sad, and of course, intriguing.

"She needs a new stone."

Dr. Steele didn't move. He'd heard her coming, of course, something she'd made sure of as she tapped a stick on the rather strange statues along the way. Knowing Mr. Nepenthe, he'd had them installed before anyone had ever even been buried here. He was the type of father who understood that his daughter Elizabeth, with her taste for the outré, would have liked them.

Such different fathers, Pandora mused. The Professor. Mr. Nepenthe. Mr. Choken. Hank Jackson. Almost complete opposites.

"She does need a new one, doesn't she? Want to help me pick something out?"

"Totally. I'm an expert on tombstones."

He smiled, but didn't look over at her. "Good. Wasn't exactly looking forward to going on my own."

"You could go with Ms. Netterson."

"I think this is more a thing that you and I should share."

"She wouldn't mind me tagging along."

"I know. But she would understand why it's best for it to be just the two of us. You know, because we both lost someone."

A warm glow spread over her. "Oh, okay." She quickly changed the subject before he could change his mind. "Say, I brought something for the professor."

He glanced over. "What is it?"

She held out her hand. "A dead butterfly I found on the way here. I couldn't think of anything else. Flowers seemed wrong. But he loved his bugs."

"Sounds perfect."

"Xavier and I want to go yard saleing next weekend. Will you take us? Ms. Netterson can come, too." She figured she should probably toss that bone out there.

"That sounds like a good idea. My place could use a few things. I've been a student for so long, and then an intern, that I'm still not used to having money."

And yet he'd given a sizable donation to help Frank and Beetle get settled.

He would make such a great dad.

"Cool."

"So you two are good?"

"I suppose. He's still a snot and a know-it-all and that mullet…it's got to go. But other than that, we're good."

"I'm glad."

"Thanks for looking after the little rascal while I was so busy." She grinned. "We didn't do anything for his birthday, you know, so maybe we could take him out to eat after yard saleing?"

"I think that's a good idea." There was silence for a few moments. "I'm really glad you came today, Pandora."

"Yeah, well, I didn't want you to be alone. Especially today, after we found out that Elizabeth's dad is a raving psycho, and you almost went to jail for punching him. I told Captain Banty that I was the one who took him out, just so we're on the same page if we get interrogated." She was really hoping they'd get interrogated.

"Thanks for that. I shouldn't have punched him, you know."

"Yes, you should have. He deserved it."

"Maybe, but I have a feeling his parents messed him up as much as they messed up Elizabeth."

"You sound like you want to forgive him."

"Maybe a little. I've been mad for so long, it feels kind of good to let it go."

Her heart started beating harder. "So what are you going to do now that the mystery is solved?"

"Keep working here, of course." She let herself breathe again. "Continue helping people. Make a difference."

"Are you going to keep trying to push that the posse should leave?"

"Do you seriously want them to stay here forever?"

She shrugged. "Would that be so bad?"

"Would it be so good?"

"I don't know. I guess I can kind of see your side now. After what you told me about Elizabeth." After she'd experienced what it was like to feel trapped in this place, and for only a month. It wasn't a nice feeling.

He glanced sideways at her. "You've changed, Pandora. Gotten softer."

"What's that supposed to mean?" she bridled.

He chuckled. "I simply mean that you aren't so prickly anymore."

"Oh. Yeah, well. Maybe I should hit my head more often."

"I'm also not as worried about you as I was." She squinted at him. Why didn't she like the sound of that? "Calm down," he read her mind. "Like you said, we're family now, and I'll always worry about you. My point is that despite some pretty big obstacles, you've proven over this past month that you've got the ability to cope when life gangs up on you. So whatever reason you had for jumping off that bridge—whether you wanted to make a point, or really kill yourself—it doesn't matter." Wait. That's kind of what she had already told herself. Was she a genius or what? "The important thing is that you're no longer the same person. You've evolved, and now you get a second chance, a chance to see and experience all the great things you're going to do for this world."

Hearing that last part, she felt like he'd pulled all the air out of her lungs. "Oh."

"Pandora Belfry, speechless? Did I just perform a miracle?"

"Very funny, doc," she growled. Though inside she was glowing, and maybe feeling a tad bit embarrassed at all his praise. But definitely glowing.

"So what do you think I should put on Elizabeth's gravestone?" he asked, deftly changing the subject.

"Can there be anything else?"

"I don't think there can."

As though they'd planned it, at the same time they began to quote Elizabeth's favorite poem… Well, Dr. Steele did, and Pandora sort of stumbled along after him.

They are not long, the weeping and the laughter,
Love and desire and hate;
I think they have no portion in us after
We pass the gate.

They are not long, the days of wine and roses,
Out of a misty dream
Our path emerges for a while, then closes
Within a dream.

"That's a lot of words," Pandora noted when they were done. "I don't think it will fit, and it's going to cost an arm and a leg."

"How about just this then, 'I think they have no portion in us after we pass the gate.'"

"Perfect."

He held out his arm. "Shall we go see the professor now?"

She drew in a deep breath, then grabbed hold. "I think we shall."

As they walked away, Pandora glanced back and saw a young girl leaning over the grave, reaching down to pick up a rose. Pandora blinked and the girl disappeared.

She blinked a few more times, and when nothing showed itself, she turned away, but not before sending a thought upward into the sky. "If anyone touches so much as one beautiful hair on his head, I'll cut them, Elizabeth. I swear it."

She thought she heard laughter, then very distinctly, "I have no doubt about that, Pandora Belfry. Now go seize your days of wine and roses. They are not long…"

Author's Note

People attempt suicide for many reasons, but oftentimes the underlying goal is to escape what for them feels like a never-ending pain (imagine having a migraine for months, with no end in sight). For many families, and for society in general, it's a scary and emotional topic, and typically taboo. But until we stop treating mental illness and suicide like a dirty secret we must hide from the world, that won't change. Plain and simple, we have to stop the stigma. We need to get to a place in society where people don't have to tiptoe around the subject, where a person can walk up to someone and say, "I want to harm myself," and not get treated like they just announced they have a bomb on them. There's often an element of panic in how we react to someone who's suicidal or mentally ill, like we're dealing with a terrible crime that's been committed. But we have to get over that. We should treat the issue like we do any physical illness or disease…with cutting-edge therapy, by giving lots of support to the individual and their family, by financing top-of-the-line research, and by endeavoring to find ways to eliminate the underlying cause. In other words, treat mental illness as simply an illness, and suicidal ideation as a symptom, not an aberration. Treat both like we would treat cancer or diabetes or heart disease. Doing so will save a lot of lives, and, I'm thoroughly convinced, make the world a better place. We also need to take some of the onus of getting help off the mentally ill. As individuals, we must endeavor to change our way of thinking about mental illness, educate ourselves on it, and reject any judgment we might feel. As a society, we need to find ways to teach our young people how to better cope with stress, train our leaders on how to recognize and manage mental illness, and create a more accepting environment all around. Then, and only then, can we defeat this scourge that is taking our loved ones from us and leaving behind a dark and lonely isolation no one should ever have to experience. We must rally, and we must overcome.

About the Author

When author, Kristina Schram, was growing up she wanted to be a star. When that didn't turn out quite like she expected, she turned her mind to achieving other goals: Earning her Ph.D. in Counseling Psychology, working as an Artist-in-Residence at local schools, being a free-lance editor and reader, coaching parks & rec basketball, protecting the earth through recycling and using green products, and publishing her first novel, a YA fantasy called The Chronicles of Anaedor: The Prophecies.

Knowing what it's like to struggle with self-doubt and lack of confidence, her biggest dream (in addition to owning a castle) is to stamp out low self-esteem for everyone, especially young people. She lives in beautiful, wooded New Hampshire with her husband, three boys, and various pets, and can also throw a tomahawk, if need be. One of her favorite things to do is walk with her dog in the woods, where she searches for the impossible around every corner. Sometimes she finds it.

For more information on Kristina Schram, feel free to make a trip to her website: www.kristinaschram.com. She's also on Facebook, Twitter, and Pinterest.

Other Books by Kristina Schram

The Pandora Belfry Adventures

Mayhem at Nepenthe Manor
The Labyrinth of Lunacy
The Eldritch Affair

The Forest Immortal Saga

The Changeling's Tale
Oswald's Revenge
Meltdown

The Chronicles of Anaedor

The Prophecies
The Return to Anaedor
The Lost Ones
The Uprising

Tales From Hawthorn Lane

Bewitching Hawthorn Lane
The Curse Is Come Upon Us

Paranormal Gothic Romance

The Wrath
I Shall Return
Moon Dweller